OF AGE AND INNOCENCE

ALSO BY GEORGE LAMMING

Fiction
In the Castle of My Skin (1953)
The Emigrants (1954)
Season of Adventure (1960)
Water with Berries (1971)
Natives of my Person (1972)

Non-fiction
The Pleasures of Exile (1960)
The Most Important People (with Kathleen Drayton, 1981)
Western Education and the Caribbean Intellectual: Coming, Coming, Coming Home (1995)
Coming, Coming Home: Conversations II (1995)
Sovereignty of the Imagination, Language and the Politics of Ethnicity – Conversations III (2009)

OF AGE AND INNOCENCE

GEORGE LAMMING

INTRODUCTION BY JEREMY POYNTING

PEEPAL TREE

First published in Great Britain in 1958
by Michael Joseph Ltd
This new edition published in 2011
Peepal Tree Press Ltd
17 King's Avenue
Leeds LS6 1QS
England

ISBN13: 9781845231453

Supported by
ARTS COUNCIL
ENGLAND

JEREMY POYNTING

INTRODUCTION

At the funeral of Walter Rodney in 1980, Supriya Nair reports the rueful admission of some young Guyanese student activists that, while they hugely admired Lamming's political stand and witnessing presence, they found his fiction 'too hard'.[1] This was a tragic confession in the circumstances since one can argue that *Of Age and Innocence* set out to answer the question, amongst others, of why the radical anticolonial movement in British Guiana had by 1954 collapsed into inter-ethnic competition, the very divide that Walter Rodney had been trying to bridge. But the response also raises the question: if Lamming's novels are indeed 'hard', for what purpose do they challenge the reader? Lamming seems to have asked himself this question when he was writing *Of Age and Innocence*. As J. Dillon Brown shows, Lamming embeds in this and others of his novels elements that make a plea for an ideal reader – one who doesn't take surfaces for granted and is prepared to make imaginative connections.[2] I first read *Of Age and Innocence* many years ago and was impressed, but suspected that aspects of the novel eluded me. How did the group of European visitors fit in? Wasn't there something rather puzzling about the treatment of the apparent opposites of the novel's title? I was inclined to agree with Wilson Harris's verdict that the novel suffers from a 'diffusion of energies', that it fails to keep 'to its inherent design'.[3] At the time it was the novel's treatment of ethnic politics that really interested me and this I felt was flawed by a lack of inwardness in its handling of the Indian Caribbean world.[4] A little later, I read the novel again, more closely, and came to different conclusions. Cultural authenticity became less important than how the novel's multiple layerings fitted together. Harris was wrong; Lamming wasn't stuck awkwardly between the conventional novel of classes and social distinctions – which he writes very well indeed when it serves his purpose[5] – and the novel of speculative imagination. Lamming brings the late colonial world into sharp focus but he also creates, in Harris's words, a 'profound, poetic and scientific scale of values'. *Of Age and Innocence* criticises ways of seeing which regard temporary 'realities' as fixed, and views of the person which, in Harris's words, 'consolidate one's preconception of humanity'.[6] Here Lamming and Harris share a similar goal. The difference is that Lamming roots such possibilities within existing history and human society, in contrast to Harris's metaphysical idealism.

Rereading the novel after twenty-five years, and looking at some recent criticism, I felt that my second, closer reading held up, but again found much in the novel that I hadn't seen before. There isn't the space to do more than outline some of these approaches, but their variety emphasises that this is a rich novel that repays multiple readings. For on, there has been the huge compliment that V.S. Naipaul paid the novel's significance in his dialogic, answering narrative of *The Mimic Men* (1967).[7] There has been Gordon Rohlehr's reading of the novel through its treatment of language[8] – a focus developed by J. Dillon Brown and Supriya Nair (though neither reference Rohlehr). There has been Wilfred Cartey's 'The Search for Polity'[9] that reads beyond the novel's political surface to see deeper temporalities and a poetic ecology of scale. There has also been the often painful compliment that Caribbean actuality has continued to pay the novel's prophetic qualities. Rohlehr, writing in the 1990s, by which time there had been ample time to see the 'mixture of folly and murder' which characterised the unsteady paths of the new nations, points to the prophecy in Mark Kennedy's vision at the political rally. Kennedy is overwhelmed by 'a constant and perceptible disintegration of things: leaves, grass, asphalt, the hooves of the animals…' (p. 198). He hallucinates the apocalyptic bloody birth of a kid and hears 'voices announcing the crowd's wish to be ruled. Vote for the star. Vote for the donkey. Vote for the aeroplane. Vote for the knife…' (p. 199)[10]. I am reminded here of Stanley Greaves' acerbic and visionary series of paintings, *There Is a Meeting Here Tonight*.[11]

According to Rohlehr, Lamming understands that challenging the 'old consolidated Western Atlantic order' cannot do other than awaken its malevolence; that the birth of a new Caribbean order is unlikely to be other than traumatic. My recent reading was dominated by a feeling that here was a novel with a tragic vision in which utopian impulses engage with darker fears of human limitation. What Terry Eagleton has described as 'tragic humanism'[12] seemed to offer another pertinent framework for reading – though whilst *Of Age and Innocence* engages with a religious world-view, it never becomes trapped in Eagleton's fixed Catholic ontologies of evil.

This tragic vision struck me most clearly in an element that no critic appears to have commented on: the relationship between Thief and Rockey and their importance to the novel. There's nothing beyond touch and the holding of hands ('Rockey turned to face Thief, and his hand moved blindly over the sand to touch Thief's' (p. 378), and 'Thief felt for Rockey's hand, and they stood, silent and perplexed...' (p. 423)), but it is unmistakeably a relationship of love, and one that points to the tension between the novel's vision of human community (of which their love is the least equivocal image) and its realistic/pessimistic view not only of historical circumstance, but of human capacity, in particular the perceptual processes which go into the making of consciousness.

Of Age and Innocence is profoundly concerned with the struggle to overcome alienation, and this is seen not only in Marxist and Sartrean terms but spiritually, too. Of Ma Shephard and her mission to bring the Word to the inmates of the asylum we are told: 'It was not the physical pain of hell which she taught, but the eternal separation from a source of love which the soul required but could no longer achieve' (p. 285). That this is a struggle taking place both inside and outside immediate human history is conveyed in Ma Shephard's story about the great flood. Her tale of the island being 'put to rest' and rising from the water again on 'that Day o' Deliverance... renewed with riches' (p. 87) is a mythical vision of cycles of defeat and renewal that connects both to the Shelleyan/Promethean reference to a 'dark and melancholy sojourn of time that happened before the discovery of speech' (p. 197), and to the vision expressed by Kennedy at the rally:

> Freedom and Death, like opposites and contradictions working in harmony, are the two facts which we cannot bargain, the two great facts, Freedom and Death, twin gods or forces or

whatever you like which haunt every human existence. Beyond these is nothing but that infinite and indefinable background against which we ramble in the service of Freedom and the expectation of Death. But here we can choose... (p. 197)

The rhetorical play on such capitalised abstractions points to the way such terms thread through the novel. Readers will rapidly pick up how terms such as Age, Innocence, Freedom, Law, Loyalty, Betrayal and others continually surface. What's worth recognising is how Lamming uses and deconstructs them. They exist in the language and consciousness of some of his characters as abstractions that cannot be questioned (the 'Law' represents, for one of the policemen, a divinely inspired value locked in a chain of being) but for others as particularities embedded in history and materiality. Lamming, indeed, uses the motifs of Age and Innocence with no less a sense of inversion and dialectical instability than Blake.

My initial route into the novel's vision was through its focus on perception and ways of knowing. I still see this as its main connective thread, but now also see its deep engagement with existential questions of being and consciousness. The sections where Mark Kennedy contemplates suicide (pp. 332-335), or where Thief debates with Rockey about carrying the name of his calling, and which came first (p. 378ff), suggest that a reading which is alert to this focus would yield a further network of ideas running through the novel.[13]

A more gender-aware reading (than indeed were my earlier ones) would no doubt query, as Sandra Pouchet Paquet does, the novel's sexual politics, particularly in the polarised gender split between Ma Shephard and the male political leadership (and Singh's and Lee's recessive wives).[14] This is pertinent, though it's worth noting how frequently Lamming finds himself having to argue, in an authorial voice, with the powerfully created presence of Ma Shephard. And if she, in the end, betrays the future, it is not because she is a woman, but because of her innocence – an innocence that is epistemic and ethical, and more fundamental than gender. There is too the vileness of Shephard's misogynistic cursing of Penelope on the plane; this seems to me a very explicit critique of a wider sickness in the male psyche, and Penelope's role in the novel is more significant than has sometimes been acknowledged – and is briefly recognised below.

I want to open my more detailed discussion of this novel with Rohlehr's focus on its concern with language.[15] He draws a parallel between Lamming's statement that the novelist's challenge is to bridge 'the world of the private and hidden self, the social world he lives in and the understanding of the reader'[16] and the ideas explored in the diary writings of the mulatto character, Mark Kennedy. (Rohlehr, indeed, describes Kennedy as 'the author's mouthpiece', which I think goes too far – indeed, elsewhere he is quite clear about the novel's multivocal, dialogic qualities.) Rohlehr locates Lamming's treatment of Kennedy's crisis as a writer, his loss of faith in his capacity to communicate what he sees and knows, in both a Modernist scepticism about the communicative capacity of language in general, and the character's particular circumstance as a Caribbean intellectual. As such, he is separated by colonial education and exile from all but the most fragile memories of the counter-world of African Caribbean 'folk'. It is only when Kennedy makes common cause with Shephard in the 'charismatic' context of making a speech to the working-class supporters of the People's Communal Movement that he 'enters his voice' in a state of possession and uncharacteristic volubility.

Rohlehr also shows how Lamming explores Kennedy's division between language and silence to draw attention to the difficulty of finding a fictional form to express the 'perhaps inexpressible quality of personal experience' (Rohlehr, p. 9). The fictional self-reflexiveness is paradoxical: Kennedy, in expressing his angst, is, as Rohlehr observes, both 'lucid and lyrically eloquent'. Kennedy communicates only too well, as the doctor reprimands him when Marcia attempts suicide after reading his diary's painful honesty about the impasse in their relationship: 'And you didn't think of the damage you might have done by letting her know how she existed in your mind?' (p. 284). As J. Dillon Brown suggests, there is a good deal of reflexiveness embedded in the novel about the kind of reader/reading that *Of Age and Innocence* requires.[17] Brown doesn't mention this incident with Marcia, but deals specifically with Bill Butterfield's *mis*reading of the fragment of Mark Kennedy's diary that he uses to bolster his irrational view that Shephard is responsible for Penelope's death in the asylum fire, and his determination to murder Shephard in revenge.

> He spread it out again, and brought it closer, searching for some further reference to Shephard. He read a line, skipped angrily over a passage which seemed irrelevant to his need… The word 'betray' had aroused his interest. He read the passage slowly, waiting for the name of Shephard to increase his frenzy. (p. 330)

As Brown points out, Mark's diary in fact carries a powerful warning about the self-destructiveness of revenge. Brown's focus alerts us to look for other instances in the novel where the issues of writing and reading are foregrounded, for instance in the clash between the narrative the fisherman Rockey wants to tell the court about finding the dying Shephard ('He is trying to invent a language of darkness and absence to convey the black splendour that surrounded him' (p. 363)), and the restricted version the judge wishes to hear. This and Singh's critique ('He did not trust words, and he had never encouraged the habit of reading, for that was like playing into the enemy's hands' (p. 271)) form another layer that connects to the novel's epistemic and ethical centre.

The other reading I want to develop further is Wilfred Cartey's brief focus on the treatment of place and time in the novel. He writes of 'the author's injunction of the necessary visceral interpenetration of man and land',[18] and quotes, as his starting point, Mark Kennedy's impassioned definition of the nationalist project:

> the private feeling you experience of possessing and being possessed by the whole landscape of the place where you were born, the freedom which helps you to recognise the rhythm of the winds, the silence and aroma of the night, rocks, water, pebble and branch, animal and bird noise, the temper of the sea and the mornings arousing nature everywhere to the silent and sacred communion between you and the roots you have made on this island… (p. 198)

Cartey directs us to 'a recurrent cohering motif throughout the novel', where '[e]nvironment and phenomena correlate and correspond to the movement of the story' (Cartey, p. 345). He gives as an example the macaw that presages the asylum fire: 'The sun made a blazing circle of flame with the scarlet ring of feathers… the vivid flame of feathers burning green above the roof...' (p. 284). The environment frequently echoes the novel's key motifs (seeing, the eye, being observed) that image the characters' states of mind. As Marcia begins to disintegrate she senses that outside her window 'the light fluttered like an eyelid closing into the shade of the window pane...' (p. 184). Worth exploring, too, is the way that ants become another connective thread running through the novel.[19] And there are the descriptions of the bats that surround Thief and Rockey as they search for consolation after the cataclysm of political failure, recalling Martin Carter's 'University of Hunger' with the 'sea sound of the eyeless flitting bat'[20] and reminding us that Lamming was a poet before he started publishing novels:

> The bats burst from the trees and swished the air in a furious swoop that pitched them sightless into the light. They grew dizzy in a mad pursuit of shapes, colliding like lines on a map before swinging skyward through the wide, soothing obscurity of the night. (p. 419)

However, Lamming's landscape does more than carry 'within it its very history', as Cartey suggests; it has a presence that predates and ignores any kind of human activity. When the boys climb the volcanic hill, what they encounter is a nature which 'rose, reckless and arbitrary, like an insurrection which had nothing to prove but the fact of its power' (p. 136). But if Cartey doesn't report this disjunction, his recognition of the intersecting temporal zones of the novel – the plot time of the action, the legendary time of the fire, the mythical time of the flood, the edenic time of the boys' narrative ('when the world know only nature an' noise [...] before sense start to make separation betwixt some things an' somethings' (p. 117)), and the primordial time of the island's volcanic eruption from the seabed – provides a salutary perspective on Lamming's sense of scale in his location of the human present.

But the way in to *Of Age and Innocence* that I want to spend longest on, because it provides an underpinning for other readings, is its exploration of the epistemic foundations of an ethics of political culture, and social and intimate personal relations.

Recently, I stumbled across Amanda Fricker's concept of 'epistemic injustice', which very neatly describes Lamming's dissection of colonial society.[21] Her distinction between 'testimonial injustice' (the failure to grant credibility to somebody's words – and more fundamentally their means of knowing – on the basis of prejudice) and 'hermeneutical injustice' (where a society refuses to ask the questions by which injustice or inequality may be recognised) is highly pertinent to Lamming's novel. How the three surviving boys are denied belief in their attempt to tell the truth about Singh's and Lee's only tangential involvement in the asylum fire is an example of the first; and, like Fricker, Lamming recognises that *how* we know is located in systems of power, and that systems of ethics cannot be separated from their epistemic roots. Shephard knows why the privileged elite will resist his project. It is not so much material retribution that they fear:

> But they are really frightened that the order of privilege which is an essential part of their conception of themselves can be revalued, redistributed, or even abolished completely. They are terrified of becoming like the chair which is defenceless against the idea of chair. I am the one who now sees them, not they me. (p. 228)

Lamming's San Cristobal is a composite of the most crucial features of Caribbean reality in the period immediately before political independence. Its present is deeply shaped by its past, an island where 'Africa and India shake hands with China', but where each 'pursues all its separate parts' (p. 81). This separateness has held back the anti-colonial movement and allowed opportunist petit-bourgeois politicians like Paravecino to strut the stage.

In the use of multiple narrative perspectives, private forms such as the diary and extensive use of free indirect speech, Lamming represents a world in which subjective realities are abnormally fragmented and partial. Shephard, for instance, sees his own psychic division as intimately related to San Cristobal's ethnic segmentation:

> I know San Cristobal. It is mine, me, divided in a harmony that still pursues all its separate parts… No new country, but an old land inhabiting new forms of men who can never resurrect their roots and do not know their nature. (p. 81)

Similarly, Kennedy's failure to commit himself to the nationalist movement has the same roots as the failure of his relationship with Marcia. Both are located in the colonialist denial of the

Other, which Lamming sees expressed archetypally in Prospero's attitude to Caliban where:

> … the real sin is not hatred, which implies an involvement, but the calculated and habitual annihilation of the person whose presence you ignore but never exclude.[22]

Lamming's emphasis on the links between personal and public relates to his view that 'what a person thinks is very much determined by the way that person sees'.[23] The peculiar emphasis Lamming gives this statement in *The Pleasures of Exile* is matched by the emphasis on modes of perception in this novel, and how the individual's idea of himself/herself is shaped by an awareness of how he/she is regarded by others. This reciprocity is summed up by Thief when he reproves Rockey for his naivety:

> 'How my actions innocent I know,' said Rockey, 'like I know my face.'
> 'But it ain't matter what you know,' said Thief, ' 'tis what the next man don't see.'
> 'I can talk,' said Rockey, 'innocence can talk.'
> 'It ain't got no language,' said Thief, 'unless the next man lend you his belief.' (p. 392)

Lamming follows Fanon in seeing that the colonial relationship concerns not only the determination of the colonised person's material conditions of life, but the consciousness that arises out of knowing knows he/she exists in the mind of the coloniser. Lamming shows how this 'regard of the other' also structures the relationships between the different ethnic groups.[24]

Shephard and Mark Kennedy return to San Cristobal as stigmatised persons contaminated by exile. On the plane Shephard has 'the face of a fugitive'; at the rally Mark is the 'angry vagrant'. Both feel that they are always judged 'in spite of' their colour and colonial status. Both are driven towards forms of madness by this constant reservation. Shephard tells Mark:

> Of all the senses that serve our knowledge of those around us, it is the eye I could not encounter in peace. It is as though my body defined all of me… So that the eye of the other became for me a kind of public prosecutor… And there were times when I have felt my presence utterly burnt up by the glance which another had given me… (p. 134).

Whereas Shephard's sanity is threatened by his acute vulnerability, Mark has evolved defence mechanisms. When, for instance, Marcia tells him that she feels ashamed that their friends have seen how he neglects her, his 'disinclination' becomes even more pronounced:

> He brought his foot down from the chair and shoved her hand away... Whenever Marcia mentioned anyone else in order to sharpen her rebuke he would withdraw. He became resentful at the thought that his life was a spectacle which others were observing, and took refuge in his silence. (p. 176)

Lamming uses the contrast between Shephard and Kennedy to dramatise his conception of the relationship between ways of seeing, experience and action. The men are two sides of the same coin: Shephard acts as if his vision annihilates the real world; Kennedy's passivity annihilates his being in the face of the world's material appearances.

Shephard's strategy is to confront his neurosis through the situation which has fashioned it. His starting point is a rigorous self-analysis of what the regard of the other has done to him. As he tells Penelope on Bird Island:

> I discovered that until then... I had always lived in the shadow of a meaning which others had placed on my presence in the world, and I had played no part at all in the making of that meaning, like a chair which is wholly at the mercy of the idea guiding the hand of the man who builds it. (p. 226)

Although Shephard wants to be a man without exterior definition, his response is to confront that regard by living through the definition which has been imposed on him:

> Similarly, I accept me as the meaning I speak of has fashioned me... But from now on I deny that meaning its authority. When it suits my purpose I shall use it, when it doesn't I shall be hostile. I am at war... What I may succeed in doing is changing that conception of me. But I cannot ignore it. (p. 228)

His method is to offer up his vulnerability to searching exposure as a man upon whom all eyes are fixed. 'I went into politics in order to redefine myself through action,' he says. But Shephard's politics are not merely the means of healing a private neurosis. As he says, the meaning imposed on him 'applies equally to millions'.

The novel repeatedly stresses that rebellion, action and struggle are essential to humanity's true nature, and there is no mistaking where between the two extremes of Shephard and Kennedy Lamming locates possibility – which is of course in the direction of Shephard. Lamming implies a very fine dividing line between the necessity of refusing to accept reality as fixed and Shephard's denial of a reality separate from his will (though ultimately his extreme subjectivity corrupts possibility). Mark has seen the disorder in their shared boyhood, when he observed Shephard preaching to the empty chairs of his father's chapel, giving him the disquieting feeling that the boy Shephard did 'not seem to see any real difference between a boy's play and what is real… If he were a man I would say he was mad' (p. 132). And on the night before the elections, Shephard's 'sense of power beyond control' destroys his last links with the real world existing outside his fantasy. 'He seemed to see the world concede its worth to his touch,' Lamming comments authorially, in one of his overt intrusions. Now his delusions of power are grand but terrifying:

> I shall hold this land in the palm of my hand, and bend it like a wheel to meet my intention…
> …You remember it? …My wooden children waiting my words… Can you see them now? My wooden children waiting my words […] you remember how they kneel at my bidding? …Tomorrow it will come to pass again. (p. 339)

Lamming contrasts, dialectically, Shephard's delusions with Kennedy's failure to exercise choice. Kennedy recalls a moment which epitomises his disease. He is sitting on a beach observing 'a pebble, a piece of iron and a dead crab'. What disturbs him is the absence of any sensuous relationship between himself and the objects, and this 'endowed the pebble with a formidable and determined power of its presence' (p. 94). This perception of the power of the object makes him incapable of reaching out to touch them. The resulting feeling of 'disinclination' paradoxically (as the Djuna Barnes' epigraph to the novel asserts) has the same annihilating consequences as Shephard's inverse relationship to things:

> This feeling of disinclination surrounds me like space. It enters me like air… I can feel it like a clutch around my throat, an annihilation of things about me, a sudden and natural disloca-

tion of meaning. And it is no force other than me which moves me. It is me. (p. 95)

Mark's mode of perception has its logical end in his feeling that the objects around him 'watch him with a silent and unerring contempt', his contemplation of suicide and his conclusion that he is unfit to make even this existential choice.

It is in the context of these two key frameworks of 'ways of seeing' and 'the regard of the other', that Lamming portrays the relationship between Indians and Africans. Indeed, Shephard's passage to joining Singh and Lee to form the People's Communal Movement is portrayed not so much as a political process but as an extension of his attempt to heal his psychic/epistemic division.

The movement that brings Africans and Indians together collapses, of course, with Shephard's murder by Baboo. But neither Baboo's motivation nor the ethnic breakdown is explored in political-historical terms. Baboo's action is located in his extreme passivity of perception – like Kennedy's – his sense of oppression by a fixed, unchangeable order of things.

Lamming has prefigured this political breakdown in the collapse of the relationship of Mark, Marcia, Bill and Penelope as part of his strategy to focus not on the obviousness of ethnic difference, but on the perceptual processes that underlie all relationships. On the plane bringing them to San Cristobal, Mark describes them as a 'little world, made by four people whose happiness... no argument can deny' (p. 52), but their experience of San Cristobal drives them apart. Mark can neither explain to his three white friends his attraction towards Shephard's Movement, nor tell anyone his reason for withdrawing from it. Marcia is destroyed by her knowledge of how she exists in Mark's mind. Bill enters the society a fastidious liberal and leaves it 'no longer averse to the ways of Crabbe' (p. 331). Penelope, in her moment of desire for Marcia, learns what it must mean to exist in another's mind always qualified by the label 'in spite of', concluding that for the Black or the homosexual, 'it is not their difference which is disturbing. It is the way their difference is regarded which makes for their isolation' (p. 174).

This connection between the suspicion of the 'eye of the other' and the consequent retreat into secrecy then threads through their relationships like a cancer. Misunderstandings occur, until the four lapse into 'solitary and different worlds of understanding' (p. 206). Penelope, indeed, is the only one who grows in the course of the novel, in her understanding of the epistemic injustice of the colonial world.

A parallel process of retreat into solitary and different worlds occurs in the relationship of Africans and Indians after Shephard's death when each group retreats into isolation to nurse its sense of defeat. Each returns to the stifling security of stereotypes that, initially external, have become self-imposed. The Africans revert to the nihilistic sullenness of the slave and sit,

> heavy, large, indolent, unwilling and destructive. They rebuked all possessions by a show of indifference. They killed time with their hands. Their labour was irrelevant and misplaced. (p. 408)

The Indians recoil to the image of the indentured worker, clannish, temporary and rootless, saving every last cent, waiting for the passage home:

> The Indians worked furiously with small push carts, hurrying up and down along the pier. They were cruel with labour to their bodies, and their faces were strained with secrecy and spite and expectation. They were going to rob the future of what was left. (p. 408)

But this portrayal of a defeat does not support a philosophy of despair. There are, indeed, tragic outcomes to Penelope's journey towards understanding, to the relationships of Shephard, Singh and Lee and to the little Society of the boys. But these are pathways interrupted, not dead ends. In each case the journey requires learning an open vulnerability to the other's way of seeing as a means of mutual enrichment or, as Lamming writes elsewhere, a 'desirable extension of reality'.[25] There are, for instance, contrary attitudes to land. Ma Shephard, echoing Kennedy's sense of oppression by objects to which he feels no connection, explains to the boys why the slaves burned down the cane:

> The men who make that fire fret how their labour went robbed in a lan' which refuse to make them brother an' sister, or feed them with a right reward for the sweat they drip night and day. The lan' come to look like a tyrant in their eye, an' they decide to burn whatever memory hol' them to the plough. (p. 91)

By contrast, Singh's son tells his friends:

> My father say education is losin' all the time… An' he tell me is safer to stay with the lan'. He is for education too, but he say you must never swap the lan' for education. Hurricane or whatever hell have can come, but hol' to the lan', hol' to the lan'… (p. 141)

His father's commitment to the land and suspicion of colonial education is the basis for his psychological independence from the white world. As Lamming argues elsewhere, the educated colonial is made absolutely dependent 'on the values implicit in the language of the colonizer'.[26] Whereas Shephard's mind is one where 'the two worlds… met in the same chaos' (p. 77), Singh has a consciousness described as 'physical, integral as a root to the branch and body of the tree… There was no difference between the thing he knew and the man he was. He was his knowledge' (p. 264). This certitude, the 'concentration, purpose and will' is a source of strength for Shephard who feels that '[Singh] was like the road itself which said there was only one way' (p. 273).[27] Conversely, in his relationship with Shephard, Singh discovers a closed-upness, a limitation in himself. The story he tells of himself as a boy on the sugar estate seems to be one he has not previously shared. Without Shephard, we see Singh becoming enmeshed in the politics of plotting and revenge, a mirror image of the world of Crabbe. As Singh tells Crabbe:

> There never was a man who make me feel more deep than Shephard… He expose himself to me in a way I never learn to do to any friends however near. An' through him I learn for the first time what it could mean to feel loyal, not only to the cause but loyal to the person too. I come as near to lovin' Shephard as any man come to lovin' a next, and it was his murder twist my heart like it was my own son dying in front my face. (p. 402)

What Singh describes is a profound remaking of the inner person and one senses that for Lamming this is (like the political imperative of love) essential to the revolutionary remaking of the colonial world. He shows, though, that the vulnerable exposure this involves is necessarily painful. When Shephard, Singh and Lee are discussing their differences and private misgivings, the labour of breaking silence is very powerfully conveyed in the rhythms of Lamming's prose:

> It had happened again: the frenzied argument, then the sudden pause like a frozen breath separating the sound of a voice from the echo you expected.... Then each would know it was his duty to break the spell of what had not yet been said. Each knew it was the moment to explode the motive which nursed this pause; and each, uncertain and yet determined, tried; so that the pause flared into a clutter of voices which left something unsaid. Then the tremor would begin, a moment after the voices had retreated into a tired procession of syllables, noiseless as petals fallen into silence... (p. 264)

Singh fears that if they cannot achieve absolute openness and trust, then Paravecino's allegation that 'the surface friendship is going to spell misery for one group or the other' will become the truth. And, of course, when there is a knock at the door of their private room, guilts over actions and knowledge unrevealed erupt. As Penelope recognises, 'Secrets are difficult to conceal because a secret is by nature contagious' (p. 172), and the words 'spying', 'secrecy', 'informer', 'conceal', 'suspicion', 'vigilance', 'treachery' toll through this episode and through the novel, connecting Mark's guilt over recording the life of Fern Row in his diary ('Shall I concede that I may be a spy and that my activity is a kind of treachery?' (p. 54)) to Baboo's duplicitous activities. Later, after Shephard learns that Butterfield had come to warn him of Crabbe's murderous plans, he tells the boys, 'Do not suspect too much. Suspicion is the end. It will rot everywhere, everything we do' (p. 310).

'Suspicion' is frequently the symptom of an 'innocent' way of seeing in the novel, less a product of deviousness than of an unthinking, perceptually passive response to the 'obvious'. Lamming's paradoxical treatment of the nature of innocence is particularly revealed in his portrayal of Baboo. When Baboo brings his murder as an offering to Singh and is shocked by Singh's horrified rejection, Baboo's voice is 'almost innocent in its cry of sad and despairing solicitude':

> ...was only for you, Singh, was only for you I do it... from infancy I dream to see someone like myself, some Indian with your achievement rule San Cristobal. My only mistake was to wish it for you Singh, was only for you I do what I do... (p. 407)

His action is rooted in a way of seeing that is naively unreflective, passively dependent on a fixed outer reality. Like Kennedy, Baboo is a victim of the obvious:

> His glances seemed effortless, incurious and without intention, as though some instinct of dumb and bored credulity had defined their function. His eyes revealed no possibility of doubt; no tendency for surprise or expectation was entertained. His eyes were casual, unhurried, almost reluctant, as though they had refused to trespass beyond those objects that interrupted the ordinary line of vision. He did not look. His attention had to be seduced. It surrendered to the thing which it could not avoid, lingered for a moment, and then withdrew, innocent, without calculation, impartial. ...He did not look. But he saw. Baboo saw everything. That look of innocent renunciation was the mask which neutralised his interest, and lead everything finally within the range of his motive. His treachery was faceless, transparent, freed from any form of visible intrigue or cunning. (p. 413)

The intensity and deliberate superfluity of this description of Baboo's perceptual passivity links profoundly the epistemic and the ethical. We are in the Blakean territory of 'the five senses whelm'd' the 'fluxile eyes' turned 'into two stationary orbs, concentrating all things',[28] where imaginative vision has met empirical death. Lamming has already traced the destructiveness of seeing but not looking in Kennedy's life. He does not need to spell out the implications of this way of seeing in a society where the most obvious 'fact' has been the apparent difference of the ethnic other.

The innocence of Baboo's way of seeing links the questions of loyalty, perception and action to the ironies of the novel's title, the paradox that whilst Age stands for action, experience and the acceptance of responsibility, Innocence is passive and profoundly conservative. The conventional connotations (as expressed by Ma Shephard when she tells the boys at the beginning of the novel, 'I feel your innocence take to me' (p. 93)) are subverted in a thoroughly Blakean way. As Lamming wrote in *The Pleasures of Exile*, 'To be innocent is to be eternally dead',[29] and as the young Bob thinks, 'Age is nothing if there ain't no doing' (p. 138). Later, the equation between innocence and existential nullity is reinforced by Mark [Kennedy]'s diary entry when he berates himself for his mere semblance of mourning for Marcia: 'I felt innocent as the clouds which collected overhead. Innocent and free' (p. 333).

In failing to see the ironies in Lamming's use of Age and Innocence in the novel, some critics seem to me to have misread the role of the four boys, Bob, Singh, Lee and Rowley. Their importance in the novel is commonly seen as Lamming's attempt to portray the germ of a true human community which unites the divided ranks of the colonised, and also includes the children of the former ruling whites who have climbed down from their ladder of privilege.[30] This may be so, but it has also been assumed that the secret society of the four boys is the Innocence of the novel's title. Mervyn Morris, for instance, quotes from *The Pleasures of Exile* of 'the distance which separates Age which apprehends, from Innocence which can only see', but then comments: 'Yet in this novel, Innocence seems in the end to see more accurately than Age'.[31] This misreading, which fails to recognise in what respects the boys are not so different from their elders, is perhaps a consequence of not really grasping Lamming's emphasis on perception. And not seeing how the same problems of relationship affect the boys, nor how much the boys are changed in the course of the novel, misses the true depth of their tragedy.

We are introduced to them, it is true, with a slightly sentimental picture of their lack of racial bias. As they listen to the altercation on the seashore between Thief and Baboo, Bob's and the young Singh's race is stressed, but, we are told, 'they showed no awareness of this difference as they listened' (p. 102).

They share a common perception of the island's past in their 'easy co-ordination' in telling the legend of the Tribe Boys and the Bandit Kings; but their boast that they had surpassed their elders, who were 'whining and shouting about San Cristobal and the future as though it had always been an impossible journey' (p. 140) is rather too obviously smug, as is their easy confidence that they were transforming 'the myth of the political meetings into some reality which no one could question', and other such self-congratulatory phrases. The comment that 'San Cristobal had contracted to a pebble in their hands' (p. 140), with its echo of Shephard's vision of megalomaniac control, ought to warn us that there is an hubristic irony at work. It should remind, too, of

the moment recorded in Kennedy's diary of the 'little world...
which no force can annihilate' (p. 52). There is, too, the boys'
enjoyment of 'secrecy' and 'power', temptations that connect
them to, rather than distinguish them from, the world of their
elders. Their growth towards experience begins when they accept Rowley Crabbe as one of the little Society, and of course,
immediately after the burst of self-congratulation this involves,
the boys make the fatal (and innocent) error of giving Singh's
father's cigarette lighter to Rowley as a token of acceptance.

The way the boys are most like their elders is in the game of
hide-and-seek they play in the woods. Separated from each other,
the boys' sense of oneness is subverted by private knowledge.
Singh knows his father burns to murder Rowley's father, a secret
that gives him a 'feeling like shame... a charge which, even in his
innocence, he wanted to avoid' (p. 156). When Bob catches sight of
his sister masturbating in the wood, he discovers an hitherto
unconscious racial shame when he considers that the person to
whom he could least confess what he has seen is Singh. Rowley
imagines inviting Bob, Singh and Lee to his house, but 'they did not
fit... the chairs would not admit of their presence' (p.160). He has
to puzzle over why his father's and grandmother's affection for him
should be at the root of their rejection of Bob and Singh and Lee.
Later, on Bird Island, where the boys have taken Penelope on one
of their 'works', and where they encounter Shephard, Rowley is
divided from the other boys by his awareness that the accident with
the boat will be known because his father is having Shephard
watched. The others 'felt he knew something which they could not
guess, and he was afraid' (p. 217). Their response is to turn inwards,
to form, as their elders do, an exclusive circle which isolates them
and threatens to destroy the very openness which brought them
together. They see themselves as a secret society taking on the rest
of San Cristobal, as in their strategy to get oil for Crabbe during the
power strike. They, too, succumb to the temptations of power,
when Rowley feels that it 'was the secret Society outwitting San
Cristobal, and his power surpassing that of his father' (p. 295).

It is Rowley's death which finally marks their passage from
innocence to experience, as they learn that they must carry the
responsibilities for the consequences of their actions, for failure

as well as achievement. They have to suffer as historically aware persons, knowing that they sought to create a vision of community at a moment when as the elder Singh says, 'The time for separating has come' (p. 269).

Their tragedy lies in their powerlessness to make anyone understand what the little Society has meant, or to save Singh's father from possible conviction and execution for the mental hospital fire. When the court refuses to hear the evidence that could have saved him, and even Ma Shephard turns against them, the boys feel that they 'had no power to persuade anyone who did not understand and could not believe what they had done' (p. 433). It is a feeling which recalls Thief's rejoinder that innocence has no language 'unless the next man lend you his belief'. They have been initiated into a society where the negative regard of the other is part of the meaning of daily life. Their tragedy is the prematurity of their bid to realise the essential unity-in-difference of the human race. This is Lamming's historical realism. The personal friendship of Singh's and Crabbe's sons does not change the oppressive structure of a colonised society. As Thief tells Rockey, '…it goin' to take a terrible crime to make them [oppressor and oppressed] meet in a common place' (p. 417). The boys have passed beyond the innocence which sees but does not apprehend. It is now Ma Shephard who says with unconscious irony, 'But I am innocent, innocent as the day that now leavin' this land. I was innocent an' whole in what I do' (p. 396). The boys have seen that mysterious abstraction 'Law' for what it is, the 'mind-forg'd manacles' of the ruling class. When they resist the curfew, we are told that 'The Law could not now enter their feeling' (p. 425).

Lamming inhabits many voices in the novel, and at no point offers either a blueprint for how to conduct the struggle for decolonisation or a vision of what a decolonised society might look like. But, besides those of the boys, the voices that I believe Lamming most wants us to hear beyond the novel's end are Thief's and Rockey's. Their discussion of the revengeful mayhem that Thief wishes to visit on the invading troops brings together the novel's core tension between the attractions of a Fanonian vision of the purifying fires of anti-colonial violence and a Shelleyan vision of revolutionary pacifism and love:

' 'Tis like the sea, Thief, life ain't got no favours to give but the favour each man can take. An' if you choose a murderin' evil, whatever reason you choose it make no difference, then you buildin' a tabernacle that can only house one breed, an' the sun goin' set a lastin' disgrace on the bones that help you build. For ever an' ever, Thief, till time change to eternity it will go on an' on...'

'But a man don't make his feeling,' said Thief. 'They just hold him an' hold him, till he an' it come together as one. An' 'tis a feelin' that hold me when I watch these troops.'

'It hold me too,' said Rockey, 'an' 'tis why I ask what will happen tomorrow.' (pp. 417-418)

It is Rockey who expresses Lamming's recognition of the endless potentiality of people and his conviction that, though particular struggles may fail, it is in the process of struggle that people begin to tap those unguessed-at potentialities:

Everyman hides many sources... an' there's no tellin' till the lids be taken off. (p. 380)

Thirty years is a lot o' years for a man to struggle with life... But when my struggle was real an' help to make more life, I could struggle again an' again till the Almighty call me home. A man must struggle, Thief, 'cause that is what man was fashioned for, but his struggle got to keep a clear meanin' in his head an' heart, or else... (p. 415)

So what might the young Guyanese radicals at the university have gained if they had persisted with the 'hardness' of Lamming's novels? In the case of *Of Age and Innocence*, they might have shared – all too pertinently for those times – with Shephard, Singh and Lee the fearful temptations and pains of political vanguardism and the bitter ash of the politics of revenge. They might have begun to understand in depth, not the appearance but the construction – historical, psychological and epistemic – of what oppressed them, why it was so hard to make changes even in a society crying out for change. They might have been drawn to seeing that this was in part because of our complexity as beings whose processes of knowing and understanding both unite and divide us. They might have understood why Lamming challenges the reader to probe beneath the surface of things. But they could also have taken to heart Rockey's vision and aspired to Thief's high praise of his friend: 'Where you get your heart, Rockey, 'tis high as any hill with hope. You never say no' (p. 380).

ENDNOTES

1. Supriya Nair, *Caliban's Curse: George Lamming and the Revisioning of History*, Ann Arbor, University of Michigan Press, 1996, p. 20.
2. J. Dillon Brown, 'Changing the Subject: The Aesthetics and Politics of Reading in the Novels of George Lamming', in *The Locations of George Lamming*, ed. by Bill Schwarz, London, MacMillan, 2007, pp. 91-111.
3. Wilson Harris, *Tradition, the Writer and Society*, London, New Beacon Books, 1967, p. 28.
4. In 'The West Indian People' (*New World Quarterly*, [2. 2], 1966, pp. 63-74) Lamming confesses to an ignorance of the inner Indian world, and in *Of Age* he deals with Indian communal solidarity as a primordial bond or as a scaled-up matter of individual psychology, rather than seeing it as culturally rooted in the kind of socio-religious institutions to which many Indians in Trinidad and Guyana then gave their loyalty. Although in this essay, he stresses Indian 'difference' as a positive value, in the novel he minimises the extent to which Indians are culturally distinctive. So, whereas the social and ethno-cultural roots of Shephard's or Crabbe's or Butterfield's feelings are acutely drawn, Baboo and Singh are defined only by their race.
5. See the acerbic satire of the 'Pink Curtain' episode depicting colonial functionaries with nebulous pseudo-jobs and locals who have prostituted themselves in one way or other to the colonial order (pp. 208-228).
6. Harris, *Tradition, the Writer and Society*, p. 28.
7. The connections between Naipaul's and Lamming's novels are worth an essay in their own right. Far beyond the superficial resemblances between San Cristobal and Isabella, there is the use that Naipaul makes of the idea of the person made in the eyes of the other (though for Naipaul the need for interpersonal witness can only be a weakness and never a strength, because he ignores Lamming's sense of dialectic).
8. See Rohlehr, 'The Problem of the Problem of Form' in *The Shape of that Hurt and Other Essays*, Port of Spain, Longman Trinidad, 1992, pp. 7-15 ('Man Entering His Voice': Lamming's *Of Age and Innocence*).
9. W. Cartey, *Whispers from the Caribbean*, Los Angeles, Center for Afro-American Studies, University of California, 1991, pp. 334-347.
10. See also Sandra Pouchet Paquet's chapter on *Of Age and Innocence* in her *The Novels of George Lamming*, London, Heinemann, 1982,

pp. 48-66, where she provides a useful summary of the narrative and locates the novel in the politics of the colonial revolt of the 1950s.

11. Painted between 1992 and 2001, the series is reproduced and discussed in Rupert Roopnaraine's *Primacy of the Eye: The Art of Stanley Greaves*, Leeds, Peepal Tree Press, 2005, pp. 160-186.

12. See for instance Eagleton, *Reason, Faith, and Revolution: Reflections on the God Debate*, New Haven, Yale University Press, 2010.

13. Confirmation of Lamming's engagement with Sartrean existentialism is given by Philip Nanton in 'Knowing and Not Knowing George Lamming: Personal Style and Metropolitan Influences' (in *The Locations of George Lamming*) on the basis of an interview with Lamming. Nanton doesn't, though, extend the analysis to the novels, and indeed there appears to have been little writing on other Caribbean authors of the period – qv Orlando Patterson – that explores responses to radical European thought in their work.

14. Pouchet Paquet, *The Novels of George Lamming*, p. 52.

15. Rohlehr, 'The Problem of the Problem of Form' , pp. 9-11.

16. Lamming, 'The Negro Writer and his World', *Presence Africaine*, The 1st International Conference of Negro Writers and Artists, Paris, 1956, pp. 324-332.

17. Brown, 'Changing the Subject', pp. 100-101. See also Supriya Nair's *Caliban's Curse* (1996), which follows Rohlehr in drawing connections between Lamming as writer and Mark Kennedy as fictive analogue. Both face the challenge of re-inventing a Caribbean literary culture under the burden of a language and forms entrenched in colonial history. Thus Mark abandons a work of colonial historiography he has been writing and asks: 'Why did I ever believe that it was possible to reconstruct the life of that three-fingered rebel?' (*Of Age and Innocence*, p.129).

18. Cartey, *Whispers from the Caribbean*, p. 334.

19. Warrior ants feature in the story of the Tribe Boys and Bandit Kings, the 'terrible cargo' the Kings return with, who cannot be fought because 'ants don't understand, an' you can't fight an enemy who don't understand...' (p. 120); as a moral epithet used by the boys to account for Thief's career ('So he behave like the ants... that is without seein' what they kill or why...' (p. 115)); and, of course, in the episode when the boys watch the ants in the woods (pp. 146-149) and then kill as many of them as they can, an episode that provides scale and a point of learning. Finally, there is the image right at the end of the novel, of 'a regiment of ants... waiting, patient and furious, to devour the flesh of the living' (p. 434), an image both of the nihilistic violence that may lurk under the surface of societies like San Cristobal, and of the fearsome energies that enable survival against the bleakest odds.

20. Martin Carter, *Poems of Resistance*, Georgetown, University of Guyana, 1964, p. 1 (first published, London, Lawrence and Wishart, 1954).

21. See Amanda Fricker, *Epistemic Injustice: Power and the Ethics of Knowing*, Oxford, OUP, 2007.

22. Lamming, *The Pleasures of Exile*, London, Michael Joseph, 1960, p. 116.

23. Ibid., p. 56.

24. In *The Pleasures of Exile* Lamming describes the arrival of the Indians as one of the three most important events in the history of the Caribbean (pp. 36-37), and in a speech delivered in 1965 he argues that in the very difference of the Indians' cultural heritage lay 'a most desirable extension of the West Indian reality'. He spoke of the Indians as 'perhaps, our only jewels of a true native thrift and industry. They have taught us by example the value of money; for they respect money as only people with a high sense of communal solidarity can' ('The West Indian People', p. 69).

25. 'The West Indian People', p. 69.

26. *The Pleasures of Exile*, p. 35.

27. There are obvious parallels between the relationship of Shephard and Singh and that between L'Ouverture and Dessalines which Lamming draws attention to in his discussion of C.L.R. James's *The Black Jacobins* in *The Pleasures of Exile* (pp. 125-150). Lamming follows James in seeing Toussaint, the educated man, as having become, at a crucial stage in the revolt, confused and hesitant about his objectives because his loyalty to the ideal of French civilisation conflicted with the revolutionary demands of the mass of the black slaves. Dessalines, the ex-field slave, narrower in outlook and uninvolved with the white world, has always known precisely what had to be done. When they discuss the rumour that the People's Communal Movement wants to kill the whites, Shephard says he does not want to kill anyone, but Singh rejoins: 'Unless it is necessary... Remember they don't think twice about killing if it is necessary' (p. 244). (Wilson Harris, characteristically, sees in Toussaint's wavering a 'groping towards an alternative to conventional statehood, a conception of wider possibilities', (*Tradition, the Writer and Society*, p. 45).

28. William Blake, *Europe*, Plate 11 (13), lines 11-12, *The Continental Prophecies*, Princeton, Princeton University Press, 1995, p. 242. There are a number of Blakean echoes in *Of Age and Innocence*, not least in the discussion of the decision to betray Crabbe by the two policemen (pp. 319-320) and the short one's claim that 'Lucifer an' Christ is blood brothers in spirit.'

29. *The Pleasures of Exile*, p. 103.

30. 'The West Indian People', p. 69

31. Mervyn Morris, 'The Poet as Novelist', in *The Islands In Between*, Oxford, OUP, 1968, p. 78.

A strong sense of identity makes a man feel he can do no wrong; too little accomplishes the same.
                                    Djuna Barnes (*Nightwood*)

BOOK ONE

FLIGHT

Suddenly the land was no longer there, and the airliner had lifted itself like a cripple grown used to his crutches. The sky was coming closer as the light turned to cloud which travelled always like a tramp. And the weather was absent. Two small bulbs, half-hidden in a roof of metal, were stammering a language of red and green flickers, and the girl with the strawberry face that smiled every wish away passed among her passengers like the air, easy and important.

But Marcia could tell from his sudden preoccupation with the diaries that Mark had felt something was going to happen. He was leaning forward, supported by his elbows and his hands fixed flat against his face in its clownish manoeuvre down and across the pages which lay on his lap. For the second time his hands slipped, and his fingers slid together to make a curve of knuckles which rested his chin; but his sense could not receive what his eyes were seeing. His attention was tarnished. The pages remained in their natural state, a familiar contrivance of words and paper which ignored all desire. And he wished that time would leap the hours and hurry without interruption to an immediate arrival. Each second was a sickening obstacle.

She put her hand on his shoulder and creased the overcoat with her nails, but he avoided her affection, and kept his eyes on the page. He was feeling in his habitual way, which great altitudes always exaggerated, that something was bound to happen. But the airliner only snored, gently, like a roomful of children carried by the same dream. The green light blinked frantically, but the red bulb was still, a scarlet socket deprived of its eye. Marcia pressed on his shoulder again. He smiled and kissed her mouth; and then, without the least delay, he continued reading as though the words needed his attention, and his attention was the only possible chance against the disaster which he suspected. Marcia took her hand away and closed her eyes.

The airliner found its course, making a grumble, low and genial like an old man singing in his sleep. A huge bank of cloud collapsed and spread into flat, white wings that sailed under its belly. And voices dimmed gradually to a whisper, cosy and reminiscent. Marcia was alone. Gradually her eyes opened, wandering across the silver grey partition with the transparent lettering which carved the order, no smoking. The yellow light which filled the space with words was already turned off, and the order was no longer effective. She was going to have a cigarette, but her eyes closed again, and it seemed that her need had also ended. The voices rose behind her, full of habit, and her eyes opened. They closed and opened in a play of light and darkness like the red and green flickers of the small bulbs which were now idle and sightless.

Mark had withdrawn into a fearful isolation. She turned away in search of Bill and Penelope who were sitting two rows ahead on the other side. She could recognise their heads turned towards each other as they talked. For a moment she felt an urge to hear what they were saying, but other voices had intervened. There was an uneven rhythm of talk which rose and fell around her like the near drone of the airliner. These passengers had already made this vehicle their transitory home. And she thought that she would do the same. She crouched deeper into her seat, and looked in the direction of Bill and Penelope, and wondered again what they were saying. But their voices were taken by the loud hum of the airliner, and gradually she felt the effort to remember them in some other place. She was coaxing her memory to revive their first meeting, so that she might relive through this flight some of the events which filled that time and finally turned their first meeting into a friendship which held all four of them so close together: Bill and Penelope, herself and Mark.

She could see Bill's head slide away over the seat as though he were about to sleep. She stretched her hand to touch Mark who was staring outside at the airliner's wing. She glanced at him, then at Bill and Penelope, but she was separated from them all by silence and reverie, and Mark's fear. She turned indolently in the seat, withdrawing her hand from Mark's arm, and wondered how he might have differed from Bill, and what, at the root of their friendship, was her real attraction for Penelope. The seat slipped lower under her, and her neck found a new rest.

Words were collecting in her head, vague and vagrant like a movement of shadows over an indifferent surface. She could almost feel them stray, as though they refused to obey their normal use. They slipped from their meaning, sailing briefly like feeble noises that stumble for a while before returning to the silence which contains them. The signs did not cohere. The ends would not meet in a meaning which would help her memory. In order to tidy the mess which they were accumulating in her mind, she thought aloud: 'I want to marry Mark and bear him children.' The words surprised her. She thought others might have heard, but Mark was still reading, looking up now and again to observe the weather. Perhaps he had heard, but she had often told him, and it was not likely that he would have taken a special interest in her slip. She glanced at him, and thought again to herself: 'But he always says he doesn't want children, and he is afraid of marriage, as he is of the plane.' Then the words receded leaving their inept traces over the surface of her mind. She would abandon them and give herself to the vague shapes of places which her memory was striving slowly to restore. She noticed Mark's hand tremble as he turned the pages of the diary, and she waited to hear again the voices which were trying earlier to make their signatures on the air. But everyone was quiet, and the airliner seemed to make its own kind of silence too.

She lay back, her head at rest on the reclining seat, and looked at the small bulbs so securely set in their cells, and felt the natural intimacy of sheets, hoping that Mark would hold her hand and love her only with his presence beside her. That was all she asked as the liner sailed the air like a hand through water. But Mark could not appreciate this pleasure. It was real for Marcia. She knew peace like the palm of her hand.

The liner slipped in a pocket of air, and a shudder shook Mark. His elbows had slipped from their rest and his hands automatically hid his eyes. When he raised his head he saw the sign EXIT painted in gold against a red margin at the top of the sliding door. He looked at the door with misgiving, and his glance moved like a man in hiding across the area of the airliner and gradually towards the life-belt which peeped out from the back of another passenger's seat. The pages remained on his lap, submissive and indifferent, while his fingers pecked at the life-belt. His nerves were screwed by a single anxiety which forced his glance past the window towards the tip of the airliner's wing. He could detect with a frightening precision where the curve of the wing came to an end, and the air in an infinite superfluity registered nothing. There was an absence of things outside; and that absence, transparent and impenetrable had taken meaning from his mind. He looked about the airliner with its quiet cargo of lives before guiding his glance again past the window towards the territory of absence which encompassed them; and nothing seemed meaningful but the arrogant little order EXIT on the door and the incalculable absence which had labelled the air. He was getting dizzy. Fear shook him like the wind, alive and real as an enemy, and he hurried his attention to the pages. But his eyes could not find the words which made an intolerable noise in his head. His ears would let nothing in but that distant and official voice, false and cheerful: FROM LONDON TO SAN CRISTOBAL... FLYING TIME... IN THE INEVITABLE EVENT... IN THE INEVITABLE EVENT... The words rattled through his head like dice rolled across a surface of dry bone. His hands were wet. He placed one hand on Marcia's shoulder, and set some of the pages down on her lap; and she knew, like a horse its stable, what she should do. She would read the pages and let her interest in these fragments of the diary become his distraction.

She settled the pages on her lap and wondered why he had always postponed his promise to let her read them. Her curiosity had almost failed but she had decided to wait. Now, like the sudden shudder of the plane which tumbled some of the pages off his knee, he had passed them to her. For a moment it pleased her to think that she would be the only other person who had seen them, and she leaned across and kissed him. He tried to smile, but his face was tight, his lips barely moved. And she thought 'it's because he's afraid, it's only in a moment of weakness that he really wants to share his feelings.' And she felt an overwhelming sympathy for him. She wanted to crush his ears between her hands, and bring his body against hers. But his anxiety had already separated them. He had drawn the small, green blinds to obstruct his view of the airliner's wing and continued reading the pages which he had kept. Marcia considered the sheets. Her hands were excited, and she was almost beyond herself with elation. There was no need to tax her memory with new errands. His first sentence was more immediate.

'Midnight and a year since we have known each other. I see this voyage and Marcia in another moment which I recognise, feel almost I can touch: my father dying, and the day looking ordinary outside where brown birds with blue necks fly over the mud shore and children are pushing their scabby fingers mining for false gold. And on the same night my father, now a naked corpse, is taken into a small room smelling of camphor, and my mother's friends assemble to wake him with weeping and coffee. Their fingers nibble pink cubes of cheese, and a voice says, "someday the clouds will roll away forever." Not only this moment on the deck but that time too waits here beside me and Marcia. It does not stretch towards anything but the sea which pursues us and connects Barcelona with the Balearic islands; and Marcia and the boat are part of the mud shore and the festival of mourning for my father, and twenty years largely forgotten, obscured with living. Now I am standing somewhere between islands and mainland.

'The sea surrounds us. The surface sparkles with light and a little sentiment where the moon charges from behind the black hump of hills. They look like men marking time, large and indifferent, and they will be with us all the way and in similar attitudes until the day returns to tell their colour and their age. But now they look splendid and I am with them under the same anonymous cover of night. The deck is wet and cold, and this voyage becomes an adventure which denies health and seems beyond reason. I try to think about Marcia, but suddenly the wind comes up, touching us with spray, and I remember Bill and Penelope who have taken a cabin for the night.

'The young German passes in his heavy wind-breaker and the thick black boots which reach to his knees. I hear the boots pause, and notice he has stopped. Marcia leans forward to make sure someone is standing there, in front of us. Then she closes her eyes and makes herself smaller under the blanket. I surrender to the wind, frozen beyond feeling. Marcia puts her head in my hands and stretches full length on the bench, and when she falls asleep I make a pillow with the end of the blanket under her head and let her lie alone. The German leans over the rails fiddling with the ropes which tied the ship in harbour. I know that he wants to talk, and I am curious to know what he is thinking. I remember his face earlier in the afternoon, lively and strong, yet without much meaning, like a coin that takes the wrong turn down a slot. Can it be that he has boarded the wrong boat on purpose? It excites me to think that this is true, so I don't shirk from his effort at conversation. He asks after Bill and Penelope.

' "They took a cabin," I say. He laughs in the crook of his arm like a child trying to conceal a secret mischief, and I wonder whether he is mad. He's serious again, making his knuckles crack in the wind.

' "It's too short a journey for a cabin," he says. "We arrive in the morning."

'I want to ask him whether he doesn't feel the cold, but I reply: "I think so too."

'Agreement makes him eager to talk, and I recall him in the afternoon sitting on the deck staring at his black boots like a refugee who has been refused. Then Marcia was asking him when the boat would sail and he suggested they should cut the ropes and let it drift. Ever since she has avoided him.

'Now he lets go of the ropes and puts his fingers in the narrow slots that slice the sides of the wind-breaker. Standing before me, he shows a face evenly divided by the night and the moon. I move closer to make sure it is the same face, narrow, tense, and hardy.

' "You were not in the war?" he asks, and suddenly turns his back to the rails, raising the ropes between his fingers. I hesitate.

' "Where were you?" I ask, and it seems that he has forgotten my answer which I avoid.

' "I was sent to Poland and Czechoslovakia," he says. He is looking down at the water as he talks, holding the ropes idly between his fingers. "They drafted me at fifteen," he says, then grins like a thief caught defenceless. He takes his hand from the rails, presses them along his body down to the enormous black boots, and I see his body bend, easy and agile, up and down in a tiresome exercise. He has refused to care. It is not the objectionable toughness of one who is callous by vocation. Just a certain obscurity of intention.

' "Well, that war is over," he says, and he makes it sound like news.

' "And you are taking a holiday, now?"

' "I'm just going," he says. He pushes his sleeve above his watch to see the time, and I suddenly think, with unaccountable malice, that he is in some illegal traffic between North Africa and the Spanish Coast.

' "Have you ever been to North Africa?"

' "As a prisoner," he says. The wind blows his hair about his ears, and he looks, in his natural indifference of manner, like one who is used to ignoring the weather.

'Marcia is getting restless on the bench, and I go over to stroke her hair. But I still think about the German, that face which does not seem to belong anywhere, and the casual, quick voice, telling his experience like one offering tips to an unseen waiter. I try to talk with Marcia about him. She is awake and there is nothing else to occupy us. We are both feeling the largeness of the night. The ship is rolling heavily. Marcia folds the blanket into a cushion which makes two seats, and we sit, leaning against each other. The wind has changed direction. The night is cooler. Marcia's speech is slow and lazy, and I suddenly remember that Marcia has always got to make an elaborate ritual of awakening. It proceeds by stages.

' "I'm not sleeping now," she says, "you know my habit."

'Sometimes this irritates me, the way she can slip like a seal into a perfect lethargy of nature.

'"We're an impossible pair," she says, and I think: "That's true, and it's probably why we're together." She confronts me as an example of something I cannot define in myself. But I am about to tell her that we are perfectly matched, and it's foolish to complain, that I am satisfied. I press her arm and kiss her on the mouth. "I don't think we can make a go of this," I say.

'Suddenly Marcia comes alive with an agility which seems almost deliberate. She warms my hands under her blouse and presses her face against my neck. We are feeding a little life to the night, but the memory of the young German alters our intentions. Slowly, she releases her arms.

‘"What are you thinking?" Marcia asks, and I answer, "Nothing."

‘But I am thinking again about the night they carried my father's corpse into the small room, and the voices singing, "someday the clouds will roll away forever." I ignore Marcia's waiting and wonder about the faith of the friends kneeling beside my father's corpse, and the wish of all who declare that the shape and conduct of our world may be contained in one mind. I try to imagine a consciousness which carries my secret and the German's, and all the secret lives that include every instance of life before and always. I see the German passing again and slowly, surely, I hear, like the plodding hoof of his boots, the words: out of touch, out of touch. He walks past, and the words keep returning like a fever, beyond my control; and I wonder what can be my interest in this brief meeting with a man who will pass me on the street tomorrow like the wind, experienced and yet beyond real human contact. Is it that he suggests myself?

‘"Tell me what you're thinking," Marcia says. I hesitate, and she adds, "Do you love me?" But she also chooses my answer before I can forget the words that echo like iron from the German's boots. "Kiss me," she says.

‘She holds my face and her eyes close on my mouth. We watch the moon trying to recover its stride behind the hills, and the sea seems to sail like our silence out of sight, leaving us with the privilege of the deserted deck.’

Marcia reread the last paragraph, but before she had turned the page the boy who sat directly in front raised his head. Mark was distracted and Marcia smiled, but the boy ignored them and turned his glance on the other passengers. They passed before him like troops for whom an afternoon inspection has become a formality. Now and again he would turn to speak with the woman who sat beside him, but she was always curt and uncommunicative in reply. He was in search of company, but the faces were all foreign, and he remembered the warnings he had heard against mixing with strangers in San Cristobal. Marcia thought it was time he sat down, and the woman, who seemed to feel her neighbour's wish, suddenly ordered him with a jerk of the wrist. He huddled into the seat, and sat quietly, looking towards the cockpit. Mark looked relieved, and Marcia reached for his arm and tried to coax him into speech.

'You think we'll meet that German in San Cristobal?'

'What German?' Her voice had surprised him.

'The man you met on the boat from Barcelona,' she said. 'He sounds like someone who would turn up anywhere.'

'I don't remember much about San Cristobal,' said Mark. 'I don't know what sort of people turn up there.'

He had avoided any mention of the diaries. Marcia reflected. She wanted to distract him from this anxiety about the plane, but the boy had raised his head again. Mark was staring outside at the airliner's wing. The boy might have spoken now, but Marcia was considering the pages. She showed no sign of acknowledging his presence, and the boy dipped his head and slumped down like a fruit into his seat. He could not find anyone to help him kill time with talk, and he started to count backwards from ten to five on the fingers of one hand. He paused, spread the next hand over his knee and started again from five to one. He looked up to see whether the woman had noticed, but his effort was in vain. She was reading the map which showed the route they were taking from London to San Cristobal.

'Granny!'

'What is it?' she exclaimed.

He noticed that he had scared her, and he hurried to say something before she turned her head away.

'Will Daddy be there to meet us?' he asked.

'What makes you think not?' she said.

He had not really thought, and the question was a way of making her talk. Now her answer had confused him and he tried to remember what he wanted to say. He saw her finger stretch to where the red lines intersected on the map and he felt he was gradually losing her attention. He told himself that he would not miss this chance, and suddenly he blundered into speech.

'Why does Daddy choose to live out of England?' he asked.

'It's his duty to live where his work takes him,' she said, and turned to check the name where the red lines showed land on the map. He wanted to interrupt her, but he felt that his attempt had failed and it would be better to wait until she had lost interest in the map.

He raised his head and looked round at the passengers. Some were already asleep, effortless and unworried as the airliner. The hostess had taken care of their fears. Sound had frozen their ears to a state of unhearing. It was as though their departure from the land had granted them a reprieve to share the freedom of the air. And Marcia was reliving through the diaries the morning of their arrival on another island.

'The boat crawls wilfully through the bay as though it wants to prolong our waiting. Marcia warns that the German is approaching. Soon he joins us, looking towards the hills which are now shaggy and brown. A desert in air claiming small pockets of life along the levelled areas of the land. I wonder what is happening there now. I would be there and here on this boat at the same time, and beyond the curve of the bay where the faces are blurred by light and distance. I neither like nor dislike the German. He is simply there, and I am here beside Marcia who is impatient to arrive. The German watches us sideways, but I pretend not to notice, and Marcia remains stubbornly silent. I do not know what he sees, but I think I shall speak to him. Marcia anticipates this and warns me with her elbow. I decide to let him alone. We shall soon disperse, and that will be the end of my interest.

'"When do you think we'll arrive?" I ask. Marcia frowns.

'"Half an hour," the German says. He smiles like a card player who knows that the game is his. Marcia avoids his glance, and I am suddenly angered by this face which seems so cunning. I remember our conversation last night, and it occurs to me that something will happen if I call him a Nazi. Say Nazi, I tell myself, and see what happens. I hold Marcia's hand and turn to the German, and I can feel the word tighten my tongue. There is something like noise in my mouth.

'"Tell me," I say, "what time is it?"

'"Ten o'clock," he says. He drops his hand and smiles.

'"Let's go on the other side," says Marcia, "we can see everything better from there."

'I have abandoned my little enterprise. But the German is rebuked. He turns to watch us go and his smile changes to a tight-lipped grimace.

'The light is sharp and clear, and the sea is a repetitive frolic. Ten o'clock. Ahead of us the houses are arranged above each other, following the slope of the hills. They slide quietly down to the shops and cafés which wait for the ship. Approaching the pier, the hills begin to close round us on all sides. The police are waiting like amiable watchdogs. The boat grazes the pier, and the crowd press forward, waving a general welcome to the arriving voyagers. A whole village has come to see. It is a morning of delight. The air is startled, and the bars stare from the edge of the street.

"What a beautiful setting," says Marcia. She is holding my hand staring through her dark sunglasses. The baggage men are beginning to crowd on to the boat, and their cries scatter in all directions.

' "These people haven't come to anyone in particular," I say. Marcia does not answer, but she cuddles under my arm, and I understand her feeling. The sun arouses her. Desire pricks her from the back, like a pistol. She is looking at me the way she always does when this happens. And I want to laugh.

' "You'll have to wait," I say.

'She leans her chin on the iron rail and stares down at the water. Then she is alerted, and stands erect, taking her hand away from my shoulder.

' "How long shall we stay here?" she asks.

' "Until the money is finished," I say.

' "I can let you have some," she says, "if you try to finish the book you started."

'I feel my skin twitch, and I pretend disinterest. I do not want to encourage this talk, because I cannot fulfil my part of the bargain. I am relieved to see one of the baggage men making towards us, but I know that Marcia is waiting for me to speak.

' "Would you take the money on that condition?"

'I reply promptly that I shall not, and Marcia looks wounded.

' "You don't want to feel any responsibility," she says, "not even to me."

' "And why did you come here?" I ask.

' "I don't know," she says. Then she adds very quickly, "because I love you."

'A baggage man is trying to rent us a small house at the top of the hill. Bill and Penelope have left the boat and are lingering in the street, and Marcia tells the man that we must consult with them before making any decisions. I point to the street to show him where Bill is standing, and I notice the German walking down the gangway. He waves a card at the Civil Guards and walks across the street. Marcia notices, and remarks, as though it were illegal, "But he has no baggage at all."

'I watch him follow the street as far as the wall which rises and spreads around the mutilated castle and the mute steeple of the cathedral beyond. Then he disappears like a rat which has found its hole, and I feel that I shall not see him again, but always I shall remember the night smelling of camphor round my father's corpse happening again in the same moment that I hold Marcia beside me on the deck and hear the iron of the German's boots echoing the words: out of touch, out of touch.'

Marcia paused in the middle of the page and tried to recall the months which had preceded that trip to the Mediterranean. She had moved to London in the hope that Mark would share her uncle's flat. It was the first serious decision she had made on his behalf, and it had caused an unbearable tension between herself and her uncle. Mark would arrive every day, and they would remain together until night and the last train. Sometimes he missed the train and had to remain overnight, but he would always leave early the following morning. Marcia would lie in bed and read until he returned. Sometimes she had not yet changed out of her night clothes, and Mark, on his return, would get back into bed. But she could not persuade him to make a permanent arrangement. Nor would it ever occur to her to insist. And she thought, as she thumbed the pages, that the interval which he always chose between morning and the lunch hour must have given him the feeling that he was still on his own. It was, she felt, another example of his refusal to take the offer which he had mentioned in the diaries. She would have liked to talk with him about the pages she had read, but she was unsure of his response.

She looked up from the pages and felt for his arm. She was surprised when he took her hand and rubbed it gently along his knee as he tapped his fingers against her wrist. He was probably getting used to his trespass in the air.

'I wonder whether San Cristobal will be as nice,' she said.

'Bill and Penelope will be the best judges,' he said, and stroked her hand again. She was warming to his affection.

'You should be very excited to see it,' she said, 'after how many years…?'

'I don't remember much,' he said with some emphasis, but his voice was intimate, and she felt that he was really trying to remember a little about his childhood. He was about ten when his father died and he left San Cristobal. The intervening years had taken him to three or four countries, and at thirty it required some effort to recall with clarity some of the events of those years.

'There used to be a boy whose name I forget,' he said. 'He used to catch worms.'

'Why worms?'

Mark continued as though he were determined to enjoy his own story. He had tightened his hand round Marcia's.

'He just went in search of them,' said Mark, 'like a man after treasure, digging up cabbage roots, grass, anything that might be hiding his worms.'

'What the devil did he want with worms?' Marcia asked.

'He used to eat them,' Mark said calmly. 'Every one he caught was chewed and swallowed. Just like that.'

He made a small hole with his mouth and slipped two fingers in and out. Marcia brushed his hand away, and rearranged the pages on her lap.

'Why didn't they feed him properly?' said Marcia.

'It had nothing to do with hunger,' Mark said. 'He just thought they looked like spaghetti.'

'But worms don't taste like spaghetti,' she said, and she made a face as though she were going to be sick.

'But they looked like spaghetti, and he thought they should taste like spaghetti,' said Mark. 'After that nobody could stop him…'

He paused as though he had suddenly remembered something which was far more astonishing than the boy's behaviour. He took Marcia's hand unthinkingly and bent her fingers back to touch her wrist. She was going to make a noise when he dropped her hand and continued with the story.

'...except the old woman,' he said, as though he were now talking to himself. 'It was only the old woman who could get him to stop...'

'What old woman?' Marcia asked.

'The old woman of San Cristobal,' Mark said. 'She's probably dead now.'

'Who is this old woman?' Marcia asked. She was enjoying Mark's secret delight with this recollection.

'She used to deliver babies,' he said, 'a kind of village midwife. Primitive perhaps, but somehow successful. She might have had a hand in my arrival for all I know...' He glanced down at Marcia to see whether she was showing sufficient interest in his story.

'And then when she must have been well over fifty,' he said, 'she had a baby. Believe it or not, the old woman had a baby, and the island was wild with rumour. Some said it was a miracle, and some said it was a freak.'

'Did the child live?' Marcia asked.

'He was alive up to the time I left,' said Mark, 'but miracle or freak, he was...'

The plane seemed to stumble and shudder, and Mark released her hand, and shifted in his seat. Marcia felt the change that had come over him. She settled the pages, and tried to take his hand. But everything was different. He did not really concede it. He was nervous. The plane moved, calm and even in its flight; but its shudder a moment ago was like a warning which predicted disaster. Mark could not trust the emptiness of the air.

'Look at that man's head,' Marcia said, trying to distract him, 'it shines like glass.'

Mark refused to share her fascination, but Marcia had found a new and absorbing interest in the shaven black object which grazed the rim of the seat. The naked black skull scraped the seat from side to side, and Marcia tried again to win Mark's attention. But the plane rubbed the clouds again with a sudden jerk, and Mark dropped his head in his hands, and stared ahead towards the cockpit. The lettered partition of the plane was illuminated, and the

46

order had returned: no smoking. He thought he saw a new terror in the warning of the sign. He glanced quickly towards the airliner's wing, and he thought he saw it flap under the pressure of the wind.

He was surrendering San Cristobal to the future and all those who would follow in a more fortunate circumstance of transport. He looked at the wing again, and it seemed quite steady. He was encouraged. The plane moved soberly; and all was well until his eye caught a flame that flashed like lightning under the wing. Another flame flew, and another; and he searched for Marcia's arm. It was like trying to say goodbye. But suddenly the boy had interrupted his terror with that curious and determined voice with which he addressed his grandmother. She turned eagerly to hear what he was saying. Her attention was like a gift, and Mark sat up and tried to listen. It was part of his attempt to forget what he had seen outside. The boy was asking questions.

'Why exit?' he asked.

The woman coaxed the boy's head to her mouth and whispered in his ear. They remained silent for a while. Then the boy spoke. His grandmother put her hands round his neck in order to cross his lips if he became too audible.

'I've been in a plane before, Granny. In a dream in the hospital.'

He scratched his ear and turned his head up to her face. 'It was the time Uncle Basil took my tonsils out,' he said. 'When they put me on the table to put me to sleep, and Uncle Basil took up the knives and told me to close my eyes.'

'You didn't see any knives,' she said. The boy checked his memory.

'I did, Granny, the knives –' and suddenly she pressed her index finger across his lips, and he lowered his head and frowned.

'But I was in a plane,' he said. 'It's the truth. In a dream. In the hospital. I don't remember getting in or sitting down like we are here, but I remember the plane won't stop. It just went flying and flying forever.'

'And how did you get out?'

'I don't know,' he said, 'but I remember being back in the hospital in my bed and Uncle Basil saying "wake up, Rowley, the tonsils are out," and I think I asked Uncle Basil what happened to the plane.'

'Well, you were dreaming,' she said, and pushed her fingers through his hair. The boy scratched his ears and rubbed his head against his grandmother's shoulder. He looked bewildered, and she held her head away as though she wanted to show a lack of interest in his story.

'But suppose our plane doesn't stop, Granny, we'd have to use the exit.'

She used her silence to discourage him, and she kept her head turned away. But he knew she was listening, and he stretched across to take a look outside beyond the wing of the airliner.

'Granny,' he said, 'we couldn't reach the bottom from here, could we? I mean if we had to jump.'

She pushed him gently away, and searched her bag for a sweet. He was still staring outside, trying to imagine the distance below. He took the sweet which she offered and said thanks before putting it in his pocket.

'Don't you want it?' she asked, and he nodded to let her know he would have it later.

She pressed her arm against his forehead, and drew him closer to her. Her affection was a bargain for his silence. She was used to these outbursts of curiosity. During his holidays from boarding school they were particularly frequent, but she dreaded their occurrence in public. At home she could cope with him as she had done for years during his father's absence in San Cristobal. But she felt something inappropriate, even indelicate, about what she would call private talk, being offered indiscriminately for the ears of strangers. She was a woman of the Sunday afternoon fire and the whispered reminiscence. She hated noise, and it was a reason people like her never spoke during public transport. It had nothing to do with shyness, or the need to conceal their feelings. But there was a certain nicety about privacy which their silence on the public occasion usually reminded them of. Moreover, you could never tell whether what you were saying might not have, even in the remotest way, some association of discomfort for your neighbour. Then you would be guilty, as Rowley probably was, of being unpleasant.

She looked down at the boy to see what he was doing, and she thought about her son and the life he had chosen. It was true that he was a man of great importance in San Cristobal, and it was his duty to remain until his work was done. But any place beyond England was for her a 'foreign part', and she had uneasy reservations about 'foreign parts'. She was relieved to turn Rowley over to his father, but she was doubtful about the decision. A 'foreign part' might serve its purpose, but it was hardly the place for an English boy who was also her grandson. She wished the boy's mother were alive, and she wondered how her son and Rowley would manage if she decided that San Cristobal was not worth her effort to adjust. She was trying to imagine what her life would be like in such a place, but Rowley had interrupted again.

'Granny!'

'What is it now?'

'You don't think this plane will crash?' he said.

'What's come over you?' she said, and her voice was at once solicitous and severe. She had anticipated an unpleasant exchange of questions and rebukes.

Mark, who had been following the boy's questions, took some of the pages from his lap. One hand found his ears, and his knees were shaking slightly under the pages.

'I'm not afraid,' the boy said, 'but I was thinking...' He paused and looked round at the passengers as though he were trying to remember for all time the order in which they were seated. He pushed himself up and looked over the seat to see Mark and Marcia.

'What were you thinking?' the woman asked, and steered him back to the seat.

'How if the plane crashed we'd try to remember the faces of those who died.'

The woman was dumb with fury. She was trying to shape some rebuke that would silence him for the rest of the flight, but Rowley was indifferent. It seemed that he could not imagine an accident which would destroy him too.

'The papers wouldn't have had a chance to photograph them,' he added.

'How monstrous, Rowley, shut up!'

Her face was scarlet, and she had become suddenly embarrassed by her own vehemence. Some of the passengers had turned to see who had spoken. Rowley had burst into tears. He buried his head in her bosom and wept his pardon.

The sobbing distracted Marcia who now shifted in her seat and shuffled the pages before setting them down on her thighs. She pushed her elbow further into Mark's side, but he was unfeeling. Fragments of the boy's sentence had strayed through his mind… 'remember the faces of those who died.' The words worked on his nerves with a smooth and gradual destructiveness like flakes of glass losing their way through flesh. Marcia forced her attention on the diaries, for she knew that in certain circumstances any gesture of sympathy towards Mark was like an act of intrusion. He had changed his position again as he always did during such experiences of discomfort… 'remember the faces of those who died.'

The boy had taken his head from his grandmother's bosom. He was towing the sweet from side to side on his tongue.

Then the airliner lurched and as quickly climbed the air, throbbing like an enormous balloon which had been bruised by the wind. The sensation was sudden, and Rowley's grandmother drew him closer and slipped three fingers into his empty pocket. They were inseparable. Mark drew the small blinds and cut off his glance from the view outside. The currents of air seemed unruly, and the airliner was riding defensively. It lurched again, and proceeded in a throbbing and cautious ascent like a boy who is bargaining with branches at the top of a tree he has not climbed before. Some of the passengers remarked that the weather had changed. The airliner leaned awkwardly to one side, then straightened with a jolt, and continued its climb. Someone called in a loud voice for a Scotch, and the hostess, in her role of comfort and apology, started on her patrol, leaning from side to side to say that all was well. Her smile was becoming absurd, but the flame of strawberry still supported her cheeks.

She had entered the cockpit, but when she returned Mark avoided her glance. He saw her coming towards them, and he pretended to be busy with the pages which he had stopped reading. Her smile was a false assurance and he suspected that she knew something was wrong. She stopped to talk with Marcia, but Mark had already turned to look outside at the airliner's wing.

The hostess passed on and his eyes found the pages again, but he could not recognise the words on the page. They had merged into the language which his imagination had already invented for the disaster he suspected. He closed his eyes and listened to his fear describe a future which he could never experience.

...me to myself after my darkest departure, laid out at my usual length like my father in a case of cedar stained in turpentine, screwed with silver... exact, uncontroversial symbol of my absence ever after... my coffin cruel and cosy in silken linen receiving me, forever unalive under false roses hired for the evening ritual of wreaths and rhyming wishes for a life hereafter... abide with me, the darkness deepens, Lord with me, me, me, carried like crockery through an avenue of flowering corpseland, carefully, carefully, carefully carried... abide with me entering earth, raising wishes for a heaven whose embassy is there alert in the vigil of angels in stone, hearing my hope and the hope of all men meeting in dust and ashes to dust and ashes... death is unspeakably cheap, cheap, cheap, cheap... there's no cheaper than the cheapness of being, as me to myself now see me, dead... dead... here lie the remains of Mark Kennedy... born... crashed...

'Crashed...' His fear had turned to a whisper like a voice talking to itself.

'You ought to take the tablets, darling.' Marcia drew his head to her and tried to kiss him. She could feel his lips in a spasm, drawn thin and dry.

'Don't you think they ought to turn back?'

'Are you feeling ill?' she asked. She had coaxed his head on to her shoulder, and she could feel the warmth which burnt his ear.

'It's such an odd sensation,' he said, as he slid easily away from her, trying to rescue the pages from falling off his knees.

'Take three of the tablets,' said Marcia, 'they'll work in no time.'

'I'll be all right,' he said, and she watched him gulp the tablets and lean his head slowly against the seat.

The airliner was steadier now, climbing through a quieter region of air. A few voices were making some comment on the interval which had shaken them from sleep. And Mark waited as though he anticipated the effect of the tablets. He stretched his legs and folded his hands across his stomach. Marcia rearranged the pages, and put the small bottle in her pocket. She hoped the tablets would soon put him to sleep. Then she continued reading.

'And one evening returns to remind me of something which seems always possible. The lane is littered with honeysuckle, and the smell has lulled us to silence. We have walked from the bay through a crooked marl road which rambles across the grass to where the potato field begins. I walk ahead with the young Spaniard who is our guide, and Bill and Penelope lag behind with Marcia who is feeling exhausted. We reach the lane of honey-suckle, and Bill sits on the grass to rest his legs. But Marcia and Penelope have stooped to examine the weed as though they have seen something which reminds them of their village. The hills appear purple and grey from the light of the sun which has reached the sea, and there is no wind. Then Marcia scales the grass which makes a hedge around the field of wheat. Penelope follows her, and they lie for a while in a curve of earth where someone has rested before. Bill raises himself from the grass, and shouts for Penelope. She seizes Marcia's hand, and trails her along, and the three hurry towards me. We stand at the brink of the grass where the honeysuckle starts on its ramble through the lane. And it seems to me, standing between Marcia and Penelope, with Bill and the guide silently watching the hills that lean so steeply to the sea, that something has happened for us. And I tell myself that formerly I have only been in love with Marcia, and Bill and Penelope were simply friends who move about me like the weather which takes its seasons for granted. Penelope has her hand on my shoulder, and I draw Marcia closer to me and not until now, which no force can annihilate, have I felt the presence of this little world, made by four people whose happiness, in this moment, no argument can deny.'

Marcia paused. She was trying to recall the incidents of that evening. It was nearly two years since their holiday in Spain, and the diaries had suddenly sharpened her memory of what had happened ever since Mark's first arrival at Fern Row. She glanced towards Bill and Penelope, wondering whether they might have shared Mark's experience of that evening. For she felt, as she read the passage, that it was probably such an evening which had encouraged them to decide on this flight to San Cristobal.

She could barely see Bill and Penelope who seemed alike in their disavowal of danger. The airliner might have travelled with the violence of the weather, and they would not have been disturbed until the worst had happened. She glanced at Mark who was dozing. His hands lay open on his thighs, and his lips had lost their edge. But she wished he were awake to talk about Bill and Penelope and his first visit to Fern Row. She remembered the evening he arrived for Penelope's birthday party. It was not long after Bill had left his job at the BBC. She lived with her uncle in the neighbouring cottage, and now and again she and Bill met at the small public house which had become their favourite village institution. Her uncle never visited the public house, and he had very definite views about strangers who did. Nevertheless, she invited Bill and Penelope to visit the cottage, and her uncle surprised her by showing an immediate affection for his neighbours. It was a triumph for Marcia.

Some months later, during her uncle's absence in Malaya, Mark arrived. He was one of a party of six whom Bill had invited from London. Two of them were Bill's former colleagues, and three were newspaper men. Mark said he had had no certain occupation, but he had been left enough money to keep him for a few years. He was trying at the time to write a book about a three-fingered pirate who was notorious in the West Indies during the first half of the eighteenth century. It was his account of this pirate which had started his acquaintance with Bill. That evening they talked about little except the pirate; and it suddenly struck Marcia, like evidence which she had not suspected, that it was she who had suggested to Penelope that Mark should stay for the weekend.

Marcia looked at the pages on her lap, and it seemed that the diary had reduced the details of that evening. They had merged into one vivid recollection of a particular experience, like the feeling which Mark had described about their holiday in Spain. There were no details to remember. He would return to Fern Row almost every weekend, and there were letters during his absence.

Three months after his departure from London, her uncle

returned to consult Marcia about her plans. He had been made Governor of an important colony which was then at peace with England. It was suggested that Marcia should join him there. She said she had decided to live in London; and since he had always known her to show an unspeakable loathing of London, he asked no questions and returned to his post in a state of bewilderment which had seldom been noticed in Sir Henry Nicholson.

Marcia's eyes fell on the diaries again, and her curiosity was quickened by a reference to Penelope and Bill.

'Shall I concede that I may be a spy and that my activity is a kind of treachery? But my behaviour that evening has never seemed part of my intention, and yet I dare not confess to Penelope and Bill. I fear that they may misinterpret my curiosity, and I do not want either of them to question my loyalty.

'I have just returned from a walk round the village. It is evening, and as I approach the house, I notice the light spread across the back garden. It means that they have left one of the side doors open, and I decide to go through that door and down the passage into the living-room. A window is open, and I can see Bill and Penelope sitting opposite each other. They are probably waiting for me to return. Then we shall eat and go out for a drink. I pause at the window, because it amuses me to watch them, not suspecting that I am there. It is like a child's game of hide-and-seek. I wait at the window, unseen, and suddenly my ears become alert, almost amused like my eyes. I listen for a moment, and as I am about to move, it seems that Penelope's voice has changed. It is earnest and firm, and I become curious.

' "It's the way I feel," Penelope says. "What can we do?"

' "I'm all for trying a new place," Bill replies, "where we can both feel that we're being useful without sacrificing any of the pleasures we've been used to. I don't want to go all over the world justifying causes, whether it's for the unfortunate in Africa or Asia, or wherever they may be…"

' "In a way I am quite happy here at Fern Row," says Penelope, "I make myself useful, and I have got you. But I don't feel I can bear it for a lifetime. It's not so much the other people's unhappiness which troubles me. It's the happiness at Fern Row, just our life here without relating it to anything. And after you have known what it is to be happy like this, it seems that there is nothing to do but go on being happy. But it makes me want for something else, and it's this waiting which disturbs me."

' "Isn't it enough to know that we love each other?" Bill asks her.

'Penelope does not reply and suddenly I discover that I do not want to go. It seems that it is not an inquisitive intention which detains me, but the substance of their talk, for I, too, have been thinking of a change of place, and I begin to believe that since our speculations are now similar, it is not really improper for me to listen. Moreover, I fear that my presence will be an interruption, and it does not seem the right moment for me to intrude. I find myself standing in the passage, unwilling to enter, and suddenly eager to go on listening.

' "You mustn't think I'm complaining," Penelope says. "I hope you don't think so."

' "Of course not," Bill says, "and even if you were…"

'They are quiet for a while, and I push my head further forward to observe their attitudes. Penelope's eyes are bright as though she will cry any minute now. But Bill stares at the floor. Now that I see their faces, I seem to feel more acutely the urgency of what they are saying. I make ready to go, but Penelope has spoken again, and I tell myself there must be no interruption. I don't believe my presence in the room will help. It is better to wait until they show some sign of coming to an end.

' "Do you want to go on talking?" Penelope asks. "I should hate to be a nuisance."

' "Penelope!"

'It is a kind voice which assures her, and I notice that Bill has leaned forward to take her hand. She seems to regard him with misgiving. Someone emerges whom she does not know so intimately as she has always thought.

' "We have loved each other for a long time," she says, "and you know that is not likely to change."

' "Of course."

' "You really understand how I feel…"

' "I understand perfectly," says Bill, "but I've never wanted to tell you…"

'Bill pauses, and Penelope seems to sit up, waiting for something quite unexpected. I think now that I shall go, because it is not their secrets that I want to discover, only the substance of their talk which relates to my own desire for a change of place.

' "It's the way I have felt for a long time," says Bill, "not yesterday."

' "But you never showed it," Penelope says. And again she seems startled, as though Bill has suddenly revealed a self which she has not known.

' "One survives it," he says. "Happiness here at Fern Row or anywhere else may not be enough, but you can't get beyond it. And when you begin to feel like you say, there is very little anyone can do. Happiness becomes a duty which you must bear."

' "You mean I shall survive Fern Row by remaining always at Fern Row?"

' "Not at all," Bill says, "although, in a way, I could wish that was true."

' "Shall we go somewhere else, some other country?"

'Bill considers her question, and it seems that he has resigned himself to Penelope's wish. I begin to wonder about their choice, and I begin to think that I must go from the window. This is becoming a secret which I want to avoid hearing.

' "Anywhere you ask," says Bill, "but a change of place won't make any difference if you feel the way you do."

' "You don't mean that we're likely to separate," Penelope asks.

' "It's out of the question," says Bill, "but it is possible that…"

'Suddenly I raise my body from the window, and make a noise in the passage. I do not want to hear anything that does not relate to my feeling about a change of place. They know that I have arrived, but I wait in the passage for a while. Then I enter, trying to avoid their eyes, because I am afraid they have suspected. The room is silent until Penelope shouts for Maisie to set the table.'

Marcia slackened the safety-belt and crossed her legs. One of the pages fell from her lap, and she waited for a while before retrieving it. She glanced at Mark who was asleep, and then at Bill and Penelope who were drinking whisky from the same glass.

The plane was like a slave who knew to perfection his master's need. There was a sense of safety everywhere.

'I wonder why Mark never told me about that evening,' Marcia said quietly. The words had left her mouth like a noise unwilled, without instructions. Then she said in a breath, 'But then he probably didn't want me to know that he was spying.'

He couldn't relate that story without explaining his presence, and it would have been difficult for him to confess that he was spying. And why was Mark spying, she wondered. Spying on Bill and Penelope, of all people. She turned to consider Mark, relaxed in his seat, snoring softly.

There was for Marcia a moment which wiped out her knowledge of everything and everyone, and made her confront Mark like a thing which she had never before encountered. Her gaze was passive like a receptacle which takes in its contents without judgement. She saw him now, for those few moments, as a mirror embraces some reflection. She was an eye poised here, and Mark was an object situated there.

The object penetrated her eye with all its visible qualities: his head almost square in its natural wilderness of bush. His nose shone with sweat, and his skin, which the stubble punctured along his chin, crawled over his bones, staining his face with the bright, hard colour of copper. The lean, brittle fingers came like roots out from his hands. The rest of him was hidden, but her eye had received its assault of copper singing through the wiry wilderness of his hair. And suddenly her eye became a glance, critical and intentional. That moment had gone, and the object was redeemed. It was Mark.

She said, smiling, 'And it's never occurred to me to question whether you really love me. Never.' She found herself watching him as she had done some minutes ago, and wishing, too, that he were awake to talk about the diaries, but the tablets had done their work. 'Just as you say,' she whispered, 'like the weather taking its seasons for granted.'

Her hands fell to the diaries, and the dialogue she had read returned with all its force of revelation and suspicion. What were Penelope and Bill really thinking as they sipped the whisky, passing the glass from one to the other? The pages which were falling into order under her hands seemed to ask her the question which was gradually forming in her mind: Why were they leaving Fern Row and England? And she thought, too, looking down at Mark's diaries, that she knew the answer. She knew but she could not explain. She understood only for herself; she could not communicate what she understood, just as the dialogue she had just read was at once final and incomplete. It was not a simple business of trying another country, and they were not, for the time being, in search of work. Moreover, they admitted, in a sense, that life at Fern Row was nearly always very happy. They were leaving England because they felt, for some unaccountable reason, that there was somewhere an alternative to Fern Row. San Cristobal was just another place which they had chosen by the accident of their friendship. Mark was going, and since it was the place he belonged to by birth, they had had little difficulty in accepting his suggestion. Also, Bill had been persuaded by his oldest friend, Peter Flagstead, who had settled in San Cristobal. They were ripe for suggestion, and Mark and Flagstead had confirmed that choice.

And why am I leaving? Marcia asked herself. She saw her reason clearly. She was in love with Mark, and she could afford to make the trip. She held the pages up, feeling the feebleness of her own interrogation. Mark was the only one among them whose choice could not be explained or understood in the way she understood Penelope and Bill. She looked at him, feeling an urge to disturb him. She wanted to talk with him, but the plane bumped again, and she remembered his anxiety. She would wait until he was awake. What she knew for certain was that Mark's choice could not be explained by the sentiment of going home. Of all the places he had known, San Cristobal would have been the last he would have thought of as home.

He turned, and Marcia felt his arm rub against her. His eyes half-opened as though he were trying to recognise his surroundings. She held his hand and drew closer to him, and his head leaned on her shoulder.

Then she said in a breath as she had done before: 'Why are you going to San Cristobal, Mark?' And in that gradual fall towards his original sleep he heard the word, and spoke.

'What about San Cristobal?'

Marcia was surprised by his voice. She said, in a hurry, 'We're getting there soon.'

And Mark, slipping deeper into sleep, said, 'Where?'

Marcia released her hand and continued with the diaries. There was no further mention on this page of that conversation; and Mark, it would seem, had made no notes of what had taken place during the evening. She checked the pages to see whether any were missing, but it seemed that the diaries followed no regular order in time. She had no way of knowing when this conversation had taken place between Bill and Penelope. There must have been a gap of many months because the next item referred to the last party which Penelope and Bill had given at Fern Row.

'It's our last weekend in this cottage. But it seems hardly the right time to celebrate, since I shall miss it. Bill looks pleased, and so is their friend Flagstead who has been living in San Cristobal for five years, and whom I have met only twice.

'The room is crowded with all their friends. The music has just come to an end, slowly like a lid coming down over a box. I have hardly disengaged my arm when Penelope's friend, Fox, cuddles her shoulder and shepherds her to a corner. It is a natural gesture, very easy and intimate like the voices chattering away through the long, low room. Bill changes the record and walks back to his seat on the sofa. The liquor has lit his eyes with mischief. His hands move wilfully over Maisie, stroking the frilled skirt that finishes abruptly below her knees. I like the way Maisie moves about this room, without the usual restraint of an employee on such occasions. She has never been excluded from a party at Fern Row, and the cottage will never be the same without her.

'She holds Bill's hands as though she wants to scold the fingers that are playing with her skirt. Then she drags him up from the sofa, and they waltz into the crowd. The voices have lowered, and the music fills the room.

' "Aren't you dancing, Mark?"

' "Not this one," I say, and step back quickly to avoid collision with Bill and Maisie who have just completed a hilarious spin which disturbs their balance, and sends them stumbling in my direction. Maisie is laughing, but Bill has found his legs again, and glides with drunken authority out of the reach of those who cross his path. It is a delight to watch Maisie's face, resting quietly on his shoulder.

'I pour a drink for Flagstead who is not dancing. He swallows it quickly, and wipes a trickle from his chin. The fire has reddened his face, and his hands work rapidly with a handkerchief which he passes round his neck, and down his collar to his chest. He shows no interest in the dance, and I turn to pour another drink.

' "Have you seen Fox?" he asks. His voice is sharp, almost angry.

' "Isn't he dancing?"

'Flagstead looks about the room, but he knows Fox is not there. He turns irritably, and saws his neck with the handker-chief. Bill and Maisie are coming towards us. When they reach, Bill slaps him on the shoulder and tells him to find a girl. And for a while it seems that he has taken this advice. He walks towards the stairs which lead to a small balcony. Actually he has gone in search of Fox. But now I can guess what is happening. Is this the reason for Flagstead's anger? Looking towards the balcony I can see Fox and Penelope barely visible between the bookcase and the wall. It is an awkward moment. Bill and Maisie sail in bliss to the possessive call of the music. Penelope, almost hidden by the bookcase, betrays her presence by a show of arms which swings Fox's head away from her mouth. I wonder where Flagstead has got to, and what is his role in these relations.

' "You haven't seen the madam?" Maisie asks.

' "She has probably gone to bed," says Bill.

' "Good night, Mr Mark."

' "Good night, Maisie. Why are you going so soon?"

' "I must be up early," says Maisie. "Shall I call you?"

' "You needn't bother."

' "Good night."

'Bill follows her out of the room, but soon I forget them, because Fox and Flagstead have returned. They are standing in the far corner, facing each other in attitudes of defiance and contempt. No one seems to notice them, but I don't like the look of their faces, and the rapid exchange of words which can hardly be casual. I walk to the end of the room and stand beside Flagstead whose face is wet. He keeps his hands in his pockets, completely ignoring my intrusion.

' "What the hell business is it of yours?" says Fox.

' "You want to know?"

' "Yes, blast you, I want to know," Fox answers.

' "Then, let's go outside," Flagstead challenges.

'He points to the door. Fox brushes past Flagstead who follows close, until I seize his arm, and ask to have a word. Flagstead turns with reluctance, while Fox waits at the door, impatient for a fight. I struggle to say something which might distract Flagstead. Then Bill, ignorant of the issue, enters, and pulls Fox merrily behind him to the bar. This interruption has worked a kind of reprieve, and gradually their tempers subside, like a burst of rain which has suddenly failed.

' "You wouldn't want to spoil the party," I say, holding Flagstead's arm.

' "The bastard," he says, trying to communicate his rage and his disappointment. "I would have crushed the life out of him."

'For a moment I feel almost crushed by the malevolence of his voice. He mops his brow, as he looks in the direction of Fox who is now helping Bill to change the records. The music begins, and Fox and Bill walk slowly back to the bar, and I see Penelope hurrying tipsily towards me. She tries to conceal her embarrassment, but Flagstead keeps his glance in the opposite direction, and when she reaches us, he says very quietly, "Good night." He pockets his hands again, and walks through the door which leads to the passage and the garden. Penelope asks me to dance, and we hold each other close, moving quietly about the corner. I pretend that nothing has happened, but I am lost for words, and I know she is waiting for me to ask her what has happened.

' "I don't know what you're thinking," she says, "but Flagstead's behaviour must seem quite strange."

'My first impulse is to lie, but it is silly to pretend that there is nothing noticeable about Penelope. I make room between us, and turn my head away.

' "It seems that he is in love with you," I say.

' "He hates Fox," says Penelope. Her manner is guarded, and nervous.

' "Is Fox in love with you, too?"

'Penelope lowers her head, and her hands tighten round mine, as though she may be considering the chances she risks in making such an admission. The music seems to isolate our voices, and Penelope comes closer, trying not to restrain the intimacy which she now feels.

' "I feel nothing towards Fox," she says, "and Flagstead has no such interest in me."

' "Why were they going to fight?" I ask.

'Penelope starts, and I am afraid that I have said too much. She relaxes her hold, and walks towards a table. I wait for a while, then follow. Penelope sits, wipes the back of her hand against her nose, and looks up at me.

' "It's on Bill's account that Flagstead behaved the way he did," she says. "He would have behaved the same way towards you or anyone else."

' "Will he be returning to San Cristobal?"

' "He has settled there for good," says Penelope. She pauses.

' "And you think he will hold this evening against you?"

' "He is Bill's closest friend," says Penelope, "it was he who brought us together."

'I try to avoid any mention of Fox, so I ask Penelope to dance again. We remain at the back of the room, trying to catch the rhythm of the music. Fox has remained with Bill on the sofa.

' "I don't want to bother you with any explanations," says Penelope.

' "There is no need to explain anything," I say.

'But I really want her to say why she went up the stairs with Fox. I feel a sudden resentment towards Fox who looks quite unconcerned as he talks with Bill. And I wonder, too, whether Penelope is lying about their relationship.

' "Does Bill know about Fox?" I ask her.

' "There is nothing to know," says Penelope.

' "Then why did you go upstairs to kiss him?" The question makes me feel involved, and I want to apologise.

' "Bill would understand if I told him," she says. "I'm sure he would."

'Penelope looks more assured. She takes a small handkerchief from her bosom and pats her nose. She adjusts her hair with both hands, then comes towards me, and we dance. My curiosity increases. It makes me almost inquisitive, and I encourage her to go on talking.

' "Will you tell Bill about this evening?" I ask.

'She hesitates, but it is no longer uncertainty which fails her. She is confident, a little puzzled, perhaps, but self-controlled.

' "There is no need to," she says, "and Bill understands, anyway."

'I am amazed by her words, because I have never thought Bill a cuckold. But I do not believe Penelope is telling the truth about Bill, and I feel that I want to be assured of his place in her affections.

' "What would Bill understand?" I ask her.

' "Bill understands why I want to leave Fern Row," she says.

'Her voice is resigned as though it is useless to explain anything to me. Perhaps she has noticed my astonishment.

' "It might not have happened," says Penelope, "but if you were with us when we discussed leaving Fern Row, you might understand."

'It is the first time I have heard that evening mentioned, and I do not want to betray my knowledge. Nor do I want her to repeat something that I should not have heard at the time. It seems to me this faked ignorance would be real spying. So I speak as though I was there. But I must have missed some part of their talk, for I do not remember any reference to Fox or anyone else.

' "Is it because of Fox that you want to leave Fern Row?"

'We have stopped dancing for a while, and Penelope takes her hand away. I urge her to answer, then she speaks as she turns away.

' "Bill can tell you why I want to leave," she says, then pauses. "But it's probably part of the reason for going up the stairs with Fox. It's nothing to do with my desire for him," she adds, "it's almost the opposite."

'Then I notice that Penelope has started to cry. There is nothing I can say, because it seems that her meaning belongs entirely to her, and I doubt whether Bill does understand such an explanation. She is quiet, thinking, it seems, about this evening and her behaviour with Fox, and her conversation with Bill.

' "Shall I pour you a drink?" I ask.

'It will give me time to recall what I heard her tell Bill that evening, and to make some sense of this strange opposition between her act and her intention. For what I understand seems only a suggestion. It is her happiness at Fern Row which makes her leave, and almost a lack of desire for Fox which seduces her up the stairs.'

When Marcia looked up from the page, considering this incident, she noticed that huge black head turn on its side against the seat. She wanted to draw someone's attention to it, but Mark was asleep and she did not think it a good reason for disturbing him. Her eyes caught Bill and Penelope close and quiet on the other side, and then she heard the boy in front tell his grandmother about the naked head which had emerged another inch above the seat. It seemed that the man was getting restless.

But the incident at Fern Row recalled her attention. She wondered what Bill and Penelope were thinking which neither could guess. Penelope was always emphatic about her loyalty to Bill, and Mark's account of the party confirmed this. For she felt no special interest in Fox, and there was never any question of seeing him as an alternative to Bill. There was no danger of disloyalty, and her dissatisfaction with life at Fern Row was no reflection on her marriage. In its way Fern Row was perfect.

Then why this meaningless behaviour with Fox? she asked herself. It seemed that this incident, like Penelope's decision to leave Fern Row, existed without reference to any logic of thinking or feeling. Or the feeling was too vague for anyone but Penelope to understand. It had occurred; that was all. She felt that there was something disturbing about Penelope's behaviour, which could not be related to any particular source of motive or ambition. In a way this absence of motive was equally true of her relation to Mark. But hers made for a feeling which was clear and vivid. It seized her and found its fulfilment in her relationship with Mark. And it was part of her duty to keep it alive. But Penelope's choice seemed like a denial of the pleasure she had known, even with Bill. And yet she needed Bill.

The plane bumped, and Marcia saw the strange black head

shudder. The boy was telling his grandmother about it again. The airliner groaned angrily at the jeering mass of cloud, and sleep was gradually losing its hold on Mark. Marcia settled the pages, and nestled against his side, waiting for the airliner to recover its calm.

2

Penelope was polishing the pink glass beads which made a pattern of islands over her skirt. She raised her head and looked over the seat to see what Mark and Marcia were doing. Then she turned to Bill and held his hand.

'You should see them now,' she said, 'they make you feel old sometimes.'

'Mark is probably trying to sleep,' said Bill, 'he gets so terrified.'

'But I think Marcia brought the tablets,' Penelope said.

She raised her head again and looked to see whether Mark was sleeping, but she could only glimpse Marcia's head leaning on his shoulder. Bill moved closer to her, and she let her face rest on his shoulder.

'You remember that evening on the island,' Penelope said, 'the evening they fell into the sea.'

'They frightened the life out of me,' said Bill.

He paused considering the incident which Penelope had mentioned. The sun had set late that evening and the sea was red. He and Penelope were lying on the pebbles where a huge brown rock leaned like a jaw over the sea. Mark had come running over the precipice, dragging Marcia like an exhausted poodle behind. She stumbled at the edge of the rock and they both plunged into the water.

'They were such a long time surfacing,' Bill said, 'I couldn't think where they had got to.'

'He nearly drowned her,' Penelope said.

Bill nodded but he did not speak. He had remembered the expression of terror on Marcia's face when she waded up the shore and stood trying to vomit the water she had swallowed.

Marcia was angry when she recovered, and there was a quarrel. Mark accepted the blame for what had happened, but after he had seen Marcia safe on the shore he seemed to behave as though nothing had happened.

'But it was almost a joy to see them quarrelling,' said Penelope.

'I remember,' said Bill.

They had crawled up the pebbles, and Penelope remembered how the four of them lay there, and the sun, large as the sea, seemed to marvel at their silence.

'I would have liked her uncle to see them,' said Bill, 'something might have softened in the old blimp's heart.'

'It is probably too late for that,' said Penelope, 'and it doesn't matter anyway because Marcia has found what she wants, and Mark couldn't care less about Sir Harold.'

They looked out at the clouds turning somersaults round the airliner's wing, and tried to follow them until they dispersed and vanished out of sight. In the distance the clouds had formed a range of mountains which the air was slaughtering into separate peaks. They looked firm and fixed like an enormous wave that had suddenly halted and hardened into ice. The view had guided their thinking towards the sky.

'One sees all sorts of things at this height,' Bill said, 'and all sorts of fancies enter your mind.'

'Look there,' said Penelope, pointing to the shape of a head, 'a real lion, all white and fluffy.'

'I was thinking of children,' said Bill, 'and fairies and harmless ghosts walking idly towards the sky. One believes it is almost possible.'

Penelope was thinking again of their trip to the Mediterranean, and the afternoon they had described. It had become her standard for comparing different sensations of delight.

'Do you envy Mark?' Penelope asked. Bill did not answer, because he was staring idly at the clouds.

'Do you?' Penelope said again, and Bill jerked his head round and stared at her.

'What are you talking about?'

'I mean in a nice way,' Penelope said, 'you can envy people in a nice way.'

'Why should I envy Mark in any way?' Bill said. 'Why should I?'

'I mean in a nice way,' Penelope repeated, 'like I envy Marcia her cheeks.' Penelope laughed.

Bill slapped her gently on her leg, and turned to look at the clouds.

'You mean whether I should prefer to be Mark's colour?'

'No, that's different,' said Penelope, 'I mean something silly, like not having to use make-up.'

Bill turned to look in the direction of Mark and Marcia, but they were hidden. Penelope reminded him that it was unnecessary to check his memory. He had always remarked on Marcia's natural colour. That was true. Her cheeks were a natural pink like her lips.

'You know what I mean,' Penelope insisted. 'Many a woman would give anything for some natural colour. I would. That's all I mean.'

Bill was turning his head indolently from the window towards Penelope. 'Do you think Mark envies me my natural colour?'

'Of course not,' Penelope said. 'You don't understand me.'

Bill paused, spying the bottle to see whether there was any whisky left. Penelope drained it clean, and took a sip before returning the glass to him.

'Mark does seem a little strange sometimes,' he said.

'In what way?' Penelope seemed apprehensive. Was Bill going to say something that she had never heard? She pressed him to finish the whisky. They covered the bottle with the glass, and Bill placed them between his legs. Penelope elbowed him.

'In what way is Mark strange?' She was excessively curious.

'I don't mean anything serious,' Bill said, 'like you and the make-up.'

'I know, but what do you mean?'

'Sometimes he seems so private,' Bill said. 'That's all.'

'Yes,' Penelope said, and stopped.

'If you didn't know him well, you'd think he was hiding something.' Bill eased round in his seat and let his leg slide the bottle flat on to the floor.

'Yes,' Penelope said again, 'I've felt that too, I mean the

privacy.' She paused, waiting for Bill to speak. Then she said: 'But it's probably because he's so warm most of the time, that his silence makes you think something is wrong.'

'I never think anything particular is wrong,' Bill said. 'It's just that his silence seems sometimes to be worse than secrecy, as though you're really shut out, not excluded from some secret, but just shut right out, absolutely shut out, from Mark himself.'

'Has Marcia ever told you that?' Penelope asked.

'Of course not,' Bill said. 'Has she ever told you?'

Penelope was quiet, then she bent to retrieve the glass which had fallen off the bottle and was rolling under another passenger's seat.

'Once, a long time ago, she mentioned it.' Penelope turned to get a view of Mark who was slouching out of sight. 'But it doesn't make him any less friendly, does it?'

Bill did not reply. He was following his own line of thought. 'You know,' he said, 'Mark once told me something very odd.'

'What about?'

'Nothing much,' said Bill, 'but he made it sound so strange.'

'What happened?' Penelope asked.

'They were just walking,' said Bill, 'and you know Marcia's passion for Christmas trees. Well, Mark said he saw a very large one beautifully lit, and he noticed that Marcia was looking in the other direction, but he never drew her attention to it.'

'Obviously he got lost in the thing himself,' said Penelope.

'No, no,' said Bill, 'that's exactly what he tried to explain. His first thought was to show Marcia. He knew she was looking elsewhere, but he made no attempt to distract her while he argued with himself, looking back all the while at the house where he had seen it.'

'But why didn't he tell her?'

'I don't know,' said Bill, 'but he just kept arguing with himself that he ought to show her before it was too late.'

'It seems very strange,' said Penelope.

'All he remembered was a sudden confusion when Marcia jerked him round and asked what he was looking at.'

'And didn't he say?'

'She didn't believe him,' Bill said.

'That he had seen the tree?'

'Mark said he wasn't looking at anything.'

Penelope stared through the window, only half believing him. 'Are you making this up, Bill?'

'Not at all,' said Bill, 'that's exactly why he told me. He said he couldn't for the life of him understand why he had lied.'

'How very strange,' said Penelope, 'he didn't want to tell her.'

'Or he didn't like having to do so,' said Bill. 'I don't know.'

Penelope was quiet, thinking of the incident which Mark had related to Bill. She wondered whether he had ever told Marcia about it, and suddenly, as though she had perceived some flaw in their relationship, she was thinking about Marcia's uncle. He was less than thirty years their senior, and already he had become a fossil in their understanding.

'I wonder what he will do now,' said Bill.

'What the devil can anyone do about two people who love each other.'

'I mean Mark,' said Bill. 'He has lived away from San Cristobal for twenty years and he was never really at home in England.'

'I suppose they will get married.'

'But you've got to have a home somewhere,' said Bill, 'and that means having some sort of work.'

'But he can always get a job,' Penelope said. 'If his money is coming to an end, there should be some kind of job in San Cristobal.'

'A job is not enough,' said Bill, 'a man like Mark needs more than a job. He has to have work. You remember what he told the people in the San Cristobal section of the BBC. They walk in and out of a studio the same way they walk in and out of the lavatory. They talk because they have to eat just as they shit because they have eaten. And he really meant it.'

'And if he doesn't find this work in San Cristobal,' Penelope said. She was going to continue, but Bill had already spoken.

'I believe it's the only place he will find it,' he said.

The airliner was still cheating the weather. It gave the passengers the feeling that its movement proceeded in a series of circles. The clouds had made a spectacle of waves frozen stiff, precipitous and immobile as far as the eye could see. The flight had not been very smooth, and the sudden interruptions of weather had created a certain suspense and impatience.

'You mustn't point, Rowley,' the woman said, and Marcia looked up to see what had attracted the boy's attention. Rowley lodged his finger in his mouth, while he stared at the naked head which came up like an enormous vegetable over the seat. But the boy could not resist his curiosity. And Marcia understood. Her interest had turned to a kind of awe as she looked at the man's head. She could see one ear like a loop of flesh untidily tucked onto the side of his face. His neck was hidden by the seat. The man never shifted, and his head remained motionless but for an occasional shudder like the throb of the airliner. She wished Mark were awake to see it. His skull was smooth and brilliant as though it had been scraped and polished like a bone taken from the sea, and she got the feeling that a stone let down gently on the top would have caused it to crack like glass. An authority of silence surrounded it in that calm and suspended pose.

'Granny, it's like his brain will walk out any minute,' the boy said.

'You must be quiet,' the woman said.

Rowley held his head down and spoke in a whisper. Marcia looked towards Bill and Penelope who were staring at that huge black head which crowned the seat. Then the airliner stopped, churned the clouds and rose again. There was no signal to fasten the belts, but the atmosphere had turned heavy with expectation and surprise. No one understood what had happened.

3

Mark was awake. Marcia stopped reading. Bill watched the conduct of the clouds. Rowley sweated. His grandmother crossed her hands. Penelope put a pill under her tongue and felt the dissolution sail her throat. The hostess hoisted her cap. A man said, 'Scotch.' A whispering chorus commended the weather. The light was firm, but the sudden absence of sound was dark, dark and dangerous; an unreliable neutrality, a cold quiet which made no clear prediction. The silence was a sieve which let peace through. Mark coughed. Rowley hiccupped. His grandmother censored a sneeze. Bill watched the weather. Penelope pinched her ear. Marcia said in a whisper, 'Mark.' But Mark would not hear. He asked his eyes to shut everything out. This was the moment his habit had predicted… 'remember the faces of those who died…'

'Please, Rowley, be quiet.'

'Granny,' the boy cried, 'I'm afraid. It frightens me, honest, it does.'

'Don't look, darling, that will help.'

'Please, Granny, please.'

'It is nothing, darling, believe me.'

'I cannot, I cannot.'

The sob had strangled his voice, and his neck convulsed in terror under her arm.

'What do you say about that, Mark?'

Mark pretended to be distracted by the airliner's wing.

'Will it really be all right?' the boy implored.

'It can't be a joke, Mark, it really can't,' Marcia insisted.

Mark would not answer. Like Rowley's grandmother, he was trying to avoid a conviction. It would have been disastrous to feel sure. He begged his eyes not to see. He resisted Marcia's hand and looked over at Rowley. The boy's body shook in his grandmother's arms, firm and ineffectual in their caress.

'Tell him to stop,' the boy cried, 'please, tell him.'

'It is terrifying,' Marcia said. 'Where is the hostess?'

Marcia caught Penelope's head, turning to confirm their fear. She brought the diaries to her face and hid her eyes.

'He is getting up,' Mark said quietly.

'Mark, darling.'

'It would be better not to look,' Mark said.

'Mark.'

'Hold my hand,' said Mark, 'and look at me.'

The enormous black skull which had been wagging from side to side like a clock's dull tongue rose gradually, showing its heavy thick neck, and the ample shoulders that sloped abruptly into arms.

'He is standing,' Rowley said. 'Granny, why did he get up?'

'Someone should do something,' Marcia said.

'He is turning,' Mark said. 'Just hold my hand, Marcia, and look away.'

'It doesn't help, darling.'

'Granny, please, Granny.'

'Try a sweet,' the woman said.

The man turned slowly, ignoring his neighbours, his hands falling stolidly down his sides, and his massive ears twitching under the naked dome of skull. He stood heavy and still, staring vacantly over the heads of those who immediately confronted him. His presence made the air thick with confusion.

'Whatever does he want?' Marcia said.

'Granny,' the boy cried, 'what will he do?'

No one knew what words would make for an adequate consolation. There were scurrying whispers of enquiry at the back, but no voice dared the silent, towering authority of that figure. He remained standing, heavy, square, and certain, feeling his ears twitch, and his fingers scrape lightly the even rim of his coat.

'There's the hostess,' Marcia said.

'What will she do?' the boy said.

'Don't worry, darling,' his grandmother said. 'Take my hand.'

'His lips are moving,' Marcia said.

'The hostess is smiling,' the boy said. But his voice cracked when he noticed the hostess's face change colour and her hands behind her back trembled. The man was repeating his request.

'Did you say fire?' the hostess said.

'To fire a pee,' the man said. His voice was solid and certain.

'My bladder is boiling,' he added, and his fingers crawled with a furtive and meticulous caution between the buttons that kept his fly.

The hostess dropped her head, and turned her back, pointing in the opposite direction to the toilet. Everyone pretended not to notice when he passed, following her direction, mumbling to himself, 'It is full to the top. Full, full, full.'

But in those moments of uncertain animation, the airliner had travelled with incomparable ease. The weather waited its approach with a soft and solicitous welcome. The winds had wandered amiably in favour of its course. The clouds had left the way clear. And nothing now changed. The storm had retreated.

The airliner paraded the miracle of its comfort, calm and unfelt. The hostess had restored herself to her role, but there was a more obvious emphasis on her assurance. She carried her magnificent figure with control. She leaned expertly to console someone, and the split of her skirt parted to show her marvellous calf. She had touched up her cheeks and brightened her lashes, but her eyes remained suspicious. She was performing in the interest of her passengers who had to be reminded that nothing disastrous could ever occur during this flight. Graceful and endearing in this prescribed deportment, she was now at war with the restraint which sullied her work. Her duty was in danger, for it was her responsibility to ensure the safety and peace of everyone's feelings. She checked the names on her list, and waited with a patient and impossible dignity for the man who had asked her the way to the toilet. She wanted specially to receive him when he appeared, so that she might lead him back to his seat and prove a courage which she knew it was hard for anyone to believe.

'Mr Shephard was just a bit disturbed,' she said, patting Penelope on her shoulder. 'It's probably his first experience in the air.'

She moved along the carpeted passage nearer the toilet, rolling the list between her hands, and smiling with a secret, conspiratorial intimacy at those who met her glance.

'It would be an awkward situation,' Bill said, 'very awkward, indeed.'

'You mean for the hostess?' Penelope was hesitant and curious.

'For everyone,' Bill said.

'No one is with him,' Penelope said. 'Of course, he might have had too much to drink.'

'You never can tell,' Bill said. 'He looked quite sinister.'

'I thought so too. But would he dare disturb...'

'Could you see very well from here?'

'Not really,' Penelope said, 'but no one served drinks to that row.'

'He is alone, I think.'

'Are you worried, Bill?'

'I think so. Perhaps you might see what the others are doing.'

'Mark is pretending not to notice anything,' Penelope said, 'but the little boy in front of them is scared, and that would upset Marcia.'

'Is there another toilet?' Bill asked.

'Couldn't you wait until he came out?'

'I would prefer not to see him,' Bill said.

'You are afraid, Bill.'

'For a moment I thought I was,' Bill said, 'but it seems all right now.'

'I think she is terrified,' Penelope said, indicating the hostess.

'She is doing very well,' Bill said. 'I would have thought it safer to be out of the way.'

Bill turned his head and looked outside and watched the sky, distant and grey, make its enormous curve ahead of the airliner. The sun had spread a little light thinly on the spreading arc of the sky, and it was a relief to see the airliner race through the elusive haze. It made him feel they were arriving somewhere very soon. Penelope rested her head on his arm and tried to share the view.

Softly, without a shudder, the airliner sailed. Its calm made a mockery of their discomfort, for their nerves were roaring the possibility of the man's return from the toilet. And their fear was loud.

'Is he still in the toilet, Granny?'

'Be quiet, Rowley, and don't worry.'

'You saw where he put his hands, like a little boy asking to pass water.'

'I didn't notice, Rowley,' she said, 'try another sweet.'

'I couldn't eat it, not until I was sure nothing will happen.'

'I'm sure,' she said. 'No one else is afraid.'

'I hope he stays in the toilet, don't you?'

'Put your head here, darling,' she said, offering her arm, and drawing him closer to her.

'I don't think he is going to come out, Granny, it doesn't seem so.'

Behind him, he could hear the crumple of paper which Mark

and Marcia were putting away. The boy rested his head and listened till the noise of the sheets was unheard.

'He has certainly been in a long time,' Marcia said, looking towards the toilet.

It was the voice which shook them, a sudden and soulful tremor of confession and prayer. The hostess shivered in retreat, bouncing her smooth round rump against a passenger's shoulder.

'There he comes,' said Rowley in tears. But his voice was lost in the great cavern of sound which rolled from Mr Shephard's throat:

> *I fled Him, down the nights and down the days;*
> *I fled Him, down the arches of the years;*
> *I fled Him, down the labyrinthine ways*
>   *Of my own mind; and in the mist of tears*
> *I hid from Him, and under running laughter... laughter...*

The words were spoken from a depth of torture and delight, and his face, like a lost piece of night carving its image upon the afternoon, was the face of a fugitive who had meandered through all weathers to a season of insanity. A red rage coaxed his eyes from their sockets, and the words churned his passion to a fury which now separated him from the memory of himself. Some animal of the air, more fantastic than beasts or birds of the familiar earth, inhabited his brain and romped with the words which had made subversion among his senses. All sense had gone away, and the music that mastered his mouth had flattered him into a recognition of himself as a poet whose lunatic contagion could not evoke pity or pardon from the passengers. They watched aghast when Shephard thrust his hands out as though he wanted to seize the rhythms which his memory had exploded.

> *I sought no more that after which I strayed*
>   *In face of man or maid;*
> *But still within the little children's eyes*
>   *Seems something, something that replies;*
> *They at least are for me, surely for me!*
> *I turned me to them very wistfully;*
> *But, just as their young eyes grew sudden fair*

With dawning answers there,
Their angel plucked them from me by the hair...

They looked at him, incapable of pardon just as their blame would have been a poor reply to his performance. And during each interval, as he waited for the words to work his tongue, they were suddenly reminded of their possible ruin. Suppose! Suppose! Supposing this man in a mad fantasy of power decided to take over from the pilot. Their faces made a unanimous supposition of disaster, and it was then they seemed to realise the evil rejection of the air. Escape was inconceivable. They were caught at an altitude where any choice was a wasteful proposition. But now it was the harmless power of ordered speech which held Shephard captive.

I am defenceless utterly.
I slept, methinks, and woke,
And, slowly gazing, find me stripped in sleep.
In the rash lustihead of my young powers,
I shook the pillaring hours
And pulled my life upon me; grimed with smears
I stand amid the dust o' the mounded years.

There was a pause, much longer than the interval which preceded each intonation of verse, and then a general sigh was felt, like a lurch of the airliner, when he seemed to fall back into his seat, overcome with exhaustion.

The attendants crowded round him, agile and indulgent, brimming over with a forced and false encouragement. It was nothing very serious. The captain suggested a shot of brandy, and the hostess who might have anticipated the order was ready at his word. They slipped the glass between his lips, and let the liquor dribble down his throat. Shephard wriggled in his seat, and opened his eyes, regarding them ungratefully. It was an astonishing response to their indulgence. His roving eyes rebuked their attentions, and his hands, trembling with rage, signalled their immediate dismissal. The hostess was the first to explain the misunderstanding, but the captain intervened, and Shephard was suddenly smitten by a need to defend himself. He sat erect, fierce and resistant to their concern, a man whose solitude had been rebuked by their presence.

'I beg your pardon, sir…'

'My pardon is beyond your begging,' Shephard snapped, and the language of verse was still fresh on his tongue. It was appropriate to his excitement.

'I was trying to explain, sir…'

'Beyond, beyond, beyond,' he raved, 'beyond any manner of meaning you can make. Let me be by Grace of God, or the power of my arm, let me be.'

The hostess tried to smile her way into his affections, but it was too late for words. He turned a malevolent eye on her.

'Your waist has made many a man weep,' he said, softly, like a gentle croon. And then his manner roughened, and the hostess stepped back, humiliated by his words: 'You are the odour of your underwear.'

The captain disappeared in the cockpit, and Shephard's sense of danger increased, and that was itself a great danger. He would not trust anyone's absence at this stage. He stood, making impatient gestures in the air, a man who had suddenly felt his authority slip. Defence was the word and the deed which would undo them in his mind. The captain, who was returning from the cockpit, was cut short by a scream. Rowley had screamed, and it seemed the end for everyone. Shephard held two pistols cocked, most carefully cocked, and anxious for action.

'Now take your seats, every one of you, be seated.' His voice was firm and cruel. It was an incredible return of sanity which had made him place himself so that there could be no attack from the back. It was the airliner against an armed man of uncertain and perplexed mind. The marvellous incantation of the verse and the assured control of the triggers were two worlds which met in the same chaos. Everyone was seated.

'And I swear now,' Shephard said, 'as a man who is not given to grossness will swear, that if you, meaning any of you, move in a wrong manner, in word or deed move mean with me, you can say your prayers. Without a word on your part, and in a matter of moments. And you must not lie. Remember, above all else, remember, you must not lie. For that poet, my poet, me, John

Isaac Shephard, picturing that pursuit that is darker than your likely death, claimed no need to diminish the truth.'

His eyes rolled to the gentle balance of his head and they thought his attention had strayed as he intoned:

> Now of that long pursuit
> Comes on at hand the bruit;
> That Voice is round me like a bursting sea:
> 'And is thy earth so marred,
> Shattered in shard on shard?
> Lo, all things fly thee, for thou fliest Me!
> Strange, piteous, futile thing,
> Wherefore should any set thee love apart?'

He stammered another line, but his voice was inaudible, and it seemed that his memory had now failed him completely. He looked around him as though he understood what was happening. He could feel power like the pistols in his hand, and he embarked upon a curious game of enquiry. He ordered the passengers to stand, as he indicated, and state the purpose of their flight. Without the pistols he might have seemed very comic, but now his occasional insistence on certain details added to their sense of danger. They were beginning to feel embarrassment. The captain tried to show his disapproval, but he was fearfully reminded that any action might be dangerous. Shephard had started the investigation.

'Going on business, if you please.'

'Just a holiday, Sir.'

'To see my family.'

'I have always wanted to see the beautiful island.'

'On the doctor's orders.'

Shephard suddenly indicated a halt.

'Are you tubercular, lady, tell me the truth.' The woman shrieked and fainted on her neighbour's shoulder. But Shephard seemed unaware of what had happened. 'Let us continue,' he said sharply.

'My brother is dying.'

'Are you happy?' he asked, fixing the man with a malicious look.

'Happy?' the man said, bewildered.

'Never mind, never mind,' Shephard said. 'Next.'

'I need a change.'

'A change of what?' he asked quickly.

'My husband thinks I ought to have a change of air,' the woman said feebly.

Shephard thought he heard someone giggle, but it was the boy, Rowley, stifling his fear.

'Your husband thinks you need a change,' Shephard said sadly. He regarded the woman with a fierce and passionate show of scorn. 'I know,' he said, his voice low and heavy with contempt. 'You have unmanned him, eh? I know the meaning of a woman's need for change. You have unmanned him, I know, but you'll pay for it. All over the world, the sperm is running dry. The vultures have sucked our sex. Sucked it up all, clean, clean.' He paused to revive his scorn: 'She says she needs a change.'

'Next, what's your business?' But he did not hear what was said, for he was still thinking of the other woman, whispering to himself: 'Even in my island, she'll wear the weapons out.'

'My granny is taking me, sir.'

That was Rowley, standing erect, trying to control the shake of his little hands. But it was hardly necessary. Shephard's manner softened. He seemed to like the boy, and for a brief moment he smiled. Rowley's grandmother smiled back, but Shephard was not to be taken in by that. His attention was exclusively for Rowley.

'You have a good, sensible face,' he said, 'courageous and strong. That is good.' Rowley did not seem to make much sense of what he was saying, but it did not matter. Shephard was lured by his own need to speak. 'I hope you shall escape the poison of your forbears' breeding,' he said. 'Of course, I prefer little girls your age, with your nice manners. I really prefer them until the mirror draws their attention to themselves. Sit down, my son, I shan't harm you.' Rowley sat, crouching against his grandmother, while Shephard, watching the pistols, intoned, 'Mirrors, it is the mirror which has mopped up all our moisture. What a pity, the mirrors.'

'Next, what's your nationality?'

'I'm English,' the man said. He had a silly animal's grin as he spoke, and Shephard seemed displeased.

'English,' he said regretfully. 'Where were you born?'

'Actually,' the man said, picking his nose.

Shephard interrupted brutally. 'Are you lying?'

'No sir,' the man said. He was hardly audible. 'I was born in Australia, but I left at an early age.'

'Australia,' Shephard murmured. 'It is a sad civilisation which starts with rabbits and rogues. Cricket is about all they're good for, and talking about developing the country.' The sweat was making wrinkles on his face. He looked angry and hateful, and beckoned the man disdainfully to sit. 'All this human dreg trying to start afresh,' he whispered, as though talking to himself. 'The new country people, Australians, Canadians, South Africans, dregs, dregs, dregs, developing the country, and the land of the future. The land of the future my foot. Just scum, comfortable scum.' He paused for breath.

'Next, hurry up, next.'

This sudden irritation had increased their restlessness. For a while they seemed slightly numbed by his talk, and they were relieved by his apparent lack of violence. But whenever he showed such irritation, his eyes rolled, and his hands trembled, and everyone expected the worst.

'You, yes you, come forward,' he said, pointing at Penelope. Mark and Marcia were cold, and Bill raised his body timidly from the seat. But he dared not interrupt.

'Ignore the hostess,' Shephard ordered. 'She is only a servant.'

Penelope stood in front of him, white and frail, watching the pistols. The moments seemed to lag, and everyone's fear was heavy. 'But you,' Shephard said. 'You are beautiful, and that is why, that's the reason…' He was stammering for breath, and Bill hoped despairingly there would not be an accident. The captain was squatting in his seat. 'I should like to see you in another form.' Shephard's voice had regained control, soft and firm and spiteful.

'Cactus, yes, cactus, I'd love to see cactus flowering from your hair and clinging only to your nipples. Your nipples are pink, I know, the ones that poison and never give milk. Let the cactus hang there weighing you down, and maggots crowd your mouth, carrying your lips off clean with their crawling, and crowd your mouth, marching to and fro through the perforated flesh up to your eyeballs, pestering them, but leaving your vision clear, for the mirror, that is, and causing you only an endless itch in the eye. I should leave your legs in all their natural lechery, but I'd have fat snails, out of their shells, slide plentifully into your womb, leaving you heavy and full with a lasting slime.'

Penelope shrieked with tears, but Shephard, fierce and unrelenting, tried to think of every malediction that would torture. They had not before seen such hate in his eyes.

'Yes,' he said, and his voice was gradually acquiring its customary intonation, 'I would rejoice to see you ugly. Ugly, ugly, ugly. You beautiful bitch.' He brushed the sweat from his brow and shoved her back. 'Bitch,' he muttered irritably, 'the bitch, like the other bitch I remember… I remember…'

Penelope fell into her seat, hardly conscious of Bill's hand pressing against her. Her heart was pounding and her lips twitched, and there was no feeling at all left in her. There was nothing Bill could do, but whisper a little cheer and press her lovingly to him.

Shephard's shirt had stuck like leather to his skin, and he could feel the sweat make rain down his face. His head shone black like glass in the night. His eye had caught a shadow of land, and they saw him smile. The pistols leaned downwards as he widened his smile; and suddenly he spread his hands out again as though he wanted to fly. He held one pistol aimed at the window where he had seen land, and they saw his lips move slowly, heavily, with sound.

'San Cristobal, San Cristobal,' he intoned. 'You let rumour argue against reason in a voyage to San Cristobal which every race has reached and where the sea is silver and the mountains climb to the moon. You do not know San Cristobal, coming up by accident one morning from water, the tiny skull of a mountain top which was once asleep under the sea. Here Africa and India shake hands with China, and Europe wrinkles like a brow begging every face to promise love. The past is all suspicion, now is an argument that will not end, and tomorrow for San Cristobal, tomorrow is like the air in your hand. I know San Cristobal. It is mine, me, divided in a harmony that still pursues all its separate parts. No new country, but an old old land inhabiting new forms of men who can never resurrect their roots and do not know their nature. Colour is their old and only alphabet. The whites are turning whiter, and the blacks are like an instinct which some voice, my voice, shall exercise. San Cristobal so old and yet so new, no place, this land, but a promise. My promise, and perhaps yours too...'

His reverie of San Cristobal had relaxed their fear, but suddenly he paused, looking at Marcia and Mark, and it seemed that he would begin again his earlier interrogations. His glance lingered on Mark who turned his head away. But Shephard had come to an end. He leaned forward, and his lips began to beat like a clown's, and his head rocked slowly into his shoulders. It seemed the moment for the captain to intervene. The pistols had fallen to the floor, and it looked as though a fit had seized his body, bending it forward. His teeth were set, and his legs were stiff. The captain and the hostess stooped over him, regarding his seizure with pity and contempt. But it was difficult for the passengers to follow the progress of his limbs. The airliner was stooping cautiously, and suddenly it bumped and rolled, making a proud circle across the land, which lay below them, incredibly patient and loyal after every hazardous survival.

BOOK TWO

SAN CRISTOBAL

PART ONE

1

The sea turned under the dull eye of the morning that moved round the trees. The branches nodded as the wind brushed the leaves into a brief and timid flutter of awakening. The stems leaned dangerously, and sometimes a sudden snap surprised their balance and threw them down in a negligible death under the dark seaweed. The sun arrived late, forcing a shift of the clouds which curled and hurried in a dark dispersal through the light. A feeble lustre touched the sand, stained brown like sugar. Many feet had minced and flattened the beach into a floor that followed the curve of the sea out of sight. The weather was appropriate.

A huge black rock which grew high out of the sea looked across the sand to the tops of the trees in a melancholy longing for the land. Ragged snatches of weed rambled up the sides, and the water shaken furiously into foam by the resistance of the rock washed them with its spray. The sea surrounded it like a captive, leaning over its wet soil, a piece of earth mourning its luck.

The crowd had travelled with their gifts to propitiate the thirst of the sea. The sand received their weight from the abrupt boundary of the weed that rambled inland under the trees to the slipping edge of the sea, and their voices journeyed in a grave echo across the water. There were children everywhere, eager and credulous as they listened to the story of their island.

'You turn in your gift?'

'Yes, Ma, I give it up.'

'An' with a good heart you give it?'

'With a good heart, Ma.'

'Time an' the water will make your reward with mercy.'

The old woman did not recognise the strange boy who stood alone under the tree, but she knew that it was his wish to join the three boys who were sitting at her feet. The boys were native to

85

San Cristobal, and they knew who the stranger was, and they felt no wish to share this privilege with him. Yet he was walking towards them, taking some confidence from the look which the old woman had turned on him as he stood alone under the tree. She put her hand out, and he said, as he glanced uncertainly at the three boys, 'Can I call you Ma, too?' And the three boys were astonished when they saw the old woman embrace the stranger and sat him down beside them.

'You make your gift?' one of the boys asked as though they were questioning his right to be with them.

'I couldn't take it myself,' said Rowley, 'my granny nor my daddy won't let me, but I ask the maid to put it.'

A tear had lit the old woman's eye as she looked out to where the small boats were waiting. The boys were surprised by her welcome and wondered whether it was a special favour because this boy was younger and also a stranger. But they did not speak.

'When did it happen, Ma?' Rowley asked, and they all turned to hear the old woman.

'A number will name the years, my son, but no mind can contain the time. The measure is too great. Some say five hundred years, an' some say many more, but everyone accept the time as a long, long time ago.'

'Will it happen again, Ma?'

'Mercy is not yours nor mine to give, so it may happen again. Who knows? The sea can be a wicked water, an' lan' is not reliable. But it happen before, a long time ago, as I choose to describe the time, the lan' holdin' us up this very moment change places with the sea, an' a total reckon' take the livin' o' the time to a sad end. Scarcely a breath it spare, of animal or bird, on that dark day. 'Twas a day with a face like today, they say, with the sky unkindly lookin', an' the water movin' silent in a malice no man can watch. These same sands you tread now, my son, slip like ice, an' the trees forsake their branches an' the leaves run lawless through the air. They say the rain let itself loose an' burst upon us like a harvest of thorns, an' the poor lan' cry till the tears that cover it like a lake of water stretch in every direction to shake hands with the sea. The birds forget how to turn a tune, an' the animals lose their tongues an' had to die in a wonder at that harvest of water.'

'You make it fearful to remember, Ma.'

' 'Twas fearful before an' after. When the sea climb every hill until it hide all recollection o' the living, it settle quiet again into itself and never stop swimmin' with the evil confusion o' corpses on top. Bone an' branch, a large comminglin' of tongues that couldn't talk their way back to the mouth that house them, beaks from their birds, and all manner of heads took from the necks that once rescue them, eyes let loose an' wanderin' blind, an' sockets takin' water in unlawful possession of their emptiness, an' the confusion o' feathers joining their many, many colours with the colour o' skin an' skull an' every manner of dead meat.'

'Why did it happen, Ma?'

'A secret, my son. Nature which is naked for us to see in grass an' flowers livin' an' dyin' before our very eyes, an' the fruit fallin' heavy an' ready for our feedin', that same nature hide a slyness on the inside. An' I don' know, an' no man know the secret that surprise us on that day San Cristobal die in a total drownin'. But men make excuses an' explanations, an' you can buy many reasons which they write in their books, but there is no certainty of sayin' in a matter so large with surprise. I believe it was the will o' the Lord, an' that is a complete reason, for His will can outlast every question which try to corner it. An' I believe in the matter 'bout our island that part o' His will was a rememberin' of all things, how they come under His care, an' not only animals an' birds an' men who are so thoughtless, but the earth also which seldom refuse our feet travellin' at all times an' in every manner o' speed across it. He remember that the earth need a rest, an' he put San Cristobal to rest for a while under the sea, so that when the sea withdraw an' grant a view of the air again, the resurrection would return a new supply for the needs o' those who come after. An' so it was. The islan' that rise from the water on that Day o' Deliverance which we come here to celebrate was renewed with riches. So that the water which take against your control and mine will, in a time no man can capture with his wish, return what it carry.'

'The boats are leaving, Ma.'

'I hope every gift go with a good heart.'

'I am sorry for the animals which have to drown,' said Rowley.

'Do not grieve the offerin', my son, do not grieve it ever.'

The small boats rocked to the rhythm of the water as they received the offerings which they were to carry out to sea far, far beyond the reach of the shore. The men had arranged the cargo carefully, testing the balance of the boats with suspicious glances. Their voices reached the shore in feeble exchanges of remonstrance, and sometimes, unwittingly, their language rose in anger, and many an ear lost its innocence by the shock of a wrong word. They were fishermen who worked the boats, and those who were listening from the shore would forgive what they heard. Fishermen were always granted a licence of language, since it was the sea which had trained their tempers and roughened their tongues. The animals were restless and afraid at first, but soon they forgot their fear and took their chance. But for a long time the air was loud with their noise. Pigs grunted their displeasure, and a goat groaned, and the fowls were in panic, making a riot that reached the sky with their scattering cackle. They never grew hoarse. Only the sheep seemed unconcerned and took their places without caution or reluctance as though their life had always been a preparation for this servitude. The rabbits were nervous but incapable of utterance, and the ducks simply waited as though they were going home. First the large boats moved forward swaying under their weight; and the small boats followed laden with the fruit and vegetables which were their share of the sea's treasure and the island's reward for pardon. And the crowd sang that it may never happen again: a tragic return of their land to water. But the old woman spoke to the boys again.

'An' not only water walk this lan' to tell San Cristobal a rule no arm can compete with in power. Not yours which the first crop o' years encourage to play rough with any weight which tease your strength, nor mine that the time turn feeble, an' none that wave round the town talkin' all night 'bout tomorrow. No arm, I tell you, in this kingdom we call land o' the livin' succeed to raise some order when the forces I see went ravin' wild. An' not only that water in the mornin' we make memory here with. Fire an' wind come after. An' I know them like my next door neighbour, only I run an' not wait to risk any welcome. They reach with a fury only prayer might tame.'

'You was alive for the Fire, Ma?'

'My eye was the earliest witness that night the rivers run red an' every house curl up and fall flat in a hot white sleep. I was a girl no more nor less the size your legs raise you now, an' feelin' free, steppin' light as a breeze with no worry for the world which start sudden to roast under my two feet. How I remember it, the ruin that reach right 'cross San Cristobal, an' make a red wonder in every corner o' the sky where my eye could keep watch. An' I was learnin' a lesson no school can instruct, how there be forces which need make no fight 'gainst any arm that raise in question or comman'. Men who make magic in ordinary time, with a voice like the sun decidin' who is who, an' how an' when you an' me might move where, I see them, those same men, how they stan' in a silence that tremble for mercy, an' their hands creep quiet to their eyes like children hidin' shame or fencin' with a fear that catch them sudden for the first time. My head hol' that sight, an' my ears keep the noise that night confess. An' I receive from those days till now such warnin' as a little wisdom will lend any sense that is willin', however simple in learnin', to receive. Sometimes I see the end o' some wild ambition San Cristobal catch, I see like it was the beginnin' takin' place in front my face. An' I pray, an' you better learn to pray, like I pray whenever a cloud collect to tell my feelin' that trouble near. My blood don't come out o' hidin' to show w'at happenin', but I feel it leave every limb, an' hold me on these knees till I make my peace with prayer. An' it hol' me that night, an' the mornin' that come next, an' wake San Cristobal like a man who let bad liquor wash him clean an' take every sense his mind use to possess. An' a mornin' as may never tame my tongue again, I beg, the mornin' I witness San Cristobal fail from every direction to stan' like a real live town once tall with stores an' trees that hoist their head wherever this lan' was a soil for growing green. Every roof crumble. Paper, an' records men make for rememberin', every garment cloth could fashion, an' the very grass scarcely green, I see them in one same colour, soft as soot which the wind was wheelin' everywhere. A black breeze only comin' 'twixt the sun and the soft face which make night-light over the lan'. It was all equal in appearance. Stone an' root an' bones where the animals finish in ashes.'

The boys remained silent as though they feared a repetition of the destruction which the old woman had related. The Wild Fire was only a legend for many who were alive in San Cristobal, but it was not beyond the old woman's memory. It had killed the finest crops the island had produced in half a century, and it had silenced the wishes of all those who depended on the island's produce for food or wealth. It had become a text for teachers. But for the old woman, it was a spectacle, real as the sun which now loitered over the trees. The boys watched her raise her head and wait for the nailful of snuff to clear her nose.

'It didn't come like the flood,' one said.

'What make it happen, Ma?'

She clasped her hands as though she were about to pray, and the boys noticed how her eyes strayed vaguely above their heads towards the horizon. And when she spoke it seemed that her memory had stretched the distance between her and the boys.

'For days we hear a singin' in the hills, an' the seventh night was silence, the night the fires crack every blade o' cane an' dry the juice that was almost ready to make San Cristobal a season o' sugar, the best season God ever give. Those who work an' those who receive smell the same fear when the sugar fires chase down the hills, an' spread wild with the wind all over the town. I was a girl then makin' much the same size you reach from head to foot.

'How those men sing before that night! How they sing, an' now this moment recollect that time, it seem that the voice was no part o' the will that start such a prosperin' red evil afterwards. It was a music that never since rejoice my ear in the same way, an' I remember how my mother stare through the window like her eyes really not seein', but followin' a vision that travel back, somewhere behind an' far outside the circle o' the house an' the endin' o' San Cristobal itself. So her eyes look to tell that her hearin' was like the wind which reach everywhere and still seem steady in one place. So her hearin' seem, tickin' two times, now an' a next, an' turnin' round two places, the hills outside which her eye could locate, an' elsewhere, more like a dream which only her memory collect and sprinkle like the voices making some secret message in her head. An' I feel how my head swell with a

90

wonder to learn what it is her heart was hearin' out o' that music. I hear it too, but she was nearer to some secret my tongue couldn't tell. An' I make my questions as you been makin' yours, to learn what she see. But she won't let her tongue utter not a single teachin'. 'Twas only after the air snap like fingers lashing wild an' not feelin', that she talk. An' her talk was clear an' true as the air turnin' red over the hills. The fires begin growin' like the very grief that encourage them. An' she say she know it was comin'. The singin' was the warnin' the men been makin' night after night, an' the fires was the way their heart complain.'

'But why did they do it ?' Rowley asked.

' 'Twas a malice on every side that start disaster. The men who make that fire fret how their labour went robbed in a lan' which refuse to make them brother an' sister, or feed them with a right reward for the sweat they drip night an' day. The lan' come to look like a tyrant in their eye, an' they decide to burn whatever memory hol' them to the plough. An' they burn every blade, young an' ol', ripe or not ready, it matter no more, an' they promise to burn an' burn for ever till those who conquer San Cristobal an' own it from afar relax their will, or choose some next han' to labour with the lan'. 'Cause they had no more home to go to. San Cristobal was the only home they know, an' it was no home. So time seem a waste in their eye, an' they put their livin' to a fearful purpose in those fires that make every workin' nerve shudder the night the silence take possession o' the hills.

'But those who remain take to livin' again like it was the beginnin' o' the world. An' we plant again, an' those who start that force which no arm could halt, even them, with their wicked remedy for the grievance they was shoutin', make their promise solemn an' true never to burn again.

'An' in a time it come to happen, the lan' wrinkle an' work, an' sugar come ripe with the same sweat, but a different looking face. 'Twas even in my time I see a new race o' labour voyage in an' come to stay, makin' all kind o' mixture here in San Cristobal. Now it was India, an' later China, an' more too I cannot recollect, from east an' west, whatever nations outside had power to sell or len' mankind, they come, an' time take whatever memory come with them 'cross the sea, an' their habit make a home right here, you an' me an' all who now stay for good or evil till eternity take them off, one by one or all together.'

Gradually the fishermen were finishing their toil. The boats slipped vaguely out of sight, and the faces brightened with the assurance that their reprieve was certain. Talk now turned to the presence of the land, and the fever of rumour and hope which had aroused San Cristobal in the past two months. The sun was working itself up to a warmth which shook the day. The light shivered with a brilliance which seemed to dissolve the clouds, and the sky screamed its magic of colour in every eye. The waves washed the black rock with leaping pearls of spray which fell and crashed wastefully over the shivering weed.

But the old woman sat quiet regarding the crowd which drifted slowly from the shore. Their talk was familiar, and she noticed how the three boys listened to the voices which were shouting prophecies about the future of San Cristobal as though they had been granted the promise of some special favour. The boys seemed eager to join the crowd, but they would not leave without the old woman's permission, and they did not know what their feelings were towards Rowley. They were all following the traffic of the crowd until the old woman stretched her hand and touched one of them.

'You want to stand?' Rowley asked.

'I want to speak one word more,' she said. The boys relaxed and waited. ' 'Tis not all gold an' glory in the colour an' sound o' the day. An' what I remin' you may happen again, 'cause malice makin' a move these days, like the time I tell you. There ain't no singin', but the town an' all San Cristobal talkin' a noise that match the wish which fan those fires, an' I only waitin' to feel the road my prayer should walk. But you better learn before your ears make you ramble wrong. There be a wrong somewhere, an' only prayer can answer when a voice tell where right is waitin'. 'Cause there be always a punishin' season. Tomorrow or later, time need make no warnin', whenever the heart authorise some evil ambition, nature may name a terrible discord which no man here nor 'cross the sea can counter.

'Like after those fires, no more girl I was but a woman beginnin' to take on life, we had some winds in San Cristobal. I see them rip roots out the earth, an' sen' the trees clappin' crazy in the sky. No man make that deed, an' no arm risk to still that wind when it come. An' it seem cruel as the fires, like one disaster tryin' to take record from the next. An' my feelin' whisper it was a punishin' season, for we must learn not to wrong the earth, or nature may make her own arrangements to correct the offence. So it work with the winds the time I watch those housetops fly like kites through the clouds, a time I try sometimes not to remember, for it may happen again, an' I talk to you like a duty tell me the four must be part o' any prayer my lips make concernin' San Cristobal.

'Now you watch me here on the sand this mornin', old, old as ever in your eye, an' I feel your innocence take to me, an' in your years the head is open to false an' different favours which the worl' always makin', so I speak to warn you 'way from any turnin' you know my prayers may contradict. An' if your heart keep a right respect for age, the little wisdom my time collect can help your understandin' too. Never you look to the ways that teach those round how to hate, an' different as you be in name an' nature, 'tis the same love my prayers will ask to favour any wish you make.'

She stood and their silence was eloquent with awe as they watched her amble up the shore. The sand had turned silver, and the sun polished the pebbles with its burst of flame spreading white to the top of the hills. A flock of sparrows hissed at the water, and trespassed the shore briefly with their breasts, before sailing, drunk with the salt singing of the sea, into the arms of the trees. The hills were suddenly loud and lavish where the monkeys seemed to ruin their throats in an effort to sing, and the birds made song their unending speech.

The boys walked away, following the crowd which turned to greet the town with music; and the streets, under their surface of asphalt, kept company with their feet, like a faithful dog. Children blinded the windows with balloons as the crowd drifted gratefully from the shore, hearing the music announce the town. It was a holy day and a wild day, the day San Cristobal celebrated its historic deliverance from the water.

2

It is with me again, and now I wonder what source of danger this feeling conceals. If I tried to describe the scene in all its detail of ordinariness, the result would almost certainly appear as a game, childish and pointless to any eye which could not detect a single relation between the objects which inhabit this beach of Paradise Point. And I have not been conscious of any relation either, but it is precisely this absence which seems to restore each thing to its completeness. A certain lack of connection had endowed the pebble with a formidable and determined power of its presence. It was there, independent, obstinate, decisive.

A pebble, a piece of iron and a dead crab.

We were separated by unequal distances of sand, but we seemed to share the same lack of power to move. They were all within the reach of my arm, and when I turned to touch them, my wish had taken the shape of an undertaking which now seemed at once extraordinary and simple.

There was the pebble, smooth as an egg, and I felt my arm crouched beside my ribs in its customary servitude, awaiting the order that would lead it forward to the glistening white stone that could not resist my touch. But I saw the pebble and my fingers lay relaxed in their brief sprawl on the beach, a little embarrassed by my indecision. I could not touch it. The sun made a ring of shadow about it, and the brief arc of sand retained its dark dry quality, wholly defenceless but undisturbed. What was the source of this dumb obstinacy? Hard, white, and delicately curved, the sea had pushed it up a little beyond its reach, a by-product of sand and water in temporary exile from the huge heart of the ocean. It was just another pebble. But here, under cover of the sun and my glance, it had acquired a quality that rescued it from the mute simplicity of stone. It presented itself as another existence, separate and inde-structible. It might arrange itself to offer another appearance for another glance, but it could not die; and this, I believe, was the secret of its quiet splendour, and its insuperable decency, its mild and relentless defiance. I was beginning to understand my envy and my curious insistence to pass my hand over its polished surface. And I looked at my fingers, five inert and uncooperative aspects of my fancy. My hand was waiting, using its servility as an excuse for its stillness, while my glance moved with a quiet and shameful caution towards the piece of iron.

Slightly dejected, it wore its rust like a mark of humiliation which it had completely overcome, a ruined memory of the black earth from which it had come. I wanted to hold it for a while before turning it gently, but my glance had already encountered the questioning dead eye of the crab. I watched it, then quickly looked at the pebble and the piece of iron, before returning my gaze on its fragile pink back. Life had withered in its claws, and the wrinkled white band of the belly opened to show the empty chamber of its back. A stiff stubble of hair covered the tips of its claws, sprawled flat on the sand. One socket had lost its eye, but the other eye stood on its hidden hinge, perpendicular and transparent. My attention did not waver. I felt a sudden impulse to crush it under my fingers and watch the shell crumble in flakes over my palm. It was there, accessible, defenceless, a promise of my power. I raised my arm, and looked at my fingers which were stretched tight over my eyes. Now they would work. I had only to give the order and complete the act which would crush the arrogance of this lifeless object. But suddenly my arm failed and I felt my fingers fall in a willed reluctance on to the sand. The dead eye shone as though it understood its triumph. My inclination had failed me. I rolled over and away from the reach of the pebble, and my hands rested on my face, and one finger slipped into my mouth, between my teeth, and I was like a child who was suddenly surprised by his failure to do something that was simple like biting his nails.

This feeling of disinclination surrounds me like space. It enters me like air. It is like my hand which reminds me of the distance between me and the object it brings me in contact with. I can feel it like a clutch round my throat, an annihilation of things about me, a sudden and natural dislocation of meaning. And it is no force other than me which moves me. It is me.

3

The landing had been delayed until late afternoon, but the weather did not change, and the tide came stronger. The currents were calm round the ship until they found the wind which cruised them swiftly out to shore, and the air turned colour with each interval of smoke lifting heavily from the solitary black funnel. The ship was ready to deliver its cargo of cattle. The ropes were flung from the deck to the boats which waited below, rubbing and tossing from side to side. The men rested the oars and hauled themselves forward. They were efficient and loud, and the work proceeded through a confusion of signs and voices which instructed the crew who laboured on the deck. The crane swung wide, stooping lower and lower until the animals made a mountain of spray as they slid down the ship into the water.

A huge crowd waited on the shore, watching the slow, turbulent traffic of animals between the ship and the boats. They could see the men through the casual drift of smoke, leaning over their boats in a swift and desperate conflict with the ropes and the sea. Each man found his beast, latching the ropes to his boat, and the oars slapped the water in a slow propulsion away from the ship. For a while the animals were completely covered with foam. The boats pulled them forward, and their heads surfaced. Two of the boats waited ahead until the others came into line, and then they started their journey towards the shore.

They came nine at a time, and the crowd shouted their impatience, arguing about the skill of the oarsmen. They were beginning to anticipate the order of these arrivals, wondering which boat would make the first landing, and who would be the first to release the animal from the stern and race across the sand to the market stall. The betting had begun, and it seemed for a while a very difficult crossing.

'This race sure belong to Rockey,' someone said.

'I put a bet 'gainst you if you care.'

'Half a dollar.'

'Matter fixed,' said the other.

The man considered the two women who were standing within arm's length at the edge of the crowd. Then he leaned forward, avoiding Marcia, and asked Penelope to hold the bet.

'He's the only man who know how to make headway in a turnin' sea,' he said.

'Time will tell,' said the other.

They glanced sideways at the women, comparing their attitudes to this spectacle outside the market stall. Penelope was checking the bet while one of the men prolonged his stare at Marcia. She seemed less enthusiastic to witness the landing of the cattle, almost oblivious of the crowd which surged round her. The man altered his glance, and bowed to Penelope.

Marcia held her head up, staring vaguely out to sea. Her eyes did not focus the boats, and her gaze seemed to ramble beyond the ship, tracing the wide, blurred swing of the horizon. The wind flew red locks of hair into her eyes, and she swept her hands across her face, and screwed the hair into little rings behind her ear. Her action was careless, almost bored, until the skin under her eyes twitched, making a sudden little shiver that rippled down her cheek like water. She curled her lips between her teeth, and worked her mouth in a taut sideways movement which relaxed the skin across her cheeks and down the sides of her face. But her attitude seemed fixed. It was part of a total distraction which now separated her from the spirited cries of those who were waiting for the boats to arrive.

Penelope seemed hardly conscious of Marcia's silence. The crowd had made her alive with wonder and a vague anticipation. She knew why they had all assembled outside the market stall, and yet she felt that there was something more urgent and ominous that shaped the expectations of the crowd. Her eyes darted, brisk and curious, like sudden spurts of light which briefly identified the faces, and she saw the shape and colour of these skins merge into some unanimous desire which surpassed the simple delight of watching the boats ride forward to the shore.

Others made a private wish and watched the sea heave and fall behind the chop of the oars. The afternoon continued heavy and windy, and the light and the water were the colour of slate. But the crowd were indifferent to the failure of the weather. Their waiting had suddenly turned to a festival of wishes and reminiscence, vivid and various as the faces which looked out to sea. It was one of the occasions which always assembled the diverse elements of San Cristobal in one place. They arrived from the town and the hills, men and women and children who made an unusual miscellany of races which joined in a single excitement.

The boats were labouring steadily through the water, and the crowd had found their patience. Their attention turned for a while to the shore and the voices which were raised in argument about the results of previous landings. An old woman was telling her memories of a visit to China where her father was born. She worked two fingers into her nose and cleared her head with snuff. Then she breathed deeply, drawing her head into her shoulders, and smiled as though her vision of the sea had been suddenly quickened. The three boys were holding roller skates in their hands, and one with features remarkably like the old woman's was conducting a persuasive argument with Rowley. The latter had come down to the waterfront with his father's maid, a thick black woman who watched him closely as she talked with an Indian in the uniform of a prison warder. The boys looked at the Indian with suspicion, and then they nodded as though they had come to some secret agreement which the Indian and the woman would never know. The maid called Rowley, and the other boys turned and walked away. Marcia and Penelope looked across to see whether Rowley had recognised them, but the woman had his head locked under her arm as he looked towards the boats.

The crowd had increased, and some of them had taken seats on the sand. Marcia and Penelope were tiring, but they were fascinated by the crowd which they had never seen in such large numbers, and they did not want to leave until the boats arrived. Some of the men had started a lively discussion about San Cristobal and the political meetings which were held every night in the town. Penelope turned to see them, and suddenly she felt her heel sink in the sand. She caught Marcia's arm, and soon the two were craning backwards, struggling for support, until the men noticed their difficulty and restored their balance. The men had paused to follow the progress of the boats, but attention was now divided between the race and the talk which rose casually from the crowds.

'Was like a new day o' deliverance,' someone said, 'the day he announce that speech when the music stop.'

' 'Tis words make him work his magic,' a woman said, 'when a man got words he can open any ear.'

'An' magic don't take no time to work,' said the man, 'before your eye clap twice you in the spell.'

'He move my heart that mornin',' the woman said, 'an' if I could have lay my han' on them who say he was mad, only if I could have lay my han' on the lyin' tongue that try to slander his brain.'

'They didn't want him to do the work he start,' the man said, 'but he choose the right day to make that speech, the mornin' we celebrate San Cristobal. 'Tis a next day o' deliverance he goin' bring.'

'An' he aint talk no lies,' the woman said, 'he aint let his tongue slip a single lie when he say that San Cristobal is his an' mine, an' how he goin' make it belong to everybody who born here.'

' 'Tis why they say he mad an' make that disturbance on the plane,' said the man, 'the spirit must have tell them what plan his min' was makin'.'

'Those who born here come first,' said the woman, 'he make it plain as scripture that we got to come first. An' for that they call him mad. But if 'tis mad, 'tis a madness we been waitin' for God only knows how long.'

Penelope looked scared as she tried to avoid hearing the voices which had turned to a rumour the incident she had witnessed on the plane. She had recovered from the shock of Shephard's assault but the events which had followed seemed more staggering than that afternoon in the air when Shephard's words worked a fear which paralysed her senses. And after she heard him speak to the crowd assembled in the town to celebrate the return of the island from water, she knew no one had the power to tell this crowd what had really happened on the plane. She turned to say something to Marcia, but they were all alerted by a voice which rose above the noise of the crowd. The man was drawing attention to the Indian.

'Baboo, who you come to catch? Who multiplying your stripes, Baboo?'

The Indian identified himself with a wave of the hand, and continued talking to the woman. He was standing ahead of the crowd, almost at the edge of the water. The woman seemed suddenly conscious of her presence, and appeared to sidle further into the crowd. But the Indian detained her, slowing his words, as though he needed her company to protect him from the man who had shouted.

'I ask you who you come to catch, Baboo?' the man shouted.

The Indian did not reply, and the man shouted again. The Indian turned, showing his contempt. There was loud laughter from the crowd, and the Indian, who now seemed uneasy, turned and said, 'When you ready with your next finger?'

'Going make them reap all seven next time,' the man said.

The crowd laughed more heartily, and Penelope turned to look at the man. There were three fingers missing on his left hand. He waved his lame hand in the air while he spoke, as though he wanted to remind them of his misfortune. He had become aware of the attention of the crowd, and he seemed eager to provoke the Indian.

'An' then I goin' try for a different kind o' trade,' he added.

The laughter increased. The man rolled his sleeves to his elbow, and showed his fat, scarred arm. He was tall and thick around the shoulders, and his face seemed unnaturally black under the bright surface of sweat.

'What's he talkin' about?' Penelope asked, turning to one of the men.

'He's thief,' the man said, ' 'tis his occupation.'

'How did he lose his fingers?' Penelope asked.

' 'Tis how he had them taken,' the man said. He was smiling as though he enjoyed his knowledge.

'Did they cut them off in prison?'

'He never see the inside o' prison,' the man said, 'nature prefer him to lose a finger.'

'Was it his punishment for stealing?' Penelope looked scared as she waited for the man to answer. She was unsure of the laws which obtained in San Cristobal, and the man disturbed her by his lack of sympathy for Thief.

' 'Tis punishment,' the man said, 'just like the accident that make it happen. Each theft one finger, an' he got seven more failures to make 'fore he put his hand to a next pastime.'

'But it's not the Law?' Penelope asked.

'Not the law o' the land,' the man said. 'Those the law catch spend time killing cows. They waitin' this very moment in the stall for the cattle to offer their neck.'

He pointed in the direction of the market stall, and then turned to see the boats which were sawing feebly through the water.

'One day they'll go mad with murdering,' he said, ''cause after a while the sight o' blood, week in week out, confuse their sense. But Thief get a right punishment, 'cause 'tis a serious crime. A murder may make one less mouth, and when population leap up, prosperity come lean. But stealin' is destructive complete, 'cause it confuse the whole meanin' o' property, an' property is the only real thing, 'cause the worth of a man, as you know, is the size o' his belongings. An' for that, nature prepare the accident that catch Thief each time. One finger he lose by bullet, an' the rest on the knife blade, an' the owners feel it wus enough recompense, an' refuse to prosecute. Was nature, miss, tryin' to correct his mistake.'

'But why does he go on stealing?' Penelope asked.

''Tis his choosin',' the man said, 'he just turn to it like a carpenter to the hammer. An' when he aint on the trade, he's just what you see him now, entertainin' any ear that give him a hearin'.'

The man glanced at Thief, fearing that he might have been overheard, but Thief was talking quietly to the men who squatted behind him on the sand. The men were silent, almost grave, in their respect for what he was saying. He was arguing with himself about the future of San Cristobal, and the men nodded from time to time as though his words had already become a part of their feelings. They surrendered their approval before they had heard him through. His manner was earnest and expressive, and his humour could turn their attention, without warning, to a sudden burst of laughter. The men were grinning as Thief raised himself, looking round at the crowd. He had prepared them for his mischief. They watched him sweep his lame hand through the air, trying to anticipate the attack which he had hinted.

'Baboo, what scandal you concoctin' now?' Thief shouted.

The Indian kept his ground, unmindful of what was said. Penelope was hoping that the Indian would not reply. Thief might have tired and returned to talk with the men. But he seemed indifferent to the Indian's response. The Indian served only as an occasion for him to entertain the crowd. But he was less facetious now. He was beginning to repeat his argument with the men, using the Indian as an example which focused his meaning.

'Look my face,' said Thief. He passed his lame hand over his nose and across his mouth. 'Like night-light in full mornin' time, an' there aint no paint can put fresh complexion where this dark set in, 'cause 'tis more than colour make me shine. Look me straight Baboo, an' see how skin curse the light like judgement evenin' for a soul in sin. But tomorrow comin', tomorrow near here, Baboo, an' we goin' all sing with the same no-colour smile. So you better get ready, Baboo. Tell your heart to teach your lip the movement when it feel joy come home.'

Thief laughed as he talked, and the crowd urged him quietly to continue. The Indian folded his arms, and played with his boots in the sand. The three boys with the roller skates glanced at the Indian and then at Thief. One boy was an Indian and the other was the colour of Thief, but they showed no awareness of this difference as they listened. They looked at each other in silence, waiting for Thief to continue. He reminded them of the speakers they had heard at night, and they tried to forgive him his occupation, and imagined that he was one of the speakers who addressed the large gatherings in the town every night. The crowd which waited on the sand looked like such a gathering, and they seemed to show a similar pleasure in Thief's performance. The boys watched him eagerly, then they glanced at Marcia and whispered among themselves.

Thief was soothing his lame hand. He pushed the three fingers through his hair, and looked round at the crowd. They seemed eager to hear him speak. He hurried his hands in his pockets and studied the progress of the boats. The crowd followed Thief's movement and some started to shout, encouraging the oarsmen whom they had favoured. They could barely see the heads of the cattle twisting painfully against the boats. The sea sailed little fists of spume that lifted with the oars in a fine, wide spray over the men's faces. The tide was difficult, and the men steered their load towards the shore with great caution. Thief grinned as though he had already discovered the result of the landing. Then his eye caught the Indian warder, and his interest was renewed. He had started to tease again.

'Baboo!'

Thief's voice came like a sudden ejaculation, and the crowd became almost hysterical. Thief showed the same elation, as he stared at the Indian, searching his head with his lame hand. The Indian was going to reply by pushing his index finger up the crease of his backside, but he suddenly remembered his uniform, and his fingers closed reluctantly against the side of his leg.

'Friend or foe, Baboo, we goin' lie down in the same future,' said Thief. 'You aint see a star pitch that aint touch my fortune too, Baboo, all two both bleedin' the lan' from boyhood with hoe and plough, till time turn my luck first an' later your own too. Now we ridin' high, 'cause time call a new tune, an' we both goin' rule San Cristobal, you an' me Baboo, an' every boy an' daughter born out o' the mixture we make. You follow the meetings, Baboo? Where you puttin' your vote? See how Singh let Shephard lead, 'cause the blacks outnumber all, but the numbers don't matter no more, Baboo, an' we goin' join the same dream that wake with the Chinese too, an' any white who willing. 'Cause San Cristobal aint got no history but a people who collect in one place by some strange chance. So you votin' with me, Baboo, an' the Powers who want to humble pride with learnin' goin' salute Thief an' Baboo in the same mornin'. An' we goin' lie down in the same future, an' you got to make your face smile with mine. You smiling, Baboo? Let me see your lip learn the movement, Baboo. Smile!'

Thief paused to look at the boats, but there was still some distance to cover before the crowd could distinguish between the men who worked the oars. The maid was taking Rowley away, and the three boys turned to watch until he disappeared through the crowd. Penelope stepped nearer to the man beside her. She wanted to ask him about Thief and the Indian. Thief was quiet, and the Indian warder walked leisurely up and down. The three boys were rehearsing in whispers what Thief had said, and now and again they glanced towards Marcia and Penelope to see what they were doing. They were obviously making some calculations which related to the two women. And they were waiting until the boats arrived. The crowd had turned their attention to the sea. Thief remained silent, chewing the end of his collar as he stared out to sea. Penelope's hand had brushed the man, but he did not notice. He had been thinking about Thief and the Indian warder, and he turned to share his observation with Penelope.

'Stay alive, an' you never know what change you'll see,' he said. He looked at Penelope who was not sure that he was speaking to her.

'A time ago,' he said, 'the Indians in this crowd won't let Thief plague the warder the way he do without trouble.'

'But why is he provoking the warder?' Penelope asked.

'No provoke,' said the man, 'he only choose the warder 'cause he wear uniform, an' gettin' promotion too rapid, but he aint making no malice there. 'Tis the warder who aint sure what Thief sayin' is true. An' 'tis true.'

'He hasn't any quarrel with the Indian?' Penelope asked.

'Not outside the uniform, and the rapid promotion he gettin',' the man said, 'but 'tis strange how the Indians on the sand here rejoice too how Thief talk. When I was a boy, would be like blasphemy to mix the two in any kind o' commotion. When one turn the corner, the other hide, an' nowadays you don't know who managin' money in this place. Both take on a new set o' power.'

'And it's all due to the political meetings,' Penelope said.

She was cautious because she was not sure of the man's sympathies. He brushed his nose, and corrected his stance, bringing his heels together as he spoke.

'Everywhere, madam, is politics,' he said, 'even over yonder on that little island where nobody live but the birds, an' even the birds change their tune. An' everywhere politics is all, everything, madam, livin' an' dying is politics.'

'You really think so?' Penelope asked.

' 'Tis the first time every son o' man goin' vote in San Cristobal,' he said. 'Education or no education, property or no property. 'Tis like openin' up a rumshop free for every passer-by. Think 'bout that. Imagine me authorisin' as I please what my thirst call for. 'Tis like that. The vote is a key, madam, use it, an' authority can take any turnin'.'

'And you know how you'll use yours,' Penelope said.

'I may sell mine, madam.' He smiled, and looked to see whether Penelope was shocked.

But the crowd had become restless. The boats were now clearly visible and everyone could see the animals' heads rising and dipping in an exhausted effort to defy the water. There were shouts of encouragement from the crowd, and the boatmen were working furiously with the oars. Marcia and Penelope were caught in the excitement. They glanced at Thief who watched the progress of the boats in silence. The sea had gone shallow where one of the boats heaved forward, and it looked as though the bull had begun to scrape the sand with its hooves. Cries of delight and disappointment rose from the crowd. The enormous bull was tugging madly away from the boat. The man let the oars lean over the boat as he loosened the rope which held the bull to the stern. The animal leapt out of the water, panting windily, in a wild endeavour to find its bearings. The man seized the ropes, wading through the water, close behind. He shouted at the bull, slapping the ropes against its sides, and gradually, like a body which can hardly bear its weight, the animal stumbled forward, and the man steered it up the slope of the sand towards the market stall. The crowd cheered, turning to watch the bull shake itself dry.

'When I speak, I speak,' said Thief, who had won.

'Don't speak no more,' said the other.

'But I must speak, man, I must.'

'If speech please your mouth, speak,' said the man. He seemed peeved by his loss. He shrugged his shoulders and looked indifferently towards the sea.

'Not my mouth, if you please,' said Thief, ' 'tis my understandin'.' He turned to Penelope who was encouraging him to take his winnings. 'I know who can do what an' when,' he added, shaking the coins in his hands. ''Tis not skill only, but a special skill for what you goin' risk, an' there aint no man born or dead who can plough the oar in a turnin' sea like that Rockey.'

He glanced over his shoulder towards the market stall. Penelope smiled as though she wanted to pay him a compliment, but he had turned to address the Indian warder who had walked further up the sand beside the three boys. The boys were showing him the skates.

'Baboo, what can I do to please you,' Thief shouted, 'what favour for Baboo?'

'Go dead,' the Indian said sharply, and the crowd laughed, waiting for Thief to renew the attack.

'Lord be with us,' said Thief, 'Indian man always meditatin' murder.'

His voice was low and cheerful as though his success had made the Indian less conspicuous. Penelope turned, forcing a way through the crowd, and immediately the three boys retreated up the sand and waited to see where the women would go. The Indian walked further up the sand ignoring Thief. The boys glanced at him, then strolled casually towards the market stall in the direction of Marcia and Penelope.

The other boats were still riding in towards the shore. The oars leapt and turned and disappeared in a slow propulsion under the water. The boats were now all in sight, separated by unequal distances. The animals wrenched their necks, but their heads remained safely latched to the boats. Their eyes looked like circles of grey marble carved into the shining black promontories of skull. The crowd moved further up the shore, and some had made a new group which waited at the entrance of the market stall, hoping to see the slaughter.

4

The market ended where a white wall rose on all sides, making a brief partition between the sea and the town. Penelope could still hear the voices of the crowd on the other side. The sound sent an echo up the wall before finishing gradually like a general sigh over the street. The scene was vivid in their minds. They stood for a while scraping their shoes against the kerb. The echo came again, fading gradually as before. Penelope saw the three boys turn off the street into a lane, but she was thinking about Thief and his prophecy about the future which he was inviting the Indian to share.

She liked San Cristobal, although she had not yet acquired Bill's enthusiasm for the place. It was a spectacle like the landing of the cattle which gave her pleasure, and she liked to hear people like Thief talk. Their language seemed to give everything the sound of ritual, and there was no end of ritual in San Cristobal. But she was becoming suspicious of the passions which Thief described and which had awakened San Cristobal to some new conception of itself. Everyone talked about the future as though they had discovered by accident a new dimension to time. Even Bill kept talking now and again about the possibilities of the place although he was not always sure that the men who aroused this desire were wholly satisfactory.

'It seems such a strenuous way to get your meat,' Penelope said, 'and they don't seem to mind.'

Marcia was still brushing the sand from her skirt. She leaned forward, flicking her finger over a stain which had made a red smudge like dry blood under the belt.

'I suppose they've got used to it,' she said, 'and it will go on until they get a deep water harbour.'

'Then that will be the end of the landings,' Penelope said, 'and I don't think they will want to give that up.'

'I don't suppose you could have both,' said Marcia, 'and they are so eager to change everything that they probably wouldn't mind.'

Penelope hesitated. She was thinking again about Thief and Bill's curiosity about the affairs of San Cristobal.

'Do you think it's good,' she asked, 'the sort of thing that seems to be happening?'

Marcia considered her answer. For a moment she was trying to remember whether Mark had ever expressed himself on this aspect of San Cristobal, but Penelope seemed to be waiting to hear her speak, and Marcia felt her eagerness.

'Are you scared?' she asked. She thought she had detected a certain uneasiness in Penelope's enquiry.

'Everything seems so restless,' Penelope said. 'It makes you feel anything can happen.'

'But Bill seems to find it exciting,' said Marcia, 'I don't think he'd like to leave here for a long time.'

'I don't think I want to either,' said Penelope, 'but I've never known this kind of atmosphere before.' She paused, and turned to

Marcia as though she wanted to elicit a confidence. 'Weren't you a little nervous when the crowd started cheering Thief?'

'Thief might have made me a little nervous,' said Marcia, 'what with his three fingers, but there wasn't anything odd about the people.'

'And the talk about Shephard,' Penelope said, 'I couldn't help remembering him.'

'You think there might be trouble?'

'There could be,' said Penelope, 'but it's also the way things seem to happen here. Take his madness on the plane, for example, and now this sudden popularity, as though nobody remembers anything.'

'Bill thinks it's the fault of the Administration,' said Marcia, 'and all those who protect them.'

'But it isn't their fault that the people favour a lunatic,' said Penelope.

'Not only that,' said Marcia, 'it's because they have created a wholly mad situation.'

'But what can they do if people are allowed to choose freely?'

'Nothing,' said Marcia, 'they never expected that such a day would ever have been possible.'

'And who is to blame?' Penelope asked. 'The present Administration have not always been alive. Must they be held responsible for all that has happened before?'

The women had hurried by chance into argument. Penelope had been trying to elicit Marcia's feelings in order to judge whether her anxiety was unusual. And Marcia had noticed this. She was simply describing her reactions to all that was topical in San Cristobal, but she was not aware of the threat which Penelope seemed to imagine.

'I don't know who is to blame,' she said, and her sudden silence seemed like a lack of interest in Penelope's enquiry.

They continued walking towards the centre of the town. The three boys appeared again ahead of them and as quickly slipped into another lane. The women followed the street as far as the turning where the boys had disappeared. They were making in the direction of the Sea Walk, a gravelled path, hedged with tall, barren palms that divided a main street down the middle. Buildings were beginning to close in around the dark passage of the street. They were silent, meandering through narrow lanes that crossed and folded like arms before arriving, without warning, at the edge of the traffic.

They stood under the awning of the Soda Fountain, waiting for the traffic to thin out. The weather now promised a change. The clouds were lifting and the sun had made dry patches over the street. The town seemed giddy with work as though everyone had been warned to expect some new emergency in their lives. Men were hurrying up and down behind small push carts laden with fruit and vegetables. The carts were all gaily painted, and some had been christened with names and reflections which the owners had chosen to describe the qualities of each vehicle: Time Will Tell, Sugar Lady, Angel On Wheels, All Is Necessary. Sometimes people would pause to make some comment on the names, and now and again one of the men could be seen steering the cart with one hand as he rebuked the traffic with the other. It was a wild and resonant pursuit of wheels and feet hurrying up and down the street. The small stores were soliciting custom with music, and people collected in small groups, beating out the rhythm with their feet as they compared the fashions on display.

Marcia was gazing through the palms towards the dome of an Indian mosque, a circular hood of grey stone, with brass balls surrounding the base and a white flag on top. The large red building opposite was the library, and beyond she could glimpse the church steeple and the wooden barracks of the constabulary. Everything seemed near and concentrated as though the pulse of San Cristobal was alive in one place.

'Did you ever find out who was Louis de Ponge,' Marcia asked. She was pointing at the tall green statue which rose in the distance at the end of the main street.

'The inscription says that he was the founder of French power in San Cristobal,' said Penelope, 'and he died at sea in 1690.'

'And no reference in the library?' Marcia said. 'It seems all their records got washed away.'

'It was the fire which took the library,' said Penelope, 'but fire or flood, there isn't much to go on but the statues and the legends.'

'There is another at the corner of one Admiral Brummel,' said

Marcia, 'he is the English counterpart to de Ponge. He died of a fever after the battle which saved San Cristobal finally from the French.'

They were staring ahead at the statue of de Ponge, which rose almost level with the top of the stores. The French admiral stood six feet in stone, arrogant and bored. One arm was raised, and the hand made an awning over his eyes as he gazed out to sea. The left leg inclined, and the other arm finished in a crooked, wide spread of fingers that clutched his hip. He had made the name of France renowned throughout the world.

Penelope was thinking of the crowd she had seen earlier on the shore, and she felt that these statues which told the broken history of San Cristobal could do little more than incite the passions which Thief had been hinting for the pleasure of the crowd. They continued loitering outside the Soda Fountain, gazing up and down the street at the statues and the stores.

'If those powers had sufficient imagination,' said Penelope, 'after they'd got what they wanted, they should have raised a statue to an unknown native of San Cristobal.'

'I believe the natives want to do that themselves,' said Marcia, 'and they have certainly found men who will make good enough statues.'

'Has Mark said anything about this?' Penelope asked.

Marcia did not answer. She shrugged her shoulders as though she preferred to avoid any mention of Mark. The traffic was moving slowly. Three men came up the Sea Walk, wearing placards with slogans about the Movement and the future of San Cristobal. The women had not noticed them. But suddenly the three boys leapt out of the lane, and scurried across the street. They removed the roller skates, and jumped over the canal on to the Sea Walk. Then they tied the roller skates round their necks, and sat on the grass waiting for the women to cross.

'I'll tackle the one on the left.'

'An' we go for the one on the right.'

'Pins?'

'No, not pins. They don't look like people who wear pins.'

'But their shoes not shape for polishin', an' perhaps they don't want to make much time now it turnin' late.'

'An' we promise not to beg, remember. No money without something in exchange 'cause the Society teach a pride we want to keep. You don't work, then you don't collect.'

'The rules rule out begging. From the start we agree.'

'Perhaps the story take their fancy. Remember we always got the story.'

'An' maybe they want to learn some knowledge 'bout San Cristobal.'

'Then we'll try the story together.'

'The one with the Ants.'

'And the Tribe Boys?'

'That one. Maybe they won't believe, but once they listen, it mean we been workin'.'

'When we attack?'

'Let them loiter first. Then when things looking scarce…'

'We move in.'

'Correct.'

They crouched on the grass showing no interest in the crowd which moved up and down the Sea Walk, but they kept their eyes on the women while they calculated in secret the chances of a bargain. They tried to look easy and assured, but each could guess the other's impatience as they rehearsed in silence the details of the story. Lee picked his nose, and glanced sideways to make sure that the women were still there. Singh buckled his legs and bent his body low, so that his head touched his knee. Now and again he looked up to ask whether the women had crossed the street, and Bob would answer with his eyes. They looked like escaped convicts who were trying to avoid the attention of the crowd. They were quiet, suspicious and intense.

'Hidin' in the open air must make your nerves tick,' said Bob. 'An' when your back turn, you feel every wind is a han' clap your shoulder.'

' 'Tis a profession,' said Singh, 'some people learn to hide without holdin' a breath.'

'But we aint hidin',' said Lee, 'we just lay low, an' when they reach we goin' move like the crowd, till the moment say when to strike.'

'Don't strike,' said Singh, 'we got to move in a natural way, excuse me, please, an' all the fairy talk that make you look gentle, an' smooth.'

'How much you think we might make?'

'Don't state no figure,' said Lee, ''cause you might call too little, an' you never know what sort o' money people like that walk with.'

'They carry such big bags,' said Bob, 'like they goin' raid the stores, or touch the bank. But you never know.'

'Sometimes 'tis nothin' more than powder and lip paint,' said Lee, 'an' tons o' handkerchief an' bills.'

They paused. Bob looked at Singh and nodded, and Lee stretched his legs making ready to stand. The women had crossed the street. Penelope had taken Marcia's arm, and they walked beside the canal towards the slab of stone which bridged the water. Then they turned left on to the Sea Walk.

The boys became suddenly active like the crowd. They pointed in all directions, observing the buildings, and inventing comment on those who passed near them. They had untied the roller skates from their necks, swinging them leisurely as they walked along. Marcia and Penelope came close behind, and the boys lingered by the brink of the grass and watched them pass.

The palms were disfigured with punctures and scars, but the avenue was still pleasing to see. Now it was quiet, for the monkeys had not yet got their orders to perform, and the parrots were feeding. Marcia and Penelope strolled down the avenue, admiring the flowers. They were arranged on trays and in baskets between each interval of the palm trees on one side, just as the animals and birds chained to their rods made the interval on the other.

People were walking up and down the Sea Walk, talking leisurely, or smoking, and the three boys were skipping around on the roller skates. Marcia and Penelope joined in the movement, gazing from side to side, comparing the animals and the birds.

'Do you think Bill would like a monkey?' Marcia asked.

'The parrots look better,' Penelope said, 'and they're not so restless.'

'Perhaps Mark would prefer the monkey,' said Marcia.

'Then let's buy both,' said Penelope, 'one for each of them.'

They stood in front of the poles halfway down the avenue,

comparing the monkeys. Marcia stepped forward and put her hand out to attract the parrot.

' 'Tis a trained bird, miss,' said the old woman, 'well trained she is.'

'What's her name?' asked Marcia. She was still trying to make the parrot peck at her finger, and the old woman was smiling.

'She takes another name every day,' she said. 'Today, she'll answer to Tara, but tomorrow, if she be not sold, I'll call her Lulu.'

'Can she sing?' Marcia asked. The old woman giggled, and the parrot shuffled its claws from side to side, and pushed its head forward in a show of amusement.

'Can you sing, Tara?' said the old woman, stroking the parrot's head. 'In a manner of speaking, you can, Tara, can't you? Can't you catch a note in your ear, my Tara, and make it curl in that little throat, can't you, Tara?'

The parrot got excited, stepping deliriously from side to side, flapping its wings and nodding its head.

'She is pretty,' said Penelope.

'Make her sing,' Marcia said, going a little closer.

'Make my Tara sing,' said the old woman, 'would be so cruel to make my Tara anything, she'll sing, miss, when the spirit move in her ear, won't my little Tara, won't you?'

The monkeys on the neighbouring poles were becoming restless, because no one paid them any attention. They jumped from the pole to the pavement and back, whipping their tails against their sides.

Then the parrot screamed, a disdainful noise, which to Penelope's ear sounded like, shut up. The old woman held her stomach, and laughed.

'They terrible jealous, miss,' she said, 'too jealous of Tara.'

The monkeys returned to the pole, and sat quietly, sulky and contemptuous.

'You want to take Tara, miss?'

Penelope looked at Marcia and then at the parrot; but Thief intervened before she could reply, and the old woman turned her back.

'Been searchin' the market all over for you, miss,' he said, 'a word, if you please.'

Penelope took a few steps away from the poles, and Marcia turned to see what was going to happen.

'’Tis the custom, miss, if you hold a bet, you take part o' de winnings,' he said.

'That's very kind of you,' said Penelope, 'but…'

'No but, miss, would be bad not to take,' he said, 'would cut my luck another time.'

'I wouldn't like you to think I'm too proud,' said Penelope, 'but it's so little you've won anyway.'

'Then I make you some present, miss.'

'It's not necessary,' said Penelope.

'Cost me nothin',' he said, 'I go to the hills this very day an' hol' a monkey an' a parrot. You can keep.'

'You mean you…'

'Not steal, miss,' he interrupted. 'All parrot an' monkey you see here come from the hills. Anyone can take. Please, miss, you must. ’Tis for my luck another time.'

Penelope called Marcia, and they consulted quietly. The old woman had made a disapproving face at Thief.

'You're sure you won't get into trouble,' Marcia asked.

'No one steal parrot, miss. Like monkeys, 'tis free. You got time and patience, miss, you sit in the hills an' wait on your trap.'

'Isn't it an offence?'

'Perhaps you offend monkey, miss, but the Law make no ruling.' Marcia and Penelope watched him in silence.

'’Tis for my luck, miss,' he implored. 'You must take.'

They looked to see whether the old woman had been following Thief's offer, but she kept her back turned, stroking the parrot's beak. Thief continued to press them with his offer, and the boys came closer, pretending not to notice. Penelope was indecisive, and a little confused. They had shown an interest in the parrots, and she was reluctant to disappoint the old woman. But Thief insisted, and she felt afraid to refuse his offer. Penelope was still trying to reach a decision, but Thief had already asked for their address, and Marcia told him. She spoke quickly as though she wanted to share part of the responsibility for accepting Thief's offer. Immediately he saluted with his lame hand and ran up the Sea Walk where the fisherman, Rockey, was waiting.

114

Marcia turned to look at the parrots, hoping that she might find some excuse which might satisfy the old woman. But the old woman continued stroking the parrot's neck, and Marcia felt embarrassed. She could not think of a way to escape without attracting the old woman's attention. She looked for Penelope who had been delayed by the boys. They were talking about Thief and the landing of the cows, and Marcia seemed to think that it would help if they appeared to be engrossed in talk with the boys. She raised her hand as though she were suggesting to the old woman that they would return, and she sidled towards Penelope.

'Did you hear that?' Penelope asked as she looked up from the boys. 'They say Thief used to be a preacher.'

'In the Spanish mission near Maraval,' said Bob, 'an' he stay a holy man till he lose his wife.'

'Was the Spanish man who own the mission,' said Singh, 'he was stealin' the wife from Thief for a long time, an' everybody was talkin', an' Thief won't believe till he find them himself…'

'One Saturday night,' said Bob, 'when the mission should be shut, they was makin' their own service behin' the organ…'

'An' from that day Thief won't believe no more,' said Lee, 'he say there was no law a man could really believe, an' he take to his trade till this day, an' won't turn back.'

Penelope was trying to conceal her amusement, and the boys glanced at each other as though they wanted to confirm that their undertaking had begun. They looked as surprised as Marcia who had been spared the trouble to encourage them.

'At first people understan' why he make the change,' said Bob, 'an' they say his conscience would come back. But it won't.'

'He say from that time he come to understan' everythin' as a kind o' takin',' said Singh, 'an' the only difference is the name they give to your action. So he just behave wild.'

'Like his head won't make the same sense as me an' you,' said Lee.

'An' he say he aint got what it take to behave like the Tribe Boys,' said Singh. 'He wish he could imitate the Tribe Boys, but his heart can't reach that pride.'

'So he behave like the Ants,' said Bob, 'that is without seein' what they kill, or why, 'cause 'tis their nature to kill.'

The boys noticed that the women were puzzled by this reference to the Ants and the Tribe Boys, and they paused, waiting for one of the women to enquire. The women were curious. They looked at the boys as they had done earlier at the statues, feeling a certain astonishment which they could not quite control. Marcia glanced at the old woman with the parrots, but her interest was now taken by the boys, and she had almost forgotten the incident with Thief. Penelope was thinking about the landing of the cattle and the exchange between Thief and the Indian warder. She stared at the boys as though she wanted them to confirm what Thief had said, for she could tell, by the way they regarded each other, that they enjoyed the confidence of a boy's enthusiastic friendship. Marcia was wondering about their reference to the Ants, but she was waiting for Penelope to speak. The boys continued swinging the skates, treating the silence which passed as a natural break in their talk. They had trained themselves to wait, and they were not going to lose this opportunity by any show of impatience.

'Who are the Tribe Boys?' Penelope asked.

'And why is Thief like the Ants?' Marcia added quickly.

The boys hesitated. Then they looked up as though they all wanted to speak at the same time. They wanted to give the story a special importance, and they were trying at the same time to make it appear like common knowledge.

' 'Tis some history 'bout San Cristobal,' said Bob. 'We learn it from early.'

'An' if any strangers aroun',' said Singh, 'sometimes we tell it as a work. 'Cause not everybody know how to tell it.'

'Let's hear if it's not too long,' said Penelope. Penelope motioned to a bench where a man was sitting, and the boys hurried ahead. They were a little nervous, and it seemed that they were uncertain about the order the story should take. Each was trying to suggest that the other should begin. Penelope glanced again at the old woman with the parrots, but she seemed to have forgotten them. She was feeding one of the monkeys, talking to herself as she brought her hand up to the monkey's mouth. The boys squeezed close, making room for the women, but the man suddenly got up and walked away. The boys seemed more relieved. Singh decided that he would sit at the edge of the grass, and the other boys eased round, making distance between them and the women.

'It aint a long story,' Bob said, 'so you mustn't think we been foolin' if we don't go on longer than you expect.'

'An' it aint anything to do with Thief,' said Lee. ''Tis only that he make it come to min'.'

Marcia noticed that they were uncertain, and she wondered for a moment whether this was a prank which they had devised against herself and Penelope. She searched her bag for some cigarettes and passed one to Penelope.

'You want to hear from the beginning?' Singh asked. He glanced at the others, urging them to come to his assistance.

Marcia nodded as she put the cigarette in her mouth, and when she lowered her head, and Penelope scratched the match, the boys decided that it was the moment to begin.

''Twas like in that time when the world know only nature an' noise.'

'Bird noise and wind,' said Singh.

'An' plain animal talk,' Bob continued. 'An' the fish dancin' wild an' makin' faces at the bottom o' the ocean, an' only the sun get permission to say the time, an' the moon only makin' plans to decide the size o' the sea, or makin' fun at some mountains which couldn't climb no more, an' sometimes collapse if a new tide turn upside down, and shake up the sand. Like such a time it was for San Cristobal, long, long before human interference.'

'Like in Genesis,' Lee said.

'As in the beginnin',' said Bob, 'before sense start to make separation betwixt some things an' some things.'

'An' food was free,' said Singh, ' 'cause there was no han' to hide what it take.'

'Except for the animals who fight an' fail,' said Lee.

'Except for them,' said Bob. 'But lan' didn't belong to nobody, an' the law, you feel, was only nature authorisin'.'

'Or refusin' to interfere,' said Lee.

'So why we say,' Bob continued, 'that San Cristobal set up a good example like the world before men make arrangements.'

They paused as though they wanted to make sure of the

women's attention. They saw themselves fixed under Marcia's gaze. Penelope sucked the end of the cigarette as she looked at them, and the boys suddenly thought that it would be disastrous to fail. The women were waiting.

'You better take over from here,' said Bob. Singh nodded quickly.

'Well just so it was,' said Singh. 'Exactly the state o' the island when the Tribe Boys arrive. Right here on San Cristobal. Nobody know where they sail from or how they favour here for a home. But just so. They set foot on San Cristobal, see it was empty, and say there an' then that it belong to them.'

'Exact,' said Lee, 'exact. It may not satisfy simple sense nowadays, but that time was when a man could set foot first anywhere, an' decide where his foot rest an' could further ramble belong to him.'

'So the Tribe Boys take possession,' said Singh, 'an' they settle in behavin' as their nature teach them. Their wife cook and make bed, an' the land begin to take a human shape, turnin' soft, an' sheddin' new food wherever the Boys put down their fingers, tendin' seed an' tiny plant for what we call harvest. An' it work like a miracle in the sky, the way things seem to respect them. An' it seem that what we refer to as family was not a mere man an' woman with the result thereof, but animals too. The land play human too, learnin' to obey, an' they had some peace.'

'A lot o' peace,' said Bob, 'plenty peace. The Tribe Boys had peace.'

'Just so,' said Singh, 'as you say, they had peace. The day was for doin', when their hand hold the lan', an' the night was for knowin' what happen in the day. That is peace, real peace.'

'No trainin' with alphabet,' said Bob, 'temptin' the brain to turn soft, an' confuse everything or go extreme.'

'Exact,' said Singh, 'as you say. Peace. But a peace which touch more than ordinary sense. The peace which touch the Tribe Boys at night take them in a trance to the top o' the world an' to the beginnin' an' end o' the ocean. An' that peace last for a time no man feel it necessary to count. An' then without any warnin' at all, like a next kind o' miracle, peace disappear. Some Kings come on the scene. Things get tight for the Tribe Boys, an' 'twas only then we see what they never show' before. The Tribe Boys had a human will complete. That is to die before takin' any kind o' defeat in disgrace. An' so the fighting start.'

'Where a man work,' said Lee, 'you can't always tell what turn his reward will take. So with the Tribe Boys. They put a seed in the ground expectin' nature to raise it up an' train it with time to make a certain taste, and sudden so, like when the Kings come, something say that taste is one thing, but what now sweeten the tongue must turn to a kind o' terror. An' the Tribe Boys use simple food to fight with.'

' 'Cause they didn't know the secret o' the gun,' said Singh, 'an' the Kings went to work with guns. An' a man aint worth too much in the eyes o' the gun. Strength or no strength, when guns begin to talk, there's only one tune to expect. A man must say "amen".'

' 'Tis true what you say 'bout the guns,' said Lee, 'an' the Tribe Boys understand. But what they understand better was the sweet talk of the Kings. The Kings talk like angels, ever so gentle like a beggar in his bags. So the Kings say they claim San Cristobal, claim was the word they use, they claim San Cristobal, but the Tribe Boys could stay an' help. Help mean serve, and serve mean, you know what? So the Tribe Boys make their intention clear. They won't serve. So they take to the hills where they had their pepper trees plant like a forest for hidin'. An' the guns follow them, and the Kings who know the strength in a man, wait for the bullets to make a silence in the hills, an' then follow after.'

'An' that fightin' stop and start again,' said Singh, 'an' last till only God know how long. An' the Bandit Kings would turn back for a time an' then come again with a next surprise o' battle. But whenever the Kings make a little retreat, an' leave the islan' for a time, the Tribe Boys work like their hands gone mad. They was makin' a hole right 'cross the ground under San Cristobal.'

'More than one way to kill a mouse,' said Bob.

'Bet your life,' said Singh, 'an' the same turn out true for Kings who carry guns. 'Cause when they reach in the forest which once use' to flavour food, the Tribe Boys had a new home that reach right 'cross San Cristobal under the earth. A hole that just open an' close at one end an' a next, holdin' nothing but a total darkness that turn left and right. The Tribe Boys went crawlin' like worms through the belly o' the lan'. An' San Cristobal, on top, where the hills use' to swim whenever wind come, poor San Cristobal was nothing but fire an' smoke. The pepper trees just burn and the Kings crawl like cripples who can't find their crutch, 'cause when that smoke wrap round them, it put the fire o' hell in every eye.'

'Ever bite a pepper in the centre,' said Bob, 'just where the seeds waitin' to touch your tongue.'

'You got to remember that,' said Singh, 'then maybe you feel for a secon' or so what it mean when some kin' pepper sit in a poor human eye. It is time an' a half before nature show itself again in a proper vision. An' by then the Tribe Boys come up to the surface o' the lan' like sharks playing hide-and-seek, an' they knife every King who couldn't make his way to the shore. Those who escape take to sea. An' the Tribe Boys creep out on to the lan' again, an' San Cristobal stay quiet for some time. But not with the peace as before.'

'Never that same peace,' said Singh, 'from then to now, preparation for food had to mean also preparation for fightin'.'

''Cause the Kings set their ambition on San Cristobal,' said Lee, 'an' every Tribe Boy know they would come back.'

'An' when they reach back,' said Bob, 'what a time it was.'

'They come back with a terrible cargo,' said Lee. 'They bring some ants. The Warrior Ants.'

'You can't fight ants,' said Singh, 'not the Warrior Ants.'

'The Tribe Boys had bow and arrow ready to do battle with the guns they remember,' said Lee, 'but ants don't understand, an' you can't fight an enemy who don't understand…'

'Those Kings forget they had guns,' said Bob, 'they just let the Ants inhabit the hole which the Tribe Boys make home.'

'An' that was the end o' the Tribe Boys,' said Lee. 'While they keep looking out for the Kings, they didn't notice those warrior Ants multiplyin', making a camp in the belly o' San Cristobal, an' when sense surprise them, it was too late. The Ants went all over the hole. They take to every corner an' the hole the Tribe Boys make under the island soon overflow with the warrior Ants. Men alone can't do nothing with creatures o' the kind, an' the Tribe Boys just drop like numbers from five to three, or nineteen to ten.'

'A terrible thing for the eye to see,' said Singh.

'Maybe we understand,' said Bob, 'if we remember some dead chicken which the owner forget to put away. So the Tribe Boys some mornings see their brother or sister, nothing but the shape of a human, only ants, ants in the eyes an' the ears, ants inside an' outside the three-days corpse, an' their numbers just keep dropping for them to see. An' soon as they creep out one by one, the guns cut them down till they was but a handful lef'. An' then they make a decision.'

''Twas that human will you talk 'bout,' said Singh.

'Nothin' else,' said Lee, 'the Tribe Boys who remain walk out like they surrender, an' the Kings wait for them to kneel an' beg, 'cause they was goin' to let them serve if they only kneel in surrender.'

'But they won't,' said Bob, 'they swear in whisper one to the next never to take defeat from the Kings, never to be victim complete. An' they walk without stoppin', an' the Kings only watch them walk like they join a trance, right to the top o' Mount Misery. An' there they kiss on the cliff for ever, an' then lean their heads down in a last minute dive to their own funeral.'

'They all drown,' said Lee.

'An' those Ants take possession,' said Singh, 'complete, terrible possession in the belly o' San Cristobal till the islan' went under water.'

'That is it,' said Bob, ''tis how it happen with the Tribe Boys an' the Bandit Kings.'

The boys held their heads down, looking at the roller skates, as though they were waiting for an opinion which would assure them of their success. The women had listened in silence, and the boys seemed uncertain of the result. Singh was trying to guess how much they might receive, but he remembered Lee's warning against stating a sum, and he remained still, spinning the wheels of the skates over his leg. Lee looked towards the old woman with the parrot, and hoped that the women would soon make some suggestion about payment.

Marcia and Penelope were completely taken by the story. They had not yet thought whether this event had really taken place in San Cristobal, but they were impressed by the easy co-ordination which the boys had achieved. Each had made his contribution seem an essential part of the story, and Penelope began to wonder about the statues of Brummel and de Ponge. Could it be that they were regarded in the legends of San Cristobal as the Bandit Kings? She had heard about the total eclipse of San Cristobal under water, but she could not recall any reference to the Ants. And yet the boys had made the whole thing sound weird, monstrous, and quite credible.

Marcia seemed suddenly distracted. She was looking sideways at the boys, trying to imagine what Mark was like before he left San Cristobal. Would he have known this story of the Tribe Boys and the Bandit Kings? She thought she would ask him to confirm it, and suddenly she turned her head away from the boys as though she wanted to avoid the thought of Mark. She had tried to forget him all afternoon, and it seemed that she had managed until she met the boys. Now they made her think again of Mark who had become as strange and obscure as the boys and their story. Penelope noticed Marcia's uneasiness. She had sensed it earlier when they left the house on their way to see the landing of the cattle, but she had not given it much importance. But Marcia had suddenly become tense and distracted, and Penelope wondered whether it was the boys' story which had recalled something that disturbed Marcia.

'And this really happened?' Penelope asked, and she felt, as she spoke, that Marcia's feeling might have been appropriate, for she had been wondering about some of the overtones which made the story more meaningful than the boys might have understood.

'Right here in San Cristobal,' one said.

'An' may happen again.'

'Only in a different way.'

She glanced at Marcia, wondering whether she had heard the boys. The two men who were sandwiched with the black placards for the Movement passed on the other side. They paused to talk with the old woman who was helping the parrots down from the perch. Penelope noticed that the boys were staring at the men as though they were excited by the announcements which the placards made about San Cristobal. And they seemed to admire the men. She considered the boys for a moment, then interrupted their gaze towards the men.

'Who says this may happen again?' she asked.

The boys seemed surprised. The men had continued down the Sea Walk, and the boys regarded each other as though they were guarding a secret. Then they pointed at the old woman who was helping one of the parrots into a cage.

'Her head hold a lot o' history,' one said.

'An' prophecy too.'

'An' already she done make a big history.'

'Who is she?' Marcia asked.

The boys glanced at Penelope, and wondered whether they should not make their own suggestions about payment. They felt they were becoming involved by knowing the old woman, and they did not want to spoil their luck. They regarded the old woman as though they were afraid to talk, and Penelope looked suspicious.

'I thought you knew her,' she said.

'She is a good woman,' said Singh, 'more than good.'

'A Christian, an' real too,' Lee added, 'an' she can heal, now she don't do the midwife work.'

'People go with all kind o' complaint,' said Singh, 'an' she always help to make a cure, 'cause they say she hol' some powers which make her special. An' she take to the wood sometimes to pray in private, but she never let nobody know when she go.'

'An' it aint good if she pray 'gainst you,' Lee added.

'I wus frighten when Thief prevent you buyin' the parrot,' said Singh, ' 'cause it could mean any kind o' downfall for him if she pray.'

'But she won't pray evil for you,' said Bob.

'So she is,' said Lee, 'no bad heart.'

The boys were looking in the direction of the old woman who had turned to face them. They seemed to regret all that they had said, as though it were a kind of blasphemy to speak about her.

'But who is she?' Penelope asked.

'She is his mother,' said Singh, and turned to the others to continue.

'Whose mother?' Marcia asked.

'Shephard.'

Penelope started. The boys stood, pretending not to be interested in what they had said. Singh held his head down, dangling the skates over the gravel. The others were beginning to settle their feet in the skates. Penelope was still staring at the old woman, but the boys lingered, trying to impress their delay on the women. Marcia noticed that the light was fading, and the evening was beginning to close in over the Sea Walk.

'There,' she said, 'and thank you.'

The boys looked in wonder at the coins, and Marcia felt a sudden pleasure in their delight and this show of gratitude. The story had brought them three shillings, and they were beginning to calculate the amount they had raised in the name of their little secret Society.

'We could come some time where you tell Thief you live,' said Singh.

'Only to make another little work,' Bob added.

Marcia glanced at Penelope who nodded. The boys smiled and bowed. Then they limped across the Sea Walk, and stood in the main street, waiting to chase the traffic on their skates. The women watched them disappear through the crowd, then got up from the bench and walked away.

5

The Sea Walk was beginning to welcome new company. The sweepers were busy tidying the gravelled path, and the vendors had started to collect their fragments. A woman was sprinkling water over the dust where the fallen petals had been swept together in two heaps. She tried the scent of the flowers which had remained, and spread some sheets of paper over the basket which contained them. Ma Shephard was stacking the parrot cages into a push cart. The monkeys waited quietly on the poles, crouching their heads into their shoulders as though they would soon fall asleep. She did not notice the women who continued towards the end of the avenue. The street lamps were beginning to show weak flickers of light as the public clock struck the half-hour. But the sun had made its last thrust through the palms, and the Sea Walk was shot with wide, red bars of light. The day was beginning to disappear.

Some girls emerged at the end of the avenue, strolling leisurely towards Marcia and Penelope. Arm in arm they made a line that filled the width of the gravelled path. Marcia could hear their voices in an idle exchange of gossip and expectation, then she saw the boys follow not far behind, looking casual and precocious, as they whispered their intentions. The evening was waiting for them.

The town was quieter, and the streets showed up in the distance, almost empty. Marcia and Penelope continued walking, following the line of the high wall which vanished and returned at intervals behind the buildings. The wall stretched its boundary beside the sand until it reached Paradise Wood where the suburbs began. There the sand and the water changed colour, and the air was light and clean. The sea had relaxed its pulse, and everything was still. The women could see where the wood rose and turned inland, obscuring their view of the houses, and the distance seemed to diminish without effort as they made towards the house.

Everything that had happened an hour ago seemed to yield willingly to the familiar intimacies of their past. At Marcia's suggestion they had taken the road that ran beside the beach, a wide asphalt path, blue black in the early evening light. They walked on that side which touched the sand, and watched the sea, a dark, deserted plain of water, washing itself. The bathers had gone home. A couple of fishing boats rocked idly in the distance. But there was no one in sight. This was their reward of time, these moments that seemed to turn with the ancient rhythm of the sea.

It was as though nothing had happened since they left the house at noon. This was the event selected and conserved for this particular point in time. The sea scarcely evoked the wet, tumbling traffic of the cattle which they had witnessed earlier, and the crowds which waited outside the market, once loud and vivid, had narrowed to nothing. An anonymous face might appear, then retire, ordinary and forgotten, like the road moving backwards behind their heels. Marcia might have spoken, but Penelope's silence was like a presence which it would have been improper to disturb. They walked along, without words, riding differently, but on a similar tide of memory that could challenge the ocean wherever it went. Penelope was silenced by the recollected spell of their life in Spain: their walks through the lane of honeysuckle, the mornings beside the pier where a village waited with an eternal welcome for people they did not know; the evening descending in purple over the limestone quarry which was always making faces at the sea. And above all, the night which huddled them together in a harmony of private fantasies: Bill drawing comic sketches under the old paraffin lamp that snored through the light, and Marcia needling her fingers in a moment of distraction, rebuking Mark for his refusal to sleep. Penelope and Mark kept diaries of what they had noticed during the day, a useless, but consuming delight which often took their labour to the brink of the dawn.

The evening was deepening into shadow. The sun waited on the edge of the sea before making its habitual plunge out of sight. In San Cristobal you could almost feel this change, increasing with every failure of the day. The clouds were putting up screens everywhere, like nurses trying to hide a dying man from his neighbour's view. But the sun was still screaming, a scarlet cry that shocked the sea and threw splinters of light between the trees. Soon there would be nothing to look at but the night, large, secure, and complete. And Mark and Bill who were waiting for them to come home.

But Marcia was crying. She would have spoken long ago, but she did not want to betray her weakness, or spoil Penelope's pleasure. Now she tried beyond her strength to steady herself, to talk with Penelope as though the substance of her thought was a casual occurrence, unexpected but quickly understood, and wholly within control. She wiped her eyes in secret, and brushed the tears off her mouth. But the effort of speech was exacting. She turned her head towards the sea and saw the last curve of the sun like a lip about to be washed away. And Mark emerged swimming through her blurred gaze like a nightmare that taunted, and refused to go long after the conscious eye had proclaimed it unreal. She was wiping her eyes again, waiting for the moment that would lead her like magic to Penelope's comfort. Was Mark unreal? she wondered. And before she could seize upon this fleeting fear to prove it false, she heard her own voice, and felt Penelope's hand take hers.

'Penelope,' she said again, and suddenly her strength deceived her, and the tears made brine in her mouth which rested, half-open, in an exhausted gasp on Penelope's shoulder.

'What is it, Marcia?'

'Mark,' she said, as though the name was enough to explain the whole burden of her anxiety.

Penelope led her across the road to the other side where a bench showed up against a white milestone.

'There, sit down,' Penelope said. 'What's happened to Mark?'

'I don't know,' said Marcia, 'I thought you might have noticed.'

'He seems very quiet these days,' Penelope said, 'but I've seen him like that before. It passes very quickly.'

'It's not like the other times I told you about,' Marcia said. 'It's worse.'

'Has he said anything to hurt you?' Penelope asked.

'To hurt…' Marcia was talking through a mouthful of saliva and tears like a child hysterical with fear. Penelope waited like one whom age and suffering had made inhumanly patient.

'Does he want to leave San Cristobal?' Penelope asked. But Marcia did not answer.

'Has anyone offended him?'

'I haven't,' Marcia said.

'Didn't you ask him what has happened?' Penelope felt for a moment out of her depth.

'I don't think he knows,' Marcia said.

It was hardly the time to try to understand anything. Penelope felt Marcia's body shaking beside her, and the noise her throat made, like a wheezing valve. She moved closer to Marcia, and held her head against her neck, tapping out a consolation that could not contain Marcia's fear. The night had made them part of its property, indistinguishable from the wood and the dark whisper of the water.

'If he wants to leave San Cristobal,' said Penelope, 'you'll have to go with him.'

And suddenly Marcia seemed to regain her strength. But she

remained where she was, shaking lightly against Penelope. It was Penelope's choice of words which had helped her. Had Penelope said 'you will have to leave us,' everything might have been different. For what she feared most was the uncertainty of her place in Mark's decisions. She could have found a way of supporting the loss of Bill and Penelope, wounding as that would be. But she could not begin, at this moment, to imagine a life which did not include Mark. She was wiping her face against Penelope's arm, wanting desperately to ask the question she knew Penelope could not answer. Would Mark leave her? Any answer Penelope gave would have been an attempt to console, and therefore to minimise the danger of what she had noticed in Mark.

Penelope was meandering halfway between memory and this moment. Now she saw Marcia in a luxury of waves and moonlight, surfacing the tide that tossed her like weed on the shore, her lips pink in the sunlight. Then, this moment which seemed to sweep time away brought her back to Marcia, leaning against her, in search of arms which should have been Mark's. And she let her arms rally to Marcia's need for comfort. Her touch was a wish and an assurance, and in the circumstances a substitute. For this was exactly the way Marcia might have turned to Mark to be rescued from some other crisis. Marcia's need became Penelope's responsibility, and Penelope, feeling again, like a rediscovery, all that had held these four lives together, entered into that role with an assurance that was complete. She was saving something which belonged to them all by restoring Marcia to her wish for happiness with Mark. That private world, in every detail of its history, was there on the bench. Penelope had to be Mark and Bill and herself, all at once, in the presence of Marcia. And the degree of participation had to follow the need that was most urgent. Marcia's need for comfort which only Mark could give and which, in his absence, became her duty. Penelope felt a sudden rush of power possess her. Her arms had taken another's strength, firm, protective and kind. Marcia's need had given her some new sense of her own resources. She widened her embrace. Marcia drew closer, sobbing heavily. But Penelope did not speak. She thought for a moment only of Mark and the role which his absence had now assigned her. She had to play Mark's part. Her voice soothing Marcia with a chosen comfort had to be Mark's voice, and her arm feeding Marcia's body with warmth was Mark's arm.

'We must go,' she said, 'everything will be all right.'

And they stumbled, arm in arm, looking for the track that led through the wood to their house.

MARK'S DIARIES

6

April, March, February... Wednesday, Tuesday... I read the months backwards, try to repeat this man-made arithmetic of days and nights to assure myself that nothing is really lost by what I have done. Why did I ever believe that it was possible to reconstruct the life of that three-fingered rebel? Three centuries separate us, and yet I believed that I could select from the dreary pile of history some truth about him. But each account can only be a fresh corpse which we assemble in order to dissect again. Nothing was lost when I burnt the last pages of the pirate's biography. I had only burnt a little corpse whose original I could never know. And who, three centuries hence, will be able to say whether Shephard was mad? Who will be able to say what happened? The facts will accumulate like tombstones over a cemetery: arrived in San Cristobal in 19..., the records show he was under observation in the San Cristobal asylum for a month after his arrival, joined the Indian Freedom Party started by Aly Singh; had this name changed to the People's Communal Movement which was now led by Singh, formerly a canecutter on the Baden-Semper sugar estates, and Joseph Lee, a retired schoolmaster who became a merchant. Plans to have him arrested for carrying firearms on an Anglo-Cristobal airliner were quietly dropped. Because... But was it true? The people believed it was a plan to rob them of a leader. But what really happened? The corpses will grow with time round the legend of this man.

The day we arrived I wanted to tell Marcia a little more of what

I remembered about San Cristobal, but I could not find a way to begin. I was confused by the general hysteria surrounding Shephard. Later I was using Penelope's unfortunate experience as a reason for postponing what I had to say. But I never stopped thinking about that incident on the plane. And I shall never forget, in the test of a lifetime's surprises, the lucid flash of those eyes suddenly turned sane upon me in a moment of recognition. I could not speak. I squeezed Marcia's hand and turned my head away. It was a minute or two before Shephard collapsed that he saw me with the absolute certainty of his memory focusing a particular occasion. They leaned over him, obscuring my view, but I could still see, like some image threatening my sight, the boy I had known before I left San Cristobal.

Now I do not have to remember that occasion. It has slipped through some aperture of time to harbour with me here in this room, a much larger room. But the morning is similar. A Sunday morning. That other room enters and embraces my memory with a pleasing muddle of furniture. At first, it seems too crowded as though the arrangement has lost its way. But very soon the boy, Shephard, helps me to adjust to his surroundings. They are familiar to him, and he understands their modest disorder. He closes a window, the light turns away, and the room becomes grave. The chairs are in shadow. I pretend to be at home, and gradually he helps me into this role of the experienced participant. Some strange ceremony is about to begin. I follow his movements which disclose secretly the orders I must undertake. I have surrendered to this little drama which no longer disturbs my feeling. Curiosity leaves me, and I am at home among the chairs, waiting for him to instruct us. His assurance has stolen my speech and covered my limbs with the same complacent immobility which defines the chairs; and by some private magic of belief, he has turned the natural silence of the chairs into an act of obedience. I wait, and the chairs wait, and the boy, Shephard, moves towards us. He does not speak, but his hands work with a total knowledge of their power. The chairs are assembled in rows like children who are eager to please. He has helped them gently to a kneeling position; their backs turned innocently to the ceiling let a needle's eye of light through. He passes slowly between the rows, and pats the chairs; and his touch, gentle and authoritative, is intended to tell his kindness. They are his chairs, now regarded as his children. It is the word he uses as he takes up his position in front of us. I hear his voice, tender and precocious, and I see his face which has not altered in expression for this mysterious act. Perhaps, I cannot tell; for I cannot remember his face any different. His eyes are bright, and his skin twitches slightly under a permanent shadow of absolute blackness. His teeth appear, from time to time, in sudden flashes of whiteness, brief and shining like the visit of lightning. And his lips seem to roll like two thick thumbs of earth turning in the air. I am sitting on the floor, head bowed, but my eyes are raised, because I do not want to miss any change which his face may make. He leans forward as though suspended, like a leaf held steady by the wind before settling softly on the ground. He kneels, and again I hear him call the chairs his children. He lowers his head to the floor, and he prays for us. I too am spoken to like a chair. But my curiosity suddenly returns, and I want to find out the meaning of this performance. I think he is a little mad. I wonder how often he has done this. My attention does not stray, but I feel an urge to interrupt. Until I hear his voice, reminding the chairs that it is time for silence. The room has the fixed, neutral stillness of light, and I remember some of his words.

'...Children in darkness, do not ask to change, and do not be angry that you cannot of your own accord make a change in your condition. Be happy to serve, and if you serve well, there will be reward for your service. Your purpose is fulfilled in your perfect service, and the rest is my burden. Love is mine and punishment too, and these are difficult to bear to children, even to you. But I shall give love and punishment as I see fit, and it is your perfect service which will help to decide. Now let us stand in silence for a while, then you may sit...'

I push myself up from the floor, but he beckons me to lift the chairs from their knees. He comes forward and we lift the chairs one on top the other until they are almost touching the ceiling. They lean awkwardly to one side, and we stand within easy reach so that we can avoid a noise if their weight tumbles them down.

A minute passes. Utter silence. Then we take the chairs away, and he assembles them again in three rows. It seems that this little dedication is over. I am almost afraid now, because his parents will soon be here. But I am still curious. I wonder whether he wants to be an evangelist like his father who preaches in the village church. For it is his father whom he is imitating. He uses the same words his father uses to the children in his church. But it seems strange, nevertheless, to treat the chairs in this way. I make to go, and I am anxious to hear what he will say. Perhaps he will say why he invited me. But he opens the door and shows me out without a word. And his face does not change. He does not seem to see the difference between real living and make-believe. I hurry down the steps and disappear, thinking that I do not want to see him again. He frightens me, because he does not seem to see any real difference between a boy's play and what is real. And I say to myself that if he were a man, I would say he was mad.

I have forgotten the pirate. I know why it was necessary to give up the study of his rebellion. I continue with the diaries, but this I do not understand. This activity has become a natural function like my breathing. It serves no purpose except to forestall that feeling of disinclination which returns without warning.

Today I remembered a young German I met three years ago. I don't think I could recognise his face again, but I can almost hear his voice talking through the night, and the words return like fragments of bird noise or an argument of wind and sea afar, out of touch… out of touch…

Is this failure to communicate a kind of illness which puts me out of touch with the others? I have looked for it in them, and I am suddenly made feeble by their fluency. I try to find a way which would enable others to enter my secret so that they might, through a common experience, lead me to its source. But my effort moves off the mark. I begin, as it were, from the circumference of my meaning, moving cautiously and with loyal feeling, towards a centre which very soon I discover I cannot reach. Then speech deserts me. I abandon what I had felt to be an obligation, and the result is silence. Yet my silence contains a need to begin again. But the difficulties accumulate. For I have hardly resigned myself to the solitude of one secret before a new enthusiasm entices me. I am once more at the centre of something I must share, and the origins which I seem to understand for myself suddenly disperse into a frantic chaos. I have thought much about this before and since my arrival in San Cristobal, and one thing seems clear. Although these situations are made explicit by very different circumstances, the nature of my experience is always the same.

But my knowledge of Shephard has produced a kind of complication. Ordinarily the people who move in this private drama disappear leaving only the forms of their influence. Today I feel that I stand in a certain relation to Shephard. He is not merely an occasion which my memory gradually restores to insignificance. He does exist flesh-real like the boy whom my memory returned yesterday amidst an obedient arrangement of furniture and words which he had taken from his father's message of humility and hope. For I see some continuity between the boy who frightened me so many years ago, and the man I saw on Saturday and shall probably see again tomorrow.

I have been seeing Shephard, and I have again postponed the moment of making this known to Marcia and Penelope and Bill. And I know now that this postponement will gradually grow into a meaningless refusal. I shall not bother to say that I have been seeing him. But they are bound to know, because Shephard is now more important than the boy I recalled. It is four months since our arrival, and already he has grown into a national legend. He rules thousands with a promise. His word is like the last refuge of the unfortunate in San Cristobal. Soon we may all be his subjects, loyal or recalcitrant. But power has chosen him, and it may be a long time before he relaxes his willingness to serve. But it is not this aspect of his achievement which interests me. I remember more vividly my first meeting with him the morning after his release from the asylum.

Can it be that Shephard has always been, in the past, afraid or ashamed to see himself? I ask this question of Shephard and at the same time I feel it is a question I have also put in silence to myself. He does not frighten me any longer, and I cannot say that I have ever felt his fear of being fixed by another's glance. It seems incredible, and I would not have believed that a man could have gone to such extravagant risk to purge himself of some private fear. But he spoke to me that morning, as he has done ever since, in an ordinary, almost cold sanity of recollection. I cannot really tell what happened on the plane. Was Shephard mad? Did he really suffer some hallucination during that flight? That terrible incident which occurred on the plane seems now almost deliberate, like the boy's behaviour towards the chairs. He has remembered the reactions of those he terrified. I would not have believed such a demonstration to be possible, and I only believe it now because I have seen him very often in the last few weeks and everything he says, derives, in a way, from the reason he tried to explain for his brutal and incredible conduct on the plane. I say brutal, but I do not feel any hostility towards Shephard, and now I have got to know him a little, it is not a word I associate with the man himself. But he did make Penelope suffer, and no one really knows the effect he may have had on others.

His explanation has had some effect on me. I was inclined to stare at people, and I looked to see whether people were staring at me. I am not afraid, as Shephard said he was, of the other's glance, but I believe I wanted to find out whether it was possible for me to feel that fear. Until recently it has been a torture for him. I made a note of what he said that morning. Word for word I tried to recall that part of our conversation:

'You may not be of a turn of mind to understand my feeling. This is private, and, perhaps, I have given the matter an unnatural attention. That is what you will say. But I could never escape, and I do not see how you can call such an awareness my fault. This is the truth. Of all the senses which serve our knowledge of those around us, it is the eye which I could not encounter in peace. It is as though my body defined all of me, and then played the role of traitor for those who watched. So that the eye of the other became for me a kind of public prosecutor. I felt surrounded by a perpetual act of prosecution. I was judged finally by the evidence which my body, a kind of professional spy, always offered. And there are times when I have felt my presence utterly burnt up by the glance which another had given me. I wanted to disappear or die. I don't think I have always had this feeling, but I was aware of it for the first time in England, and then a certain relationship helped to put it beyond my control. It was no longer a private fear. It became an obsession which possessed me completely...'

I do not know whether Shephard had tried before to create the sort of disturbance we witnessed on the plane. But he seemed to see it as a way of satisfying his fear and at the same time releasing himself from his fear. And the plane seemed the best occasion, for it represented a world which was for the time being self-contained. No one could escape. There was the nearness of disaster, so that the eyes which saw him could not afford to be casual. They had to look. And that was what he wanted. He wanted to be looked at as he occupied the centre of that world's attention. He wanted to rob his mind of its concern for the other's regard, and he tried to do this by making his body serve as a real traitor.

Now he is free to ramble a larger world, freed from his fear by the very attention which started it. I would like to write about that one day, but I do not really know the truth of what happened. No one knows. I do not think his followers are really interested. He is now like any other man in San Cristobal, and the appearance he prepares for this world is enough; the promise he offers has made him heroic. There is already talk about a statue to the memory of this man. And it is only my feeling of disinclination which prevents me from swearing some kind of allegiance to the People's Communal Movement. His friends and his enemies are alike in this way: Shephard is not only a man (ordinary or mad, I cannot tell), but a kind of magic which caught everyone asleep.

7

The landscape had come fully into view, and the boys paused, staring over the ridge of the hill at the wild, green cone of vegetation which opened below them. The sides were thick with trees. The wind had carved it hollow, and they could see, looking directly below, the huge hole which made a circle extending from the top, wide and deep within, to a black, dead crater of bush at the bottom. It reminded them of the legend which told of their island's formation: the ascent of the land from water which now surrounded the peaks and valleys and inactive craters of San Cristobal. The vegetation was wild and nameless and silent but for the swift, warm passage of the wind hissing round the trees.

Some miles away they could see the town hurry to an end at the village of Milot. The land changed contour behind the small wooden houses; and nature rose, reckless and arbitrary, like an insurrection which had nothing to prove but the fact of its power. It leapt and divided into a broken family of hills and foliage crawling at random to an altitude of two thousand feet above sea-level. They considered the distance they had covered, gazing now and again at the wide, restless geography of the clouds and the sky swinging over the island. The sea broke the coastline everywhere, carving the land into a series of semicircles. They could see them for the whole length of the visible coast, a smouldering blue remnant of some volcanic eruption.

Ships were at anchor, familiar as the water which made their home, and a few fishing boats frisked about in the distance. The sea sparkled, heaving slowly towards the land where it collided with rock and flowered into a bristling white rush of spray that fell, harmless and bored, a dead, dissolving foam over the weed. Then the land seemed to crawl out and away from the sea, across a natural formation of asphalt and marl; and gradually the roads slunk and reappeared and receded again behind houses and stores and churches that showed the giddy, complicated transactions which people had arranged for living in San Cristobal. Soon the land seemed to pause, lingering round a flat plain divided into tennis lawns and bungalows; then an abrupt segregation of hovels made distance further south where they could see other contingents of colour and shapes, the green pasture shorn by grazing and the sun, and finally the fields of sugar cane, natural as grass, continuing for miles in a green, repetitive journey out of sight. Turning north, everything seemed to relax before making a sudden, precipitous climb up the wooded summit of Mount Misery, erect and still, under a peeling skin of mist like a hand wrapped in gauze.

They had been walking for hours, but they felt they could go on for ever. They turned their eyes away from Mount Misery to consider for a moment the furthest limits of the land which stretched far beyond the houses until it joined the light and turned like space to the sky. This was San Cristobal. And they were thinking of the wish which had lately aroused the island to a sudden frenzy of rumour and promise and expectation. Last night they had listened again to the speakers in the public square, and they were reminded that they too were a part of the promise which everyone had heard. They too were together, and in a sense which was more immediate and intelligible than the wailing excitement of the crowd. They had come together as a little Society which worked in secret, and the unity which the speakers were urging San Cristobal to achieve was for them a fact. It seemed that they had, in some way, surpassed their elders; so that they behaved, during these expeditions, as though they were no longer dependent on the decisions which others were making for them. It had made their age irrelevant, compared with the wasted experience of those who were so much older. Sometimes they felt that the others would have to catch up on what they had already accomplished.

In the past they had often played at being sailors or cowboys. They would make wooden pistols and imitate the endurance of horses in pursuit of an enemy, claiming as their own experience the violent drama of courage and toughness which they had watched in films. Sometimes they would wage war among themselves, pretending afterwards to count the dead. One boy might represent a regiment of fifty or sixty, according to his size. And sometimes they assumed the roles of policemen, keeping watch outside their houses. Then they would choose the stray dogs and cats for their victims, and the watch would continue until an act of violence forced their parents to intervene. The result was always the same. The world which they had learnt at first hand was transformed into a myth or a farce.

But the secret Society which they had formed was different. It was as though they had transformed the myth of the political meetings into some reality which no one could question. In the first place it was, unlike the other games, a secret experiment. They had succeeded in avoiding attention, and they did not have to resort to the artificial roles which the other games required.

There was no need to change their names or choose occupations which could only be filled by men. Above all, the secret Society was directly connected with what was happening in San Cristobal. Their behaviour was no longer a boy's imitation of his wish to be different, for the Society had achieved the secrecy which each had pledged at the start. Inevitably, it had given them a new sense of power. They were agreed on their own rules of conduct and duty, and they had decided on their own rewards.

They looked for the last time towards the houses crouching at the foot of the hills that rose behind Milot. The Society was at work again, and they considered the distance as though it were an obstacle which their ambition had made too simple. Their shirts were wet under the armpits. They could feel the sweat like a wet hand feeling clammily down their backs. But they had finished with this landscape of blue craters and precipitous hills. The green cone of rock and bush which rose like a giant's paw receded, and they continued in silence up the hill.

Once a man twice a child, Bob was thinking. That they say, once a man twice a child, but twice a man once a child, never. Never ever twice a man once a child. That I know. And Singh and Lee too. But twice a man once a boy. That we do when the Society work. Twice a man once a boy like now when man and boy happen at the same said time without dividing line. Like me and Singh and Lee. And talk of age, talk of age; age is only numbers except for people like Ma Shephard. Age is nothing if there aint no doing. Age is me and Singh and Lee. Age is the Society start young and behaving old without any show of numbers. Take me, and take Singh and take Lee. Take what we see happen. Some people grow from child to boy, from boy to man, and then backwards to boy and child again. But some start and end different. Then child, boy and man all seem to happen together without distinction of years and time. Like how we moving here this morning to start something new. The Society at work again, doing what the big ones talk. Shephard and Singh's father and Lee's father. Last night I hear them again and I wonder what my father... Now take me, and then take my father... take my father...

The road had started to climb ahead, surpassing the neck of the trees which rose on either side from a shallow ravine of weed and grass. The earth was beginning to take on the dull brown grit of the encroaching sand, and he could see Paradise Wood rise and spread beyond the tall black samaan tree at the curve of the hilltop. He rubbed his knuckle into his eye to clear the film of dust which clouded his iris. And he heard Singh and Lee breathing hard and close behind him. He thought of his father, but he was uncertain of his words. He did not want to conceal any feeling which he knew the Society should share, but it was difficult to remind them of the difference which he felt when he thought of his father. It was his father's lack of importance which seemed to rob him of the status which Singh and Lee must have known. He did not envy them, and he did not think they were aware of his misgivings. Yet he wished that his father was a man of more importance in San Cristobal. He would have liked to hear his father speak from the platform where everyone saw Singh's father and Lee's father and Shephard. He would have liked his father to be like Shephard himself, a voice which could summon music or silence in the night. Or even like Singh's father and Lee's father who shared the platform with Shephard. Yet there is the little Society, he thought. The little Society is more different than anything. He was deciding to make his peace with their experiment. Singh and Lee had now come abreast. He felt an arm hug his shoulder. He lengthened his stride to keep pace with them, and they trampled up the hill as though it were something to be conquered.

Bob was now frank, easy and talkative. He had found a certain confidence in this role of the independent man. He was no longer a boy, or at least he was a man and a boy at the same time. He had become his role, and he could feel the emblems of this new status cleave to him. It was an ordinary part of his feeling which now surpassed any recollection of his father's failure to be like others. The Society had made his father irrelevant. He felt his authority like a mole in the skin, casual and complete.

'Some people start from scratch an' go gradual,' he said, 'from one learnin' to a next. But for some, learnin' just happen without any stages. The middle an' the beginnin' come like the same said thing.'

' 'Tis like the little Society,' said Lee. 'What Shephard say they got to learn an' live by is what we know.'

'We know,' said Bob, ' 'tis true we know, but they make it sound like a learnin' too, 'cause we got to learn not to lose what is natural, like how we here together.'

' 'Tis true,' said Lee. 'Some people got to learn by stages from scratch as you say, an' some just got to learn not to lose what they know is natural.'

Singh nodded and they seemed to repeat, in different ways, a similar chorus of approval. This kind of reflection had become a habit whenever they met; for the secret Society which they had started as a game had given them a special relation to their parents and also to the claims which they had heard Shephard make for San Cristobal. They had followed the political meetings as they might have attended a bazaar or a visiting circus. For it seemed, at first, that Shephard and his friends were part of a game which they were going to improve upon. They had begun the secret Society as a kind of satire on the political meetings which they attended at night. Now they had condensed those enormous crowds which assembled at night into a private circle of three boys who represented the details of every speech which they had heard. They started to see themselves as a flattering example of the wish which Shephard and his colleagues had made. San Cristobal had contracted to a pebble in their hands, until an attitude of anarchy or irreverence had gradually troubled their views about their parents, whining and shouting about San Cristobal and the future as though it had always been an impossible journey. It was an attitude which made them seem important in comparison.

'An' I wonder if my father know what he sayin' sometimes,' Bob said.

'What it is he tell you sometimes?' Singh asked. 'Not before he beat you, but in plain peace talk, like one man to the next.'

'He only talk to me when he workin',' Bob said. 'Not any time else. But he talk to my mother when he drunk.'

'An' what it is he say?' Singh asked.

'He always say I must be different from him,' Bob said. 'I go in the shop, an' when he cutting the meat, that's what he say all the time. You must not cut meat like your father. There aint no future in meat.'

'Meat always got a future,' Lee said. 'That's what my father say, meat always got a future.'

'Meat got a bad future,' Singh said, 'it aint make to last, raw or cook, it just aint make to last.'

'My father mean that I aint to cut meat like him,' Bob said. 'My position in the future got to be different. Meat aint need no education, an' he want me to follow education. That's what he mean.'

'Education is very one-sided,' Singh said, 'that's what my father say. He say that's where certain people always lose, because they think only 'bout education.'

'Education can rule everything,' Bob said. 'I think my father right 'bout that. Education always goin' to win.'

'My father say education is losin' all the time,' Singh said. 'An' he tell me it is safer to stay with the lan'. He is for education too, but he say you must never swap the lan' for education. Hurricane or what ever hell have can come, but hol' the lan', hol' to the lan'. That's what my father always tellin' my mother.'

'What your father say?' Singh asked, looking at Lee.

'My father don't say much,' Lee said. 'He say a man must not say much but keep his eyes open, and learn.'

'Nobody eyes can stay open all the time,' Bob said.

'My father scarcely sleep,' said Lee, 'that's why he say keep your eyes open.'

'What it is he lookin' for?' Singh asked.

'My father only look,' Lee said, 'he ain't looking for anything. He just think he ought to look.'

'He will go mad,' Bob said. 'I know a man who went mad 'cause he just look, look, look all day at nothin' in particular.'

'If he wus goin' mad,' Lee said, 'he would done do it already.'

'Tell your father to rest from lookin',' Bob said. 'My father say there is a time for everything. A time for lookin' like your father, an' a time for not lookin'. My father is happy only when he sleepin', an' not lookin' at anybody.'

'It is bad sometimes to sleep,' Lee said. 'You don't know w'at you losin'.'

'My father say he ain't got nothin' to lose,' Bob said. 'Sometimes he sing a funny arithmetic which say, nothin' from nothin' leave nothin'. So he go to sleep happy.'

'It is wakin' up my father think most 'bout,' said Singh. 'Whenever he lie down to sleep, he think most 'bout when he goin' get up again.'

'He ain't a Christian,' Bob said, 'or he would sleep like my father.'

'My father ain't no Christian,' Singh said. 'He is a Hindoo, an' Hindoos go a long time without sleep.'

Bob was going to laugh when he suddenly remembered that he was not a Hindoo; nor was Lee. He was going to ask Singh whether he was a Hindoo like his father, but Lee had already spoken, and the talk was guided naturally back to the familiar consideration of their parents.

'But everybody must be different,' said Lee, 'an' we different already.'

'I only listen to my father with one ear,' said Bob, ' 'cause I talk to myself through the next, an' hear what you say.'

'San Cristobal goin' look like what we doin' now,' said Singh, 'an' we'll be the first to start what the big ones always talkin'.'

'My father say they goin' keep San Cristobal,' said Lee, 'like how we have the Society, but he don't know 'bout the Society, the way we three different an' still alike.'

'They talk 'bout the future like a war,' said Singh, 'how the future goin' come only with the struggle.'

'An' we have the future already,' said Lee, ' 'cause we make a little Society for three, an' we see how it work.'

' 'Tis 'cause they live so long before,' said Bob, 'that the future look hard to reach. But we reach already.'

They were approaching the wood which rose between the sea and the chalk white suburb of bungalows. They could see the wood in the distance, thick and still with leaves; and they were now eager to arrive at the clearing which they had made under the barren grape tree which bent like a dwarf within a prickly, green patchwork of cactus and wild fern. This was the meeting place of the secret Society. Here they would discuss new chores and bury the money which they had earned in the name of the secret Society.

The carnival of San Cristobal was an annual event which would take place in about six months' time, a fortnight after the political elections; and they had already decided to divide their savings for the purchase of costumes. It was always an incredible spectacle. For two days the island would be possessed by some strange, relentless fury. It was neither joy nor a passionate longing which made San Cristobal utterly defenceless against the weird, and rowdy sorcery of its music. It was as though some general contagion of madness had made all equal to the elements of nature. The hills would shake under their dancing, and water and wind and the intangible night surrendered their secrets to the dark, ancient demand of the drum.

The boys were going to use their savings to celebrate in public the secret achievement of the Society. But today, they were not thinking of the carnival, or the elections, nor were they going to bury any money under the grape tree. They were remembering the morning they saw Rowley walk across the sand and ask Ma Shephard's permission to sit at her feet. And they were hoping that this meeting which they had arranged with him under the grape tree would never endanger the secrecy of the little Society.

They entered the shade of the tree with its wide shelter of branches spreading over the slope of the hill. Bob slid down quietly to rest his leg on the fat worn root that crawled like a reptile above the ground. Singh was looking towards the houses that made a little compound on the edge of Paradise Wood. Lee followed the thrust of the branches turning to a lake of black shadows over the road. They were waiting for some sign of Rowley; but their talk had now turned to a silent and grave deliberation of their plans for the day. An unusual event was about to take place.

'How it is he seem to fit so natural?' Singh said, flicking his fingers over the lighter in his pocket.

' 'Tis because he, too, different from his father,' said Bob. 'Like me an' you, he too take the future in his own han'.'

'Why you think he so different from his father?' Singh asked. He had tightened his fingers round the lighter, and his hand was emerging slowly from his pocket.

' 'Tis not a matter for why or wherefore,' said Bob. 'Seems to me he just different like you an' me different, an' that is that.'

'His tongue make such a strange noise the mornin' he ask Ma Shephard if he could call her Ma too,' said Lee.

' 'Twas that mornin' somethin' move in me,' said Bob, ' 'twas there an' then I feel how he different from his father.'

'Then we goin' celebrate as we promise,' said Singh, 'an' I bring this as a kind o' badge which we can keep.'

He held the lighter out for them to see. The shade of the tree had given it a pale grey surface. Singh was waiting for the others to sanction this as a gift from the Society. Bob turned his finger over it several times as though he wanted to make sure that the surface was smooth. Then he passed it to Lee who wanted to know whether it would work.

' 'Tis only the letterin' which make it not quite perfect,' said Lee.

'It won't be a worry if your father miss it?' Bob asked.

'He won't miss it,' said Singh. 'Lighters an' clocks he keep by the dozen as if time an' fire is all he understan'.'

'But the letterin',' said Lee, 'you don't think the letterin' make it not safe?'

' 'Tis only his name,' said Singh, 'an' that ain't make a difference, once Rowley don't let his father know where he get it.'

'He promise to keep the Society secret,' said Bob.

'Exact,' said Lee, 'once he keep it secret my father name can't matter.'

'But why you give him a lighter?' Lee asked.

' 'Cause it make in England,' said Singh. 'He can remember here an' his home at the same time, the Society an' San Cristobal all in one.'

'I like to think here is his home,' said Bob. 'I like to think it that way.'

'It could be,' said Lee, 'whatever happen it could be.'

They passed the lighter round again examining the fine grains that crossed into several splinters of lines showing like scales. Bob pressed the lid and tested the frayed cord of wick, and they watched the small blue flame wobble and sputter in the wind. It was real; it worked. And it was the Society's symbol which

Rowley would have as a reminder of his pledge to keep the Society secret. Lee tried the wick again, and Bob drew closer to keep out the wind. They leaned together approving the strength of the small blue flame which tapered and trembled within the hollow of their hands.

'We goin' wait for him in the wood,' said Singh. 'We goin' ask him to swear again, an' then take the day off for some kind o' celebration.'

'Penny for your thinkin',' said Bob, ' 'tis a good game to test when a man will tell the truth.'

'We goin' test him with that,' said Lee, 'penny for your thinkin'.'

'You can test yourself with it too,' said Bob, ' 'cause when the next person don't guess right, you have to say what you think 'fore any money can pass.'

'Not everybody play that way,' said Lee. ' 'Tis usual not to tell if the next person don't guess right.'

'We leavin' what is usual behin',' said Singh, 'we goin' play penny o' thinkin' our way. If I guess wrong, then you got to say what you been really thinkin' 'fore any money pass.'

' 'Tis better that way,' said Bob. 'Makes a man's pledge more real.'

'Much more real,' said Singh.

He took the lighter and polished it over his pants before slipping it into his pocket. They looked towards the houses, hoping that Rowley would soon appear. The street was empty, but Singh saw someone pacing up and down in the large white house with the brown shingled roof at the edge of the compound. Three houses away he could also see the wide balcony which enclosed three sides of the house where Rowley lived. But the windows were closed. He had the feeling that no one was there, and he suggested that they should continue towards the stunted grape tree where they had arranged to meet Rowley.

Mark noticed the boys again, but something had reduced their steps to a feeble crawl. Now they stood still at the brink of the track which led into Paradise Wood, equally intent in their scrutiny of the earth. Bob's foot scraped an inch of dust away, and he fumbled forward. They looked like three young cripples caught in a similar wish for strength, asking the earth for pardon. The sun blazed over them. Behind the street stretched out of sight in a blank and burning desolation. The heat had emptied the houses. They were alone.

Bob made a sudden leap aside, and stooped, tracing a line with his hand in the dust. He let his arm rest flat on the ground, making a blockade with his fingers. Then he looked up at the others as though he were about to ask their advice.

'You think these can bite?'

'Don't touch them,' said Lee, 'I want to see where they goin'.'

'Don't touch them yet,' said Singh, 'they will get suspicious.'

'I believe they know already that we watchin',' Bob said. He raised his arm and stood, looking down at the ants which were rapidly moving towards a patch of grass.

The boys stood still as though they could not resist the magic of this journey. The scene had altered their calculations of distance and time, and the grass grew a miracle of labour before their eyes. The ants continued to crawl under parcels of food that seemed impossible for their size. It was a desperate and determined struggle to succeed. Now the boys did not think of destination or search or escape; it was the idea of success which ruled their minds. The ants swelled their ranks climbing the treacherous cliffs of pebble and grass. The earth was surrendering to their will. The boys watched, silent, and incredulous. The tiny pleats which the ants had printed in the dust behind them deepened into valleys that seemed to hurry, steep and impassable, to the heart of the earth. A pebble was a frozen planet threatening to halt the progress of these heroes, minute and yet surpassing all ordinary notions of strength. Each scribble of weed was a peak of mountains, long submerged, demanding their release from the bowels of the sea. But the ants travelled in a drama which made obstacle and endurance equal, infinite. They continued like the sky always and for ever there, forged by some blind, original need to last. The ranks multiplied, diminished here and there, or marched, for a while, out of sight. But always they remained. Their advance was pushing the scene slowly further to a new decor which would soon swell into a sudden density of wilderness and jungle and sea-size rivers at night. Nature was crowding nearer. But the boys did not want to lose sight of the ants so soon, and their curiosity turned.

'It would be damn easy to kill all o' them one time,' said Singh.

'How many you think they can be,' said Bob, 'in this one line here?'

' 'Bout twenty,' said Lee, 'perhaps less, perhaps more.'

'I say more,' Bob said.

'Count them,' said Singh, 'an' see who is right. I say thirty.'

They all stooped, leaned forward and tried to count the ants.

'Count fast,' said Singh, ' 'cause they beginnin' to separate.'

'You think they hear any noise?' Bob asked.

'Ants don't have ears,' Lee said, 'they have to hear with their eyes.'

'But these don't have eyes,' Bob said, 'they see with their legs.'

'Who say so?' Lee asked, supporting himself with one arm.

'I say so,' Bob said. 'Even if they had eyes they couldn't see 'cause of where they carryin' the food.'

There was a pause. The boys squatted, uncertainly balanced, waving their hands in the air.

'I think they hear,' Bob said, 'look how they scatterin'.'

'I count twelve so far,' said Singh, 'but they scatterin'.'

'Don't let them scatter,' said Lee, 'they droppin' the food to scatter.'

'I count nine,' said Bob, 'but some gettin' away.'

'Corner them,' said Singh, 'corner them before they reach the grass.'

'They getting near,' said Lee, 'don't let them pass.'

'One passing,' said Bob, 'but I 'fraid he might bite.'

'If he bite kill him,' said Singh.

'An' I will still have the bite,' said Bob.

'Then kill him first,' said Singh.

'One gone,' said Lee, 'I kill him.'

'Two, three, four,' said Bob, 'four dead for certain.'

'But they still scatterin',' said Lee, 'they know what happenin'.'

'Block everywhere and kill quick,' said Singh, 'we can count after.'

'See who kill the most,' said Bob. 'I got seven.'

'I goin' still count the ones that get away,' said Lee.

147

'We ain't takin' word for what we ain't see,' said Singh.

'I agree,' said Bob, 'it is easy to overcount. I got thirteen.'

'I got twelve,' said Lee, 'and two more ready, not countin' the one that get away.'

'You killin' some o' mine,' said Singh, 'don't cross my line to kill mine.'

'Who say you got a line,' said Lee.

'I say so,' said Singh, 'we start from the beginning with a different line.'

'That is fair,' said Bob. 'I finish my line. I count nineteen.'

'I think they all dead,' said Lee, 'I got twenty-three.'

'You see what you do,' Singh said, looking at Lee. 'You make some of mine cross over. For that I only get twelve.'

'How I make them cross,' said Lee, 'they just run wild to get away.'

'I think they was a hundred in all,' Bob said. 'Plenty get away.'

'Where you think they was goin'?' Singh asked.

'They was going home,' said Bob, 'takin' home food.'

The boys stood, staring in silence at the dead ants as though they had forgotten to check their count. The marl was spotted with small black freckles like seeds which had failed to make roots. The weed had suddenly lost its stature, and the grass lay withered and simple in the sun. The magic of the scene had escaped with the death of the ants. But the boys waited as though they expected the ants to come alive and continue their journey into the wood.

'We murder them,' said Bob.

The others did not reply. Each was waiting for the other to make a move.

'Suppose we wus one o' them,' said Lee.

'We'd just lay down dead,' Bob said, 'an' no more movin' after that.'

'Would be the end o' the little Society,' said Lee.

'But we ain't ants,' said Singh, 'an' what use is ants?'

'Not much,' said Lee, 'they can't do more than live an' work.'

Singh was going to speak when they heard the rustle of the leaves behind them. Rowley had crept up quietly to see what had happened. The boys were not aware of his presence until they heard the leaves, and Rowley had spoken.

'Who killed them?' he asked. He had never seen so many dead ants in one place, and he was intrigued.

They hesitated. Singh was feeling in his pocket for the lighter. Rowley looked at the boys and the dead ants, and they seemed equally strange. He could not understand their secrecy and he repeated his question. The boys seemed afraid to admit what they had done. And suddenly they replied, almost in unison: 'Me.'

'Why did you kill them?' Rowley asked. He looked as though he were at the heart of some new adventure. He was waiting for them to answer, but they did not seem to remember what had happened.

Then Bob said: 'We been countin' them.'

Rowley was satisfied. He looked at Singh who was feeling for the lighter in his pocket, as he glanced at the others. They hardly spoke. Rowley looked over his shoulder to see whether there was anyone in sight. Then he leapt over the patch of grass and ran down the track which led through the wood to the barricade of cactus and wild fern which surrounded the grape tree.

Mark had walked down to the track where he had first seen the boys staring at the earth. It seemed an ordinary part of the ground, a little more wrinkled where the dust had received the broken signatures of footprints and fingers. He looked further ahead, hoping to find the reason for the excitement he had noticed from the window. But everything seemed perfectly ordinary. He scratched a finger through the dust which settled in a little lump on his fingernail. He shook the lump back to the track, and he saw an ant, still, and surprisingly conspicuous at the centre of the scattered lump of dust. He tried to disturb it, but nothing happened. He flicked his finger through the dust again, and the sprinkle fell over the pebble which showed an ant, quiet as the sky. But he had hardly noticed the ant. He tapped it lightly in the dust and took the pebble between his fingers. It could not have been the pebble which delayed the boys. He let it fall through his fingers on to the patch of grass. He pulled a handkerchief from his pocket to wipe his face, and an inch from his eye, his hand fluttered the handkerchief back, and he brushed away the speck of dust he had seen. It was an ant, the size of a pinhead, almost flattened. He was going to swear at this uncanny repetition of dead ants. He looked more closely, wondering, for a moment, whether it was the same ant. But that seemed unlikely, yet the three ants he had noticed, almost shocking in their obvious stillness, confused him, and he thought about the boys. They had deluded him. It must have been some strange idea of fun, waiting for the earth to offer things that did not exist. He had lost interest, but his curiosity bullied him, and he stepped forward searching the patch of grass where the pebble had fallen. But there was nothing to see, only an ant labouring furiously, stumbling through the deep valley of grass, behind its huge burden of food; and like the boys, the spectacle seemed to surprise him into a sudden awakening of the ant's persistent journeying. But he had almost forgotten the boys. He looked towards the centre of the wood where the trees rose like a wall to the sky. He turned to leave, and his eye caught the ant again, hurrying feebly through the weed which rambled over the stout roots of the trees that comprised the dense and devious acreage of Paradise Wood. The ant was now out of sight. Mark gave up his interest in the boys and turned his back on the wood.

Paradise Wood had enclosed their view and held them captive. They were glad. Here they had enacted a private fantasy. Rowley had made his pledge and taken the lighter. Secrecy was their bond. They felt free to rebuke their parents or revile the law. They felt safe and free in the shelter of the wood. They spoke their names to the trees and the wind carried their wishes out to sea.

'I swear to keep the Society secret,' said Rowley.

'You have to call your forebears first,' said Singh.

'I'm sorry,' said Rowley. 'Let me begin again.' He paused and made a face at Bob. 'I'm Rowley, Crabbe's son… I swear to keep the Society secret.'

'I am Singh, same name as my father, an' shall be a rich man.'

'I am Lee, the teacher's son, an' shall be a rich man an' wise too.'

'I am Bob, the butcher's boy, an' shall be a…'

'Shall be a fat man,' Lee interrupted. There was a giggle which was cut short by Singh's order for silence. Bob was reminded of his wish.

'…Bob, the butcher's boy, an' shall be a great man.'

'No more men,' said Singh, 'so let's begin with penny for your thinkin'.'

'Be a fat man,' said Lee, looking at Bob, 'a good man must be a fat man too.'

'No more fun,' said Singh firmly. 'Now hide, quick. I shut my eyes till I hear no noise.'

The wood was a vast acreage of trees and vine which reached from the sea to where the roads and houses began. It served every purpose. People went there to be at peace, to make love, to ease their bowels, and sometimes to rehearse quarrels with their friends. It was a public private place which received every possible confession. And it was a kind of miracle the way people seemed to know by instinct the areas that were appropriate to their needs. The lovers had their quarter which included all lovers without exposing any couple to the privacy of another. There were familiar tracks which pedestrians used from the road on their way to the sea; but these never seemed to trespass on those areas which served some other purpose. The boys were going to ramble far, but it was part of the game that the entire wood was their domain. It was only with boys that all the rules of the wood were broken. They might trip over lovers, or interrupt the solitary lunatic, or appear at the moment of some hideous adult bargain. Then they were simply dismissed with a single wave of a hand, or a corrective stare, or the threat of a voice which meant no harm. And they accepted their dismissal as part of their privilege.

Singh, like the others, knew this privilege, and he kept going farther and farther, with no guide but the feeling that he was sure to find them. Lee heard the stems of the leaves click every now and again, and for a moment he thought of Singh's approach. But soon he had abandoned Singh to the world of things, loitering or drifting. It was his business simply to wait, and Singh's to listen and look. But the clicking of the leaves increased. It interrupted his peace, and he was now convinced that Singh was near. But he did not stir. He was simply getting ready to recognise Singh whenever he appeared. The leaves snapped again, and then he heard a body turn as though it were crawling through the foliage, and a bramble clicked and fell, and he got ready to recognise Singh, but he did not stir.

The leaves shrieked again and in a flash he was sure that he had seen Singh, but he remained still, like the sandy floor of the wood where he sat. He had become a thing like the roots of the trees which surrounded him; for it was not his business to be aware of Singh. Having chosen his hiding place, there was nothing to do but wait; and instinct, it would seem, had trained him for waiting. He had abandoned Singh to the world of leaves and birds and insects that crawl at random. It was Singh's duty to find him, and if he arrived and found his target, Lee would simply surrender himself patiently and in silence. Like one who understood unerringly every occasion which involved his presence, he also seemed to know what rhythm that presence should have for each occasion. His was not the assured persistence of Singh. It was rather a case of being alert without the least display of effort. So he waited, like the wood itself, in a state of passive authority which could not be disturbed even after he had been found. Instinctively he had found a value for any loss, and that value was a certain protection against defeat. For it was defeat that was his ultimate enemy.

The search was exhausting, and although Singh's spirit never failed, he had become aware of his fatigue. He retraced his steps more than once as though he doubted his knowledge of the wood. A branch bruised his knee, and he limped to a standstill over the root of a tree. He was talking quietly to himself, soothing his scar with a finger of saliva.

'Maybe they think it better to hide together,' he said. 'Maybe they feel two in one place will make me wrong from the start, wonderin' if to turn left or right. Maybe they feel to hide together. But I remember my father sayin' always in anythin' you keep goin', go, go, go. Who they think Singh is at all? What they think? Maybe, they do not hide together, but I will find out. Sure thing I will.'

He stood, patting his knee as though he wanted to test its strength; and it seemed that his will had been revived by the memory of his father's advice. It was not a quick result which hastened his steps, but rather a strange curiosity about his ability to keep going. He was talking to himself again, as he stood, passing his hand up and down the smooth black bark of the tree.

'Maybe it is the tree my father talk 'bout sometimes,' he said, 'a tree which only show the leaves but not the richness it can give. Maybe it is the tree he feel he can turn into money, but it is hard to do a good thing for people who want to prevent you, yet you have to keep goin', go, go, go. Who they think they can fool, hidin' together, maybe, but I will find out...'

Rowley clasped the lighter and repeated his pledge. 'I'm Rowley, Crabbe's son... I swear to keep the Society secret...' It had taken him like a guide showing the way to this hiding place. He could never deceive them, or he would have betrayed also the luck which had made this friendship with the boys. Now he would be able to endure the tyranny of affection that ruled his father's house. He was going to put his father's importance in its proper perspective. His secret was a challenge to his father's authority. 'He's chief of police,' he said, 'chief of this and chief of that, but I swear, I swear to keep the Society secret...'

He lay flat, squirming under the vine which hung heavy with thorns and black berries above his head. He caressed the lighter and thought he heard the monkeys and the parrots celebrate his secret in the hills. 'Swear to keep the Society secret, I swear to keep the Society secret.'

The wind swayed the vine and a thorn scraped his chin leaving a little red head where his skin was pricked. He leaned his head and the blood was quashed into three red freckles which turned dry on his hand. He was insensitive to the prick of the thorn or the brief spasms of movement which the vine was making above his head. He polished the lighter over his shirt and watched the shine squint above his eye. 'I swear to keep the Society secret... I swear to keep the Society secret...' And he thought of his father moving about the house with the face of an angry teacher, important and mysterious. His father was not an ordinary man who lived and worked in San Cristobal. He was like those strange numbers which appeared in tubes on the wall, telling secrets about the weather. He liked his father, but he could never find the courage to speak with him about the things which mattered to a boy. His father was always beyond his reach like the moon which, on occasions, he felt he could touch. His father was a man who knew what was happening. His head was sacred with knowledge, a harvest of facts which many people in San Cristobal would have liked to share.

He continued polishing the lighter, letting his memory play with these recollections of his father. 'Sometimes I was like a prince in the crowd when people saw me and remember who my father was. I would feel like a prince. But now I am bigger and better than a prince. I swear to keep the Society secret… I have a secret he cannot know…' He had found a privilege which made him equal in the house which his father's silence ruled. 'He knows what he knows,' he said, 'and I know what I know, and he cannot know what I know if I keep the Society secret…' His father was a fallen hero.

His chest was sore from the gravel, and he raised his body an inch or two from the ground. His heels split the leaves which lay dead around him, and he paused for a moment before completing the swing which would let him lie flat on his back. He stretched, and the leaves and the bramble dissolved into a shriek which reminded him that Singh might hear. He lay still, watching the vine droop down to touch his chest. The thorns pointed like spears towards his eyes, but he did not shift to avoid their touch. This morning was an adventure which had swept him beyond any recollection of danger. He could not now remember when he had ever been afraid, and he stared at the thorns and the black berries as though he wanted them to challenge his power. He was no longer a prince in a crowd which would not know what had happened this morning. He made eyes at the thorns and the black berries and ordered them, in the name of the Society, to deny the wind and stay still until Singh was near.

He was hoping that Singh would find him soon. He knew that his father would never let him ramble with them on errands which brought the Society money and helped them to prove its success. But he was determined to meet them in secret, and he wanted to know how he could contribute to the funds. He had to play his part, and he needed their help.

'There's always my bicycle,' he said, 'I can always lend them the bicycle if they have to go somewhere for the Society… and there is…'

He stopped to consider this risk. He was polishing the lighter over his shirt as he looked up at the thorns. The sea was scarcely an echo, and the wood was still as though it waited for the trees to stir. His eyes fell on the lighter, and then rambled away with a noise of footsteps, soft and near. Perhaps it was Singh, but it did not matter. He was thinking that there was nothing he could not risk for the Society. Nothing. He was no longer a prince in a crowd which could not guess his secret. He was bigger and better than a prince, an equal in the house which his father ruled. I know what I know, he thought, and he cannot know what I know.

'There is the boat,' he said, 'the little boat my father has… perhaps I could take it now and again if the Society needs a boat… The Society may have some way to use a boat…'

Singh was getting tired. He sat again, nursing his knee. But he nursed it with a casual and almost aloof competence as though it were a harmless nuisance to which one might show a little kindness. It was not so much a part of his body which modified his movement and therefore interfered with his desire. It was a thing which his body had made a part of his possessions and which he could arrange and direct according to his will. The crawl of his fingers over the bruised flesh seemed to be no part of his feeling which was given wholly to his search for the others. A little sea crab scrambled out of a hole and raced madly along the sand in search of another hole, and suddenly he leapt to his feet in an attitude of pursuit, and as quickly the memory of his father's voice dismissed the spectacle of the hurrying crab, and Singh kept going. He patted his knee like an old man trying to comfort a child, and then set off as though it were no part of his interest. He was going to find Bob, or Rowley or Lee, and if they were together, then they would all be his victims at once.

His thought wavered from the hidden power of the tree to the whereabouts of his friends. For a moment he rebuked himself for wasting a thought on the tree, and yet it seemed part of the same ambition. The tree reminded him that he had to keep going, and it was as though he withdrew his rebuke. He mumbled to himself again: 'Who they think Singh is? Maybe, they think Singh is not like his father. Maybe. I will find out.'

And he continued, earnest and daring, burying weed and pebble under his feet as he leapt from the branches that crossed his path. His body had become a slave to his purpose, and his eyes penetrated the leaves like lights that offered a view of the hiding place he was after. He was finding his way about the tangled thickness of the wood with utter certainty, and he seemed to know beforehand where it would lead him.

'They will find out, like my father say, like my father say, my father…'

His silence was immediate like the clap of a hand on his shoulder; and then he repeated the words, like my father say. 'But my father…' He paused, astonished by the image of his father bursting with hatred; and for a moment he seemed to forget the reason for his presence in the wood. 'Like my father say…' The words had produced a silent agony in his ears. He wondered about Bob and Lee. What were they thinking? Could they guess what he had remembered his father's voice say? Could they guess the wish which he had heard his father whisper? Could Bob or Lee guess what made him uneasy? The thought of Rowley was like a charge which, even in his innocence, he wanted to avoid. He could not bring himself to think of Rowley when he remembered his father's wish. There was a feeling like shame which silenced him. Many a night he had heard his father whisper his ambition to murder Rowley's father. He could hear his father's voice barely audible in its wish for the death of Crabbe. And he felt a sudden revulsion against his father, but he could not share his knowledge with Rowley. He could never let Rowley know this recollection which hung like a shadow over the Society. Neither Bob nor Lee had ever stirred such sympathy in him, and he felt for a moment that something like duty had told him that Rowley needed them. His father's wish for the death of Crabbe seemed to make Rowley more solidly a part of the little Society. But he could not let him know the wish which he had heard his father whisper in the night. 'If only, if only…' He leaned against the tree and listened for a sound which might lead him to Bob or Lee. For he did not want to be alone when he found Rowley. He did not really want to find Rowley this morning.

Another stem snapped, and the leaf fluttered down, and Bob put out his hand to take its fall. But the leaf veered, and lodged finally between the space of his toes. He looked at it with enormous satisfaction, then jerked it in the air, and shifted to take it into his mouth. The bramble cried, and his movement travelled through the trees in a whisper of crushed, dead leaves. If Singh were nearby, it would not have been difficult for him to find his way to Bob's hiding place. But Bob did not care. He had grown tired of waiting, and his restlessness was, in a way, an attempt to help Singh. He wanted a change. It would have been better if he had shared Lee's hiding place, for they could have kept each other company. But he was not at home in this chosen isolation, and he was hoping that Singh would arrive. At first it seemed exciting, and the fact that he knew something the other did not know gave him a feeling of power. But this knowledge was becoming stale. In order to restore life to the game, he felt it necessary to surrender himself.

He was talking to himself. 'Singh, man, come if you are comin'. Stop comin' an' come, 'cause I don't want to hide no more. You lookin' everywhere except where you should. I done tired now, Singh. If you comin', come.'

He heard the noise again, much louder, and he raised his body and spied through the leaves. The bramble broke again, and a foot stumbled through the leaves. The noise moved further away. He thought Singh was taking a wrong turn and he decided to surrender himself. He was impatient and a little peeved. He leaned forward under the leaves and tried to follow the direction of the noise. But everything was still, utterly still.

The trees were swaying and he saw the dry leaves flutter and spread like a falling canopy over the air. The wind was shaking the bramble before his eyes, but he could not hear. He wanted to creep from under the shelter of fern and dry cactus which hid him to prevent the shame which he was about to witness. He wanted to shout, but his voice had failed at the wonder which was taking place before his eyes. His sister had stolen quietly away from the crowd on the beach, and entered, alone, this deserted shelter in the wood. He recognised her, and some instinct ruled that he should close his eyes, but he could not. He glanced to the right, barely shifting his head, and hoped that Singh was not near. He could not bear another witness to this solitary and indecent desire which she was trying to soothe with her own hands. The sound of the wood was subdued, but his head contained the roar which he wanted to make. 'You, you, you, you…' The words trampled like feet from ear to ear inside his skull, but he could not speak. He was afraid the others would discover where he was, and he was ashamed that they might know what he had seen.

She had spread her legs and covered her head with a large red towel which fell like a shawl down her neck. It smoothed the wrinkled bark of the tree against her back. Something shouted that he should close his eyes or make a noise which would end the indecent play which her fingers made up and down the bathing costume. Now she was observing herself in an agony of effort to start some ecstasy in her flesh. Bob could not move, nor could he shut his eyes against the terror which she had struck in his body. He watched her aghast and felt his skin thicken and crawl like a claw under his clothes. He had lost the urge to move. He did not feel the need to shout at her. His accusation gave way to a sudden paralysis of will which made him shiver with wonder and fear, as though he had agreed to join her in some rebellious secrecy against those who were not present. Everything yielded to a moment of greedy and searing curiosity. His eyes had become a furious appetite, consuming his sister's hands.

The silence had seduced them into a reckless acquiescence.

He was seeing her nakedness for the first time, and he was afraid. He had begun to tremble with suspicion. Something shouted at him to shut his eyes, but he could not move. He could feel his eyes itch, and his skin rebel against the frightened instinct which held him to the sand. He wanted to move, but he could not bear the thought which warned him where he would turn. And he was afraid. For a moment he saw the sky open and smother him with anger. His body shook, and he could hear his breathing like a noise behind his ear. But his sister's hand was a force more terrible than the wrath which threatened to come upon him if he moved. It was the awful movement of her hand which he could not resist. Then he felt, with a shudder which revolted every nerve, that he wanted to shut his eyes and become his sister's hand. And he was afraid.

'I couldn't tell Singh that,' he said quietly, 'I couldn't tell him that. Penny or no penny I couldn't tell him that. Not Singh, not that. It never happen before, but I couldn't tell that. Couldn't tell that.'

Suddenly he felt outraged by what had happened. He wanted to chase after his sister and crush the hand which had corrupted his feeling. She was standing with the towel thrown over her shoulders. Something had happened to relieve the passion which swelled her flesh when she lay back on the tree. And Bob felt angry and ashamed. He held his head down and wished her away. She was walking slowly between the trees and the fallen fence of cactus, and he looked up in time to see the branches swing behind the red towel and the dry noise which her feet were making over the dead leaves…

Rowley heard the noise of feet striding over the leaves and he crouched further under the vine. He held his breath and waited. He would have liked Singh to lose sight of this hiding place until he had decided what he would do to serve the Society. He was thinking about the boat and the bicycle, but the feet were near, passing swiftly and lightly over the leaves. He put his face in his hands and peeped through the space his fingers made. He was sure Singh had reached, but the noise of feet had stopped and he saw a dog lift its leg and spray the leaves. The dog sniffed the leaves and lifted its leg again, and soon the noise of feet returned. Singh was not near, and the silence reminded him of his pledge to the Society.

Now he was thinking of Bob and Singh and Lee as he had thought earlier of his father. For a moment their absence made him less certain about the Society. He was trying to think of a way of showing his loyalty, and he thought it would please them if he invited them to the house. He would ask his father's permission. Perhaps his grandmother would offer to help as she had often done with his friends in England. There would be no mention of the Society, but each would know the secret which held them together, and neither his father nor his grandmother would be any the wiser. Perhaps it would please them to come, and it would be the first test of the privilege with which the Society had made him powerful in the presence of his father. He could display his secret before his father's eyes. The idea delighted him, and suddenly he wished that Singh would arrive. He wanted to be found, because he wanted them to know what he had wished and what he had been thinking. There would be no need to finish the game. He would have paid the penny to tell his own thoughts. 'I swear to keep the Society secret,' he whispered, 'I swear to keep the Society secret.'

'But would they come?' he asked, and it seemed that he had heard other voices asking the same question. The sensation was strange, and he shifted and put his hands to his ears as though he could not believe his hearing. The voices seemed to break the question down to mere words which were not arranged as before. Would… but… come… they… He took his hands from his ears and repeated the question, 'Would they?' And for a moment he did not seem certain what it was they would do. 'Come,' he whispered. 'Would they come? Would they come?' He was talking involuntarily, repeating the word, they. Then he mumbled, 'Would Bob come? Would Singh come? Would Lee come? Would… they… would… they… they… they… Bob… Singh… Lee…'

His lips made a faltering movement with words, but everything was still. There was no other voice. The question had been cancelled. It disappeared like a chalk mark from a slate, and he tried for a while to think of his father and his grandmother. It was his father who had cancelled his question. He saw his grandmother like a law ordering his obedience. And he could not understand. He tried to imagine Bob and Singh sitting beside him in his father's house. He was arranging the furniture, but something suddenly went wrong. They did not fit. Neither Bob nor Singh nor Lee. The chairs would not admit of their presence. And he could not understand.

'But why? Why? Why?' He was waiting as though he expected to hear his father's voice. 'Why? Why? Why?' It was like asking why four is the result of two and two, and he was striving to hear someone promise an answer. 'I am Rowley, Crabbe's son…' He paused, trying to understand why he felt he needed the company of Bob and Singh and Lee while his father needed to live at a distance from Singh's father and Lee's father. He recalled that he had often heard his father say that he needed to have him near. His father needed his company just as he had felt a need for the company of Bob and Singh and Lee. 'It's what he says,' he whispered, 'and Granny too. It's what they say. They need me near. They need my company.' But he could not understand why their affection for him should also be their rejection of Bob and Singh and Lee. It was not only because of Singh's father and Lee's father speaking on the platforms. 'It's more than that,' he was thinking. But he could not understand.

'They would not come,' he said, 'they could not come.' And he wondered how he would begin to explain to Singh what he had been thinking. How could he begin to tell them that he knew they could not come? He could not lie, for the truth, like their secrecy, was a part of his pledge to the Society. He crossed his fingers and hoped that Singh would give him time to think of a way out. 'I swear to keep the Society secret,' he was thinking, 'I swear to keep the Society secret…'

Bob was no longer afraid, and his shame had given way to a feeling of pride and indignation. He looked at his hands as though he wanted them to confirm his innocence. Then he glanced towards the tree where his sister had committed a terrible blasphemy with her fingers. 'Fool,' he whispered, 'the little fool, exposin' herself in the open air without knowin' the trouble she could have make this mornin'. The bold-face little fool.'

His eyes avoided the recent stain which showed on his trousers. He straightened his legs and made his seat further into the sand. He was shaking his hand against his leg, looking now and again towards the tree where his sister had encouraged her longing. The tree had assumed the insolence and grossness of her hand, and he could feel his anger urge him to follow her wherever she was and let her know that he had seen her. He would beat her on the sand in the presence of the crowd, and she would be speechless because she would know why he had done so. The leaves lifted and danced like fingers above his head, and he turned his eyes away from the tree. He stared at the sand, talking to himself. 'What sort o' cross she want to make my father carry,' he said, 'what sort o' cross? 'Cause if 'twas a next kind o' man sittin' here this mornin', look what would have happen. I know what would have happen. A man with different intentions from what a brother know he owe his sister would have crucify her feelin'

161

under that tree this mornin'.' His voice lowered to a whisper, and he raised his head, pondering the crooked trunk of the tree. 'Any next man, seein' her in that open-air position would have pounce like a cat on what she got, an' tear her insides open with his iron. Look what would have happen this mornin'. And in two shakes of a dog's tail her belly would be burstin' with baby. Now look at that. My sister swellin' with chil', 'cause it ain't any fingerin' she finger that bring all this breedin' in San Cristobal. It ain't no finger make that mess. If only 'twas a next kind o' man sittin' here this mornin', examin' what it is she was doin' there with her lawless hand. What a cross my father would have to carry all 'cause the girl ain't got nothin' to do. An' 'tis as I hear him say mornin' noon an' night, whenever you see people ain't got no work, a breedin' spree will always take place. Just like in San Cristobal. As work get scarce your population swell. An' there she come this mornin' with her idle prick-promptin'…'

He paused and cocked his ear for a sound which drifted in the distance. He was unsure of his feelings about Singh's arrival. Earlier he did not want him to come. Now he felt a certain need to forget his sister. But Singh would probably make the usual enquiry about what he was thinking, and he did not know what he would say. He could not say what he had seen. Not to Singh, he thought, not to Singh and not to Lee. He thought of Rowley lost in some tangle of cactus and trees. And gradually he felt that Rowley had become a special presence in these circumstances. He was making an exception of Rowley as he thought of his sister and the Society. He looked across at the trees, but it had now lost its power to remind him of his sister. He could think of her in her absence as he thought of Rowley hidden in some haphazard cave of bramble and leaves. He waited for the sound to return, but a silence had settled through the wood.

Why I should make him special, he wondered, as he thought of Rowley. He was arguing with himself about the difference between Lee and Singh and Rowley. He had known Singh and Lee for a long time, and it was probably this long period of acquaintance which had made him uneasy about saying what had happened when his sister sat under the tree. He was sure he could not let them know; yet he could not understand why he had thought that it would be different with Rowley. He had a feeling which he could not explain that Rowley would make it easier for him to talk. He would feel less embarrassment in the presence of Rowley who was younger and a stranger. 'But he is not a stranger now,' he told himself, 'he is no more stranger. He belongs to the Society.' Rowley had sworn to keep the Society secret.

It was difficult to explain his feelings by the argument that Rowley was a stranger. And it was not because Rowley was Crabbe's son. But there was something about Rowley which seemed defenceless. He thought of his sister and her ignorant exposure under the tree. Somehow Rowley reminded him of that open and vulnerable display of longing. If he told Rowley what he dare not tell Singh or Lee, it was because he felt that Rowley needed a greater intimacy than the others. He recalled the morning when they had sat at the old woman's feet, and they had seen the strange boy walking towards them. He remembered Rowley's face, young, friendly, but estranged. He thought that Lee and Singh were not only older but more privileged in the community of men and women who were claiming San Cristobal, and he wanted Rowley to belong to San Cristobal because he remembered the morning he walked towards them and begged their permission to sit at the old woman's feet. She had sanctioned his wish. 'Not only his years,' he said to himself, ' 'tis that here and now he need much more than Singh or Lee.' He was trying to see some flaw in this feeling as he looked towards the trees. In spite of his connections and his importance as Crabbe's son, Rowley had struck him as the one most in need of confidence. This was the reason he could tell him what had happened, and how he had felt when his sister shook his restraint with her visible longing under the tree. He heard a sound again and crouched lower under the roof of cactus which hid him.

The sand had made an arch under Rowley's elbow and he could feel his arm shovelling forward and away from his side as though some force were sliding him gradually down into the sand. His elbow looked like a knuckle of bone which the sand had indented with scarlet pores. He rubbed it over his shirt, and propped himself up on one side, letting his bruised elbow incline upwards to the berries and the near points of thorn. He followed the length of his body from his knees to the ashen dead leaves which his feet had buried. And he thought that his skin would always be evidence against him in any day's adventure with the Society. It would always be difficult to deny that he had left the house on his own; for his grandmother could tell from the permanent flush of his cheeks and the blistering sunburn at the back of his neck that he had gone out and stayed longer than he should have done. His face was now crimson as though the sun would spill his blood. But he was unfeeling. He watched his knee like an animal's dead paw, and then jerked his head up to rest on his arm. For a moment he was indifferent to the orders and the warnings which they had given him at home. He was polishing the lighter which the boys had given him. But he did not know how he could explain what he had thought.

There was a noise like the cracking of fingers, and he saw a leaf wobble slowly down to the sand. He tried to think about the boat and whether Singh was getting nearer. But his glance was halted, and his eyes were fixed on the sudden splendour of the colours which flashed and wriggled through the crossed sticks of bramble making an X where the lizard was caught. He rubbed his eyes and looked more closely at the lizard, fat and green as young grass with a yellow tuft of throat hanging like a fried yolk under its head. The eyes were the size of peas, restless and black with fear. The lizard was caught a little above the base of the tail. Its body stretched and swelled like rubber on either side of the bramble. Now and again the head lunged forward in an effort to escape, and the throat widened and trembled, until the lizard tired and the head leaned wearily down to rest on the bramble. The mouth was open and the tongue showed like a disc of spit, frozen red and hanging at the edge of the breathing lip. The feet shrank visibly over the bramble, and the tail started to change colour. The lizard was going to die unless someone separated the sticks of bramble and made way for it.

He crept from under the arch of thorns, steering his head slowly beyond the last barricade of cactus to see whether anyone was in sight. He looked in the direction the dog had taken, but there was no sound of feet. He did not want to surrender to Singh. He did not know what he would say if Singh had found him now.

But he wanted to free the lizard, now swollen blue-black with pain. He crept towards the bramble and separated the two black branches. The lizard rolled on to the leaves. He saw the eyes close and he shook the tail with his toes, but it did not stir. He was going to cover it with the leaves, but he heard the sound of feet moving near. Someone was coming towards him. He thought of returning to his hiding place, but they were bound to hear him. He knew he would be caught before he could scramble back to the little cave of wild berries. And he wondered what he would tell Singh. He was polishing the lighter as he darted his head in search of a place to hide.

'Rowley... Rowley...' The voice was a whisper, soft and nervous as the leaves. 'Fin' Singh, fin' Singh quick...'

Lee was beckoning him forward. He turned and stared at Lee. He could not understand what had happened; but he could see Bob some yards away, spying through an opening in the cactus fence.

'Fin' Singh quick,' said Lee. 'She kneelin' in the wood.'

'Who?' His voice was hardly audible.

'Ma Shephard,' said Lee, 'makin' her prayers.'

Lee put his fingers up to suggest silence, and Rowley turned to see Singh who was shuffling towards them. He could not understand why they had surrendered themselves; but he felt relieved. He did not want to question Rowley. He looked sideways as he approached, then followed Lee's hand indicating the fence where Bob was waiting.

'Make a quiet step,' said Lee, 'make a quiet step. I believe she prayin' for the Movement an' Shephard.'

'Who prayin'?' Singh asked.

'Ma Shephard. I believe she blessin' what goin' happen,' said Lee, 'an' makin' a special prayer for her son.'

Singh did not speak. The boys crouched towards Bob who now lay flat, staring through the opening that showed Ma Shephard. She was kneeling; her eyes were closed, and her head rose high above the frail, black hands. And the boys could not believe the strength of her voice or the grave revelation of her prayers.

'Las' night, O Lord, I hear him again swear in his sleep, an' I say to myself a nightmare run 'way with his senses. I do not know where he find such words, not in my house, Master, nor in all the years o' my trainin' of him for the life to come. It is a matter You must take into Your own hand, good Lord, as he want to take the life o' this islan' into his. An' go with him, good God, go with him in a gradual way. He is not out of his head, I know, but a new ambition hold him in bondage, an' all because o' that England, an' some woman who wear him out all night with worry in his sleep. It is a war, it is a war he would like to purge his feelin' with. An' that is bad, You know, my Lord, that is bad. A man must clasp his feelin' like a shirt, fit it right, an' move on clean as the sun an' in courage. Help him, Lord. An' help me too to fin' whatever sin now punish my feelin' for my son.

'Perhaps I give way in the early days, tryin' to spare him the temper o' his father. 'Twas natural for a mother, an' his father was hard, hard, very hard. You know how hard, Lord. That man was a ram with horns in makin' up his min', a bull without blinkers or a dangerous dog let loose, an' takin' no muzzle. An' perhaps from the very start they hate each other. Somewhere in a part o' the heart decency will not let any man express, they hate each other. An' the chil' begin early walkin' with an evil ambition. He start out wantin' to prove that he would be bigger an' better than the man. He was goin' to teach his father the nature of a fool. 'Tis an evil ambition which turn a father's age to disrepute. An' there it would remain if the father didn't die. 'Twas only when my husban' lay down dead that the chil' soften his heart to his father. In death he was meek. But his will to conquer remain, an' there like the devil watchin' every movement he make, the women enter. My child take to women, an' they in their different deceits take to him an' work wonders on his weakness.

'An' then England, that England, Lord, that journeyin' out in blind ambition is always bad. That England like his dead father spring a new ambition in his brain, an' he keep sayin' it all night in his sleep, he just keep sayin' how he see his way to save this islan'. Whenever the memory of that false woman make room for other matters in his head, he just keep sayin' how he will save this islan'. So help him, Lord. Go with him in a gradual way, an' heal him in this mission or help him soon out o' his mistake. Help him, Lord, help him, for I feel his pride will teach a new sorrow in San Cristobal. I fear, I truly fear the time that is teachin' us change. Change us, Lord, You change us first...'

PART TWO

PENELOPE'S DIARIES

1

The month of May

It was an awkward hour for me to retire, but I thought it safer to be alone, for a feeling, in such circumstances, very easily escapes one's control, and I didn't want Marcia to make any discoveries. It would have been better if I could explain what had happened and asked her to understand. It was a relief to be in my room. When I closed the door and threw myself on the bed I felt such a sense of protection. The walls were safe. For a while I had escaped. I could consider more carefully what had happened. But when I tried to remember the details, I found that there was a lack of incidents which might have helped towards a beginning. It might have been easier if a glass had fallen or the door was suddenly opened, or the parrot had screamed. Something which had definitely occurred would have helped. But I recall only a sudden awareness of my feeling, and the curious enquiring press of my fingers into my thighs. It was then that I leapt from the bed, almost afraid of what I was doing. I thought it was Marcia's body which I was searching. I was afraid. She pushed herself up with her elbows and asked what had happened, but I could only grin and lie. I said something had stung me. She laughed and lay back, careless and relaxed as before. I sat at the edge of the bed and tried not to see her. But I could still feel my fingers rambling across my body which at that moment was Marcia's body.

I can't tell at what moment the transference took place. We were lying on the bed, tired after the sea-bathe. Marcia was wearing her bras and white shorts. I had changed into my petticoat. But there was nothing I could feel at that moment between my fingers and my skin. I hadn't lifted my petticoat, but it was a naked leg under my hand, slimmer than mine, and smoother. It was Marcia whom I was touching. It was then that

I stopped and was afraid, the moment I became aware of the absence of my petticoat. I tried to look at her without being seen, because each time my eyes turned towards Marcia, I felt my fingers against my thighs, and I thought that she was becoming gradually aware of my touch. My gaze was an accusation. I held my head away and wished she would fall asleep. I wanted to leave the room without inventing an excuse. My hands had grown suddenly nervous and uncertain as though they had escaped some disaster, and when I placed them on my thighs again, trying to recall what I had felt, my flesh for a moment seemed unfeeling. I raised my petticoat, and pressed with all my strength into my thighs, and suddenly my whole body shook with fright when Marcia, in a state of utter bewilderment, spoke to me. She asked what I was trying to do to myself, and again I grinned, but I had no lies ready. She came forward and examined my thighs, passing her hand over them, and it was then that my feeling seemed to return. I could feel her fingers sliding lightly off my knee as I lowered my petticoat and stood beside the bed. She couldn't understand what had happened, and I was glad. I walked away and left her preparing to lie back as before.

But her absence didn't help. Whenever I looked at my hands I saw her lying on the bed, her long hair wet and tangled, falling over her bras, and her thighs stretched in a slumber under my fingers. It was my feeling which pursued me. I had no warning of a desire for Marcia, and I do not recall any such intention towards her, and suddenly I tell myself with a loud and certain conviction that I didn't really touch Marcia. It was my own body which I held. But then I look at my hands and examine again my thighs, and it is the image of her which contradicts my eye and enlarges my feeling to an unnatural fear of my own desire. My senses had lost their conviction, and it was then, in the room alone, that I suddenly became aware of my feeling being wrong. And this feeling pursued me like an enemy. I went under the shower, and turned the water on full blast, and tried to occupy my attention in a furious act of bathing, and always I came back to the bed and my nervous hands and Marcia's legs, untouched, in an imaginary wriggle under my fingers. I say vehemently, 'I didn't touch her,' and this feeling returns a verdict that confuses my senses. I thought it was Marcia's body under my hands; therefore I have only got to touch her to confirm the feeling which preceded my disturbance on the bed. But I never asked myself at any time whether I wished it was Marcia's body which I was touching, and as soon as this occurred to me, I suddenly began to think of my loyalty to Mark and Bill.

It is safer in the room with the one dim light and the trees shaking inattentively against the window. A feeling arrives like a stranger and refuses to be dismissed. It emerges without warning, possesses you with a ruthless insistence, and then becoming a part of you, it leads you into a perplexing conspiracy against yourself, no longer thinking of the feeling itself, you are engrossed by all its consequences. After I have forgotten my experience on the bed, I am thinking of loyalty, loyalty to Mark and Bill. It is a concession to my feeling that it was Marcia whom I touched, and finally it is not Marcia who occupies my thought, but Bill and Mark. Suppose I conceded my hand to Marcia's body!

June

Formerly it was my feeling which confused me. I felt I had done something which, on more careful recollection, I had to convince myself was false. So far I was innocent; and I feel my innocence until I try to understand the origin of my mistake. How could I have failed to distinguish my body from Marcia's during those moments on the bed? I do not know, and I have tried to forget the importance of that question, because I must minimise the danger which it conceals. Today it is my imagination which I follow. An indolent day dreaming led me, defenceless and apprehensive, to a state of near delirium. I had not anticipated this. It seduced me slowly until I was hardly conscious of any meaning which I might place on the scene enacted before my eyes.

The trees outside the window receded from my view, bearing Marcia, awake, on their branches. She did not see me until I floated past the window and settled on the leaves, looking down on her body which was bare but for the deep violet spots which the leaves had made in shadow on her limbs. I smiled and Marcia smiled back, more in bewilderment than understanding. She curled on the branches like a cat, warm and relaxed, and I tested

170

the spots on her skin with my fingertips. But Marcia did not move. There was no mistake this time. It was Marcia's body under my hands, and her legs did not resist my touch. She was soft and receptive, and my hands played at random over her thighs. I expected Marcia to disturb me, but nothing happened, and I was restored to a state of absolute innocence. It was Marcia who welcomed me, and they were my hands which cleaved to her slumber. I had descended gently, and my face slid lightly against Marcia's, and my arms embraced her neck, delicate and white in the sun. Marcia shrugged with a child's impudence in my arms, but she did not disengage herself. She squeezed her body to me, restless and indifferent of my touch. And I stayed still, unspeaking, wishing that she would fall asleep while I caressed her throat and stroked her arms.

And time passed devoured by the sun and the deep foliage of the trees which concealed our embrace. I relaxed my arms and stared at the grass which rolled wide and singing beyond the green hedge that surrounded our house. But my legs were still sprawled indolently across Marcia who was asleep. Sheep were rambling across the pasture, but there was no one in sight. I was alone with Marcia; but suddenly she turned and made as if to speak, and my body raised itself from the branches, and before she had spoken I had disappeared through the leaves and back to my room. I stared incredulously from my bed, and suddenly Marcia too had gone.

They rise from some hidden, unfamiliar source within you: feeling and imagination. These are forces which invade a territory that was always familiar to you, and then one must contend with them for the sake of peace. I had not wished anything to change. It was not an intention which fixed Marcia in this relation to me, but there it is, a fact which I have forced myself to contend with. Was it true? Was Marcia there on the branches under my arms? I try to recall the stages of my journey, and I am suddenly reminded that I was not asleep. I go to the mirror and look for a long time at myself. My face betrays my curiosity. I clasp my hands and throw them around me to feel my body, but nothing unusual has happened. It is my body, and no one is here with me. The house is empty. I draw the chair closer and sit before the mirror regarding myself. I cannot see my feeling, and I cannot touch my imagination; but they surround me with an evil and insistent solicitude. Is it true that my body has desired Marcia's without any deliberate act or choice of which I am conscious? I regard my limbs enquiringly, but they do not speak. My hands fall dumb down my sides, and my legs are carelessly thrust forward. They do not understand anything. They fall about me in their natural and innocent posture awaiting any action I may urge. It is intolerable that I cannot speak to my body. I would like to ask my hands to surrender whatever secrets they possess. My body is dumb, a living servitude whose conduct has perplexed me. I learn nothing from my body but the risks it undertakes without my order. It has nothing helpful to report.

Perhaps I should speak with Marcia. But how would I begin? What could I say that would not seem like a stage of my insanity? And how would Marcia react to such a confidence? I could not disturb Marcia with such a confession of my fancy. Whom should it be then? Bill or Mark? And I suddenly think of their affection and my loyalty. I could not bear to be put outside the scope of their normal relations, but I am not able to support alone the feeling which lied to me about my fingers pressed against Marcia's thighs, or the imagination which led me towards Marcia's body on the branches outside my window.

End of July

Secrets are difficult to conceal because a secret is by nature contagious. It confronts you with such dubious isolation; it makes a special exception of you; it modifies your relation with everyone else. It changes its shape and size with every fresh encounter, until it is no longer enough to have one secret, but two or three. I cannot commit myself to Bill or Mark or Marcia, but my refusal must take a different form with each. If they notice that I seem different, it must not be different in the same way. They must vary in their feeling, their suspicion about my change. Bill must think, perhaps, that I am growing tired of this place. Marcia must assume that I am not feeling well. Mark must suspect that Bill and I have not been getting on well. Because I do not know how to explain what happened.

This morning Bill asked me again whether I remembered what I said before he turned away from me to switch on the light. I said I was dreaming, but he insisted that wasn't possible, not at the time he was speaking of. I remember vividly what was happening, but I remember it differently. Bill had turned off the light, and we lay together under the sheets talking quietly in the dark. It was late. I remember Bill's voice fading away gradually, and soon I was asleep. After a while Bill too must have gone to sleep. I woke once, and heard him breathing heavily beside me, and I drew closer to him, and put my arms around him, and went back to sleep. And some time later, I felt my body stretched tense and ecstatic against another. It was warm and energetic. My arms were locked tight around the thin breathing neck, and I could feel the gentle excitement of the other flesh, heaving and falling against mine. My energy was eager, a prodigal distribution of my flesh which could barely support its fury. My body was being eaten up by another, and finally our delirium subsided, and I felt an infinite relaxation possess me. I would have liked to express my satisfaction, but my tongue was lazy, and I remained quiet until my fingers rambled lazily across the wet warm thighs which pressed against me, and I said, 'Marcia, Marcia, Marcia…' It was then Bill turned away and put on the light. I was awake, and he was sitting at the edge of the bed, staring at me, bewildered and exhausted. I was hardly conscious of what he was saying, and I turned heavily on my side, and pulled the sheet over my head.

My imagination had played no part in this deception, nor was it the feeling which was the first sign of my difficulty with Marcia. These were inactive during my sleep. It was one other part of me which substituted Marcia for Bill. For the first time I felt ashamed. Not only my hands, but my entire body had deceived me. Daydreaming, I say to myself, was perhaps a way of testing my response to something that might happen. So my innocence remained. But my dream was a fact, a definite undertaking which I experienced with all my senses. Now my body must avoid Marcia. I cannot let my eye rest on her without a sharp feeling of rebuke, and she notices my caution as I pass her. She can feel the timidity, the uncertainty of my hands passing a cup, and some-

173

times my eyes are late in averting their glance, and my expression must arouse suspicion.

I had never thought it possible to alienate Marcia from my affections, but it seems inevitable, unless I can explain to her what has been happening. I am afraid to explain anything lest it alters my status in their eyes. And that is bound to happen. If I made a confession to Marcia, I might overcome my guilt, but I should immediately become a different person in her presence. They will all begin to reconsider me, and this is a kind of alienation which I could not bear. Is this the fate of the abnormal? It is not their difference which is disturbing. It is the way their difference is regarded which makes for their isolation. Their status is altered for others as though they had undergone some malevolent conversion. They must carry always a mark which denotes the measure of their fall from some general order. I could not bear to be myself minus what the others had always thought me to be. But any confession makes that inevitable. And we shall have to be together in these circumstances: at meals, in the living-room, walking the streets. They will not say anything, but their eyes will confirm their feeling. Pity, shame, perplexity: these will modify their acceptance of me. I shall become Penelope in spite of being Penelope. They will never use the accident of my experience against me, but I shall always feel the mark, 'in spite of', branded on my presence. Penelope in spite of... Penelope in spite of ... It would be better to lose one's status completely and be seen wholly as a new thing; much better than to have one's status granted with a certain reservation. It is the reservation which occupies the mind of the other, until one feels it like a scar, or a defamation. I believe this is what those people who are called inferior experience, and find resentful and intolerable. If their difference, whether it took the form of colour or religion or occupation, were regarded as their whole condition, all would be well. They could settle comfortably in their status, knowing that they were, in fact, their status. The Negro, the homosexual, the Jew, the worker... he is a man, that is never denied, but he is not quite ready for definition until these reservations are stated, and it is the reservation which separates him from himself. He is a man in spite of... I shall be Penelope in spite of...

'My God!' Penelope cried, 'she understood what I meant. She is going to tell him.'

She heard Marcia running down the stairs, and she hurried to the window to see whether Mark had left the house. She hoped he would go before Marcia could call him back to say what she knew. The lawn was empty. The sun had set a dark still flame like wine upon the neck of the hibiscus flowers leaning out of the hedge. She beat her hands on the sill and waited for someone to emerge. It was quiet in the room below. Mark did not appear, but she could not catch the sound of Marcia's voice, and she told herself that they were alone, Marcia and Mark, preparing some judgement on the secret which she had betrayed. She walked back to the bed, tumbled the cards on to the floor, and buried her head in the pillow.

Bill wanted to avoid the scene. He had noticed Mark slipping quietly through the back gate when he shouted 'goodbye', and immediately Marcia appeared, galloping down the stairs. She called out to Mark from the adjoining room, and he could feel the angry and determined plea in her voice. Mark had stopped suddenly. Soon he continued a few steps beyond the gate as though he were trying to decide what he should do. Marcia did not call again, but Mark had paused by the gate. Then he turned, angry and reluctant, to hear what Marcia wanted. He was walking back to the house.

'He's going to make her do something terrible one day,' Bill said.

He heard their voices in a muted frenzy and he walked away, wondering whether there was anything Penelope could do. He did not want to intervene. He walked across the lawn and stood at the front gate. He hoped that Crabbe and Paravecino would be late.

Marcia dragged the chair closer, but Mark would not sit. He saw the tears swell her eyes and shiver down the ridge of her cheeks. Her breath was hot against his throat. She clung to his arm and tried to pull him down to the chair. He put one foot on the chair and kept his balance without appearing to resist. He felt her hands relax and withdraw from his arm like a total failure of strength. She fumbled over the chair and pillowed her hands under her face. Her body seemed to contract with weeping, and her voice shuttled a quick, sharp spasm of noise like an animal's frightened yelp heard from afar. It made him angry and ashamed, and he wished that Marcia would say something. But the agony of this encounter was familiar, and the end was always the same. It seemed impossible, in this moment, to deny her anything; yet he knew that he had already chosen to do so. He would not stay.

'Couldn't you try, Mark, just a little?'

He had hoped to hear her speak, and now he realised that it would be more bearable if she were silent.

'I shall try to be back soon,' he said. He lifted her hand up to his chin and rubbed it gently up and down his face.

'But couldn't I come with you?' Marcia cried. 'Just to be with you.'

'Not today,' he said. 'I would prefer to be alone.'

'But that's what you always say,' she said. 'Yesterday, the day before. It's never today if I ask you to stay with me. What have I done?'

'Please, Marcia, please.'

'Can't you see what you are doing to me?' she shouted. 'Can't you see? Aren't you ashamed that the others know how you treat me? They don't say anything but they know. Bill and Penelope see how you treat me.'

He brought his foot down from the chair and shoved her hand away. This was always the moment when he failed to respond. Whenever Marcia mentioned anyone else in order to sharpen her rebuke he would withdraw. He became resentful at the thought that his life was a spectacle which others were observing, and took refuge in his silence.

'I have to go now,' he said. 'You can talk about this later.'

'Don't lie to me, Mark,' she said. Her voice had found its ordinary tone of resignation. 'You know there's never any later with you. Later you'll be too busy writing your diaries, or there will be another engagement which you can't miss, or, or something. There's always something else when I ask simply to be with you. Just to be with you.'

'Go back with Penelope,' he said, turning towards the door.

'But I don't want anyone's pity,' she cried. 'That's what Penelope was trying to avoid a minute ago. I believe she had us in mind when she was talking about the way she feels towards me sometimes. I don't want Penelope or anyone else to feel pity for me.'

She got up from the chair and followed him to the door. He lingered for a moment on the grass, and it reminded him that the order of their reactions was always the same when these scenes took place. He did not want to add to her discomfort, yet there was nothing he felt like doing to put her at ease. It was always Marcia who made her own peace.

'Will you be very long?' she asked. She had stretched her hand out to touch his shoulder. She wiped the tears from her cheeks and tried to compose herself.

'I'll be back soon,' he said, 'and then we can talk.' His voice was innocent of intrigue or bribery, and in the moment of believing him she also knew that they would not talk about this afternoon.

'Crabbe and Paravecino are coming for drinks,' she said, as though she wanted to distract him from thinking. 'Is that why you're going out?'

He hesitated, and she hastened to apologise for the embarrassment she had started. She wanted him to go and return as though nothing had passed between them, and she tried again to shepherd his thinking back to the harmless domesticities of their life.

'I'll talk with Bill about his job,' she said. 'I think that's why he has asked Crabbe and Paravecino to come. And to hear the recording of the boys' programme.'

Mark drew her closer and kissed her on the tip of her nose. He wiped her eyes with his lips, and smoothed the hair back from her forehead. She wanted to cry, but she threw her arms round his neck and stifled her sobbing against his throat. She felt calmer when she raised her head and drew her arms away. They kissed and waved goodbye.

She watched him hurry round the bend of the hedge, and she sat on the grass, turning the stems of two hibiscus flowers into a single plait, which finished in a large red bun, bell-shaped, that drooped into her hand. She untied the stems, and the flowers dropped, lifeless, on to the grass. In a moment of idle fancy she had killed them. Then she started up, taking the flowers in her hands as though she wanted to ask their pardon. She looked at the stems which made fearful green points descending towards the grass, and finally she brushed the flowers between her fingers, and walked away from the hedge into the house.

Bill was standing at the edge of the grass. He saw Marcia staring at him from the farther side. She had been standing there for some time, trying to share the wonder which had taken him like a secret across the garden over the hedge to the red tail of land which vanished through the trees. The sun was beginning to label the leaves with its quick and customary mixture of crimson and gold. She knew this interval of light would not last very long. It never did in San Cristobal where the afternoon was only a pause, a brief and extravagant interval between two major items of time: daylight and darkness. But she had never noticed Bill so completely taken by this spectacle of an early sunset, and she was at once curious and pleased.

'What's happening outside?' she asked, and her manner was careless as though she wanted to distract him from her own surprise.

'Nothing,' said Bill, 'I was just thinking.'

'I thought you were dreaming.'

'Not then,' said Bill, 'it's this job Flagstead has offered.'

'I've never seen you so excited,' said Marcia. 'One would think you'd never worked all your life.'

'Does it really show?'

'Of course it does,' she said, 'you're like a child getting ready for his first excursion.'

Bill laughed and walked past her to the small table where he had placed the tape recording machine. He played with the knobs and watched the tape slide like a worm round the spool. Marcia had come up behind him.

'What time are the others coming?' she asked.

'Any time now,' said Bill. He turned the knobs, and the tape imitated itself, hurrying backwards. There was a click, and a small green light suddenly went out.

'I think the boys were even better on the radio,' she said, 'much better than the afternoon they met us on the Sea Walk.'

178

'They have got imagination,' said Bill, 'that's what I noticed in the studio. Whenever they were in difficulty they invented.'

He paused as though he were rehearsing the scene in the studio of Radio San Cristobal: the doubt which Flagstead had expressed about his experiment, and the look of bewilderment on the faces of the boys as they waited to tell the story of the Tribe Boys and the Bandit Kings. He recalled Penelope's nervousness during the rehearsal, the atmosphere of panting chaos in the engineers' room and their final stupefaction when it was over. He had used all the resources of his experience as a producer to make it work. And it was a triumph.

'But why didn't they let you use their names?' Marcia asked.

'I'm not sure,' Bill said. 'They probably thought they might have been a failure.'

'You think Crabbe and Paravecino will enjoy it?' she asked.

'Why not,' he said, walking towards the door. 'Everybody else did.'

His assurance had suddenly reminded her of Mark. She walked to the window and leaned her head out as though she expected to see him in the garden. Thief was hurrying past the garage with a bunch of lemon berries in his hands. The leaves cracked and trembled with heat over the grass, and she heard Bill's voice as he turned from the door and walked towards the window to take her hand.

'The house reminds me of so many things I don't want to forget,' he said, 'like the holiday in Spain when you and Mark brought crabs for supper.'

'But what's so special about this job?' Marcia asked. She had lowered herself lazily into the chair, and her hands reached the floor. Her head was turned away like one whom fatigue has made inattentive. But when Bill spoke, she turned sharply as though his explanation was news.

'San Cristobal is special,' said Bill, 'I feel that very strongly, and after that ceremony, I understand how easy it would be to get something worthwhile done. Look what that man Shephard has achieved in a matter of months.'

'But do they listen very much to the radio?' Marcia asked.

'They don't,' said Bill, 'and that's the whole point. I'm sure there is a way to make them listen. Take the success of the boys' programme. The place is small, and that helps. You can tell right away what kind of result you're getting. I could really make radio a living institution in this place, not like the poor clots who see their jobs as a temporary contrivance which keeps them going until something better comes along.'

'But why do they feel that way about their jobs,' Marcia said, 'if San Cristobal offers your kind of challenge.'

'You can only see a challenge if you are ready to see it,' said Bill, 'and there are lots of people for whom there is no real connection between a job and work.'

'Is Flagstead like that?' Marcia asked. She was showing a new interest in his excitement, and she sat up, leaning towards him.

'I don't think so,' said Bill, 'but he probably needs help.'

'Is that why he has encouraged you to join Radio San Cristobal?'

'We've worked together before, you know.'

Marcia had turned to speak again, then hesitated as though she were uncertain of what she wanted to say, or the reply she would get. But Bill had almost convinced her of what he was saying, and her attitude, formerly sceptical and discouraging, had quickened to a desire to believe. She saw Bill turn towards the machine again, testing the knobs, as though he were impatient to hear it talk. She wanted to laugh at his impatience, and suddenly she remembered what she was going to say some minutes ago. Bill turned away from the machine and walked towards the door. The garden had widened its grin before him. Marcia went beside him and they stood looking over the hedge.

'Do you think Mark feels the same way about San Cristobal?' she asked. And it seemed that she was hoping Bill would say yes, but her voice had unsettled him, and he looked at her a little puzzled, unsure of his answer, and with that urgent concern which one might feel for another's happiness. Then he said: 'I think he should.'

But Marcia did not press him, because she noticed Paravecino and Crabbe making their way towards the house, and she pointed in silence at them. Bill hurried across the lawn to meet them, and she turned back to the room and sat in the chair, wondering whether Mark could feel the same excitement about San Cristobal.

Crabbe had brought a large bouquet of roses, arranged in tiers against a wide green leaf of elephant foot. Marcia took Paravecino's hat and showed him to the chair. Crabbe had walked to the writing-desk. They seemed to measure their paces with infinite caution through this brief interval of greeting. Crabbe was trying to choose the seat which would allow him a direct view of Paravecino. Bill straightened the tape and clicked a knob on the machine.

'Penelope may not be down for a while,' he said, 'she hasn't been well all afternoon.'

'What a pity,' Crabbe said, 'and I was hoping so much to see her again.'

'I suppose she has heard the programme already,' Paravecino said.

'She was in the studio with us,' Bill said.

He put a few cubes of ice into the jug and stirred the punch. Marcia brought in a dish of lemon berries on a tray and set them down on the table. Bill filled the glasses with rum punch, and Marcia passed them round.

'You haven't seen Rowley around?' Crabbe asked. 'He left after lunch and hadn't been back ever since.'

'He has probably gone down to the beach,' Marcia said.

'I would like to use him next time,' said Bill. 'He might make a good Bandit King with the other three boys as the enemy.'

Crabbe laughed and raised his glass.

'I don't know how he will hit it off with them,' he said, 'he doesn't seem to mix very well.'

'But he raved about the programme,' Marcia said. 'He thinks the boys were better than anything he has ever heard.'

'I know,' Crabbe said, 'that's partly why I'm so anxious to hear it.'

'You will,' said Bill, 'but let's have some drink first.'

He drew up to the table and sat beside Marcia. Crabbe and Paravecino were sitting at opposite ends of the table. They made a semicircle with their heads turned towards the door as they watched the gradual movement of shadows over the garden where the dead leaves rose and drifted beyond the hedge.

Crabbe's shirt opened at the neck and his skin showed scarlet with a wet, red cluster of hair sprouting from the sink of his throat. His eyes were large and moist, set deep under the sharp, precipitous cliff of his brow. There was a surgical scar behind one ear where his neck turned rubbery like a plastic surface of skin that shone, hairless and smooth. Paravecino sipped the punch slowly, looking over the rim of his glass at the scarred patch of flesh behind Crabbe's ear.

'Try some of the lemon berries,' Marcia said. 'Thief says they are very good.'

'They are,' Paravecino said, 'but I won't. They make me cough.'

'Where do they grow?' Bill asked, throwing one into his mouth.

'All over the place,' said Paravecino. 'In the south they run wild through the sugar cane, but you can find them in the mid-country, too. And in the north. But I would say the place for them is the south.'

'That's Shephard's place too, isn't it?' Crabbe said.

'Did you know him before he went to England?' Bill asked.

'I never met him,' Paravecino said, 'but he had something to do with a Youth Movement. And there weren't any Indians in that.'

He frowned and wiped his sleeve across his chin.

'You think this alliance between him and Singh will last?' Bill asked.

'But he has got things done,' Crabbe said. 'Whether or not it lasts, we have to admit what he has done.'

'But it's false,' said Paravecino… 'The Indians here don't know any other Motherland but this island. Their talk about being isolated is not true. They really want to rule the place. And that's where Shephard is useful. They can use Shephard.'

'Why did you go into politics?' Marcia asked.

'There was nothing else to do,' said Paravecino. 'I had money and I was idle. But it was only after I started the party that I realised that I should have made my decision long before. You've got to get into politics, the way I've got in, to see how wrong you are in staying out. Now I know somebody has got to expose the Indian menace, and it was working until Shephard came along. That's why they acclaim him. He is their answer to me.'

'You don't think Shephard is sincere?' Bill asked.

'I don't know what he is,' said Paravecino. 'Perhaps he wants to get some of the Indians' money, perhaps he's just working off his anger against the well-to-do Creoles, perhaps he's really mad. I don't know. But he's going to make a mess of things.'

Politics was like a fever. It obsessed everyone, and it would often strike, sharp and violent as the weather, into the most harmless exchange of feeling.

Bill was anxious to hear Crabbe's views on the situation in San Cristobal. He knew that Paravecino, who was a nominated member to the Legislative Council, was too feeble an opponent for Shepherd; and he wondered whether Crabbe might have said something to suggest what the Administration were planning against Shepherd. He could not believe they would allow him to seize power without a more determined opposition. But Crabbe was noncommital. His opinions were confined to a disagreement with Paravecino on the origin of Shephard's success. He spoke as though he were a mediator who had heard the case from both sides.

He held a lemon berry between his teeth, grinding it slowly into his mouth. It seemed he had lost interest in Paravecino's appraisal of Shepherd, and he turned his head away, slowly, discreetly, and pondered the curve of the grass where the garden finished. Thief was sweeping his feet through the dry skeleton of branches which had fallen from the hedge. He hugged the branches under his arms and limped under the trees which threw their shadows behind the house.

'Do you still call your yard-man Thief?' Crabbe asked.

Paravecino felt rebuked by the levity and irrelevance of Crabbe's interest.

'It's not we,' Marcia said, 'it's he who insists that we call him Thief.'

'Is that a threat?' Crabbe asked, and glanced at Paravecino.

'I don't think so,' said Bill, 'and he is not really a yard-man. He runs the whole place from shopping to cooking and arranging for guests.'

'He is much more honest than those who put a new name on what remains the same,' Paravecino said.

They were silent. Bill felt the overtones of Paravecino's reflection, and he saw Crabbe shift in the chair and continue his silent survey of the grass and the tall flaming hedge of hibiscus.

The wind slipped through the trees, soft as feathers, and the afternoon loitered over the house. The clouds came apart, travelling slowly out to sea, and the sun caught a fragment of glass that suddenly sprang a burning circle on the window. A multitude of leaves swung out of the trees, and the light fluttered like an eyelid closing into the shade of the window pane.

Penelope was pacing up and down the room as she swung her hair into a bun. She pushed up the window and the light darted on to the mirror. For a while she stood at the window, staring over the hedge of the garden. She turned, shaping the bun with both hands, and walked back to the mirror. And suddenly her eyes fell on the light like a hole in the glass. She passed her hand over the mirror, as though she wanted to erase the flicker which it made under her eye. But the light seemed to stare at her, and she raised her head to avoid the glimmer, and considered the face which the mirror reflected.

But nothing had changed. The skin stretched tight across her cheeks and down the sides of her chin. The sun had given her hair the colour of sand. But her eyes, in a soft, brooding fullness, were still trying to leap out of their sockets. She could recognise every line and curve which the skin made, and yet she felt, as her eyes fell down the glass to the circle of light at the centre, that there was a change which now eluded her. She could not recognise the growing lack of confidence which her feeling had charged her with. It contaminated everything she did, and finally plunged her into a solitude which would soon be obvious to everyone.

Now she was trying to decide whether she should join the others in the living-room. Mark had gone out, but she could hear their voices making animal noises as they rose and drifted through the house. The parrot let off a petulant scream, and for a few moments the house seemed shocked into a brooding silence. She glanced round her room, considering the disorder which had accumulated since morning. One stocking was hanging from the door-knob while another rested like a ball of muslin on the dressing-table. The bed looked like a plague of ill-assorted articles. Two hair clips stuck out of the open pocket-book, which was surrounded by small bottles of perfumes and cosmetics. There was a stale scar of lipstick on the pillow, and rings of red hair curled up like insects on the sheet. She closed the window and scraped the cards aside into a corner with her feet. The voices had faded to a low grumble.

'If I had to choose,' Marcia was thinking, 'it would have to be Crabbe. At least he knows what he stands for.'

Paravecino polished his fingernails, flicking them deftly over his sleeve and watched Marcia slide the crushed cube of ice into her glass. The sun made a nervous shadow where the hair turned grey behind his ears. The light showed up the ageing pallor of his face with its narrow, indecisive stub of chin and its small brown eyes. A mole burnt black on the tip of his nose. His mouth was wide, soft and full at the corners, and his lips were smooth and dry. He pushed a tuft of hair back from his forehead and watched his hands, frail and elegant with sharp, deep lines like scars, disfiguring the palms. They looked almost yellow in the late afternoon light.

He was reflecting on his privilege in San Cristobal, postponing the moment he would choose to show his candour in the presence of Marcia and Bill. He did not like Crabbe, who was his rival for the Governor's friendship. They were frequent guests in each other's homes, and they often met at the Governor's Palace. But these encounters were always conducted with a subtle achievement of reservation and compromise. They could never agree on any device for obstructing Shephard, but they always avoided any error of behaviour that might have demanded an apology. They had worked out a delicate and exacting diplomacy of self-accommodation. But each had some idea how he existed in the other's imagination. And it was only an atmosphere and an appropriate argument which they needed to unburden their silent antagonism. Paravecino considered his hands as though they held the secret of all his misgiving.

'The history of a political career is never complete,' he said, 'until we have heard from the women who had influence in the life of a public figure.'

He saw Crabbe wince and fidget with his glass. Bill was smiling, a curious and perplexed distortion of his mouth which quivered, half open, above the glass.

'The women or the wives?' Crabbe said in a cautious and jocular tone of voice.

'The wives are only summoned in moments of crisis,' Paravecino said, 'but the others are always there. It is the record of a man's success which they hear. And that's what we want to know about a public figure. What, after all, was his private ambition?'

'Are you thinking about Shephard?' Marcia asked. 'There used to be rumour about a woman in England.'

'Nonsense,' Crabbe interrupted. He smiled and looked at Marcia, amiable and apologetic.

Paravecino grinned, and Crabbe hurried the glass to his lips and swallowed a mouthful of the punch.

'You've got something there,' said Bill. 'It was one of the great South American liberators who devoted his life to the revolution after his fiancée died, or deserted him. I don't remember which.'

'Is it that the women enter the convent?' Marcia asked, 'while the men throw themselves into politics?'

'I wish I could tell them what I mean,' Paravecino thought. He avoided Crabbe's glance as he looked at the bowl of ice. It was their practised diplomacy of approval which reminded him that it would be indecent to embarrass Crabbe. He was playing with the empty glass, turning it thoughtfully between his hands.

'Haven't you heard that I have a weakness for black girls?' Crabbe said.

'Mr Crabbe!' Marcia whispered.

Bill chuckled and made a hole with his finger in the ice. 'What's wrong with that?' he asked.

Marcia had become suddenly aloof and austere. She wondered whether Crabbe was trying to make some reference to her relationship with Mark. Paravecino held his glass out for some punch while he rubbed his legs under the table. 'And he thinks that clever,' he thought, glancing briefly up at Crabbe. 'He thinks he can distract us from what is true by talking casually about it. Of course he sleeps with black women. He doesn't like the niggers until he has got them in the dark. And tries to pass it off as a joke.'

'There may be something in the theory that opposites attract,' Paravecino said. 'Isn't my wife an example?'

Crabbe was waiting for the moment to strike, an animal emerging in patient fury from its place of ambush.

'But you wouldn't call yourself black, would you?' he asked.

There was a passage of uneasy silence. Paravecino was staring at his hands as though he relied on their evidence for a reply. He was not sure that it was the moment to abandon his code of secrecy. Marcia looked at Bill, then made an appropriate excuse for her departure. She was going to chip some ice.

Thief was alone. He rose from the bench and offered to take the bowl. Marcia declined his help, but he was irrepressible. He coaxed the bowl from her hand and begged her to sit until he had chipped the ice. She watched him punch and pick into the surface of the ice that cracked into frozen splinters of water. She could hear the voices raised in argument on the other side, and she wished that Thief would delay this chore. She had felt an angry resentment towards Crabbe, and she did not appreciate Paravecino's mannered and ingratiating courtesy. She was reluctant to go back into the room until they were ready to hear the recording of the boys' story. Thief put a piece of ice in his mouth and chewed it noisily. The water spilled over his lip and ran a cold, transparent line down his chin and under his shirt. He stuck the pick into the grey, packed flakes of ice and held the bowl out between his hands. Marcia rested the bowl on the table and made room on the bench. He looked uncertain, almost shy as he removed his cap.

'They r'ally crankin' up inside,' he said. 'What it is plague them now?'

'What would you expect ?' She watched him chew the ice and soothe his frozen teeth with his tongue.

'Shephard is a engine without any room for brakes,' he said. 'They can talk till their tongue run out o' saliva, nobody ain't stoppin' him now.'

She swung her arm round to reach a box of matches from behind the bowl. Thief was staring past the window out to the garden hedge. Marcia alerted him with her elbow and passed the cigarettes. He put his hand out for the matches and lit the cigarettes. Marcia noticed the shake of his hands and the look of melancholy which had dulled his eyes. She had found him sitting alone, and now she felt that her delay was an intrusion on his solitude. She wanted to tell him that she preferred his company to the deceptive courtesies of Paravecino and Crabbe. But she refrained from maligning Bill's guests, and she did not want to betray an indelicate confidence with Thief. He sat quiet on the bench, hardly noticing the cigarette which hung like weed from his mouth.

'We thought you were going to Shepherd's Rally,' she said, looking behind him for the matches. His cigarette had gone out. She struck the match and waited for him to speak.

'Was my wish,' he said, 'I was wishin' it all week.'

'But you could have gone,' she said. 'We didn't need you to help with Paravecino and Crabbe.'

Thief did not speak, and Marcia was reluctant to press him. She watched him blow the smoke over his shoulder and lean forward to scratch his toes. The voices were eloquent in the living-room. He took another puff of the cigarette before putting it out. He crushed the black stub of ash under his heel, and put the burnt half behind his ear. Marcia was pushing herself up from the bench.

'Aren't you happy with us here?' she asked, moving closer to take the bowl.

'I was,' said Thief. He paused and shifted on the bench.

'But not any more?' she asked.

He looked up at her as though he wanted to accuse her of cheating. Marcia stood erect, glancing from the bowl to the door where the voices seemed to halt, in a sudden denial of their anger.

'Why you didn't tell me Mr Mark was leavin'?' he asked as though he felt a conspiracy of silence had excluded him from the privacy of their life.

'Mr Mark leaving!' Marcia said.

'An' all along I say it was such a good an' happy foursome you make,' he said, 'with me growin' fast in the family feelin'.'

'Who told you that?' Marcia asked, and her voice was neutral as though she were accepting her part in the deception which Thief suspected.

'I wouldn't have guess a thing,' he said, 'if I didn't pass by the Pennywern Market a little while back. Was the agent dealer who ask me to tell him that the house now free whenever he ready.'

Marcia was silent. Thief lowered his head on his hands and stared at the floor. Bill was calling for the ice, but Marcia did not stir. She was frantic with speculation about Mark's departure, and she was trying to conceal her ignorance about the house from Thief.

'Mr Bill callin',' said Thief, and passed the bowl to her. 'But it was that made me miss the rally.'

Marcia took the bowl and walked like a drunk, eager to avoid attention, slowly, nervously, into the living-room.

Penelope had come down to the living-room. She was astonished by the angry eloquence which Paravecino displayed. But she could not join in the argument until she was sure of Marcia's approval. She was waiting for the men to pause so that she might evoke some response from Marcia. She heard her put the bowl on the table and she glanced up to make sure that her suspicion was false. Marcia did not speak. She was unaware of Penelope's presence or the furious exchanges which passed between Paravecino and Crabbe. She sat on the edge of the chair, and rested her head on her hands. Penelope was nervous. She took a sip of the punch and tried to give her attention to what Crabbe was saying.

'You were born here,' said Crabbe, 'and I grant your superior knowledge of the place.' He smiled and bowed like one who graciously concedes an error.

'It's not a question of superior knowledge,' Paravecino said sharply.

'There must be,' said Crabbe, 'just as I would know England so much better than you if our roles were reversed.'

Crabbe thought that his meaning had become too obvious. He saw Paravecino's eyes narrow and sparkle with resentment, and he tried to distract their attention by a sudden show of generosity. He stood and passed the cigarettes round the table. Paravecino refused, but Penelope put out her hand and selected two. She was trying to make Crabbe's gesture seem appropriate. Bill sucked at his pipe while he held the match up for them to light. He reached for the jug and filled Paravecino's glass with more punch.

'You don't believe Paravecino is right about Shephard's background being a help?' Bill asked.

He did not want to encourage the antagonism which their attitudes had betrayed, but he was interested in the conflict which this argument had started.

'Of course Shephard's background helps him,' said Crabbe, 'but if anyone else born here had used Shephard's method of attack, the result would have been the same.'

'You sound for a minute as though you could be on Shephard's side,' Paravecino said.

Crabbe understood the purpose of the retort, but he did not want to deviate from his line of argument. He lifted his glass and took a hurried sip of the punch.

'I'm on the side which has to understand what Shephard has done,' he said. 'You remember the speech to the crowds the morning after they came back from the beach? For a moment I thought he was mad to bring up all this business about India and Africa. The racial thing was bad enough already and to make people think in these terms was crazy. But don't you remember how he developed this racial theme?'

'But all this talk about India and Africa is just false,' Paravecino said irritably. 'What do we know about these places?'

'That is precisely where Shephard scored,' Crabbe answered. 'He wanted each group to get an idea of who they were and that must include where they originally came from. When he had planted that in their heads once and for all, what did he do next? He showed them that there was no difference between them, Indian, Negro, Chinese or what you like, in their relation to people like me and the Governor and what he calls the fellows at Whitehall. That's what he made clear, and there isn't a soul in San Cristobal, literate or illiterate, young or old, who didn't understand what he was saying. Whatever difference there was between them, they had one thing in common: a colonial past with all that it implies.'

Crabbe drained the glass and sawed a handkerchief under his nose. He looked angry and impatient for revenge.

'But what the bastard never mentioned,' he said, slapping his hand on the table, 'was the benefit which that colonial past had also brought them. It is this complete amnesia on the part of all people like Shephard that is a kind of madness.'

'And you would expect him to?' Paravecino asked. His voice was low, cold, and aggressive, as though he were calculating the chances of insulting Crabbe.

'Some men have heard of the word, honour,' Crabbe said, and focused his glance on Paravecino.

'It is exactly that kind of reply which has produced Shephard,' Paravecino said. He raised himself from the chair and pulled it further under the table. 'You gave Shephard an image of yourself, and then circumstances provided him with the opportunity to examine that image. If you had never allowed these colonials to flock to your country as they please, Shephard might not have happened. So they went, and you know better than I what they found. They found you in a state of disorder which was worse than anything they knew in the colonies. And it was their experience of this disorder that suggested to them what could happen when they got back home. In fact they returned for no other reason. It was you, not the colonials, who started the colonial revolution. But you can't have your cake and eat it. You can't pride yourself on liberty and deny them the experiment too. Nor can you go on enjoying the privileges of a lie at the expense of people who have discovered the lie. The image of a superior animal doesn't make sense after these men like Shephard work in a London factory or sleep whenever he pleases with some little progressive slut from the London School of Economics. You treat these men like children and forget that children have a way of growing up. And what they understand is always different from what the parents had imagined.'

Paravecino reclined further into the chair. Crabbe was dragging nervously at the cigarette. His manner had grown defensive and aloof. He motioned the glass towards the jug and smiled at Bill. He was trying to weigh the chances of a reply that would not seem too personal an assault on Paravecino's role in San Cristobal. Paravecino, he thought, the stooge of every Governor who had worked in the island during the last ten years, crawling his way like an undetected leper to some future list of royal honours. The Hon. Reginald Paravecino, knighted for services rendered. To whom? he wondered. And he talks about a colonial revolution beginning with those who ruled San Cristobal. It was not only

Shephard whom he had to fight. It was men like Paravecino whose history was like fuel which Shephard used to demolish the edifice of British influence in San Cristobal. What useful purpose could Paravecino serve against the national frenzy which Shephard had aroused? If he were not a coward and a fool, he would have led this revolt. The mob would have been astonished and intoxicated by his prestige in the island. With Shephard, one could always argue that he wanted to surpass his humble origins. But Paravecino had spent his life in an obsequious trespass on the fringes of white society. Now he had emerged with the sour and irrelevant message of moderation. And talks about an image! What image of himself has he given San Cristobal? With his English wife and his children sent abroad for their primary education?

Crabbe heard Bill chipping the ice into the bowl and he raised the glass and invited Paravecino to share in a toast of San Cristobal. Paravecino was smiling, casual and assured. He indicated the cigarette case, and Crabbe rose from the chair and passed the cigarettes round. Bill was washing his hands with the ice, and Penelope felt in his pocket for the matches.

'I think it's time for you to hear the recording,' she said. 'Bill won't say it, but I'm sure it's the reason he asked you to come.'

'Penelope!' Bill shouted. 'How dare you?'

'I wouldn't hold it against you,' said Crabbe, 'only this morning the Governor remarked on the programme.'

'Are you going to do this sort of thing when you go on at Radio San Cristobal?' Paravecino asked. His voice was suave and approving.

'If they let me,' said Bill.

He wiped his hands and poured more punch into the glasses. He could not conceal the pleasure he felt now they were beginning to turn their attention to the radio programme. He walked towards the writing-desk where he had set up the machine. They watched him play with the knobs as the tape slid like a worm round the spool. Penelope had come up behind him, leaning over the desk to see the machine.

'It was really Penelope's idea,' he said.

'Nonsense,' she said. 'I told you about the story and you never had a day's peace until you found those three boys.'

'Who are they?' Crabbe asked.

'One is Singh's son,' said Bill, and suddenly stopped the tape. He turned and shoved Penelope to one side. She walked back to the table and filled her glass. They were all filling their glasses so that no one would have to interrupt after the recording had started. Bill looked nervous and pleased. He was enjoying their silent enthusiasm for the recording. Then he raised a hand to indicate silence. A green light went on. The tape crawled slyly round, and suddenly they heard the knob snap like a finger and saw the green light fade. Bill stamped his foot and swore. The telephone was screaming like an angry voice. Someone wanted to speak with Crabbe.

They heard Crabbe's voice in a dour and sullen whisper of monosyllables. Once he glanced at Bill, but no one noticed. The exchange was brief and incomprehensible. He walked back to the table, but he did not sit. There was a look of utter astonishment in his eyes.

'I hope you don't have to go,' Penelope said.

He stooped his shoulders forward and drew the chair nearer.

'Do you know anything about your friend, Mark, and Shephard?' He was looking at Bill.

'Mark!' Penelope answered.

'Shephard is holding a rally at Sabina Square,' said Crabbe, 'and Mark is on the platform. He is going to speak.'

'Mark!' Bill said, and dropped his hand from the machine. He was ambling slowly towards the table.

'Mark to speak on a platform?' Penelope repeated, trying to attract Marcia's attention.

'On Shephard's platform,' said Crabbe, and he noticed Paravecino looking at him as though they were agreed on one issue. They were sitting in the enemy's camp.

The light had receded, and the wind swept holes through the sombre crust of clouds that spread an early twilight over Sabina Square. The hills grew dark as the mist spun slowly through the empty spaces of the sky, and the fields of sugar cane made a blue-green barricade of quivering blades that leaned like spears over the rim of the valley. The evening was a world of bees murmuring some fearful prophecy through the land. Horse-drawn, by public transport, or on foot, the enormous crowd had journeyed from every corner of San Cristobal to swear their allegiance to Shephard. He had become a frontier which they could follow without fear, a faith which had made their future certain. The voices were paying their tribute to the message which he had made his theme. His speech was a long, historic rhapsody on their grief and their reward. He had turned the short and turbulent history of San Cristobal into an intimate and familiar chronicle of gossip, a sad and shocking alternation of fact and rumour. And the voices burnt the air and echoed everywhere to the summit of the hills with the fever of his ambition. They were hypnotised with song; while Shephard sat, imperturbable as stone, hearing the slow, demented chorus of their discovery:

> *Over land and over sea*
> *Freedom shall prevail,*
> *Man was made for liberty*
> *And freedom shall prevail.*

Singh raised an arm and the voices dribbled obediently to a hush over the last syllable of their wish. Mark let the words linger in his ear, and turned to look at the dense multitude that spread like insects blinding his sight. On the outskirts of Sabina Square he could see the houses emerge like obstacles in their way. The hills seemed to lean in fear, and he wondered whether there was some source of terror or solace in that mood which Singh's arm had achieved. The silence was like a possession which had clutched their throats ordering every breath to be still. And it lasted until Singh stepped back from the microphone and lowered his arm on Shephard's shoulder, as though he were about to remind them of an honour and a burden which he himself did not want to bear. Mark saw how Shephard trembled, and wondered whether it was the touch of Singh's hand or the sound of the words which Singh declaimed. They followed like an epilogue to Shephard's speech.

> *The people that walked in darkness*
> *Have seen a great light;*

They that dwell in the land of the shadow of death,
Upon them hath the light shined.
Thou hast multiplied the nation, increased the joy;
They joy before thee according to the joy in harvest,
And as men rejoice when they divide the spoil.
For thou hast broken the yoke of his burden,
And the staff of his shoulder,
The rod of his oppressor,
As in the day of Midian.
For every battle of the warrior is with confused noise,
And garments rolled in blood;
But this shall be with burning and fuel of fire.
For unto us a child is born, unto us a son is given;
And the government shall be upon his shoulder...

Shephard bowed his head as though he wanted to cry, but Singh had taken his hand away, and the hills were suddenly loud with song:

Over land and over sea
Freedom shall prevail,
Man was born for liberty
And freedom shall prevail...

The voices droned to an echo which was suddenly cut short by a sound like a million hands prolonging their applause. It was Mark's turn to speak, and he was afraid. The silence had returned, and he felt like a willing captive offering himself to their ferocious embrace. He stood in front of the microphone waiting for memory to return the speech which he had prepared. But it was hopeless. The silence was made more frightening by his delay. Hands were waving, and he recognised the three boys standing with Ma Shephard near the platform. He looked like a man who had come with some intolerable item of news. The crowd did not know that he was afraid, nor did they know that it was the boys who had now rescued him from a speechless failure. He made a step towards the microphone, and suddenly it seemed that they were no longer there. He was talking to himself, churning his memory for the details of his early years in San Cristobal, angry vagrant in pursuit of that certainty which this crowd had made ordinary and accessible. He had spread his hands wide, embracing the microphone that gave his words to the wind and the patient, empty spaces of the sky.

'What I remember now is the legend I heard as a boy of the Tribe Boys and the Bandit Kings. We have received it in many different versions, but the end is always the same. The Tribe Boys, in an attitude which the enemy could not predict, walked to the top of the cliff, embraced and kissed, and then made their peace. It was a terrible decision, but it was made in the name of that freedom which you sing. And it had to be made... Freedom is not a habit which may be overcome, nor is it a fashion which changes with opinion. It is an instinct; it is a nerve. And the spirit which gives life meaning revolts when that instinct is threatened. It was not pride which carried the Tribe Boys on the cliff, and it was not fear or cowardice, as we know from the way they fought before their numbers were so terribly reduced. It was their last act of homage to the spirit which gives life meaning; and they saw even in the death which they chose that spirit which feeds man with a will to overcome... And the Tribe Boys won... We have a version of that legend which tells us how the Bandit Kings lost nerve when they saw the Tribe Boys make their plunge into the sea. It was an act which reminded them of themselves. It reminded them of that will which ruled them too, and they felt a respect for their enemy. The legend says that they withdrew for a while from San Cristobal because they could not enjoy on this soil the victory which they had won. And this is the lesson we learn from that legend. The freedom which you sing is not freedom for San Cristobal only. You are only servants of a spirit which possesses all men... and when you rejoice in the knowledge of your own freedom... you are rejoicing on behalf of all men. The legend of the Tribe Boys is being enacted again in the history of this Movement for freedom. For the enemy may make many retreats but will not surrender, and many may have to die. ... But it will be a death which chose freedom as it was an instinct for freedom that made the Tribe Boys choose death. And you are not the first or even unique in this collective demand for freedom. In other countries and at different times, there have been others, among them those who now dominate San Cristobal, who have had to win this freedom, sacrifice it and win it again and again... Freedom and Death, like opposites and contradictions working in harmony, are the two facts which we cannot bargain, the two great facts, Freedom and Death, twin gods or forces or whatever you like which haunt every human existence. Beyond these is nothing but that infinite and indefinable background against which we ramble in the service of Freedom and the expectation of Death. But here we can choose. And our choice is not complete until it becomes an act, for it is only action which can help us out of error... and only through the discovery of error that we may be able to define some truth...'

The rhythm of his voice had changed. The edge was now much softer, less militant, soothed by some echo of nostalgia or regret. It seemed that he had survived an argument with himself; the air was charted like a sea with familiar cues for his safety, innocent of danger. He was being borne towards a harbour that welcomed him home. The crowd had become his anchor. They formed a centre, vital and still as a root, whence he could report on what he had seen. He had entered into some agreement with them. The valley was silent and serene, but his voice throbbed like a nerve in everyone. His words were an echo made permanent in their ears, naming a faith which was old and necessary as the sun. Their silence was something terrible and free, a contagion of wonder that stained the air and acknowledged the mute importance of the trees: a dark and melancholy sojourn of time that happened before the discovery of speech. It was an act of pure participation in this vision which he was trying to describe: the image he had of men who had laboured to tame the wild and truculent wastes of nature until it had become their harbour of refuge, felt and familiar like a hand. And their attention was like worship until his voice broke, making a troubled pause in his reverie, and suddenly rose again.

'Nationalism is not only frenzy and struggle with all its necessary demand for the destruction of those forces which condemn you to the status we call colonial. The national spirit is deeper and more enduring than that. It is original and necessary as the root to the body of the tree. It is the source of discovery and creation. It is the private feeling you experience of possessing and being possessed by the whole landscape of the place where you were born, the freedom which helps you to recognise the rhythm of the winds, the silence and aroma of the night, rocks, water, pebble and branch, animal and bird noise, the temper of the sea and the mornings arousing nature everywhere to the silent and sacred communion between you and the roots you have made on this island. It is the bond between each man and that corner of the earth which his birth and his work have baptised with the name, home. And the freedom you sing... freedom...'

And suddenly his voice rose and gradually failed, like a light going out, over the word, freedom. It was the beginning of the next sentence, but he could not continue, and when he held on to the microphone, raising one arm for support, the crowd was sure it was his signal to sing the chorus. But Mark was dizzy. Singh and Shephard embraced him and lifted him to the chair. It was an honour which they paid every speaker who had moved the crowd to such excitement. They slapped Mark on his back, and joined in the chorus. But he could not follow what was going on. He was struggling quietly to recover from the awful spell which gradually possessed him. It increased with the sound of the voices until he felt imprisoned by this hallucination which now possessed his senses. The weather had turned to a furnace which boiled the sound of the voices acclaiming his speech. It was as though a terrible heat had dissected everything, like a plague producing permanent scars over the earth. He was part of a constant and perceptible disintegration of things: leaves, grass, asphalt, the hooves of the animals which waited, patient and enduring, over Sabina Square. Only the density of the hills seemed impenetrable although in parts the surface was rusting.

Suddenly the worlds of post offices and hospitals had populated his head with letters and telegrams lying silly and solitary in foreign hands. Small tubes of blood were being prepared for some tremendous measurement before his eyes. The grass suffocated, and it seemed that the earth was about to open, and life was slipping reluctantly down its cracks to be held under. It was a strange and monstrous diversity of forms and noises which inhabited his mind. And amidst this natural corrosion he could hear voices announcing the crowd's wish to be ruled. Vote for the star. Vote for the donkey. Vote for the aeroplane. Vote for the knife. It was as though the voices existed in their own right, faceless and inhuman. And gradually they gave way to the cry of a kid, the petulant, despairing shriek of the new born. The infant animal rose before his eyes in a scarlet mess which the heat slowly turned to pure fire. But he could see the revolting spectacle of its birth. It was clinging horribly to life. Then he heard the loud-speaker again, like an obscene hole depositing its remains every-where, and voices collided in the air: 'Men are equal and free. Men are equal and free. Me go to the meetin', sir, but me no listen, sir.' And someone approached with a malevolent face and black eyes, wide open and sightless, and a voice spoke: 'What is the origin of that voice which calls you to freedom? It is life on the level of pure participation. Man entering his voice.' The blind seer and Sabina Square and the liquid red birth of the animal were one. And the words came tumbling through his head again like thunder... 'life is an occasion one of whose aspects is man, but there are innumerable deviations which make for one differ-ence... consciousness... consciousness... consciousness...'

They had lifted him back to the microphone to acknowledge the applause of the crowd. He stood between Shephard and Singh, but he could not free himself from the hallucination which confused the scene before him. He leaned against Singh and he could feel only the soles of his feet. It was this portion of his body which he experienced most vividly. He thought his hands had turned pink and soft with the heat, and it seemed that his feet would soon melt and make red puddles from which his bones would emerge like poles in water. He could barely see where the old woman was standing with the boys, and his senses returned him slowly to the scene. Her face was hard and cracked like mutilated rock-face. Her eyes were covered with age; and he saw the boys shouting like an innocent class that played at being drunk sailors. But he could not identify their voices. All was lost in the sweat and passion of the crowd repeating their chorus:

Over land and over sea
Freedom shall prevail,

Man was made for liberty
And Freedom shall prevail...

The men were returning Mark to his chair, and the chorus was taken up again. The crowd wanted to prolong this occasion, and long after the rally had come to an end, they would linger in the Square rehearsing the speeches they had heard. The singing was like an illness which they encouraged. It possessed them. The afternoon spread around them like a harvest which showed their labour. But Ma Shephard was persuading the boys to take her home. She did not want to lose her way when the crowd separated, and she did not want them to continue much longer with their speculations on this freedom which they had heard.

'It never seem real till now,' said Singh, 'what those Tribe Boys do. It never seem so real till now.'

'An' the Society, too,' said Bob, 'the Society never seem so real, too.'

'You think you could ever prove your freedom the way those Tribe Boys prove it?' Singh asked.

'I could,' said Rowley. 'If a time came to prove it in the name of the Society, I could. I really could if you agree to do so, too.'

'The Society never feel so real,' said Lee. 'It never ever feel so real.'

The old woman could not hear what they were saying, but she felt that it related to the speech they had heard, and she ambled through the crowd, signalling them to follow. For a moment they hesitated, but suddenly they looked at each other, and agreed that Ma Shephard was someone whose wish they could not deny. She was not only Shephard's mother. She was also a source of some authority which was above any argument, a seer which San Cristobal would always seek. In their eyes the old woman had become Age itself. So they saw her wave, and they knew her wish, and they followed.

'I must go ahead,' said Rowley. 'I have to get back now.'

'Tell her first,' Bob said. 'Tell her you goin'. She might guess that you come without permission, and she won't like that.'

'I'll tell her that I must hurry,' Rowley said.

They fought a way through the crowd, following close behind

Ma Shephard. But it was a long time before they emerged behind the houses into the empty street. They could still hear the singing drift in harmony like the clouds to the hidden white rim of the hills. They thought only of the Society and their triumph with the legend of the Tribe Boys.

'Tomorrow we must make another work,' said Singh.

'Till tomorrow,' said Rowley.

He put his hands in Ma Shephard's, explained his hurry and then ran to the end of the road. The boys waved until Rowley was out of sight. They walked in silence all the way, but Singh knew that Bob and Lee were thinking of the next task which the Society would set themselves. And they hoped that Rowley would not get into trouble for what he had done. He had left the house without anyone's permission. He had sworn to be with the Society at Shephard's rally, and he had kept his promise.

An hour later they were standing on the steps which led to Shephard's house. A car passed, and they recognised Mark in the back seat, but the old woman had already interrupted their wish to wave. The car cruised slowly up the asphalt road carrying the echo of Mark's voice and the memory of the afternoon at Radio San Cristobal when they had challenged the strangeness of lights and microphones to tell the legend of the Tribe Boys' conflict with the Bandit Kings. The Society was a secret and a public success. Ma Shephard had rested her hand on Singh's head.

'You make me recollect a time when my son was like you,' she said. 'Your same age, an' what I tell him then, I can tell you now, 'cause the world is the same, "Lay not up for yourself treasures on earth where moth an' rust doth corrupt…"' She thought they were not really paying attention, and she did not continue.

'Make way straight home,' she said.

'Good night, Ma.'

'Don't you hear everythin' you listen to,' she said, as she swung the door open.

'Good night, Ma.'

''Night…'

Mark saw the car crush its shadow in reverse. He stood in the garden and tried to compose himself. On his way back he had found it difficult to concentrate his feeling. He believed what he had said, and yet he would have liked to find a way to correct the general impression that he was really supporting Shephard in this campaign. It was the legend of the Tribe Boys which had aroused the feeling which he made the theme of his speech. He could hear his voice like the echo of the crowd pursuing him across the garden. Freedom and Death. He had spoken a language which they understood, but there was no way of uniting his personal fear with the collective hope of the voices which acclaimed his words.

The crowd was a discovery. At first they had appeared like a vast receptacle which would swallow him without harm, an anonymous force like the night which he could let consume him in silence. The crowd was a frozen presence which hardened his identity. He existed. Mark Kennedy existed. No force could ever alter that private experience which the crowd had now made sacred. His existence, like death, was a fact. This was a knowledge beyond argument, independent of reason, absolute, irreversible. He had chosen the legend of the Tribe Boys by chance, but his speech was a report on a certainty which he could not really share. He had been talking to himself. His speech was a fragment of dialogue between Mark Kennedy and himself, and the theme was his identity. But he could not control the feeling which the crowd had aroused; and when he raised his arm, and clung to the microphone, the word, freedom, had rung in his ears like a leper's bell, and he wanted to explain that he had no right on Shephard's platform, that he had not really earned their applause.

He saw the light which framed the window and fell like a pane of glass over the garden. Someone was standing in the living-room. But he could not resist the thought of the crowd which had made him speechless by their faith, and his tongue was heavy with a feeling of guilt which he had never known. He wanted to break his silence to someone. He remembered Marcia and he made his way towards the light, then paused and tried to think what he would say.

Marcia and Bill had accompanied Paravecino to his house. Penelope was alone. She was stroking the parrot's neck, lifting the beak as though it were a live ear which she wanted to persuade with words. The bird blinked and shook its head against her hands. The claws slid restlessly over the perch, and Penelope removed her hand. She could not bear the dumb indifference of the bird, and the silence of the house and the fear of betraying her feeling for Marcia.

'I don't think Marcia understood,' she said, 'I don't think she understood what I was doing.'

The parrot nodded impatiently, then nibbled at her hand, staring at her with a curious and insane dismay.

'I don't think she understood what I was doing,' she repeated, as though she wanted the parrot to agree.

She was thinking of Marcia and the method of deception which she had used to tell the truth. She had tried to tell Marcia about the diaries, but she wanted to be sure of her sympathy before she gave herself completely away. She was afraid that Marcia would disapprove, and she had chosen to tell the truth by a method of deception which she had often used before. She had spoken with a casual and disarming innocence about something which was serious and urgent. It was a way of testing the other's response, and it was always possible to confuse the listener by meeting their horror or surprise by a show of agreement. You, too, would always feel the same way. But she was not sure that it had worked, for she could not remember, precisely, the expression on Marcia's face when she had left the room. She could not be sure what had happened, and they did not meet again until Crabbe and Paravecino arrived. She wondered what had passed between Mark and Marcia.

'But why didn't she come back?' Penelope said. 'Why didn't she come back?'

Then the parrot made a noise. Penelope heard the footstep on the door, and she saw Mark enter. He walked towards the table where the drink was kept. And suddenly Penelope felt that he had been spying on her. She had forgotten the telephone call which told her where Mark had gone. She was trying to control her suspicion.

'You frightened me,' she said, and she noticed that something was wrong.

'Would you have a drink?' Mark asked.

'Did you hear me?' Penelope asked. 'I was talking to myself.'

Mark hesitated, and Penelope suddenly thought that Marcia had understood. Perhaps she had said something to Mark before he left for Shephard's Rally. Her suspicion had detected a sharpness in Mark's voice. She could not guess his feeling, but she knew something was wrong. She tried to relax on the couch as she watched him walk towards her with the drink.

'What were you saying?' he asked.

The question had come too soon. She thought Mark had anticipated the difficulty it might cause. She felt the glass shake in her hands, but Mark did not notice. Penelope turned aside, trying to conceal the shake of her hands. But she watched Mark walk to the chair. He sat and lifted the glass as though it were an unfamiliar object which burdened his arm. She was going to wait until he repeated the question. Then she would try to say what had happened.

But Mark remained silent, almost morbid. He knew now that he would never try to tell Penelope or anyone else what had happened this evening. He was isolated by this failure to explain the guilt which he was feeling. He knew he would not be able to say why he had gone to the Rally. He would not be able to say why he had agreed to speak. He was not going to try. And it was not secrecy which made for his silence. It was a total disinclination which paralysed his tongue, and he knew that while he remained in this house, Bill and Penelope would always be anxious to make sure that his silence was no more than a day's discomfort, a passage of difficult feeling which they had learnt to accept. Their affection would not waver, but he would always be isolated by this failure to explain this sense of guilt which seemed to swell like a silence round the house. It would be better to leave. He lifted the glass again, and looked at Penelope.

Penelope was still uneasy about the shake of her hands. Mark was pouring another drink and she felt that this was the moment to be frank, Marcia had understood what passed between them this morning, and Mark knew. She watched him lean the bottle from the mouth of the glass, and she was determined to put an end to her former trick of communication. It had failed with Marcia. Her manner had changed, and she was almost aggressive in her sudden effort of self-control.

'I wonder whether it ever happened to you,' she said, trying to avoid Mark's glance. She was fingering the glass again as though her nervousness had returned.

'Without any warning,' Penelope continued, 'a feeling emerges and is a part of you. And when it's there you can't deny it.'

She turned her eyes on the glass, and argued with herself about the risk she was probably taking. Would Mark really feel any sympathy with the state of feeling which she had described in her diaries? Her confession was not a form of bribery, nor was it a way of reconciling herself to the possible loss of his friendship.

'And after it's there,' she went on, 'it seems to feed on the very presence of those who made it possible... it just grows inside you ...' She looked at Mark and wondered whether he had paid much attention to the word, those; and she told herself that she was beginning to lie. It was not quite right to say those, when she was really thinking of Marcia. But she would wait. She would wait for his reply before she made this effort of honesty final.

'And the more it grows,' she went on, 'the more it becomes a part of you, like a hand. It crawls through you... and sometimes you are taken by surprise... and you can't deny it, and you can't go through with it... because there are always others... friends, or family or whatever they may be, there are always others to whom you owe some loyalty... there is always someone you have to account to for what you do...'

She thought she heard voices in the garden and she noticed how Mark stiffened in the chair as though an ague had seized his limbs. He shot a glance towards the garden, then straightened himself in the chair. The voice was becoming audible. She thought it was Bill's. And she was suddenly afraid that she would have to go through all this again in Marcia's presence. She wondered whether it was too late to spare herself this ordeal. Did Marcia understand what she was trying to say this afternoon? Was Mark angry? Couldn't he really see! Couldn't he really feel any sympathy for her?

She saw him shift in the chair again. The voices had died over the garden, and Mark thought that he would tell Penelope what he was finding so difficult to say. He did not know why she was trying to prepare him with such caution for this example of feeling, but the word, loyalty, had suddenly twisted his hearing. He owed some feeling of loyalty to his life with Penelope and Marcia and Bill. Loyalty required explanations, and he did not want to explain anything. He was not inclined to say why he wanted to leave the house. But he was going. He would not continue to live in this house. Penelope watched him cover the glass with his hand.

'Are you feeling all right?' she asked. The question was a preparation for what she was beginning to suspect. Marcia had understood.

'I am all right,' said Mark.

'I think I hear the others,' said Penelope.

'It's only Thief,' said Mark, 'but when Bill comes would you tell him that I have decided to find another house. I don't want to tell him myself.'

He was going to add that he regretted having to tell her. But he noticed she was about to cry, and he thought it better not to speak. He saw her gulp the drink and clutch the glass between her hands. And she thought that it would have been better if she had told them about the diaries. This method of telling the truth by deception did not work. But at what point could she have done so? At what point could she have been frank about what she did not understand? And she remembered the afternoon on the cot when this feeling, like a stranger, deceived her sense of touch and confused her memory of Marcia. She was sure they would meet again but she would have liked to bury the memory of this evening with Mark. She brought the glass to her mouth, then slowly returned it to the table.

'Promise none of us shall ever talk about this ever,' she said.

She saw Mark brush his nose and she thought she had detected a tear swelling his eyes. He nodded.

'I hope Bill will understand,' he said.

And for her sake Penelope hoped so too. They were both silent, retreating with grave and similar reminiscence into their solitary and different worlds of understanding.

3

The night was clear and cool, and I tried in a moment of idleness to count the stars. I was leaving Penelope and Bill. I had no explanation to offer them. But I remembered a similar departure: the day my mother travelled to Southampton to find out whether it was true that I had already embarked on a ship for New York. I knew that she had not come to rebuke me. She wanted simply to understand my silence which then seemed like an act of resentment against her. And I wanted to say that nothing had changed and that I was grateful for the life we had shared after my father's death. But I watched her all morning from the deck. A gentle, affectionate and generous woman. My failure was complete. And when she died, two months after my arrival in New York, I felt an incredible sense of relief. It was as though her death had purged my life, and then I wished her alive in the certainty that I could at last explain. Now it has happened again.

I felt no moral compunction to invent an excuse for Penelope and Bill. I was going because I was disinclined to stay. Thief carried the luggage to the truck while Bill and Penelope talked with Marcia at the gate. They kissed Marcia. We shook hands, and I wanted to say that nothing had really changed. The truck drove us away, and I heard Marcia beside me, hysterical with weeping, but I felt no urge to take her hand although it seemed that I had stolen her life and made my impulse hers. This feeling of disinclination had throttled my tongue.

PART THREE

1

Bird Island is a flat surface of rock almost completely covered with trees and nettle. It forms a narrow neck of land to the north, then fattens and swings like a shoulder at its southern tip where the sea turns shallow and finally peters away over a wide passage of sand. On the maps of San Cristobal it looks like a little smoked ham thrown half a mile from Paradise Point. At noon it seems utterly deserted, but it meets the sun each morning with an incredible chorus of song, and in the evening there is a similar traffic of birds returning home. The sea makes a slate-grey lagoon still as glass on the west side, and at low tide some people may be seen wading out to the island to honour an old legend that the lagoon was once a sulphur spring which could wash any sickness away. Rheumatism and gout, asthma, bronchitis, madness and the loss of memory are some of the afflictions which have been washed in the still, healing waters of the old lagoon. And once a month it is streaked scarlet with the punctured heads of fighting-cocks, dripping blood. The birds migrate and the island becomes the hideout for this forbidden sport.

'Once I see a cock watch his eyes drop out right in front him,' said Bob, 'an' he couldn't move for not knowin' where to turn.'

'Did they stop the fight?' Lee asked.

'When the whistle went,' said Bob, 'they stop it there an' then. But the next cock which win was bleedin' bad too, like his head was a pipe leakin' all night, an' the owner grab him up, put the head an' the beak in his mouth an' lick it clean with spit. Then they jump in the lake an' bathe like two people who understand what happen.'

'But there doesn't seem to be anyone on the island now,' Penelope said.

208

'Perhaps we too early,' said Lee.

Penelope paddled her hand through the water and watched the boys spar with the oars. Rowley had changed places with Bob at the halfway mark. He leaned to one side of the boat with his legs drawn high up to avoid contact with Penelope's naked thigh. She had removed her beach dress and was reclining astern in a gold and black polka dotted swim suit. She did not notice Lee's uneasiness whenever his eye caught the soft, red waves of hair which sprouted like false weed over her legs. She was looking at Rowley and Singh slapping the oars in the water.

Behind them, at the far end of the boat, Bob was crouching with his hands buckled round his knees. She noticed how Rowley interrupted his glance whenever his eyes met hers, and she wondered whether he had taken the boat without his father's permission. She wondered too about his relation to the other boys. She had never seen them together before, but she had heard Mark telling Bill about the morning he had watched them staring at the ground before chasing into Paradise Wood. It was Rowley who had begged her to make this visit to Bird Island, and he was taking the boys, he said, as his appreciation of the story which they had told on the radio. There was nothing to suggest that he really knew them. They hardly spoke during the crossing. Rowley was unusually quiet, she thought, and Lee's face never changed its expression, patient, taciturn, almost severe.

She was observing the three who sat directly in front. Rowley was her neighbour, and she was more familiar with the Crabbes than she might have been with Bob's father or Singh's. She was used to Rowley running in and out of the house on his way to Paradise Point; but her acquaintance with the boys was limited to the afternoon they told their story on the Sea Walk and the similar meeting in the radio studio with Bill. She thought that Rowley was also a stranger to them, and she was curious to see whether their faces showed any sign of an awareness that he was Crabbe's son. She could not help thinking of the roles which Lee's father and Singh's were playing in San Cristobal. But she did not want to start any questions which might make them more estranged than they appeared.

Bob was preoccupied. He was not aware of Penelope staring at him through the space which separated Rowley and Singh. He was thinking only of the bargain which they would make on their return from the cockfights. That was their purpose in bringing Penelope to Bird Island. They had loaded three sacks of sand which were left under the grape tree, and they were hoping that she would agree to buy the sand. Rowley was using her presence as a way of distracting attention from his association with the boys; but they had all agreed on the Society's work for the day. The trip to the island would be a free gesture on Rowley's part, but the sale of the sand was their real motive for this journey.

Penelope glanced slowly, critically, from Bob to Singh, observing, as though by instinct, the obvious physical difference between them. Bob was working his little finger round the rim of his nostrils, black and pancake in shape. The bridge hardly rose from the wide socket of bone between his eyes, and the skin sagged like a lid coming down to close the space of his nostrils. One eye looked crosswise with a scarlet patch like fresh blood showing in the junction of the lids. His forehead was low and narrow, receding slowly into the frugal shelter of hair, tar black and crisscross like spools of wire recoiling on itself. His neck rose to an unusual height from the sturdy plunge of his shoulders backwards. But his lips were thin and sharp where the edges turned in at the corners of the mouth, and his skin slipped sudden and rigorous to a dimpled point at the base of his chin. It seemed an abrupt and distorted conclusion to the slack folds of skin which crawled out from under his nose across the loose-hinged bone that traced his jaws up to the wrinkled flap of his ears.

Penelope observed his ears more closely, struck by the way they grew out from his skull, hanging like question marks from his head. There was something about his face which made her suddenly conscious of Rowley and Singh and Lee. Bob's face seemed irregular, problematic, unfinished. It wavered between a perfect symmetry like that of Rowley's and Singh's, and some early derangement of features. She looked again at Singh plunging forward with the oar and felt the difference which made Bob stranger and less accessible than Rowley or Singh. Singh's face was tidy, precise. The hair parted and fell in a logical disorder over his brow. His nose was high, elegant and strong. The line of the mouth was sharp and clean, and the skin showed everywhere an easy graduation of shade, rich brown like sugar round the mouth up to the shadow of the eyes.

Singh felt her glance turned on him and he wondered for a moment whether she had suspected their motive for this ride to the island. He glanced at Rowley and Lee, and Penelope pretended to show an interest in the island.

'I can't see anyone yet,' she said, sweeping her hand through the water. She felt a little embarrassed by her own curiosity, and she did not look up to observe Singh's face.

'Perhaps we too early,' said Singh.

Bob glanced over his shoulder and repeated what Singh had said. But he was not sure. They were getting near, and he thought it was time they saw some signs of preparation for the cockfights. Usually you could hear the men's voices arguing about the order of the fights, or placing bets. He had to control his own surprise at the silence which Penelope had remarked, and he thought he should say something to forestall Penelope's curiosity. Lee looked a little uncertain too, and Rowley did not speak. But Singh increased his effort with the oars, and hoped that someone would talk with Penelope.

She was wading her hand in the water while Singh and Rowley sparred with the oars. Bob glanced over his shoulder towards the island, and repeated what Lee had said. They were arriving too soon.

'The islan' hold some history too like if it was a next San Cristobal,' Bob said. 'The Tribe Boys use to wash in the lake before they make ready to do battle with those Bandit Kings.'

'Like it was a kind o' good-luck beginnin',' Singh said.

'An' the Poor Pilgrims use it,' Bob added. ''Tis the lake they use to baptise those who want to born a secon' time. Like Ma Shephard. She was like me when she born a secon' time, an' in all those years she say she never ever slide back into sin.'

'Were you born a secon' time?' Rowley asked. He was smiling, but he noticed that Bob seemed suddenly uneasy, and he turned his head and watched the end of the oar cut through the water. Bob was going to say something about the secret Society when his eye caught Penelope peering over his head towards the island.

211

'I only watch them once come up from the water,' he said. ' 'Twas when my mother decide to get her soul save. The preacher dip her in three times, an' then they all sing, "up from the grave she arise," like it was true–true resurrection…'

'An' what happen after?' Singh asked.

'Nothin' happen any different,' said Bob, 'but she was always talkin' to my father, tellin' him to get born again, but he say he was not gettin' born again, 'cause he done sign his treaty with Satan an' he would always be slidin' back…'

'But your mother stayed born again?' Rowley said.

'She say she slide back twice,' said Bob. 'One time in word an' one time in deed. But she never say what the word was or the deed she do.'

'I think I'll go in the lake before the cocks begin,' said Rowley.

'We almos' there,' said Lee.

'There's only one boat on the beach,' said Penelope.

Lee was offering to relieve Rowley of the oars. The current had slowed them down, and Penelope noticed that Rowley was now much slower in lifting the oar out of the water. He bared his teeth and strained backwards, tightening his grip as he levered the oar up from the water. But Singh was trying to test his resources against this unfamiliar change of current.

'Go easy here,' said Bob, ' 'tis where the sea turn like needles till you hit the shallows.'

' 'Tis only two minutes' sweep,' said Singh. The oar twisted in his hand and the spray flew over them. He was coughing as he tried to renew his effort. ' 'Tis only a two minute sweep,' he repeated.

'How you goin'?' Bob asked, and slapped Rowley on the shoulder.

'Going,' said Rowley, 'I'm going.'

Penelope drew her legs up and spread the dress over her shoulders, but the boys had lost interest in the hirsute thighs and the dark sunburn that shadowed her chest. Lee could not understand why they did not hear any noise from the island, and he could see one boat only on the beach. Something must have happened to prevent the cockfights from taking place. The island looked empty.

'Two more sweeps before the shallows,' Singh shouted, like a man trying to encourage himself.

'Not so fast,' Rowley said.

But Singh did not seem to hear. They had reached the middle of the passage where the water hopped and spun. The boat felt rubbery under them dipping and lifting with each thrust of the oars. Lee was looking anxiously towards the island, but Bob watched the sea and glanced from Singh to Rowley. The current was sharper than usual. The waves capped and sprang behind the oars. And the boat crawled reluctantly forward. The oars had lost the rhythm of their plunge down and away through the water.

'Two more sweeps before the shallows,' said Singh.

''Tis not the first time you say so,' said Bob, 'the oars not listenin'.'

'I don't mean one an' one exact,' said Singh, 'why you tryin' to cross my luck.'

''Tis your technique,' said Bob. He was teasing, and he wanted Rowley to take some comfort from his criticism of Singh. 'Seems to me the islan' goin' out to the ocean.'

'I would follow it,' said Singh, chopping the oar into the water.

'Go easy,' said Rowley.

'Only two sweeps,' said Singh. 'This water not behavin' natural today.'

'It know who to fool,' said Bob. He saw Penelope smile, and he added: 'I goin' have to save your face from some shame.'

Singh did not reply. He had lunged forward with a violent thrust of arms, and Rowley felt an elbow jam into his ribs. He scrambled to balance himself, and the oar slipped from his hands into the water. Singh's stroke had swerved the boat away, and the oar drifted out of reach. Penelope spread her hand out, felt the oar rub the tip of her finger, and lurched over the boat in a grab for the oar. The sea jerked the boat to the side which supported her weight. She missed her balance and toppled into the water. The boys were in panic. They leapt after Penelope who had clutched the oar and was swimming fast towards the shallows where the waves had buffeted the boat ahead of them. They had some distance to cover before they could touch sand, but Singh had forgotten his oar which was drifting away from the boat.

Rowley's shirt looked like a sail ballooning over his hands. He had discarded the oar and was fighting to reach the shallow. Singh heaved the oar towards the boat drifting jerkily ahead. Lee was helping Rowley to surface as he struggled towards the island, but Bob and Singh made for the boat, pushing the oar ahead with each stroke of their arms. They believed Rowley would soon reach the shallow with Lee. And they were determined to retrieve the other oar before making for the boat.

Singh saw Penelope swimming leisurely towards the shore, and he changed direction. He shouted at Bob to follow him and they swam towards the boat. Penelope could swim, and Rowley and Lee were crawling safely towards the shallow. Their panic had subsided. It was now no more than an exercise in adventure, familiar and simple as the stroke and paddle of limbs which propelled them forwards. Bob and Singh swam abreast, determined to recover the boat and row it to the brink of the sand ahead of the others. They were sure they could overtake them. But Rowley and Lee were almost there, and they settled for a race with Penelope. She had put some distance between them, but she was no nearer the shallow, and the boys rowed furiously forward. Rowley and Lee scrambled up the sand, laughing and panting. They were recovering slowly from this hilarious adventure when they realised that Penelope had taken a dangerous route towards the shallow.

Her voice did not reach the shore, and they could not distinguish the ordinary wailing of the waves from the furious and demented pounding of Penelope's arms. She was too far away, fighting wildly to escape the sudden pull of the tide down and away from the shore. She had drifted where the currents crossed and made a whirlpool. She leapt forward, beating her fists as though the sea had made a barricade which surrounded her. She had kept her head above water, but she was getting giddy. She wanted to wave to the boys, but she could not determine their direction, and she could not distinguish the shapes ahead of her. The trees and the beach were blurred. She remembered that the shallow could not be very far away, and she renewed her effort against the threat of the tide pulling her down. Her legs were tiring and her shoulders seemed to swell under the weight of the water which blinded her eyes. She tried to think only of the nearness of the shallow, but whenever she lowered her body to explore the depth with her feet, the water pulled her deeper, and covered her head. She had disappeared. A moment later she had surfaced. Now she felt suspended above the water. Her feet had emerged, and she felt an arm rub her waist, towing her backward. The whirlpool seemed to spin and slip angrily away from her reach. She was moving without effort, but she was too tired to talk. She clutched the arm round her waist and paddled her feet. The clouds were brightening above her. The water was familiar. The shallow was waiting to support her feet. Which of the boys, she wondered. The arm was strong and sure under her. But she could not see the boys who were all waiting on the beach. They stood there, astonished and terrified. They had not seen anyone enter the water, and they were speechless now they saw Shephard emerge with the beach dress and settle Penelope on the sand.

She lay on her back and Shephard took her hand like someone nursing a wound. Gradually Penelope raised her legs from the sand and tried to prop herself up with one hand. Shephard was standing. The boys hurried forward to hear what had happened, all except Rowley. He did not move, but the others did not notice. They stopped suddenly, waiting for Rowley to join them. But he stood where he was, and they thought he was afraid of meeting Shephard. They did not press him. It was Penelope who had made them uneasy. She was now looking up at Shephard as though she did not recognise him. The boys were near. They could hear Shephard saying something about the cockfights. Penelope saw them approaching and waved them away. She did not want them to crowd round her. They stood, uncertain and a little ashamed. They thought she had rebuked them for what had happened. Shephard was walking away, but Penelope did not welcome them. They hesitated, wondering what would happen.

Then they turned back and ran towards Rowley.

He had walked a little nearer the boat which Singh had tied with a rope round the rock. They stood beside Rowley who was staring at Shephard and Penelope. They had not seen anyone else on the island, and they assumed that the other boat was Shephard's. But they did not speak. They watched Penelope pull her legs slowly up and press them against her hands as though she could not remem-

215

ber where she was. Shephard was turning the bend of the sand towards the tree whence he had witnessed the incident in the sea. The boys gazed round the rock and nettle behind them, and tried to compose themselves. They would not move until Penelope had called them. But it seemed that she was still trying to understand what had happened when she felt the strange male arm round her waist and saw Shephard retreating past the rock and nettle through the passage of trees which almost hid him from sight. Penelope did not seem to remember them. She was staring towards the tree where Shephard now sat. She stood, brushing her hands in a nervous flick down the back of her thighs. And the boys waited.

'It look like she nearly drown,' said Bob. He was spitting salty saliva as he spoke. 'But I say she was an all right swimmer an' she know the currents that side.'

'How Shephard get out there?' Lee asked.

'I didn't see nothin',' said Singh, 'nothin' at all.'

'It look like she nearly drown,' said Bob, 'it look we nearly cause terrible trouble.'

'I didn't see nothin',' said Singh, 'nothin' at all.'

'What goin' happen?' Lee asked.

Rowley was silent. He seemed to be thinking of something more terrible than Penelope's misfortune. He was staring up at the trees, turning his eyes everywhere as though he expected someone to emerge from the nettle and attack them.

'What happen to you?' Bob asked. 'You feel bad?'

'What you lookin' for?' Singh asked. 'Your stomach turn?'

Rowley did not answer. He was staring through the trees, glancing now and again at Penelope who had raised herself from the sand. Penelope sat up and turned to see what Shephard was doing. Rowley crossed his fingers scratching nervously against his leg.

'What happen?' Bob asked.

'I wouldn't have come if I knew this would happen,' he said.

'It ain't your fault,' said Singh.

'She won't mind,' said Bob. They were trying to console him.

'We didn't make it happen,' said Lee, 'an' it seem she all right.'

'Not she,' said Rowley. 'It's my father. He is going to know about the boat.'

They were silent. Bob looked at the boat, and then glanced towards Penelope. She was shaking the water from her hair, looking up from time to time to see where Shephard had gone. It seemed that she had forgotten the boys. Singh turned to Rowley.

'You think she goin' tell your father what happen?' he asked.

'Not she,' said Rowley. 'It's because of Shephard he will know.'

'Shephard!' Lee whispered, as though he was shocked.

'What you mean?' Bob asked.

'Since when Shephard seein' your father?' Singh asked.

Rowley did not answer. He was staring through the trees again. The boys were waiting for him to speak, but they did not press him for an answer. They were only curious about this strange relation between Shephard and Rowley's father. They noticed the change which had come over Rowley. He was silent now. They felt he knew something which they could not guess, and he was afraid.

'You don't see any more boats?' he asked, looking towards Penelope.

'There ain't no cockfightin', it seem,' Bob said.

'What you thinkin'?' Lee asked.

But Rowley did not answer. He stood staring through the nettle and round the bend of the beach where Shephard had gone.

Penelope stood and continued to shake the water from her hair. She signalled the boys to wait and looked at the tracks which Shephard had made on his way back to the tree. But she did not move. She was trying to trace the stages of her feeling from the moment she felt the hand drag her up the sand and settle her gently to a rest. It was Shephard who had rescued her, and she was grateful. That was all she remembered: the casual embrace which lifted her up from the water, and the slow sense of relief as she felt her legs stretch over the sand. But her first awareness of him hurrying back to the tree had revived her memory of the episode on the plane. She was not afraid, for she remembered how he had lifted her arm to examine the burning patch of skin which the pebbles had made over her elbow. She held her elbow and watched the traces which his feet had left. One danger had helped to obscure another, and Shephard's assistance had had the effect of reducing the episode on the plane to the moment when she felt him struggle to rescue her from the whirlpool which had locked her in.

It was a simple exercise for Shephard, but the urgency of his manner, at once personal and disinterested, had influenced this double feeling which now troubled her. She was grateful and curious. She thought she would speak with him. It was her duty to thank him again. But he had shown a lack of interest in her presence when he walked away. He told the boys that the cockfights would not take place, pointed to show where they should row on their way back to Paradise Point, and walked away. That was the end of his interest. Yet Penelope felt that he had looked at her with some misgiving as though he wanted to say something which a personal embarrassment had made impossible. He was firm, uncommunicative; yet there was something gentle and easy in his manner until he turned away and walked back to the tree where his blanket was spread.

She could see him in the distance imprisoned in the wide shadow of the tree. He held his head down, reading. And her gratitude seemed to recede like any ordinary response that was momentary, correct; and her curiosity persuaded everything she thought of doing. She wanted to speak to him.

She glanced behind her to see whether the boys were still there, but there was no one in sight near the boats. Rowley had taken them in a fearful pursuit round the island. She hesitated, looking up and down the track of sand which Shephard's feet had made back to the tree. She stared towards the top of the tree, impenetrable and dense with leaves. The cluster of branches was thick like a solid mass of black cloud hanging over the evening. She walked forward slowly, wondering whether Shephard had noticed her. He had not yet raised his head from the book. She looked over her shoulder again, but the boys had rambled out of sight. And she wished Marcia were present. It would have been easier if there was someone who knew all that had happened during their flight from England to San Cristobal. She was getting nearer. Shephard had seen. She could not turn back, but she was unsure what would happen. Her memory of the plane had resisted every other recollection of Shephard as the popular leader in San Cristobal.

Shephard closed the book when he saw her approach. Penelope

was trying to smile, but she noticed that Shephard paid little attention. He watched her as before, unsmiling but relaxed. She decided that she would make an apology for this interruption, thank him again, and go in search of the boys. But Shephard's manner was now courteous and precise. He had saved her the trouble of making an excuse for lingering. He put the book away, and made ready to meet her.

'You are welcome to sit,' he said. He got up and spread out the blanket to make another seat. Penelope was trying to offer a polite objection, but Shephard had already taken his seat. He indicated the opposite end where Penelope might sit. She paused, trying to show her gratitude for what he had done.

'If you think I do not look cheerful,' he said, 'it is because I can laugh only when it seems necessary. In England you smile when there is nothing else to do, and it has always seemed to me a sensible convention. There are some faces which you find it difficult to look on without the protection of a smile. I have learnt to look in the other direction. It is boorish, I know, but it is more in keeping with my conviction.'

Penelope was not prepared for an answer. She could not overcome the surprise which this sudden fluency had wrought. She had not hoped to hear much from Shephard. At best, she believed that any conversation would have created itself from the usual, preliminary noises of goodwill. But Shephard had made these stages obsolete. He had surfaced from his silence, without any show of regret, into the middle of a whole life's obsession. Words offered themselves like honesty, free.

Penelope was indecisive. She tried to avoid Shephard's glance as she stooped slowly on to the blanket which he had spread. She looked at the book which was lying face down beside him, and wished that the boys were near. She was not afraid, but she needed company to help her support this feeling of estrangement which Shephard had aroused. She felt utterly foreign in his presence. She thought she heard a noise of feet, but the boys were not in sight. Shephard leaned his head back and stared up at the trees as though he had heard it too. But he did not speak. He was observing the hair on her legs and the shake of the hand which supported her weight. The leaves showed dark velvet shadows over her face. Her suit hung loose and wet about her. Penelope could feel his eyes exploring the swim suit and the beach dress dripping with water across her waist. But she could not find the courage to intercept his glance, and she leaned to one side and wrung the dress with her hands.

'Mrs Butterfield…'

Penelope started, and Shephard pretended not to notice. He lifted the book and looked for a moment at the page before putting it back on the blanket. Penelope was curious to hear him. The dress had fallen on to her legs and she waited for Shephard to speak. He rubbed his hands over his naked chest and stared beyond a little cliff of stone and nettle towards the sea.

'What we both remember now is that afternoon on the plane,' he said.

'I had hoped we wouldn't talk about it,' Penelope said easily. Her voice was cautious, apologetic, as though she wanted to avoid offending him.

'I had not hoped to mention it to you,' he said, 'but since we both know what we're thinking, it is better not to pretend nothing happened.'

Penelope was feeling for words. She wanted to relieve Shephard of the need to express his regret, but he showed no embarrassment while he spoke, and she wondered why he should have chosen to remind her of the incident on the plane. She saw him draw his legs up and spread his hands over the blanket.

'What would you think if something of the kind happened again?' he asked. Penelope was trying to say something when he added: 'Not with me this time, with someone else.'

Suddenly the episode on the plane had become uncomfortably vivid in her mind. Penelope seemed to ease away, making distance between them. She was trying to control the fear which his question had started. She was going to say that she would think the person crazy when she remembered what had happened that afternoon. She checked herself, and tried to steady her gaze on Shephard.

'I wouldn't know what to think,' she said, and hoped that he would not bother to think about the plane.

Shephard hesitated. He had nodded as though he approved her

answer, and Penelope saw him turn to stroke the cover of the book. He seemed controlled, even harmless, as he tapped his fingers on the book and thought about what he wanted to say. Penelope's fear was gradually giving way to a new curiosity.

'Why did you ask that question, Mr Shephard?' She was trying to make a show of courage by returning to the incident on the plane, but even as she spoke, she felt it was unwise to renew his interest in the plane. She looked to see whether the boys were near, and Shephard could feel that she was uneasy.

Shephard was slow to speak, but he wanted to assure her that nothing would happen. He turned the book over and over on the blanket, playing idly with the covers. Then he stopped and looked up at Penelope.

'Suppose the same thing happened to you several times within the next year or so? What would you think?' He was looking at Penelope as though he needed her to answer. She hung her head and wondered what Shephard was trying to say. Was he still mad? But his manner was easy, almost gentle as he watched her.

'But if that happened...' said Penelope. She paused, showing her surprise at this extraordinary suggestion. 'I should probably be worried to know why I attracted this sort of behaviour...'

She thought she saw him smile. She stopped suddenly and stared at Shephard, wondering for a moment whether this was his idea of a joke. But his manner was calm and thoughtful. There was no suggestion of play as he spoke, and Penelope became suddenly tense and uncertain. What was it he wanted to say? She thought of the boys, but she did not turn. Shephard was still looking at her.

'I would be worried in the same way,' he said. He looked away for a moment, reflecting on what Penelope had said. Then he added, as he turned to watch her again, 'I simply ask the question to find out whether you and I, in similar circumstances, might feel the same way. It is clear we would. That is all.'

Penelope could not be sure of his intention, and his explanation did not help to make his meaning clear. Ordinarily she would have thought there was something odd about the way he said, 'that is all.' It seemed to arrive at the wrong moment in his talk, a conclusion which was in no way connected with his original enquiry. Nor was it his idea of a joke. Shephard was serious and calm. There was no suggestion of callousness. He was relaxed, thoughtful, sure.

Penelope was waiting for him to continue, for she had come to feel like an audience in his presence. He had emerged as a speaker who deliberately postponed his point, waiting, perhaps, to bring his listeners more into line with his feeling. But this did not strike her as a calculation on Shephard's part. His manner was spontaneous and free, so that the silence which followed was restful. It was an interval during which he seemed to have forgotten what he had said. Penelope imagined that his mind was like a room with several doors, through which the same person entered every now and again, using a different door, but appearing always to have come from the same direction. There was no break in the passage of his thought, and yet each stage was a new beginning which moved always to an end he had not disclosed. Penelope looked temporarily distracted. She was looking towards the sea where the boys were walking, but she did not see them. She turned suddenly, and the break in their silence was like a clap of a hand on her shoulders.

'Let me tell you now,' Shephard said, 'and there is hardly need to repeat it, there was nothing personal in my attack that afternoon on the plane. I did not know you.' He paused. Penelope was intent like someone waiting to receive an order. She seemed apprehensive and impatient. Shephard continued: 'But I did not have to know you. It was enough to see you.' He had put a sinister emphasis on the words, 'see' and 'you'.

'But why?' Penelope asked, and her analogy seemed to have found its total shape. Shephard had not spoken when she repeated the question. Then he turned, imploring her to be patient. She was waiting for him to speak. She saw him smile like one reminded of his folly.

'I can remember exactly what happened,' he said. 'When I attacked you on the plane, it was another woman I saw.' He paused, but Penelope always knew when he was going to continue. She was silent. He looked at her in the manner of a drill instructor asking the ranks to close.

'This is not too difficult to explain,' he said. 'When I saw you, it was another woman who was standing before me, and when I attacked you as I did, it was neither you nor the woman I was attacking. It was myself. It was me. I think I was very clear-headed by then.'

He was looking at Penelope in a way which had already asked his question. He was not sure whether he had made himself clear. Penelope felt no urge to interrupt. She was thinking about what he had said, completely silenced by the earnest and persuasive concentration of his face. He was utterly absorbed by his own understanding. 'It is so clear to me,' he said, 'now that I have completely got over it. And that is why my life is what it is today.'

He had leaned forward while he spoke the last sentence, and now he was coaxing his back gently against the tree. His hands closed in a union of fingers across his stomach, and he glanced at Penelope as though he had said all that he wanted to say.

Penelope tried to speak, faltered and tried again. Shephard pretended not to notice her difficulty, but the words had already warned her of the sympathy which she felt for Shephard.

'This woman,' said Penelope, 'she was the one you were in love with?'

She looked apologetic when she noticed Shephard's agitation. She was hoping that he would not bother to reply, but it was soon clear that he did not care to be secretive.

He nodded, brought his hand to his brow, and then glanced at Penelope.

'And she resembled you,' he said, 'almost in every detail.'

Penelope seemed no longer uncertain about her safety. She had become a little more relaxed and sure, and she looked at Shephard as though she wanted to say something which would console him for this loss which had threatened his sanity. He is not really mad, she told herself, he is not really mad. But he is not safe with himself. He will never be safe… Suddenly she checked her thought and tried to speak with Shephard. But he seemed distracted. He seemed to be thinking about all that had happened before he returned to San Cristobal, and Penelope became suddenly aware of the interest which she was taking in Shephard. She was staring at him, the smooth, heavily muscled chest and the naked skull. This was the same man who made San Cristobal tremble and rejoice with promises and threats. But now, alone, in the solitude of this barren island, Shephard seemed harmless. Above all, he seemed to need someone to share his private torment. Penelope wanted to stretch her hand and touch him. She could hear the sea turning noisily behind them; and above, the trees, whipped gently by the wind, hissed and swayed. The sun spied them through the leaves crushing the still black shadow of leaves into her skin. And she thought of Marcia and the diaries and the evening they walked from the market stall when Marcia collapsed on her shoulder and wept for fear that Mark might leave her. She could hear Marcia's voice as she watched Shephard. The two had become inseparable in her mind as though they shared a common bond of misfortune. Shephard must have loved this woman as Marcia loved Mark. And she remembered that evening, vivid as the episode on the plane when she embraced Marcia and felt some terrible male resource overcome her with sympathy and power. Was that the beginning of my feeling for Marcia, she wondered. Was it then that something went wrong? She remembered the diaries and tried not to think of Marcia.

Shephard was still staring at the book, turning his hands over the covers, and Penelope watched him, now quiet and brooding, almost innocent in the candour and dismay which his silence betrayed. And she was feeling again, like the power which Marcia's anxiety had aroused, this sudden urge to touch Shephard. He was alone, abandoned. It was a private grief which had brought him to the solitude of this island. She looked at her hands and remembered Marcia. She could not trust them to deny the power which might lead them to Shephard in a gesture of sympathy. She held the dress and squeezed the water on to her knees. Marcia and Shephard were equal in their need. Their names were synonyms for a feeling which she had never really known. She had never known this crushing sense of loss which was the price some people paid for loving. But she felt again that primitive power which it aroused when she confronted those who were its victims. A power which seemed to feed and increase on their admission of defeat. Their private suffering was like fuel which nursed her own confidence. Was this the bond between herself and Bill? Was it Bill's dependence on her which had sealed their life and made him hers? Bill, safely kennelled in this power which now reminded her of Marcia and the soft, black brooding face which Shephard raised as he looked up at the trees.

She thought she heard someone stir in the trees, but she did not move. She was looking at Shephard while she worked her fingers aimlessly over the blanket. She saw the whites of his eyes, flawless and familiar as fresh milk. And she realised that there was something set and ominous in his expression. Shephard was thinking, and while he showed this restless preoccupation, she felt uneasy. She could not be sure that he was wholly defenceless against his loss. He could feel her eagerness to speak, and he looked at her. Penelope had become cautious and defensive again.

'But it is not unusual for these things to happen,' she said.

She was trying to console him. Shephard seemed to understand her sympathy, but he was not moved. He was beyond anyone's sympathy at this moment, wholly concerned with what he wanted to say. He wanted to leave Penelope in no doubt about the value he had placed on this experience in England. It was not a sense of loss which had seduced him to share this confidence with her. And there was no longer any trace of regret in his feeling for the woman or his life in England. Experience was like an instrument which he had learnt to use. He had spoken to Penelope because their meeting on the plane had somehow put him in her debt. He owed it to her to disembarrass himself from any feeling of guilt towards her. She need have no reservations about him or the incident on the plane. That was what he was thinking when he remembered what she had said and looked up to answer. She noticed the change which had come over him, but she was beginning to treat this variety of mood as natural. She was not afraid, only curious and a little impatient to hear him speak.

'It may not be usual,' said Shephard, 'but it was through her deception that I discovered something about myself.'

Penelope was growing uneasy. She felt it would have been improper to speak, but the silence was like an interval during which Shephard was preparing himself for speech. It seemed that he was trying to put words together after a long period of separation from them, like tools whose use he had to learn all over again. But the voice was calm, almost devoid of feeling.

'Most people do not discover anything,' he said. 'They learn things, or they hear about them, but that is different from seeing, really seeing something. I discovered that until then, until that experience, I had always lived in the shadow of a meaning which others had placed on my presence in the world, and I had played no part at all in making that meaning, like a chair which is wholly at the mercy of the idea guiding the hand of the man who builds it.'

He paused to find an example that would make things simpler, but now he seemed in a hurry to speak, as though his vision had some way of escaping if he did not hurry to pass it on.

'Take the chair,' he said, 'that may help. It is impossible for a chair to object to the way it is being made, to say I prefer to look like this. A chair can have any size or shape, but a chair could never object to being a chair.'

He paused, steadying his hands as he watched Penelope.

'Now take me. I am not a chair, but this meaning placed on my presence in the world possessed me in the same way that the idea of chair is from the start in complete possession of any chair, irrespective of its shape, size, usefulness. Any chair is a chair. Similarly, the meaning I speak of had already made me for the other's regard. A stupid me, a sensible me, a handsome me, any me you can think of always remained me. But like the chair, I have played no part at all in the making of that meaning which others use to define me completely.'

His voice had grown sharper. His eyes flashed, and his hands were shaking with the excitement which gradually shaped his words. He was staring at Penelope who tried to conceal her agitation.

'And it was only through her deception that I discovered this,' he said. 'When I attacked you in the plane, I was attacking the meaning which had made me and to which I was exposed utterly by the woman who looked like you in every detail.'

He glanced over Penelope's head as though he wanted to summon some witness to prove his point. 'That meaning of which I speak applies equally to millions, but I say I was attacking myself because this me was the example I knew most intimately. I was beginning with myself.'

He had become quieter now, guiding his hand gently over the

book, reflecting, it seemed, on what had happened and what he had said. Ordinarily he might have noticed the change in Penelope's expression, but he was too eager to make himself clear. He leaned forward as though he wanted to share a confidence, and his face tightened again. His voice was severe.

'It is too crude an explanation, but quite forgivable, to say that I went into politics because of my experience with that woman. That experience was only a condition which precipitated my decisions. It is truer to say I went into politics in order to redefine myself through action. And just as it was a certain deception which preceded a certain understanding, it would seem that a certain regression is necessary for any leap I may make, for any other me to emerge.'

He brushed a trickle of sweat off his nose and rubbed his hands slowly over the blanket.

'Take the chair again. I begin by behaving like a chair. Now I have reached the stage of behaving like an extraordinary chair. I am like a chair which understands and which revolts by saying, fine I accept that I am a chair, for all practical purposes of human regard, I am a chair, but I shall behave on occasions as though I were not a chair. For example, I will only let you sit on me when I feel like it! Similarly, I accept me as the meaning I speak of has fashioned me. I accept. For all purpose of simple understanding, I agree that I am that me. But from now on, I deny that meaning its authority. When it suits my purpose I shall use it, when it doesn't, I shall be hostile. In fact, I am at war. That is a statement I make often in my speeches. I am at war. But neither the whites who get scared, nor the natives who are glad, quite know my real meaning. And the whites are terrified because I say that if I win power, and there is no doubt about that, I shall begin my business by changing the whole curriculum of privilege in San Cristobal.'

There was a pause, sudden and deliberate. And soon his voice returned, quiet and grave in its new emphasis. He had found some peace in the knowledge which he was about to impart.

'And you know something,' he continued. 'It is not the threat of losing jobs, or living in less extravagant circumstances, which really worry them. They're used to enough personal poverty in Europe. But they are really frightened that the order of privilege which is an essential part of their conception of themselves can be revalued, redistributed, or even abolished completely. They are terrified of becoming like the chair which is defenceless against the idea of chair. I am the one who now sees them, not they me.'

He leaned back against the tree. He looked weary, resigned. His eyes wandered past the nettle which ran wild around them; then settled patiently, unseeing, on the book. He did not see Penelope's face twisted and charged with weeping. Her eyes were sore, her nose red and quivering.

'I come here when I want to be alone,' he murmured, 'but this meeting was accidental. And I talked because I thought I ought to tell you that I am not a cut-throat. I am just a particular brand of man who, in certain circumstances which are old and may remain with us for a long time, refuses to be that man. When I speak of regression I simply mean that my rebellion begins with an acceptance of the very thing I reject, because my conduct cannot have the meaning I want to give it, if it does not accept and live through that conception by which the others now regard it. What I may succeed in doing is changing that conception of me. But I cannot ignore it.'

His voice was barely audible when he spoke the last two words. He was overcome by the sudden and terrible conflict of emotion which Penelope had betrayed. It was beyond anything he could have foreseen during this exchange with Penelope. She could not control herself any longer. Shephard stared at her, startled and speechless. He could feel the pressure of her hands clasping his, and he watched her eyes open and close, springing a shower of tears down her cheeks. For a moment he was lost for something to do. He did not know whether to withdraw his hands, what feeling it was which her action had betrayed. She understood what he had said, but he could not tell what prompted this show of feeling. She was beyond herself with weeping. He waited for her to recover, and glanced at their hands hanging together like living objects beyond their understanding. Was this pity? Or her guilt? Did he make her think of herself as one of the enemy whom he was waging war against? He could not tell, but her sobbing was difficult to bear. He eased his hands away, and tried to raise her head. He wanted her to compose herself and explain what had happened. This spectacle of Penelope had become more important than anything he had said this evening. Her pathos was a match for his anger. He was struggling to say something which would help, but Penelope seemed distracted, remote. He could not reach her with any show of sympathy. She was alone, left wholly to herself, irrevocably outside Shephard's power to understand. She dried her eyes. She wanted to speak, but words were going to be a waste of effort. She was thinking of the diaries and the sense in which she had seen herself condemned in relation to Marcia. To be Penelope in spite of… in spite of… To be a man in spite of… in spite of… She tried to avoid looking at Shephard as she dried her eyes, for this was the meaning she had extracted from all he had said. To be a man in spite of… in spite of… It is the other's regard which he has set out to alter. She could hear his voice return in all its obstinacy and pride. He would begin by accepting the verdict of his enemy as a way of changing himself and the enemy as well. He would begin by accepting all that he had set out to rebel against. To be Shephard in spite of… To be Penelope in spite of… To be a man in spite of… The phrase stood out like the origin and end of all her understanding. In spite of… in spite of… She raised her body from the blanket and held her hand out. She wanted to go, but she wanted to let him know that she understood this feeling which had disfigured his innocence and separated him from himself.

She would see him again for she felt he ought to know that he was not really alone. Perhaps she too was his enemy. She could not avoid that. But she wanted to let him know that those he called the enemy were equally torn by a similar contradiction which had made him a hero in San Cristobal. There was only this difference, she thought: his enemy was without the energy which had urged him seek some release in action. They could not recapture this turbulent peace which would always haunt his life with anguish and promises of reward.

She heard a rustle of leaves above, like a branch slipping down the tree, and she remembered the boys. Shephard lifted the blanket and wrapped the book inside it. Penelope pointed towards the boat and waited for him to walk ahead. He did not move, and Penelope noticed the look of regret and apology in his hesitation. But she did not speak.

'If there's anything I can do,' Shephard said with some caution.

'To meet again,' Penelope faltered. 'If it is possible to meet again.'

The boys stood on a small precipice of stone wringing the shirts dry, but Rowley could not overcome the fear that his father would discover what he had done. He was trying to think of a way to explain his meeting with the others without having to say anything about the secret Society. He thought he had seen the end of his adventure with the boys and a return to the loneliness which he felt at home. He flapped the shirt again in the wind and beckoned them to continue with the search. Bob and Singh were trying to persuade him there was no one else on the island but Shephard and Penelope, and that everything would be all right. But his future with the boys seemed uncertain. He was helpless with suspicion. He crept past the drooping fence of nettle, and the others followed, each making a line with one hand that gripped the waist of the other from behind.

'Sometimes I hear my father say he goin' do somethin' which he never do,' Bob said, 'he just talk 'cause it come into his head, an' he want to hear his mouth say somethin'.'

'Sometimes my father do that too,' said Singh.

'This is different,' Rowley said. His voice was breaking. 'It wasn't me he said it to. It was the Attorney General he was talking to when I heard them.'

The boys hesitated as though the sound of the word, general, had given them some fearful inkling of what Rowley meant. Bob was wondering, too, what his father would say if he met the Attorney General in their house.

'But even if what you say is true,' said Bob, 'they can't get one man to follow a next wherever he go. One man can't keep up with a next like that night an' day.'

'He got to go to sleep some time,' said Singh, 'but I hear my father say that sometimes people follow people just the way you say.'

'My father knows where Shephard sleeps and when,' said Rowley. 'Every night, it makes no difference. My father knows. I tell you I hear when they agree to have someone different from time to time follow Shephard wherever he goes.'

'But Shephard bound to see the man sometimes,' said Bob.

'Shephard wouldn't know,' said Rowley. 'The way my father can arrange it Shephard wouldn't know. He could be talking to the same man and not know what was really happening.'

'A man can't follow a next man like that,' said Bob. 'It ain't natural.'

'But even if there was such a man here now,' said Singh, 'perhaps he only tell your father 'bout Shephard. He won't got time to remember he see you too. 'Tis Shephard he lookin' for, not you.'

'I know,' said Rowley, 'but you never can tell what he will remember.'

Rowley was trying against hope to believe them. They stooped under the nettle and crossed a pond of stale water before following the track which led to the lake. Then they saw Shephard waving to them from the strip of beach. They hurried towards the boat trying not to show their suspicion. Shephard was helping Penelope into the small boat which was tied to the rock beside Rowley's. Shephard and Penelope were ready to go. The boys could not delay them, but Rowley had paused. They were standing under the tree where Shephard and Penelope had sat.

'Did you hear that?' Rowley asked.

'You mus' be hearin' things,' said Singh. ' 'Tis only leaves up there.'

He looked towards the tree, but Shephard was waving. They had to go.

'We'll row side by side till we reach the Point,' said Shephard.

He watched them enter and wade forward. The air was beginning to swell with the sound of birds cruising high up towards the island. The boys worked the oars through the water in silence, and everything was still except the familiar bird song above their heads, and the dark distant noise of a launch crawling slyly from the shore towards the old lagoon.

2

The Indian waiter looked at his watch and swept past the counter into the adjoining room. The cashier was waiting. The voices made an anonymous noise in the far corners, and she noticed that the faces were similar in the half-dark. She stretched her arms and yawned, gazing vaguely past the doors and the tall poinsettia fence to the massive screen of trees waving in the shadows. The voices rose and petered away without any echo, indeterminate and obscure like the intervals of twilight between the tables. The air was idle and cosy, waiting for the familiar traffic which would soon start the night. The girl was casual as the trees overlooking the fence, climbing her fingers up and down the keys of the cash register. And suddenly she felt the astonished silence of the room. The voices had fused to a hush. The air was startled by the glitter of chromium and glass, and the faces, now nervous and discreet, turned to make a wordless apology for their surprise. The lights had gone on in the Pink Curtain lounge. The Indian waiter had returned. The cash register gave out an angry shriek, and a hand clapped for service. The faces became individual and familiar in the light, and the voices gradually resumed their muted criss-cross of talk.

'What it is bring Mr Chance so early,' the cashier said as though she were talking to herself.

'I wonder,' the waiter said, and glanced over his shoulder to check who were sitting with Chance.

The table was at the end of the lounge under the window which framed a wire basket of fern. Chance sat with his back to the door that led out into the garden. There was a similar arrangement of tables and chairs in the garden. An old man was sitting alone under a ceiling of plaited grape vine, sipping his sherry. His stick was hanging from the chair, and his Panama was turned upwards on a smooth slab of stone that came loose from the walk. Under the dark green alcove, where the twisting ribs of the fence embraced, a barbecue was smoking. The air turned blue from the spitting glow of the coal. The old man sat still, staring over the fence as he strained to hear what Chance was saying. The voice was audible, promising always, it seemed, to reward his patience; but the words would not connect, and the sound surrounded him like the night, elusive and near.

Chance took another sip of the beer and fixed his eyes on the Indian who sat opposite. The man never lifted his head as though his neck had been trained to lean at a certain angle, avoiding a direct exchange of glances. The woman sat in the middle on the other side, neutral as the spectacles that cut her nose. She had nothing to say that might satisfy Chance or embarrass the Indian.

'But word must have got back to your department,' Chance said. 'The Public Relations office isn't all that tight.'

'Tighter than the journalists believe,' the man said. 'You can ask her.'

The woman gave no indication that she had an opinion.

'Then I'm telling you,' Chance said, 'the week after Assistant Commissioner Parnall saw Singh and Shephard I knew there was going to be trouble. Do you believe that?'

'It's possible,' the Indian said.

'I also knew,' Chance added, 'that they made a mistake when they got tough with Parnall. He knew too much for them to take chances, and it was Crabbe who begged him to stay after they dropped the charges against him.'

'Did you also know that he had already made up his mind to go?' the Indian asked.

'That I didn't know,' Chance said. 'Nobody knew that as far as I can see. But they might be in a hell of a mess after the elections because he was the only man in the whole official set-up who understood Shephard and Singh. And I believe he had influence over them.'

The Indian lowered his head to the rim of the glass and sucked up a mouthful of orange squash. He raised his eyes level with Chance's shoulder and watched the blue-black tide of smoke drifting from the barbecue over the fence. There was a gradual hum of voices in the garden where a few couples were collecting for drinks before supper.

'I think Parnall was a good chap,' he said, 'don't you?'

He did not raise his head, but the woman felt the accurate probe of the shoe under the table.

'He was always very nice to me,' she said. The voice was austere, and her eyes, eager and intelligent behind the clouded lenses, remained incomprehensible.

Chance drained his glass and swung his legs out from the table. He had seen Butterfield approaching the lounge from a small side door. He watched for the Indian's reaction, and then pushed himself slowly up from the chair. The woman realised that Chance had been waiting for Butterfield. She felt more relaxed, and stretched her hands against his, urging him to stay. The Indian was smiling.

'Let's know what he's up to,' the Indian said, twisting his mouth to indicate the table which Butterfield had taken.

'Are you sure the two of you will hit it off?' the woman added.

'About as well as you…' Chance checked himself, waved his hand in a reluctant gesture and walked across the room to join Bill Butterfield.

Butterfield stood and the two men shook hands. Chance put a hand on Bill's shoulder and forced him gently into the chair. Bill was glad to see him. He clapped his hands for the waiter, but Chance insisted that it was Bill's turn to be the guest. They ordered a large rum punch and a Cristobal beer.

'What's that?' Bill asked. He had barely caught the angry mutter of Chance's voice.

'The little coal-face wretch behind me,' said Chance. 'Ever since the father screwed her she can't tell black from white.'

Chance intended his gossip as a show of confidence, but Bill did not respond. He had the stranger's nervous sensitivity to questions of taste, and he did not understand why Chance, who had the same complexion, should have emphasised the woman's colour. But Chance had lost none of his ardour. He unbuttoned his jacket, and waved the waiter to hurry.

'How do you manage in this heat?'

'I manage,' said Bill. 'It's quite cool here.'

Chance took another look round the Pink Curtain lounge as though he were looking for the temperature. Someone waved at him from the other side near the restaurant, and in a matter of minutes, it seemed that he was waving to everyone.

'In our work you just get to know everybody,' he said.

'You like working in Radio, don't you?'

'It's hell,' said Chance, 'but I like it.'

He was waving again as he spoke. A girl, the colour of red brick, with a ginger wig and clipped blue eyelashes shuffled towards the table to have a word with him. He spoke and passed her on like a package sliding down a shoot. She smiled all the way as she disappeared through the door towards the restaurant.

'Something's cooking,' said Chance, 'and I'm not sure what the devil it's all about, but Flagstead has been on the telephone to Government House all day. He asked me to say that he won't be long.'

'Have you just left him?' Bill asked. He looked at his watch and thought that it was rather late for Flagstead to be still in the office.

'I gave him a lift,' said Chance. 'He went to have a word with the Governor's A.D.C. It must have been urgent.'

'I've been here once before,' said Bill, 'but it was almost empty. Is this the regular crowd?'

Chance nodded. He was pouring the beer as he talked. His arm was expert, and Bill watched him, fascinated by the assurance which marked every gesture he made. The glass leaned, and the beer churned smoothly within the glass until the foam reached level with the rim.

'One or two live upstairs,' said Chance, 'but the majority come for an evening out. The faces are different, but the kind of majority is always the same. Business, the Civil Service, doctors and lawyers, and sometimes a teacher.'

'The English at the bar are merchant seamen,' Bill said.

'How did you know that?' Chance asked.

'We are branded on the tongue,' Bill said.

'Funny, isn't it?' Chance said. He sipped his beer, looking over the glass at a couple in the corner. The woman's back was turned to them, but the man had a perfect view of the whole lounge. He was chewing a sandwich, looking up every now and again, as though he were expecting someone.

'That's Crabbe's Information Officer in the corner,' said Chance, 'and his wife.'

Bill glanced discreetly in their direction. He could hardly see

235

the man's face for the bush of beard which burnt red above the plate.

'What's his job here?' Bill asked.

Chance was not sure he should speak. But he realised that his delay was obvious, and his refusal to be caught off balance forced him into speech.

'I don't know exactly,' Chance said, 'Very few people know. He's just known as the expert.'

'Hasn't he an office somewhere?'

Bill thought that Chance was being cautious, and he took a pleasure in watching his assurance at work.

'His office is in one of the Government buildings,' Chance said, 'he's a sort of contact man. He advises Crabbe and the Governor on public feeling. It's his business to know what's going on.'

'Does he get about very much?' Bill asked.

'Everywhere,' said Chance. 'You'll probably see him again somewhere else before the night is out.'

Chance had looked across at the table again, and their eyes met. The man waved, grinning from behind his flaming beard.

'Crabbe just got the whole lot where he wants them,' said Chance. 'He's Chief of Police. He runs the Government Information Services, and he has shares in Radio San Cristobal.'

'His mother is going to be president of the Red Cross,' said Bill.

'I know,' said Chance, 'is only his son left without position.'

The waiter was standing beside the table. Chance took the drinks and tugged at his sleeve.

'Ram!'

'Yes, Mr Chance.'

'When you going into politics?' Chance grinned.

'When you put my name in the radio, sir.'

The waiter laughed and watched them knock their glasses.

The lounge was gradually filling up, and Chance's hand was waving like a flag which knew everything about the place it ruled. He liked Bill, but there was one flaw in his affection. He felt that the meeting with Flagstead was important, and he did not know what it was about. Instinctively he saw himself involved, and that rattled. He was the sort of man who is most deeply humiliated by exclusion of any kind. He could not be flattered by an invitation, but he would always feel insulted if he had not been invited. And if the error occurred with people whom he had offered friendship, then it seemed a kind of treachery. Flagstead had learnt how to deal with him. If you did not think Chance an appropriate guest, it was always safe to invite him, making it clear that you were absolutely sure he would not enjoy himself, and arranging, perhaps, to meet him afterwards. Once he had been convinced of his exception as a privilege, his absence was certain.

Flagstead had mentioned his engagement with Bill, and he had asked Chance to keep him company until he arrived. But it was clearly an appointment that Bill had arrived for, and Chance suddenly felt a certain vagueness about his place in Flagstead's arrangements. But he was expert at concealing his doubt. He swallowed a mouthful of beer, and went on talking eagerly, with excessive goodwill like an irrepressible guide educating tourists in the imaginary names of tropical fauna.

'That's the editor of *Truth*,' he said, jerking his head towards the door. The waiter was arranging chairs round a table in the small garden. The waiter settled the table not far from the barbecue, and waited for an order. The editor waved his secretary to her seat and called for lemon squash.

'He never drinks hard,' Chance said, 'and I don't think he ever asks the secretary what she'll have. In any case he doesn't need to. She's not the sort of person who ever chooses anything.'

The editor was leaning over the table, twiddling his fingers. The secretary sat erect, almost shy, staring at the table. The editor was talking, and then the girl raised her head, a movement of studied caution and reserve, to see who occupied the other chairs in the garden.

'You understand what's happening?' Chance said. He was smiling, leading Bill with a casual benevolence through the mysteries of social intercourse in San Cristobal. 'That girl has never been here before.'

'Is it the sort of place…?'

Chance had interrupted. 'Nothing to do with colour,' Chance said, 'as you can guess from me. She's first generation middle-class.'

237

Bill seemed a little puzzled, but Chance went on, scraping the glass as he talked. 'She was born in a place called Ruby Lane, about a mile or so from here. It's slum area. She still lives there.' He finished the beer. 'With a figure like that, shorthand and typing will take care of the rest. The trouble is she dare not live on her own while her mother is alive, and the mother won't ever leave Ruby Lane. It puts the girl in a hell of a spot, and the mother isn't what you'd call a lady. "If those so-called bigshots like the look of you," she tells her, "let them come and see who help you and where it happen." She's never been taken home before midnight, and insists you leave her in the main road, because the house is just round the corner, and the mother might be awake.'

Bill was not sure why Chance had been so informative about this couple. He thought there might have been a touch of malice in his story. But he was delighted by the girl's presence. She was slim and dark, almost Indian in the fineness of her features. Her hair was very long, iron-combed, with a faint gloss like glass glinting in the sun. The teeth were firm as rock and milk-white. They emphasised the fullness of the lips when she smiled, and gave a pleasing lustre to the whole face. Her eyes had a strangely oriental shape, large and full at the centre, but narrowing lazily upwards, into the arches of the brows. In different circumstances, Bill thought, those eyes might have given her face a startling radiance, matching the brilliance of her teeth. But now they worked under a peculiar constraint. Sometimes her glance darted, object-like, as though a certain surprise had alerted them; and when she turned again, rearranged and at ease, their light seemed to close in a willing failure, like those petals that retreated from an approaching hand. Her timidity had returned. There was something contradictory about the impact which the man beside her made.

He was short and square, with plump shoulders which seemed all one with his neck and his chin, aggressively compact in his attitude of precise and daring self-assertiveness. He seemed to know exactly where he was and what he wanted. Bill watched him and thought he represented a long and difficult achievement: a history of peddling, promotion, setbacks, surprising recovery, a long postponement of goodwill, some cataclysmic conversion to love of his neighbour, disappointment at himself, and a new beginning in a life that had waited with vindictive patience for its final achievement. He had vindicated himself. He knew who he was and the kind of world he lived in.

Chance said, looking outside towards the garden where the couple sat, 'They say he is a crook.'

The waiter returned with the two glasses of lemon squash. He set them down and lingered a while round the table. The editor was still twiddling his fingers, talking to the girl, darting his head here and there in casual nods of recognition to those who passed. Then he snapped his finger, as the waiter had anticipated, and ordered a snack. The girl's attention was divided. She looked at the menu with an air of careless bewilderment, thinking carefully what she should have, remembering at the same time to guess with her feeling the moment she should begin her squash. The editor passed his finger down the menu as though he were drawing her attention to an error, and then she nodded. They had chosen alike.

As the waiter turned away, she brought the glass to her mouth, taking a quick medicinal sip, examined the glass in her hand, and then returned it to the table. This was the manner of her drinking, a kind of domestic operation which had been arranged in stages. Her long, slender fingers held the glass by the tips as though the palm of the hand resented the shape. But her eyes kindled, betraying the spiritedness which they concealed. It was always then that Bill noticed the beauty of her eyes in that swift and individual scrutiny of the glass. But the editor's movements seemed all bundled together, like soiled linen which had been collected for the same future. His large, square head made a little plunge forward, and his arm caressed his chin, and the glass slid through his hand on to the table, half-full. Another arrangement of his arms and a sudden thrust of the chin upward, and the glass was on the table, like a magician's trick, empty. The girl was still going through the stages of that delicate and demure exercise.

Chance said: 'But frankly, I don't think he's half as dangerous as Crabbe. Bellows would murder you mercilessly with an axe, and then order anyone present with the same axe to clear the mess. But Crabbe will bury you alive, without a trace of death, and with infinite mercy.'

Bill glanced across at the English couple who were talking quietly, almost with an air of secrecy, like a family whom exile has brought closer together. The wife was beautiful, blonde, with blue-green eyes and fine, black eyelashes. There was a trace of disdain in that easy and relaxed survey which she made now and again round the lounge. It was the manner which Chance described as, having class. He believed that in England this couple had class, which simply meant money.

'You wonder why such people choose that kind of life,' Chance said. 'He is little more than a Government spy, and she, well, what the hell can she be in a place like San Cristobal, meeting the same dead crowd every night. It's almost pathetic to see the two of them walking out in the evening, just walking, three or four blocks to the right, three or four blocks to the left, and then it's either supper with the same people or back upstairs where they live, talking about what happened in the day, always the same day, the same talk. Work.'

The couple were about to leave. The woman walked ahead towards the door which led to the stairs. The man lingered behind, sawing his handkerchief under his nose. Then he quickened his pace, slapped Chance on the shoulder, saying in an affable, almost endearing way, 'How is Sinclair?' and continued through the door.

'You'd think,' Chance said, 'that people with money would have a feel for living.'

'It's people without money who don't care about it,' said Bill. 'They can afford to. The rich are more practical.'

'With the kind of money they've got,' said Chance, 'South America or Casablanca would be more my line.'

'I suppose they have their reasons for choosing San Cristobal,' Bill said.

'And a job like that which doesn't allow you to ease up ever?'

'Some people need to be anxious,' said Bill.

'That's a kind of sickness,' Chance said, 'real sickness in my opinion.'

'And so is idling,' Bill said. 'Perhaps Crabbe too feels that an exacting job in San Cristobal makes more sense than the irresponsible and extravagant pleasure which Casablanca might offer.'

When Flagstead arrived, the lounge was feverish with laughter and talk. The whole town seemed in the mood for extravagance. The Pink Curtain was a very expensive restaurant. The food was never very good, but the place had a reputation for catering to people of importance in San Cristobal. Its exclusiveness was, as Crabbe or Bellows would have argued, wholly economic; but the economics of status, as Chance would have reminded them, bore a very close relation to what he called, having class; and this was, in turn, modified, and often made very complicated, by the most intricate distinctions of colour. There were no rules, no discrimination for which any definite and final label could be found. This was a matter which, like instinct, was known, but could not be formulated. It regulated conduct, and yet it would have been difficult to explain conduct as wholly the product of it. In many cases, and Chance was a good example, it would have been arbitrary and illogical to argue the fact at all.

Flagstead did not speak to Bellows who had raised his head from the plate and was anticipating Flagstead's greeting. The girl noticed his surprise, and watched Flagstead until he reached the table occupied by Bill and Chance. Bellows looked at her as though he were suggesting that it was not her business. Flagstead had not spoken to anyone, except the waiter, whom he asked to take an order.

It was then Chance noticed that something was wrong. He got up, immediately Flagstead had sat, and pretended to be in a hurry. The waiter had passed the menu to Flagstead who gave it to Bill.

'You're sure you won't have a drink before you go?' Flagstead said. Chance hesitated, just long enough to suggest that his departure was not deliberate. Then he said, 'No.' Flagstead ordered two rum punches, and said he would probably see him later. Chance left.

'He's very good company,' Bill said, laying down the menu. 'And very informative.'

'Very,' Flagstead said. Then, as though he were trying to put Chance out of his mind, he added: 'I'm sorry I'm so late. Let's move into the corner.'

Bill would have liked Chance to stay, partly because he found him fascinating, and partly because he would have liked to see how he and Flagstead behaved towards each other. There was a side to Flagstead which Bill had not known. They had met each other as undergraduates, and later in London. He had seen Flagstead several times since his arrival in San Cristobal, and both he and Penelope had remarked about the change in his manner. He was still amiable, warm and frank. But there was something, at the same time, which seemed obscure. And this was the first time, Bill thought, that he was seeing the old Flagstead. This was Flagstead of the old days. Bill recognised him, and he laughed. Flagstead was angry, and, it seemed, a little hurt. The Pink Curtain seemed transported to another world with different faces, and Bill was about to behave as he had always done in the past whenever he caught Flagstead trying to control his anger. He was going to double the quantity of his drink.

'Have a large rum punch,' Bill said.

But Flagstead replied very promptly: 'No, thank you.' Bill was shocked by the abruptness, the angry assurance of his reply. It was not, after all, the old Flagstead.

'The last time I saw you like this was at the cottage in Fern Row,' said Bill. 'The night we had the party.'

Flagstead stared through the prints of his fingers on the glass. 'How is Penelope?' he asked.

'Not so good since Marcia left,' said Bill, 'but we'll get used to not seeing them every day.'

'Did you know all along about Mark and Shephard?' Flagstead asked.

'Nothing,' said Bill, 'not until the meeting at Sabina.'

'Even you he kept in the dark.'

'I wouldn't put it that way,' said Bill. 'Did I ever tell you about his experience with Marcia and the Christmas tree?'

Flagstead nodded and took another sip of the punch. He was trying to postpone the moment when Bill would hear why he had asked him, at such short notice, to meet before supper in the Pink Curtain. But he was growing impatient, and Bill's innocent lack of suspicion made him nervous and clumsy.

'Do you really want to stay in San Cristobal?' Flagstead asked.

'But, of course,' Bill said. 'And I told you why. I think I could help.'

'And Penelope, it's all right with Penelope? She likes it here?'

'I've no reason to think otherwise,' Bill said. 'Do you?'

Flagstead hesitated. 'I only wanted to be sure how you felt,' said Flagstead, 'and now it makes everything more difficult.'

Bill wavered, trying to guess Flagstead's meaning.

'Has something happened to make you cancel the job?' Bill asked.

It was not like Flagstead to hedge like this if he wanted to confess to Bill that he could not employ him. After all, Flagstead was the manager of Radio San Cristobal, but he did not own it, and all his decisions had to be approved by the directors. Radio was a business like any other, and Flagstead was an employee.

'I've been overruled,' said Flagstead. 'It's the first time it's ever happened to me here.'

'But you said they had confirmed the appointment,' Bill said. 'What happened to make them retract?'

'It's your letter,' said Flagstead, and he noticed that Bill was, for a moment, completely lost.

'What letter?' Bill was not yet in touch with his memory.

'It's the letter you sent to the Press,' Flagstead said.

'But it hasn't appeared,' said Bill, and his mind was now concentrated on the letter. He saw no connection. 'I was going to telephone today to ask them why they hadn't published it.'

'They won't,' said Flagstead.

'Then why don't they return it? I enclosed a stamped and addressed envelope in case they didn't think it worth the trouble.'

'They can't find it,' said Flagstead.

'But how do you know this?' Bill asked; and then, very quickly, before Flagstead could find a way back to the question of the job, he added, 'and what has my letter to do with Radio San Cristobal?'

Flagstead leaned closer across the table, and his voice was a whisper. He glanced at Bellow and the girl, and then steered his glance down at the table as though he were talking to the glasses. Bill recognised for a moment the old Flagstead, apparently cornered, trying to explain something which he felt very strongly about.

'I didn't see the letter,' said Flagstead, 'so I can't criticise it. But your references to the Governor's speech at a time like this would

243

never have been allowed. And that's the trouble. Sir William Bird had dinner with the Chairman of the Radio board, and they both agreed that you would be a risk…'

'Sir William Bird is the Governor,' said Bill as though he were giving Flagstead a new piece of information.

'But Crabbe has shares in Radio San Cristobal,' Flagstead said.

Bill paused. He was expecting that, but it was no part of his enquiry. For the time being he could not care less who had shares in Radio San Cristobal. It was the importance they had given the letter that interested him.

'Sir William saw the letter?'

'Of course,' said Flagstead. He looked up at Bill as though he thought the question was childish.

'But the editor had no right,' said Bill. He glanced across at Bellows. 'What right had Bellows to show my letter to the Governor?'

Flagstead raised his body from the table. He looked at Bill as he would have done in the past if they had found themselves together in a similar situation.

'Listen Bill,' he said. 'It's the way things are done here. Chance wouldn't have turned a hair about it. No native of San Cristobal would, except people like Shephard.'

Bill started at the name Shephard. But Flagstead had stopped. 'And it's not Bellows who showed Sir William the letter,' he said. 'It's not that direct. Bellows might have published. He likes that kind of sensation. But he passed it on to Crabbe to find out whether it was safe in the first place. Crabbe naturally showed it to the Governor who might have let it pass. But Crabbe advised him against allowing it. Crabbe always knows where there's danger, and Sir William trusts his judgement. I wouldn't doubt that it was Crabbe's suggestion that you would be a risk at Radio San Cristobal.'

'My letter was quite simple,' said Bill. 'I merely said that if the authorities were going to risk giving a constitution that would soon make San Cristobal completely self-governing, they should accept all the consequences of their risk. Let San Cristobal decide as the Dutch would in Holland or the British in General Election. The Governor has no right to interfere, and he was interfering when he made complimentary references to Paravecino whom everyone knows is involved in the coming elections. There was nothing offensive, and nothing particularly dangerous about that.'

'You have no power to say what is dangerous,' said Flagstead.

'But in any case,' Bill answered, and his tone was angry, 'the editor had no right to do what he did, to me or anyone else in a similar position.'

'Bellows does what he is told to do,' said Flagstead.

'But *Truth* is not a Government paper,' Bill argued. 'It's a commercial venture like Radio San Cristobal, and it's wholly independent of Government. It's not even subsidised. It doesn't owe Government money. It pays taxes. It is independent. So is Radio San Cristobal. If they want to support Government policy, fair enough. They have their reasons. But they are the only two means of public communication on the island, and if they have to take orders from the official administration, you know what that is. There is a word for it. I didn't say it in my letter because I didn't know, but that seems to be the case.'

'Nobody ever gets shot here,' Flagstead said.

'But it's because you don't have to shoot anybody,' said Bill, 'and it's why you can say that Chance wouldn't have turned a hair if he discovered he was being treated like a louse. Chance can be fired at the snap of a finger.'

They stared at each other as though they could not explain what they had understood. Bill waited while Flagstead scraped the glass aimlessly over the table.

'I'll tell you something,' Flagstead said. 'Five years ago I would have raised the same hell. We know each other well enough to talk. If you needed the money, I would have put up an argument. But this morning I simply tried to explain that I knew you, and I didn't think there would be any risk.'

He paused and looked at Bill for some kind of understanding. The corners of his mouth quivered slightly. His voice had become apologetic and regretful.

'You see,' he said, 'I too was thinking in terms of risk. I didn't argue that they were acting immorally. If I argued at all, it was simply against their charge that you were a risk. It gets you, Bill. Places like San Cristobal lure you into a position which makes

245

you a wholly different person. Here you are talking about the Governor's duty, and the risks of somebody like Chance. I simply think of risk, and yet you know that I'm not cut out for a job like Crabbe's. But once you're in the situation, you do find yourself playing some part which ultimately supports people like Crabbe. And there is nothing you can do. You can even justify it.'

He stopped suddenly and waited for Bill to say something. But Bill had refused to interrupt. The silence was like a lack of sympathy on his part, and Flagstead was determined to make him understand.

'I do believe that if certain people took over from the official administration, they'd cut our throats,' he said, 'yours and mine, and every European in San Cristobal. You have to protect yourself against such a possibility. Crabbe has no feeling for somebody like Bellows, a little hack he picked up rotting his way from a rag in Streatham to odd jobs in Fleet Street, but they are together, and so are Crabbe and Sir William, although I doubt they like each other very much. But in any crisis, they're all on the same side. And I find myself with them, and for the same reason. And then the evidence of the whole situation has a way of proving you right. If I weren't here, Chance would probably be made manager of Radio San Cristobal. Somebody like Shephard would take over the Governor's place. And you know, however liberal your views, neither I nor Sir William Bird could ever believe that our jobs would be more efficiently done by them. You seem justified in holding on, and if holding on means protecting yourself, then you protect yourself. And you use power to do it. It's perfectly natural. Shephard and his group would do it too, if they were in the same situation. It doesn't justify victimising people, but that happens in the process, and all you can do is try and limit that victimisation, short of taking risks. You see what I mean?'

Bill hesitated. He thought of Bellows and Crabbe and the whole conspiracy of privilege which Flagstead was trying to justify. Flagstead's face reddened. His hands shook violently round the glass.

'What aches my guts,' he said, 'is that the Chairman assured the Governor that the appointment wouldn't go through. And he did this without having a word with me. When he calls a meeting, as he will do, he will talk to me as he did to the Governor. We'll become partners. He will ask me to reconsider the matter, and he will expect me to agree. Not even to agree, but to admit that there's no difference at all between us. And I admit, Bill, if I didn't know you as I do, I wouldn't have given the matter much thought after hearing about the letter.'

Bill glanced towards the garden as though he had lost interest in what Flagstead was saying. He had pushed the chair back from the table.

'Suppose I go over and tell Bellows who I am, and ask him whether I could call at the office for my letter?'

Flagstead pondered Bill's question. He felt that Bill had been refusing to sympathise with the position he had explained, and he feared that Bellows might have guessed his relationship with Bill.

'That would put him in a spot,' said Bill, 'but he'll probably make some excuse. I don't know who was the last person to see the letter.'

'But if I insist on calling at the office,' said Bill, 'he'll have to explain why it isn't there.'

'It isn't difficult for Bellows to say that he lost it,' said Flagstead. 'That's as easy as counting your fingers.'

'And didn't think of informing me?'

'There will always be reasons,' said Flagstead. 'He was waiting to see whether it would turn up. He could dismiss somebody for negligence, just to prove how he felt about the matter. It's simple. Any action of the kind could be a bread and butter issue for a simple printer, a stenographer, or a messenger.'

Bill felt his knees shake under the table, and a rush of anger confused his thinking. He had forgotten the job and Flagstead's explanations. He would have liked to hold somebody's head between his hands and crash it on the table. Flagstead's words had lingered, 'a bread and butter issue for a simple printer'... He looked at Flagstead, determined and ruthless, seething with a fury which was bent on humiliating Bellows.

'Suppose I tell him,' said Bill, 'that I know the Governor has seen my letter. That he failed in his responsibility as an editor to keep his word to a correspondent. Suppose I have it out with him, the whole goddam story as I know it.'

'Then you would have betrayed me,' Flagstead said anxiously. 'Only one person could have told you that.'

Bill dropped his head as though he had not even thought about that.

'It wouldn't have occurred to me to make up a story about the job,' said Flagstead. 'You know that.'

And Bill saw the old Flagstead, warm, frank and endearing.

'It would be better to leave Crabbe and the Governor out of it,' Flagstead said. 'You can have it out with Bellows if you like. It's your letter.'

Bellows was getting ready to pay the bill. The secretary had gone to the toilet. Bill spilt the glass of punch as he rose from the chair. Flagstead was apprehensive. He got up and walked ahead towards the table which Bellows was about to leave. They greeted each other, and Bill walked up beside them, looking straight at Bellows who grinned lavishly and stuck out his hand. It was the first time they had met. Flagstead made a joke about the secretary, and Bellows assumed an air of resentment, facetious and severe. He looked at Bill as though he had forgotten what he wanted to say.

Then Flagstead said: 'I don't think you met each other before.'

'No,' said Bill, 'but you probably know the name.'

Bellows hesitated. 'I hadn't associated it with you,' he said, 'but Chance mentioned it earlier.'

There was a pause. Flagstead hoped Bill would leave.

'I hear you're going on at Radio Antillia,' Bellows said. Then he looked to Flagstead who was becoming uneasy at this turn of conversation.

'Is it too early to mention anything about it in *Truth*?' he said.

Bill stiffened. Flagstead pretended to be unsure. 'You're one ahead of me,' Flagstead said. Bill was about to ask about the letter, but Bellows had already spoken.

'Do you do any writing?' he asked. 'I was thinking of asking you for something for the paper. Impressions of San Cristobal or something of the kind.'

'I sent you a letter a week ago,' said Bill, 'I was hoping to hear from you.'

'For publication?'

Bill nodded. The secretary was approaching the table, and Bellows signalled her to hurry. He asked whether she had seen the letter. The girl shook her head in ignorance.

'Why not give me a call tomorrow,' Bellows said. 'I've just about had it up to my neck all last week.'

He paused and looked at his watch. 'Believe me, and you can ask him,' he said, indicating Flagstead, 'there isn't one of us here who doesn't do the work of five men.'

Flagstead showed no sign of agreement. He was anxious to avoid any conflict between the two men. The secretary was checking her watch by the clock in the Pink Curtain. Bill bowed to the girl, made a vague signal of departure to Flagstead and Bellows, and followed the bend of the fence out of the garden into the street.

The old man had come in from the garden. He saw Flagstead walking back to the divan at the far end of the lounge. He paused at the door and looked around to choose a seat. The lounge was crowded and the grinding of the voices made him peevish. He surveyed the mirrors, repeating his reflection round the room until he felt dazed by the weird multiplication of faces which seemed to jeer at him. It was like a circus of clowns who had all missed their cues and made their entrance at the wrong time and in a place which their presence had desecrated. They did not belong here. The black and the yellow faces and many of the pale ones too. It made him angry to see them devouring, with such raw and thuggish greed, the comfort and leisure of a room which he had known as a child. And he reflected bitterly on the change which had assaulted him in his old age. This lounge was once a nursery, and the restaurant which followed straight ahead was their living room. Crystal Cove, as it was then called, was one of the great houses of San Cristobal, and would have been, but for an accident of business, his inheritance. Now he lived upstairs quietly and alone in a bachelor apartment with a view of the sea. He came down every evening for a glass of sherry; and after supper he would return to his solitude.

He hooked the stick round his neck and walked past the tables to the large divan where Flagstead was sitting. He preferred the company of people like Flagstead to that of the local whites, while his traffic with the natives of colour was strictly limited to domestic service or official business. He had stopped accepting invitations to the Governor's Palace, and many of his friends had died or betrayed him by their spineless compromise with the forces which had turned Crystal Cove into the Pink Curtain. He was very much alone these days until someone like Flagstead came along. He could tell Flagstead, without restraint, about the things that mattered; and then he would feel, like the harmony of the flesh over his bones, the splendour of his name and the memory of who he was.

'How's Mr Baden-Semper this evening?' Flagstead said.

'Peter, my boy,' he chuckled, resting the stick on the divan, 'I'm alive. And yourself?'

'Would you have a sherry?' Flagstead said, 'I shan't be staying much longer.'

Baden-Semper was indecisive. He patted his hand against Flagstead's knee and shook his head. He was alive to the tense and secret preoccupation which he had interrupted. He was beginning to feel something like regret towards Flagstead.

'Are the rotters giving you trouble?' he asked.

'San Cristobal is getting a bit trying,' said Flagstead.

'I know, I know, Peter. You can just imagine what I feel sometimes.'

Flagstead jerked his head back and finished the rum punch. He could feel the old man's uncertainty as they sat, for a moment, in silence. And he had to restrain himself, for he had suddenly felt an overwhelming resentment towards Baden-Semper. The old man stared ahead, trying to avoid the hideous satisfaction of the faces which surrounded him. He took some comfort in Flagstead's displeasure with San Cristobal. It made him feel less isolated, and it offered him a vision of the world his father had known. But his loyalty was a sour and decaying passion. He did not want to distress Flagstead with his loathing of the sordid ruin into which his father's world had fallen; yet he felt he owed it San Cristobal and Flagstead and himself to evoke the memories of his past.

'There was a time,' he said.

'It is no longer,' Flagstead interrupted. 'I know what you're going to say, but it's better left a secret.' His voice was aggressive.

The old man was startled. He thought he understood Flagstead's dismay, and he patted his leg again. There was a look of sad and lonely wisdom in his old eyes.

'The rotters are really getting you down,' he said. 'Is it this business of Parnall resigning and going off without warning anybody.'

'No sir,' said Flagstead, and the old man seemed shaken by the salutation, sir, and the angry readiness of Flagstead's voice. Flagstead did not want to continue. He was afraid of what he might say, and he did not want to hurt the old man. But Baden-Semper leaned towards him, patient and solicitous. He wanted to be of help to Flagstead.

'I trust you, Peter,' he said. 'I really do. And you can put it to me as an older man who knows this place. Whatever it is getting you down. Don't ever be afraid to let me know.'

Flagstead decided to go. He got up and offered the old man his hand and he felt, as he remembered Bill, that he was entering some conspiracy against himself. He knew that he would regret this meeting, but it was impossible to control this feeling he had towards the old man.

'It isn't Parnall or Crabbe or the Governor,' he said, 'or any of us who've come to work here against people like Shephard and Singh. It's those who were born in San Cristobal, men like your father who've bitched the whole show up and left us in this goddam awful mess.'

The old man was speechless. He could not turn to watch Flagstead who had walked past the door and across the garden. The voices had crippled his hearing, and he could barely distinguish the face of the Indian waiter who was helping him to his feet.

'You all right, sir?' the waiter asked.

'Thank you Ram Lal, thank you.' His voice was nervous and abrupt, as though he had to make a special effort of breathing.

'Supper is ready, sir,' the waiter said.

'Would you tell them to send it up,' he said, and pulled himself round the curve of the stairs to his room.

The waiter stood at the foot of the stairs and watched until the old man was out of sight. The cash register rang and he heard a voice

251

call for service. The cashier was furious at his delay, and she kept her finger on the button that made the wires screel like a human voice behind his ears. But he did not stir. He was staring through the skylight at the cold black crust of the night, wondering how it feels to be old and obsolete and alone.

Bill had rambled like a vagrant to the brink of the town. He knew the layout of the street, but he was not familiar with the life of the poor beyond the precincts of the Pink Curtain. He had often heard Thief describe the part of the slum which started behind Ruby Lane, but he had seen slums in Europe and he felt no special sentiment about those which disfigured San Cristobal. They were all the same, undesirable and unnecessary. It was not the physical seediness of the slum which aroused his sympathy for San Cristobal. The island was, for him and Penelope, the future of those boys who had told the story of the Bandit Kings. He thought of the boys when he remembered this meeting with Flagstead, and he tried to imagine the distance of privilege which separated them from people like Bellows and Crabbe. He was not going to get the job with Radio San Cristobal, but he tried to find some consolation in the thought that he might have aroused something creative in the boys. He was recollecting the details of their evening in the studio. Suddenly he recognised a voice and felt someone brush against him. He turned and it seemed that the memory of the boys had suddenly deserted him.

'Thought I knew who it was,' said Chance as he opened a case and offered his cigarettes. They had not stopped walking. Bill refused the cigarette, and looked round to get his bearings.

'Where are we now?' he asked.

'That's the Bandit Kingdom,' said Chance, 'it's not your cup of tea.'

He followed Chance's arm indicating the large, wooden build-ing on the other side of the street. There was a faltering wail of instruments preparing for music; and he could see some women strolling idly outside the door.

'Would you like to take a look?' Chance asked. 'I promise to get you out without any trouble.'

He nodded and crossed the street behind Chance. When they came abreast under the light, he glanced sideways to catch a glimpse of Chance; and he thought, as he watched his profile, that Flagstead might have been right about places like San Cristobal. He thought of Chance lurking in the shadows, calculating the moment to introduce himself. He was sure that he had been followed. He had to control this feeling of contempt which Chance had aroused. He turned his head away to look at the women who had become alert under the light. And this feeling seemed to pursue him, urging him to say something that would let Chance know there was no need for deception. But he did not speak. They are all the same, he thought, as he shifted to avoid the solicitous welcome of the women. Then he checked himself as though he were secretly ashamed of his own judgement, and thought again: but when people are so physically different, it is not difficult to think of them as being a wholly different kind of creature, human and partly human.

'The night can be very promising out here,' Chance said.

'Let's get inside quickly,' Bill said.

The whores had formed a little battalion outside the door. The light showed up the curve of the yard, hard and sharp with its surface of concrete and gravel. A woman was tugging at Bill's jacket, and Chance wheeled sharply round to chase her away. The women tittered, and made faces.

'We got licks for them don' vote with Shephard,' one of the women said.

'All kind o' licks,' another shouted. 'You better tell the foreign gentl'man which road to follow.'

Chance smiled and made an obscene joke with the woman. She sidled up to Bill and held onto his hand. He wanted to get into the room, but he did not resist. Chance was enjoying the little scene. The woman brought her head up to Bill's shoulder and squeezed his hand.

'You can get it for nothin',' she whispered, 'if you with we on Shephard' side.'

The woman was beginning to guide Bill's hand down the crease of her backside. He shoved her off gently, and Chance suddenly intervened and ordered her away.

'Take we all in a row if you can make it,' she shouted, 'an' for nothin' once you ridin' with Shephard.'

The women laughed and danced round each other as they watched the two men hurry between the chairs and settle quietly in a corner near the band.

Chance noticed Bill's annoyance and he became very active, smiling and waving at the little group of musicians. They seemed flattered by his attentions, and a woman came over to ask what they would like to hear. It was a sign that they appreciated the company. Bill had no feelings about the matter. He was still thinking about Flagstead and the boys and the Pink Curtain.

'Whatever you think best,' said Chance.

The woman walked back to the group, and they went through the motions of tuning the instruments, looking at each other for a sign of agreement.

The woman who wore spectacles and a wide Panama hat played the trumpet. Another woman hugged a concertina, and the other two members of the band were men who performed with a guitar and a drum. It was an odd assortment, but they seemed to form a perfect coalition of interests. The woman shouted from the corner, 'Too-lah a little hoarse today,' and the others laughed. Too-lah, Bill learnt, was the name of the trumpet. They started tentatively, as though they were not very familiar with the tune, but suddenly they seemed to get into stride, and the room rocked with noise. They were playing the theme song of the club: 'Everything You Need'. Chance showed his pleasure by an occasional nod at the woman.

'They are here all day,' he said, 'but they don't really come to life before about nine o'clock. Then you see what they mean by the song. The man in the corner is there at nine o'clock in the morning, and he never leaves till midnight. He is the fortune-teller. The wife had a church round the corner with a big sign painted in blue over the door, FOR THOSE WHO ARE FINISH WITH SIN.'

When the band stopped, the woman walked over to ask whether they were satisfied. Chance assured her that the music had never been better. She laughed and looked at the trumpet, holding it out, like one actor coaxing another to take a bow. Bill gave her a shilling for the band, and immediately she drew a chair, and fetched a glass from her bosom.

'Be ready with the necessary always,' she said, pouring herself a drink. 'There be three possessions a man must travel with in these times of make-believe, a knife, a vessel that will not leak and a mind knowing its own business.'

She finished her drink at one shot, and reminded them that her friends would expect a similar favour. Chance agreed, and she walked off with the bottle which she passed to each of the musicians. They drank from the same glass which the woman later slipped into her bosom. She returned to the table with the bottle. Her friends had had their share. She was grateful. In a matter of seconds they were coaxing the instruments to a common rhythm, ready for another number.

The Bandit Kingdom was novel, and in different circumstances Bill might have responded to its raw exuberance. The musicians were labouring madly to prove the reputation of the place, but Bill lacked the spirit of the occasion. His attention was an obvious effort of courtesy. He wondered whether Penelope was waiting. Chance realised that there was not much he could learn from Bill this evening. Although their energies might have craved that curious, dark miscellany of pleasures which the Bandit Kingdom provided, their desire was now dormant, and their private interests intercepted. Bill was pouring himself a drink.

Chance looked up in astonishment. A woman had swept through the door. She wore a slip and a patched, yellow cardigan pulled across her shoulders. They could see the brief, black underwear clinging to her buttocks. She stared angrily at Bill before kicking a table out of her way. Chance looked nervous, and Bill was suddenly alerted by the fury of her voice. She was shouting her question at the man who stood behind the bar. The band stopped playing, and everyone seemed to imitate the man behind the bar. He was shaking his head in ignorance. She shouted again, bullying them to say whether they had seen Thief. The musicians looked at Bill and shook their heads like a group of children who had been warned not to speak. She went nearer the band, and Chance tried to hear what she was saying. She was talking in a low, furious mutter to the woman who played the trumpet. They continued to shake their heads, and she turned as though she were going to say something to Bill. The man walked from behind the bar. She glared at him and then rushed through the door.

'Who is that?' Bill asked.

'You remember what I told you,' Chance said, 'about the girl with Bellows. That is the mother.'

He smiled, waving his hand over the table with an air of wise and capacious resignation. 'God only knows what it is she has lost.'

The woman who played the trumpet came over to apologise for the interruption. She was not angry, only surprised and curious.

'Once a gentl'man always a gentl'man,' she said, 'and the sex may be different, but the same says me right, once a lady, you know the rest.' She paused, hugging the trumpet under her arm. 'If you know your life ain't always straight,' she said, 'you shouldn't lie down too deep in the night. 'Cause what you steal you may lose again. See what I mean, gentl'men?'

'What has she lost?' Bill asked.

'Only those who know can know,' the woman said, 'but she just ask to tell Thief that if he don't see her tomorrow before the sun make a noise, he can count his fingers again. Poor Thief. Once a thief, you know the rest…'

Chance looked at Bill as though he wanted to apologise for the failure of the Bandit Kingdom, but he was slow to speak. The trumpeter had hurried back to the band. They were anxious to obliterate the memory of the woman's arrival.

'Seems they're on Thief's side,' said Chance.

He started to pour a drink, but Bill refused. He felt a pressing desire to be home with Penelope. He rose from the chair and bowed to the band. Chance saw him put a dollar bill under the glass and heard him mutter something about the evening, and the Pink Curtain, and meeting again. Like someone familiar and unexpected the night was waiting outside.

'Where has he gone?' Penelope wondered.

She was pouring herself another drink. She tilted the bottle back, interrupting the flow of the rum and listened to the radio announcement. Someone had been badly injured in an accident near the Pink Curtain, and the relatives were being asked to go to the Carlisle Hospital at once. Then the voice, clinical as a knife, continued with the news: the Governor had been advised to intervene in the dispute about the electricians; the Hon. Albert Paravecino was holding a political meeting at Milot the same evening; a fortune-teller was charged with receiving money on false pretences when he predicted the result of the elections. There was a sports item and an appeal for funds to send a steel band to New York.

'Thank God, it's not him,' she said, thinking of the accident. She mixed the rum with some ginger ale.

Penelope was getting impatient. She had already telephoned to Flagstead's house and the Pink Curtain, but no one could suggest where Bill had gone. The night was warm and she was becoming a little tipsy with rum. She thought of Marcia and Mark and felt the utter solitude of the house. She got up and walked to the door to see whether Thief was in the garden, then she walked back to the table and fingered the small parcel which Thief had asked her to deliver to Bill. She was going to call for Thief and ask him to keep her company for a while, but she changed her mind when she saw the light in the garage. She knew there was someone with him. She picked up the small parcel and threw it on Bill's writing desk, cuddled the parrot's beak with her fingers and returned to the table. There was only the drink and the sullen croaking of the frogs in the wind. She leaned her head on to the glass and wished that something would happen.

The night bristled and sang with the whispering traffic of the fireflies over the lawn. They breathed bright holes of fire into the air like the smokeless ends of cigarettes lifted and carried for a while by the burning wind. They rose above the garage sailing their brilliance down to the low wet summit of grass that sucked them into the night. The wind charged through the tall black hedge, and the lawn slipped back into the night like a city losing its lights from afar. The grass sweated and one light showed like an eyelid blinking through the creases of the garage.

Thief was nervous. He had interrupted his story again to ask Rockey's advice, but the monkey began to stir in the corner and Rockey was alerted. The noise was like a warning which had suddenly turned them silent. Thief crossed his legs again and made his knuckles crack.

'You think I should have let her know what it was?' he asked.

'It ain't make no difference,' said Rockey. 'She goin' know when Butterfiel' get home.'

The monkey had spread its legs wide apart to lick the base of its tail. It glanced slyly at Thief and Rockey before nibbling the corners of its behind. Then the tail curled upwards like a spring of wire round its neck. The hair glistened in the lamplight, but the men paid no attention. The wind made a creaking noise with the broken gate. The monkey had lifted its head from between its legs. It wrapped its tail round its waist and watched the men.

'Then it is true,' said Rockey, 'what they say about the girl from Ruby Lane.'

'How else I come by that wallet,' said Thief, 'I see them myself. My own two eyes watch how Crabbe ride her like the devil self makin' for hell. I tell you, Rockey, I watch him prance like a demon inside him, an' nothin' short o' miracles could have make believe that Crabbe was like that. He hold that girl down, an' when his motion catch steam, it seem all his powers was tryin' to get where it ain't possible for any man to reach. But he just keep ridin' her deeper an' deeper.'

'An' they didn't hear nothin' movin' 'bout the shed?' Rockey asked. ''Cause if they catch you out, this would be worse than any time.'

Thief turned and glanced at the gate as though he suspected someone outside. Rockey leaned sideways and lifted the chimney to light a cigarette from the lamp. The monkey craned forward, scraping the chain along the floor, and watched the smoke make tottering, blue rings round its head. The wind loitered with a low sound outside, and Thief turned to look at Rockey.

'It was my easies' operation ever,' he said. 'The shed Crabbe got at the back twixt here an' where he live is whole an' sound at the sides an' on top. But the floorin' got flaws. It got a fair openin' here an' there, an' one board loose complete. I was on my back looking through when Crabbe was ridin' in all his glory. You should have see him, Rockey. Was like his bones goin' burst, or something inside him explode an' catch fire. The way he fight an' rummage on top that girl. An' all she do was lie back patient as a cow expectin' something out o' this world. I couldn't move myself for what was happenin' in front my eyes. But I could see Crabbe change colour while he wage that war, pouncin' an' paradin' like he was a whole army invadin' fresh country. And the Ruby Lane girl spread out flat under him like a animal beggin' for slaughter. I couldn't move, Rockey. An' I nearly catch myself talkin' like I was in some spell their performance put on me.'

He paused and glanced again at the gate. The garage was silent.

'Tell me, Rockey,' he said, lifting his head up to the light, 'what it is a man lookin' for when he get in that state? What it is driving him the way I watch Crabbe punish himself like he see some victory near?'

Rockey did not answer. He dragged leisurely at the cigarette and pumped the smoke out through his nose.

'What it is?' Thief repeated, 'an' the way that girl wait there under him. What it is she was expectin' other than what happen ordinary? Is what I ask myself when I watch them. An' then something hold me like a bad jealousy. An' I feel my blood rise in a kind o' vengeance 'gainst Crabbe, an' I tell myself he should pay for what he getting. He should pay for whatever jubilation that girl from Ruby Lane was givin' him. Was then my eye catch his coat hanging from the chair. An' I move that floor board back, quiet as a crumb falling from your hand. I move it back, an' like the old days, my fingers find their form. Was like lickin' your tongue or breakin' wind in a public place. Cool an' easy, I look an' see his wallet in my han'…'

'An' if Butterfiel' tell him who take it?' Rockey asked.

'It wasn't stealin' I steal,' said Thief. 'Was just that feelin' o' jealousy 'gainst Crabbe. The feelin' that he should pay with his own true feelin' for what he get.'

'You didn't take nothin' from it?' Rockey asked. He was flicking the ash down his trousers as he watched Thief.

'Nothin',' said Thief. 'It had nothin' but papers, an' one envelope with Butterfiel' name on the back.'

'An' if he decide to tell Crabbe who take it?' Rockey asked. 'What you goin' do if he turn you over to the law?'

'I got to face Butterfiel',' said Thief. 'I hold it in hidin' these days past 'cause I didn't know how to face him. I didn't know how to tell him why I take it. But it wasn't steal I mean to steal.'

Rockey pressed his heels together, forked his feet a few inches and turned his toes down, making dimples in the dust. The cigarette was a stub of wet ash crumbling over his lip. He dragged at it for the last time, lifted his head and sprayed the smoke against Thief's face. The butt fell from his mouth and made a dull spiral of smoke over the ground. The wind had abated, and the garage was still. They could hear the shrill lament of the frogs in the dark. Rockey got up from the bench and paced up and down the garage. He rattled the monkey's chain with his feet, and then walked over to the gate. He was giving Thief time to decide what he would do.

'Is some days you ain't put a foot near the Bandit Kingdom,' he said, turning to look at Thief.

'I was tired,' said Thief, 'an' thinkin' 'bout what might happen when Crabbe find out.'

'What 'bout goin' round now?' Rockey asked. 'I could do with a rum.'

Thief hesitated. He had cupped his hand behind his ear again. He thought he heard someone call, and he walked towards the gate, leaning his head to one side. The noise came again, and he unwound the bands of wire that held the gate tight. He pushed his head past the gate, and signalled Rockey to take a seat. It was Bill's voice summoning him to the house. He shouted to let them know that he had heard, and then turned to ask Rockey's advice.

'He goin' ask me how I come by it,' he said, sidling past the gate on to the grass.

'Just tell him the truth without any particulars,' said Rockey. 'An' beg him to keep it quiet.'

'I shame to let him know what I was doin',' said Thief.

'Forget all that,' said Rockey, 'an' fix your min' on gettin' him to talk mercy with Crabbe. 'Cause if I know these white folks he goin' suggest that you carry it back to who it belong.'

'Don' go till I get back,' Thief said. 'If he settle my min', then we can walk down to the Bandit Kingdom.'

'I goin' wait,' said Rockey, lowering his body on to the bench.

The grass felt springy under Thief's feet. The light was an elusive blur that broke and shivered round Butterfield's body at the door. Thief could barely control the shake of his hands as he approached the house. Bill watched him amble up to the door, and then walked back to the table where Penelope was sitting. There was something ominous in the atmosphere of the room. But Thief could not yet guess what they were thinking. Butterfield looked angry and excited, and Thief thought he saw Penelope turn on the chair as though she preferred not to hear his excuse. He needed Rockey to help him through while he waited for one of them to speak.

Bill sat with his back to the door, fingering the wallet which lay on the table. He had passed his letter to Penelope while he read for the third or fourth time the other pages which the wallet had contained. Penelope looked up, trying to draw Bill's attention to Thief. She had left everything intact, and now she waited for Bill to tell her what he had found. Thief could not guess what would happen. He noticed Penelope's anxiety, as though she too were afraid of what Bill might do. He wanted to get it over quickly and return to the garage. But Bill was absorbed with his reading. They saw his face tighten and his mouth contract. He looked up from the page and stared at Penelope as though he expected her to give some advice. She was about to speak when Thief intervened, nervous and penitent.

'It wasn't steal I mean to steal,' he said, and paused, trying to think how he might begin his explanation.

Bill turned the chair round and faced him. For a moment there was utter silence in the room, and Penelope leaned across the table to take Bill's arm.

'Does anyone else know about this?' Bill asked, holding the page up.

'The papers I didn't bother to interfere with,' said Thief, 'but it wasn't my intention…'

'Just a minute,' said Bill, and his voice betrayed his lack of control. 'You didn't read this.'

'I didn't read nothin' but your name on one envelope,' said Thief.

'You're sure?'

'Me nor nobody I know of till you,' said Thief.

Bill's hand turned slowly down to the table. He looked relieved, and Thief wondered what he had decided. Penelope was suspicious.

'Then remember this,' said Bill. 'Listen carefully and do as I say. You won't mention the wallet to anybody until I tell you. Not one word about it to anybody.'

His voice was deliberate and austere. He waved his hand towards the door and turned to speak with Penelope. Thief lingered behind the chair. He was astonished and relieved by Bill's decision, but he wanted to say that he had spoken with Rockey. Bill had spread the pages under his hands, waiting for Thief to leave.

'I just want to say sorry,' said Thief.

'That's all right,' Bill said. His voice was hurried and firm. 'Just do as I say.'

Thief knew they wanted to be rid of him. He glanced at Penelope who was trying to spy the writing through the spaces of Bill's fingers. Thief retreated slowly to the door, paused, and finally whispered, 'Good night.' But no one seemed to hear.

The room was nervous as a hive. The parrot had swung its head, displaying one eye like a circle of fire. The air was hot and still. Penelope clasped her hand round Bill's arm, and tugged frantically at his sleeve.

'Is it anything to do with us?' she asked.

Bill relaxed his hands and straightened the pages.

'I wouldn't have believed it,' he said, lifting the pages slowly from the table. 'This is a personal letter from Parnall to Crabbe saying why he wouldn't stay in the job. And this…' He paused, watching the paper tremble between his fingers. 'And this is a note in Crabbe's handwriting with the plot to have Shephard murdered…'

'Murdered!' Penelope whispered, tightening her hold round Bill's arm.

'A fortnight or so before the elections,' said Bill. 'That's what Thief has stolen.'

He dropped his hand and shoved the pages across the table for Penelope to read. She had not yet released his arm, and she seemed reluctant to confirm what Bill had said. She was thinking of Shephard and the boys and the cold, decisive passion that forged Crabbe's will. She held the pages up to the light, but she saw Bill's hand creeping towards the bottle, and she knew by the nervous quiet of the room that he was waiting for her to say what they should do.

3

This room was the party sanctuary: a private cell which Shephard had offered as a hideout for special meetings. It was an ordinary study with the simplest furniture for reading and writing, but the presence of Singh and Lee, on these occasions, made it formidable in its atmosphere of religious fervour. There was something almost sacred about the room; but now it had closed in on them, rigid, obscure and a little resentful. The tension rose like a fever. The light was little more than an interval of shadow between their faces. And it seemed, as they listened to the irrelevant mutter of the rain outside, that they were depending on some accident to clarify their misgiving.

Lee looked towards the door and regretted that there was no other place to turn, no one else whom they might consult. He wished someone would arrive; but that, he reminded himself, could not happen on such an evening. For it was a principle accepted by all three that no one else should visit this room. When it was necessary to break this rule, which was very rare, they would all discuss the matter beforehand. The room was a kind of top secret, and it was this exclusiveness which had helped to emphasise its character. Lee felt like a victim of some unnecessary punishment. He tried to guess Singh's feelings, but the man's anger was too obvious. It obscured everything else about him. Shephard was the opposite and therefore similar. He had become too calm. It was difficult to tell what this extraordinary patience concealed.

It had happened again: the frenzied argument, then the sudden pause like a frozen breath separating the sound of a voice from the echo you expected. A gradual tremor, like light and air fighting to occupy the corners of the ceiling, agitated their hearing until the room itself became an omen which made them nervous, impatient and suspicious. Then each would know it was his duty to break the spell of what had not yet been said. Each knew that it was the moment to explode the motive which nursed this pause; and each, uncertain and yet determined, tried; so that the pause flared into a clutter of voices which left something unsaid. Then the tremor would begin, a moment after the voices had retreated in a tired procession of syllables, noiseless as petals fallen into silence. It was the second time in the last hour that this silence had come upon them; and now they looked like animals, trapped by their own fury, ignorant, speechless and outraged.

Shephard nursed his jaw and brought his head slowly down to the table. Lee held a pencil up, considering the point. Singh had turned his glance on the pages before him. Like animals moving by instinct, sensitive to danger, they were gradually finding their way back to a centre of reference. They had to begin again, but they had not yet found their clues. And they could not pretend to forget that something was wrong somewhere. But they were trying to reassemble their arguments in order to return to the purpose of the meeting. Perhaps it would help them to disagree without disturbing the harmony which they had always known when they met in this room. Lee was ready to speak, but he noticed Singh's agitation. Shephard had seen it too. They were both waiting. Singh was not now angry, but his eyes looked more troubled. His mouth made that familiar nervous quiver which no strength of will can ever control. There was something unbearable in his expression of melancholy understanding. He was possessed by some kind of knowledge which was beyond learning. Others might have known the same thing, but it had not entered their life in the same way. His knowledge was physical, integral as a root to the branch and body of the tree. He did not have to summon it according to his need. There was no distance between the thing he knew and the man he was. He was his knowledge. And when that knowledge was shaken, the man was in danger. It was Singh who radiated this sense of danger. It was the first time they had ever felt this mood which ruled his hands and his voice and the simple choice of his words. Shephard had lost his composure.

'Once and for all,' he said, 'let us get it over, whatever it is.'

He had leaned forward, his hands spread wide across the table in a manner that showed authority and doubt. Lee had withdrawn, and for a moment it seemed that this was a direct exchange of feeling between Shephard and Singh. There was something between these two men which was at once inviolable and tragic. Lee watched how they regulated their movements, wilfully but imperceptibly, until their eyes had met in a common level of scrutiny. Singh steadied his hands and spoke as though he had forgotten where he was or the purpose of their meeting.

'I was a boy,' he said, 'no more or less the size of my own son, following my father like a sheep behind the shepherd, workin' an' livin' on the ol' sugar plantation where Milot now is, when me an' my father an' all nearby share the same life as the animals we pasture for those who own us. An' I remember the mornin', I remember it like the first day an' time o' somethin' I can't name, the voices from outside reach me where I was, alone in the range where I live. Those two voices: one familiar to me was the white bastard Baden-Semper, an' the other I learn later was the visiting Lord Carlisle who then own it all, every square inch that part o' the islan'. That mornin' I remember, I remember what happen somewhere in me when Lord Carlisle ask, his voice like the Almighty, kind but absent, "When will we get them out this squalor?" An' Baden-Semper, talkin' like the knowin' angel on the spot, an' believin' every word he say, tell Lord Carlisle to put his min' at ease. "It might surprise you, sir, but they are as happy here as you or I in our different ways." Just so, an' then a little argument o' logic follow before they complete their agreement, that it would take some time to unteach the squalor, some time for me an' my father an' all before or who come after to unlearn what, in the circumstance, we could only be. Was then, I believe it was then I know in a way learnin' can't teach how one man might exist in a next man's head, an' no change o' simple circumstance can alter what each understan' an' accept. Is that recollection harden me today, harden an' at the same time, for certain reasons, scare my purpose an' my faith.'

He paused and let his glance wander slowly back to the papers under his hands. Lee looked incapable of speech, and Shephard seemed nervous, like a man who hears a warning which is real, and whose relevance to his own life he cannot discover. He did not know quite where to begin. Singh kept his head down as he passed another page of the Governor's letter to him… He did not stir. His eyes were fixed on the print, but he could not yet distinguish the words. Lee thought something had to be done. He looked at his watch, and wrote the time at the top of a cigarette box.

'In case no common agreement is possible,' said Singh, 'we must vote an' stan' by that.'

Shephard understood the meaning of that digression about the past and the sullen abruptness with which Singh was calling for a vote. He did not want to lose his way again, and he tried to forget what Singh had hinted about losing faith. He wanted to remain calm until they had reached agreement about this crisis for which the Governor had invited their help. He was sure the strike of electricians would take place, but he thought it would be a mistake to ignore any compromise which came from the official Administration.

'Remember above everything else,' Shephard said, 'we have no authority to act in the name of the union. They may want to charge us with inciting a strike which we are not properly authorised to do. And they are very quick, as we all know, to speak about disturbing the peace. We must consider that. We must pretend, somehow, to be fighting to keep the peace. We can't let them get the better in any business about peace. Remember that. I think if we accept this invitation, as political leaders, to discuss the strike under the Government's supervision, we have a defence. At least we tried. But the strike will go on.'

'Remember too,' said Singh, 'that they decide what is the peace. And I say simply that I would not lend a hand to help when I know they can say what is peace and what is not peace. I think only of the people in this matter. And we cannot afford to disturb the confidence of the people. There are enemies waiting to use any mistake we seem to make, and I feel going to the Governor's Palace is a mistake.'

'If you feel now that the people trust you,' Shephard answered, 'you have to trust them. I believe we can explain anything that looks like a mistake. When we speak to the people, it is only to say what is happening. They have no reason to doubt what we say. That is the truth. We have started something new here in San Cristobal.'

Lee was looking at the watch as he listened. He was less sure than the others, and he was waiting for some error in the argument to tell him where he should speak.

'You know what Paravecino is saying,' Singh said. 'We only want to get into the Governor's Palace.'

'Paravecino is saying something else too,' said Shephard. 'He is sayin' that this union is false, and every Indian knows what every Negro feels, and the surface friendship is going to spell misery for one group or the other. It simply depends who has the most power.'

'Yes,' Singh said gravely, 'I hear that.'

'But we cannot pay attention to that,' said Shephard, 'any more than we can to the talk about getting into the Palace.'

'I know,' said Singh. 'I learn to listen with my ears shut. I know what to hear, and what not to hear. More important is what the people say. My son was saying this morning that he was listening to people talking, and some say that you will keep the oil, and I will keep the sugar, and Lee has his mind on shops, business and nothing else. Now we have to prove to be together in a way that will make that talk impossible. Now remember, only one of us can go to this meeting. One representative only. Now suppose I go, you know the stories that the enemies can make out of that?'

'But I would go,' said Shephard. 'I am not afraid of stories.'

Lee raised his hand as though he had suddenly discovered something important.

'What would they say if I went?' he asked.

Singh looked at Shephard, but they were slow to speak and Lee continued.

'They might say that you use me to appear where you did not want to be seen.'

'That is true,' said Singh.

'But if we did not go,' Lee continued, 'that would seem to everybody a kind of real unity.'

Singh nodded, and Shephard waited to reply.

'But if nobody went,' Lee said, 'the Governor and Paravecino and that lot can make stories too.'

'What stories can they make that we don't know already?' Singh said.

'They may want to talk about charging the leaders,' said Shephard.

'I'd go to gaol,' Singh said in anger. 'I am prepared to go to gaol.'

Shephard considered this commitment as though it were a challenge to his own courage. He had not thought of going to gaol until Singh mentioned it, and suddenly he felt sure of his own strength.

'Gaol is nothing to worry about,' he said, 'but the trouble is we can't do much from gaol.'

'We could win from gaol,' said Singh. 'I am sure we could win even if we all three were in gaol.'

Suddenly Lee saw himself imprisoned, and the vividness of the cell made the charge all the more obscure.

'Also, the Governor has no wisdom that I respect,' Singh added.

'Rumour is like the wind here,' said Lee, 'we must be careful. My son says that people keep saying we want to kill the Europeans, and that is why we join together, and people in San Cristobal don't want no killing.'

Shephard thought for a moment about that.

'I don't want to kill anybody,' he said.

'Unless it is necessary,' Singh added briskly. 'Remember they don't think twice about killing if it is necessary.'

He paused as though he wanted to reconsider what he had said. Then he looked at Shephard and Lee, glancing from one to the other as he spoke.

'The point is that we must never trust them,' he said. 'That is like a golden rule in this movement. We cannot afford to trust them. It does not pay, and in the past it has brought ruin. We are fighting today because of the mistake we make of trusting them.'

He paused, folded his arms and leaned forward. His manner was quiet, intimate.

'Can you imagine that the Governor could ever wish you and me well in this business? Can you really imagine that? This is not for logic, or brains, or any of these things. Can you in the part of your mind that defeat all reason with the truth imagine they can mean well for you and me? Answer that.'

Shephard smiled. He said: 'We do not have to answer. The matter before us has nothing to do with disagreement. We are simply talking over different tactics. Of course they cannot mean well, but we can learn from their own deceit. That is it. We cannot afford to dismiss their tricks. It's the way to beat them, by using their own tricks.'

'I'm completely above board with them,' said Singh. 'I want them to know exactly how I feel, and to see that I am not joking. I refuse help in this matter. Let Paravecino deal with the electricians himself. Let the Governor pack his things and get ready to leave. Everything is clear to me. They want to appear as though they are helping. They are not against us. When we win, you will hear that. Impartial, impartial. All they wish for is our good guidance, nothing against us. I have nothing to do with that game. The time for separating has come. It is now, and that is all I want to make clear to them. For the time being, we think of nothing but ruling this place, well, badly, it does not matter, but ruling it ourselves. That talk of experience, and lack of experience, is not for my ears. I am prepared to blunder and die, and let another like us blunder and die, blunder, blunder until we blunder into hell, the whole lot of us, or into a different kind of life in San Cristobal. I feel this in every nerve of me, every nerve, and I drop dead the day that feeling stop. It is now or never, we at the helm of this ship, or no ship at all.'

There was silence. Then he added casually, but with the same conviction: 'And you feel that way too.'

Both Lee and Singh waited, feeling for words which might restore Singh's patience. But it would have been awkward, probably impossible, to deviate from the line of passion which Singh had taken. He had reminded them that passion was a vocation which should hold them captive until this great work was accomplished, and he had made it even more binding by this unusual reminder of his honesty. He was not indulging tricks. His candour was to be taken as the very signal of a war which could not be obscured by occasional gestures of truce.

Shephard suddenly remembered his conversation with

Penelope on Bird Island, and felt the same sort of surprise and awakening which the woman's silence had suggested. He knew that Singh's conviction was no greater than his, but it was still revealing to see himself reflected so vividly in another's words. He felt for a moment that he was wholly under Singh's control. He accepted this experience because he knew how to extricate himself, but he wanted to do so without creating conflict among them. A conflict between himself and the woman on Bird Island would have been perfect, but here it was a flaw in their undertaking. He watched Singh leaning over the table, examining his hands, which looked in the light firm, sure, and unusually eager for action. Lee read the numbers on his watch, and made pin-size lines with his pencil on the cigarette box. He was about to speak.

'We are together in what Singh says,' Lee began, 'not one of us could begin to doubt that. But rumour, rumour is what we must work against. Take those fires two days ago. You know they are saying we order the workers to set fire to the sugarcanes.'

'The workers are the best judge of that,' said Singh.

'True,' said Lee, 'every word of that is true. But there is talk that we might not have the election if the atmosphere is dangerous.'

'You know what would happen?' Singh shouted.

'Let them try that one,' Shephard said sharply. He and Singh were suddenly together in the violence of their response to that suggestion. Lee nodded.

'I would not like to say what would happen,' he said. 'I need not say it here. We know. But nothing must make that possible. And my boy says that people say how the authorities have ways of getting information. We cannot afford to give too much. Plans must be secret. It is so easy to be deceived by friendship. This meeting the Governor wants is a show of friendship, friendship in the name of the people. If the strike happens, he says everyone is to lose, and he begs us to remember the sick in hospitals, and all the institutions which depend on electricians for keeping things going. He is addressing us in the name of the people.'

'Are you saying that we should attend this meeting?' Singh asked.

Lee hesitated. 'I am weighing the matter,' he said. 'With two views before us, we must see which may be to our advantage.

Shall we call a meeting and tell the people about this invitation, say why we will not go, or why we decide to go, as the case may be. We have a day ahead of us?'

The question had stalled their progress. There was a lull which reminded Lee of the silence which had happened before. Lee was waiting for an answer; but no one seemed capable of speech. There was nothing he could do.

The rain seemed to wash everything away, and the room had suddenly become a vacuum, where the echo of the water entered and dissolved over the books and the papers which were arranged on the table before them. Singh was drawing circles with a red pencil over the margin of the pages which he read. He was alert, ruled now by an overwhelming sense of purpose which hardened his stare. He never raised his head from the humble arrangement of those words which reached from end to end of the page, a guide to his understanding, gathering their different senses together to produce a meaning that was unique and final. The print offered itself in full approval of his enquiry, reminding him that he was right. He understood. He did not trust words, and he had never encouraged the habit of reading, for that was like playing into the enemy's hands. But this fear of print had been completely shattered by the conviction that he was right. His purpose was good. Words could no longer mislead him, because he knew his way. And what they attempted to describe or deny had already been made clear to him by the authority of his own feeling which was whole, clean and always in harmony with his purpose. Whenever he doubted words, he would return to his feeling which was at once a secret and an ambition made known by his work. He had nothing to hide.

Lee was holding his pencil up to the light as he counted some figures on a page. He did not doubt his accuracy, but he looked at the figures as he might have looked at a corpse which he had recognised before life had written it off. He was familiar with figures. They were a language which he used in a simple sense of being for or against himself. Six meant six more or six less, three for me, and three for the other, one to the other and five for me. And he could always predict their future if he knew their worth at the given time. What he liked about figures was their docility and their silence. He did not have to argue with them, because they never showed a desire to change. They always seemed at peace on paper, and sometimes they looked alike. But their silence made you conscious of error. Every calculation began in an awareness of error. You always started with the determination to avoid a mistake. When any calculation was finished, and the result seemed satisfactory, you would check the figures to see that there was no mistake. And if a result was not satisfactory, you did the same. Any check of a count was an attempt to discover a mistake. Accuracy was simply the absence of a mistake, but it was always that chance of error which reigned over a calculation. That seemed strange, for he had never made a mistake. He had found some way of persuading figures to lead him to their proper result.

The wind was making a noise with the door, but it became part of the intense preoccupation in the room. Singh was still referring the meaning of those words to the judgement of his feeling. Shephard, who sat with his back to the door, looked round the room, observing the order of the books on the shelves. This room had become a place, alive with all the familiarities of habit and appearance, like a face. He could have recognised it at any time of darkness. And in the light, it seemed to say that there was no need to stare. Nothing had changed, and it would always be the same. Small, privileged, a little nest which received secrets, plans, anxieties. It was their room. It was safe and private, a hole in the ground which no one paid any special attention. Even Shephard had taken it for granted, for he was always too busy to sit in it, relaxed or alone, an inhabitant whose peace might have shown his gratitude for shelter. He returned only to sleep, and even in sleep, it seemed that his wish had taken him elsewhere. He had not grown tired of it. He treated it like a companion whom he could trust. They shared the night, and they understood each other in a way which was independent of questions.

Shephard wanted to speak, but he was waiting until Singh and Lee showed some sign of readiness. They were still occupied, rehearsing their separate convictions which were part of the same wish. He looked at Singh and Lee, as though he wanted to check his memory of their faces. But he hardly saw their faces. They were all concentration, purpose, and will. And he felt a sudden pleasure with their presence in the room. They reminded him of a road which knew where it was going, and how far the end was. He would not hesitate to go with them, for he was like the road itself which said that there was only one way. He knew how they felt, and he knew that they had added his feeling to theirs, and the result was the same which was their duty to San Cristobal. The future was on their list of possessions. But he could not understand the reason for Singh's behaviour this evening. There was more to it than a difference of tactics in dealing with the Governor's letter. Something was left unsaid, and he was going to probe for the secret which separated them. He raised his hands from the table and made ready to speak. Suddenly there was a knock on the door.

Neither Lee nor Shephard seemed to feel that anything was wrong, but when the knock was repeated they noticed Singh's agitation. Shephard made to stand, and Lee was glancing like a scared convict from Singh to the door. Singh was already on his feet. He was going to open the door, but he wanted to let them know what he had done. He felt something like betrayal, a gnawing sense of intrigue. It seeped through every limb of his tense, fragile body. The knock came again, a stronger and more determined thud of the fist on the door. It was as though the hand had warned that it would not strike again. Singh was feeling his way between the table and the small partition of books.

'Who could that be?' Shephard asked. He was trying to help Singh out of his secrecy.

'I will send him away,' said Singh, 'but I will tell…'

'Who is it?' Shephard interrupted.

'It is Baboo,' said Singh, 'but I will send him away.'

'You asked him to come here tonight?' Shephard asked.

'Yes,' said Singh, 'and I will tell you why.'

His voice was apologetic, regretful, and embarrassed. He walked towards the door while Lee and Shephard stared down at the table. He stood between Shephard and Lee, speechless and sullen. He looked like a man who had now seen, in the flesh, the terrible anxiety which had tied him to his secrecy. The door was still open. Lee and Shephard turned to see what had happened. It was not Baboo. Singh had taken his seat and they all seemed to wait for someone to speak.

When Bill Butterfield entered the room, the silence had already ripened into something other than a lack of sound. It was like an order to stand by for action, although no one, except Singh, had any idea why there should have been a war. Singh stared at the table as though he was refusing to be a part of what was happening. Lee crushed the cigarette box in his hands. Shephard glanced at them both before turning to Bill who had remained for a moment at the door. He had a sense of being very rudely shut out. He observed their attitudes as he walked forward to the table, and immediately he felt that it was the wrong time to talk with Shephard.

'I thought you might be alone,' he said nervously, 'or I might not have come tonight.'

Shephard had lost his composure. He was curious at first, but when he glanced at Singh who seemed to understand Bill's visit he felt a double suspicion undermine him. Bill's presence had isolated him from his friends. He was defensive and violent at the same time.

'What is it you want here?' he asked.

Singh looked up before Bill had replied. He felt uncertain about Shephard's voice, but he pretended not to care what this meeting was about.

'I think I shall leave it for another time,' said Bill.

'We can leave for a while,' Singh said, and Shephard winced under the rebuke of this offer. The sarcasm had suddenly placed him, against his knowledge, in some secret which Butterfield knew. He became wholly defensive, clinging desperately to the memory of his work with Singh. He was refusing contact with Butterfield, summoning prejudice like a dagger to save what existed between himself and Singh. And Butterfield, innocent and uncomprehending, could only feel this aggressive rejection which Shephard was trying to perfect.

'There is nothing you want to say to me which my friends here can't know,' said Shephard.

Bill took a step back, then lingered halfway from the door in silence. He wanted to leave them immediately, but when he remembered why he had come, their response seemed to work an unspeakable effect on his body. He felt crippled in every limb. He considered his reasons again, and reminded himself that this visit surpassed any simple error of intrusion. Perhaps he might have told them all why he had come. But he could hardly speak. It was the look in Singh's eyes, and the absolute approval of Shephard's voice which had silenced him. It was a perfect example of teamwork in ill-will. He did not know what he would do, but he was trying to recover from the spell of their resentment. And he felt, as he turned to face the door, that his love of San Cristobal had been outraged. But he was still uncertain what he should do about Shephard.

'It concerned your personal safety,' he said lamely, and turned to see how they had reacted.

'There is nothing you have to tell me now or any time that they can't hear,' Shephard said.

Singh heard the steps making towards the door. It was difficult to tell what he was thinking. He glanced at Shephard who was still trying to overcome the shock of Butterfield's presence in the room.

'One moment,' Singh said.

The others looked up. Bill paused at the door, but he did not turn to look at them. Singh felt a sudden fury burn his body.

'How you get to know about this room?' he asked.

There was a silence which seemed to prepare them for some disaster. Bill had turned slowly, wilfully, as though he had sensed their confusion. There was a sudden angry flash of retaliation in his eyes, and it was clear that he intended something destructive when he said: 'Ask Shephard. He can tell you.'

The door remained open, and they had all turned in time to see him charge like a shadow into the night.

The silence had changed to a kind of dumb bewilderment. Singh's feeling worked on him like an informer, collecting a new set of evidence to prove his wisdom. It was not by accident that Bill had arrived that evening. He knew it, and he wondered why Shephard would not admit that the man was no ordinary visitor. Of course, his message was personal. It had to be. He told himself some kind of injury had warped Shephard's sense. Was he returning to his former illness, or was there something else which he had managed to conceal from his comrades? He did not want

275

to think, for his feeling was already suggesting reasons, and he did not like them. He turned to Lee to suggest that they should continue with the discussion, but Lee was still trying to guess the nature of Bill's visit, and the degree of knowledge which Shephard might have shared with him. He wanted always to be cautious in his dealing with them both, and particularly at this moment, when things were likely to go wrong. He thought he saw a crack somewhere, a feeble wriggle which reminded him that unity must be won. Like the figures on the page, that man's visit was a simple fact which now challenged them to prove their unity. He did not want to appear as a mediator, for that would have been to suggest that there was a division at work. He turned to Shephard and asked whether he had accepted the suggestion to hold a meeting. There would be time to consider the Governor's invitation. But Shephard seemed suddenly awakened from some reverie of regret and dismay. He folded the papers before him, hinting that there was hardly any need to bother. The meeting was going to end with a decision which sealed their argument and their suspicion, a unanimity which might for ever contain some riddle.

'No need to hold any meeting,' Shephard said. 'We're not going to the Palace.' He looked at Singh whose wish had been granted.

'I'm with you both,' said Lee.

'Then that's that,' Singh said, and he looked like one who was conscious of a victory which demanded his permanent vigilance.

Shephard was silent, and Lee glanced at his watch. He wanted to draw their attention to something. He feared that war of silence which had already strained their nerves. If their decision was final and there was nothing more to discuss, he would prefer to go. He looked at his watch again, and his restlessness caught Singh's attention. Shephard made no stir at all. He sat still, desperate and alone, watching his hands.

'That's that,' Lee said, trying to enliven the room.

'Except for the plan,' said Singh. 'The workers won't strike till we fix up a supply of oil. Whatever happens our friends must have light.'

'I will take charge there,' said Lee. 'I got all the shops under my finger. I goin' give the order in secret that they store all the oil they got, and during the strike no sales to any but the people, that is our people.'

'Tell them to watch out for the servants,' said Singh, 'the servants may try to buy for those who bribe them.'

'As good as done,' said Lee, 'we goin' give them a little darkness to play with.'

He started to pile the sheets of paper into his briefcase. Shephard noticed his eagerness to go, and Singh was glad. Lee paced about the room creating a frenzy of movement with his hands. He had warded off the silence which unnerved him all evening, and now he would leave them alone. Shephard thought of asking him to stay, but he realised it was too late to try. Lee was ready.

'Until,' he said.

'Until,' said Singh.

Shephard raised his hand and gave him a long, solicitous and familiar look. He heard the door close, and for a moment he was afraid. 'This is the way things happen,' he thought, 'without warning or reason. From now on I must be careful with Singh. But already we have lost. The moment he was in doubt about me everything was threatened, and the real thing between us finished. The real thing...'

His mind was frantic with guessing about Butterfield, and he tried to remember the details of the afternoon on the island, wondering what Penelope could have told her husband. He had mentioned the room during their crossing from Bird Island to Paradise Point, but it was only an item of information, innocent of motive, which emerged from his passionate reverie of power and promise for San Cristobal. There was nothing unsafe or secretive about his personal exchange of experiences with Penelope. And he wondered how he could convince Singh that he did not know himself why Butterfield had come.

But the silence was their bond, articulate and unequivocal. It seemed to chart a current of meaning between them, relaying its messages without enquiry. Speech was an aid which might have failed them. Neither could find his way with words, but the room had relaxed. The light displayed itself across the books and the ceiling of worn, red pine. Was it for a second or a minute? They did not know. They could not measure the time which had restored them to the equal embrace of the room. But it had become theirs again, and the silence was broken. One word which seemed to hang in alarm on the air reminded Shephard of his name; and then the pause, like an echo which knew its end, slipped, gradual as mist, through Singh's voice.

'Isaac,' Singh had said, and Shephard, astonished by the novelty of the noise which that name had made, was still waiting for Singh to continue. The name was at once so strange and natural a substitute for Shephard. Singh, too, had surprised himself. He was looking at Shephard from the opposite end of the table.

'I will accept anything you say about the afternoon at Bird Island,' said Singh.

'Bird Island,' Shephard said, and he made it sound unknown.

'Baboo was there,' said Singh, 'an' it wasn't me who send him.'

'Baboo,' Shephard whispered.

He felt that he had started to create new difficulties for his innocence. He remembered Penelope and the boys and the circumstances which led to their meeting. He might have been able to tell Singh about all that, but the mention of Baboo was like a premature defeat.

'Where was Baboo?' he asked.

'In some tree where you been sittin',' said Singh, 'but I do not look or ask for explanation. I want you to know that it is days and days I ponder what Baboo relate 'bout your meetin' with the wife at Bird Island. And today it was with me all during our meeting.'

'Why didn't you tell me before?' Shephard asked.

'I had to talk with myself first,' said Singh, ''cause if I was wrong in what I believe, if it was true...' the voice had grown suddenly feeble, and Shephard saw him lift his hand slowly up from the table in a gesture of surrender. There was something innocent and vulnerable about the way he regarded Shephard, and when he tried to speak again, they both knew for the first time what really existed between them.

' 'Cause in this work which is all my life,' said Singh, 'the one and only man, the one, believe me, one and only man...' and then his voice failed, and his eyes sprang tears like a child, while Shephard seized his hand between his, and tried to hear him through. But Singh could not continue. He raised his head slowly from the table as though telling himself that he had missed his chance to let Shephard know that he was the only man who made any kind of betrayal impossible, the only man who could shake his faith in the movement. But he could not now carry on where his voice had failed him. He looked at Shephard for a moment before sweeping the papers in a heap before him.

'There must be no secret of any kind between us,' he said, 'no secret where the work is concerned.'

'None,' said Shephard, 'not one… And that's why I wonder why Butterfield came. I don't know, Singh, I really don't know.'

PART FOUR

1

The floor was covered with water when they broke into Marcia's bedroom. She had locked the door. The rain was pouring through the empty spaces of the broken pane, and all the taps were open. Mark bent the edges of the wood into the crevice of the sill and blocked the rain. The doctor had turned off the taps and the room was suddenly still. Marcia did not stir. She lay on one side, watching the queue of paper boats which she had made from the pages of Mark's diary. The doctor sat at the end of the bed, wiping the blood off her feet. The glass had slashed her ankle, but she did not feel the cautious probing of the doctor's hand turning the bandage round her leg.

They heard the thunder gradually gathering sound. There was a pause as though the clouds were collecting in a silent congestion above the house. Mark waded through the water to the other side of the bed and waited for the doctor to speak. Marcia was fighting to free her shoulder from his grip. Then the clouds broke, and Marcia, frantic with a strength they had not expected, leapt up from the bed. She was sheltering her head with the pillows, binding the sheet around her legs and screaming for mercy. Mark crept up from the back of the bed and tried to pin her shoulders down. The doctor came forward and tried to lock her legs under his arm. He glanced at Mark who had worked his way round the bed, trying to attract her attention. Her muscles had relaxed under his hands, but she did not open her eyes. The doctor could feel her legs give way under his arms. He wanted Mark to pass the bag with the morphia. But Marcia was beginning to kick again, and Mark was trying to talk with her.

'Listen, Marcia, listen to me. This is Mark.'

The doctor slipped from the bed, but he managed to hold his

grip round her legs. Mark lay against her, trying to soothe her brow with one hand. Her face was hot and wet, and the sweat poured like rain down the back of her neck.

'This is Mark. You must listen to me, Marcia. Listen to me.'

'The bombs,' she said, opening her eyes, 'now you want to use the bombs.'

'I don't have any bombs,' Mark said softly, 'it's the thunder. You know I love you, Marcia. I love you.'

'And the ropes,' she cried. 'You wanted to cut the ropes and sink the ship.'

Tears flooded her eyes, and they could feel her body relax. Mark made his body lighter where it leaned against her chest, and brought both hands against her face. She was calm, but for the sudden spasm of noise which her weeping made.

'There is no ship,' Mark said. 'We're in our house, and it's raining outside. But we're quite safe. We're just a little tired, that's all.'

She turned and saw the doctor smiling at her. He was passing his hand gently over her feet, and patting her knee. She looked at the doctor as though she understood who he was. The doctor prolonged his smile, but she had turned to see Mark. She gazed at Mark for some time before speaking, and then they felt her body tighten and saw the tears streaming down her face. She was speaking with the doctor who tightened his grip against her knee.

'His father died when he was a boy,' she said, 'and then the Germans sent him to Fern Row. He came to Fern Row with a black man who had three fingers, but the black man disappeared. He killed the black man. That's how we met.'

Mark put his hands over her face and tried to distract her from her fantasy. She thrust her head up and her forehead bruised his lip. She was becoming furious again, but the doctor nodded his head as though he believed what she was saying. Then she lay back, silent and frantic, collecting these ruins from her memory.

'I remember the evening he tried to cut the ropes,' she shouted. 'You can ask the others, ask them now, Penelope and Bill, call them now. They were on the ship too, and he was wearing this uniform, with the tall boots. Ask them.'

She paused and brushed Mark's hands from her face. Her

voice was steady and strong, almost casual as she leaned forward to be nearer the doctor.

'Ask them,' she said, 'ask them now.'

She eased her legs from under the doctor's hands and turned to look at Mark. They made no move to restrain her as she sat up, wiping the sweat from under her chin.

'Isn't it true, Mark?' she said, and now the voice quavered as she stared into his eyes. 'You cut the ropes and tried to sink the ship. You remember? But I would not let go. I would not let go. I wanted to get to the island. I wanted to get to the island. You remember?'

'I remember,' Mark said, 'I remember the island.'

'You see,' she said, turning to the doctor, 'you see it is no lie. He tried to cut the ropes. Then he talked to me about the war at Fern Row. He was a spy in the war at Fern Row. He wanted Penelope to give the secrets, so he took her up the stairs, you remember, Mark, you remember how you took her up the stairs, and then Bill saw him. He was raping Penelope. But it was in the war. It was all in the war…'

'Marcia,' Mark said, 'you must listen to me.'

The doctor intervened. He touched Mark's arm and suggested that he should not encourage her to argue. It was better to let her have her way until she grew tired.

'You will be all right,' the doctor said, taking her hand, 'I'm sure you'll feel better.'

'Then he walked off the boat,' Marcia continued, squeezing the doctor's hand. 'He walked away with nothing in his hand, nothing but his photograph, and he would not touch me. All he cared for was his photograph, but I would not let go.'

She slid further down the bed, clinging to the doctor's hand, and brought her face close to his ear. She wanted to exclude Mark from this secret interrogation with the doctor…

'Would you let go?' she asked. 'Would you?'

The doctor took her hands between his, and she leaned her head slowly down on his shoulder. She was tired. Mark wanted to soothe the back of her neck, but he saw the doctor signalling him to leave the room. He shook the water from his feet, and lifted the chair nearer the bed. The door made a noise like the snap of a finger, and Marcia looked up. The doctor was watching to see what effect

Mark's absence would have on her. She stared round the room as though she could not understand what had happened. She was shaking all over, slipping gradually into the state of hysteria which the noise of the thunder had aroused. The doctor pushed himself further along the bed, and leaned her head on to the pillow. He could see the whites of her eyes swelling with tears. Her mouth was half open. The doctor felt in the bag for the needle while he nursed her brow with one hand.

'You'll be all right now,' he said.

He was soothing the area where the needle would enter her arm. It seemed a good time to give her the injection. The needle was poised an inch above her flesh. Suddenly she sprang sideways and plunged over the edge of the bed. She lay face down in the water which covered the floor, and her voice rose in agony, burning their ears.

'I won't let go,' she screamed, 'I won't let go. I won't let go.'

Mark rushed back to the room. They struggled with her on to the bed, hearing her screams like a siren from afar. She was much weaker now, but the voice unnerved them. The doctor nodded to Mark to hold her down. The screaming grew more demented, but Mark closed his eyes and used all his strength to smother any movement of her body. In less than a minute the room was still, but for the sound of Mark's chaotic breathing. He turned her over, and rested his head against her face.

The doctor went over to the sink and washed the blood off his hands. He looked exhausted and afraid. Mark pushed himself up from the bed, shaking the water off his feet. He watched the small boats totter and swim round the bed. Marcia was asleep, her face turned up to the ceiling. The doctor seemed obsessed with drying his hands. He stepped over the rubble of the door, and waited for Mark to lead the way into the living-room.

'Why should she confuse me with that man on the boat?' Mark asked.

'Have you really told me everything you wrote in the diaries?' the doctor asked.

Mark hesitated. He glanced at Marcia, and the doctor continued wiping his hands as he walked away. He wanted to take off his shoes and dry his socks.

'I think so,' Mark said, 'but I don't know how much she actually read.'

'But you did show her the passages about the trip to Spain?' the doctor said.

'I showed her that.'

'But why?' The doctor had stopped unlacing the shoes to look at Mark.

'I don't remember,' Mark said.

'And you didn't think of the damage you might have done by letting her know how she existed in your mind?' The doctor's voice was loud.

Mark did not answer. He had become unnerved by the doctor's angry insistence. His hands fumbled over the table for the empty box of cigarettes. But he saw the laces hanging idly from the shoes, and the doctor's leg, blue-veined and wet, shaking in his hands.

2

The afternoon sparkled hard and clean as ice, but clouds were piling up behind the hills for a change of weather. The night would probably be black and heavy with rain. A huge macaw strayed over the wall and alighted on the roof of the hut where a warder kept guard within the iron gate. The bird craned its neck down and under the wide green wing of feathers, raised a wrinkled black claw up to its head and washed its face in the wind. The sun made a blazing circle of flame with the scarlet ring of feathers which turned like a collar round its neck. The eyes looked dazzled by the heat, but the head was held high, erect and calm as it stared through the flawless space of heat and wind which warmed its breast. There were patches of yellow feathers blossoming like marigold over the bright green coat which covered its body. The colours seemed to startle the air, and the small wooden hut looked as though it would collapse and be consumed by the vivid flame of feathers burning green above the roof. The bird was still, almost imperious in its pose of imperturbable calm. The mental hospital buildings were far away, the walls hid its view of the street, and the hut was still; but the air was suddenly rent by a violent squawk. One feather fluttered towards the grass and the bird had flown out of sight, leaving an echo of panic over the hut. Everything seemed to move to a still dead centre of surprise as the echo passed into the silence of the afternoon.

The guard looked over the half-door, surveyed the grounds for a while and then drew his head slyly into the hut. Singh stood close behind wondering about that tremor which had disturbed the air. Some minutes later they heard a step approaching the hut, and the guard looked out again. He motioned Singh into the corner, but it was too late. Ma Shephard had already leaned her head over the door. They saw the small black Bible wrapped in brown paper under her arm, and they knew they had to listen until she was ready to go.

'How's my boy?' Singh asked, as he slipped his hands under him and reclined on the bench.

'I leave him home,' said Ma Shephard. 'Your work weary him out an' 'tis a rest he restin' now.'

'Which ward you doin' today?' the guard asked.

'I come to spen' a minute only,' she said, 'an' I goin' visit Mr Kennedy make-believe wife. She need the Word.'

'Don' pray too long,' said the guard, 'you work yourself too much.'

'It ain't my life nor my strength,' she said, 'but the strength o' Him I serve.'

The men were silent, hoping that she would continue towards the wards. It was a voluntary service which she had rendered every week for years. She visited those patients who were off the danger list to read from the Bible. She was free to go wherever she pleased in the mental hospital, and sometimes a guard would accompany her to see those who, it was felt, were not yet well enough to join in the reading. Her favourite text was the story of the man from whom Jesus had driven the devils. She held to the view that madness was intended by God and as an example of the state which men would have to endure if they died without forgiveness. It was not the physical pain of hell which she taught, but the eternal separation from a source of love which the soul required but could no longer achieve.

'You need the Word no more an' no less than them,' she said, looking at Singh.

'I believe you, Ma, but give me a little time,' he said, and smiled as he watched her turn to look across the grounds. Her eyes caught the wires hanging slack between the poles which rose above the grass and showed in the distance beyond the wall.

'When we gettin' back the electric light?' she asked.

'It ain't me to decide,' Singh said.

She frowned and scolded him with a look. The men were getting uneasy. If she started to chastise Singh over the strike of electricians, it would be some time before she decided to leave them.

'They will turn back to work if you give the word,' she said. 'But you only think 'bout scarin' your enemy. An' my boy, too. You have no heart for forgivin'.'

'It will soon be over,' said Singh, 'strike, riots, everything. When we win you will see a San Cristobal you never know.'

'This ain't my Kingdom,' she said, pointing to the ground, 'this nor no corner on the earth.' She paused and eased the Bible from under her arm, raising it high above her head. 'I know a place where your riot an' strike won't ever take place,' she said, 'but it ain't here, not here.' She made a circle with her hand to indicate the absent horizon of the land. Then she walked away, patient and kindly, but without a word. The guard was relieved.

'I hope nothin' happen while she in here,' Singh said. He had got up to see her making her way towards the wards.

'Everything arrange,' the guard said. 'We put away all those who show any sign o' danger. The ones you may see rambling the grounds won't notice nothin'. They on the safe list.'

'The guards know the instructions?' Singh asked anxiously.

'They know, I sure they know.'

'The demonstration is jus' a fake,' said Singh. 'The moment they smell trouble with any lunatic getting beside himself the demonstration should stop.'

'There won't be no such lunatic outside today,' the guard said.

'Fine,' Singh said. 'Report when it over.'

He peered over the door, made sure that no one was in sight and quickly hurried out of the hut past the iron gate and into the street. The guard came out and patrolled up and down. He could see some of the patients frolicking in the distance. A man sat alone paddling his hand through the lake, and everything else was as he had predicted, ordinary and still. He looked again at Crabbe's car parked in the driveway which led to the main building, then cast his eyes in a weary glance towards the sky and walked back into the hut.

Rowley lingered at the door, trying to avoid his grandmother's attention. She was standing on the wooden stairs, a head above Ma Shephard, discussing the crisis which had come upon San Cristobal. Ma Shephard's face had turned serious, almost cheerless in its expression. She nodded her head and pressed the Bible between her hands as she listened to old Mrs Crabbe. It seemed that she had a power which told her more than she was hearing. Mrs Crabbe continued in a clipped, monotonous voice, fretful and fearless.

'I call it an outrage,' she said, 'depriving us of electric, and then refusing to sell oil to those who need light. The inconvenience of it and the injustice.'

'It is bad, I know,' Ma Shephard said. 'Bad to undo the wires, an' bad not to sell oil to those they call enemy.'

'And they want to lead this country,' Mrs Crabbe shrieked. 'You know what would happen if they had their way.'

'They must learn to forgive,' Ma Shephard said quietly.

'Forgive,' Mrs Crabbe exclaimed, 'but what have we done? We've tried to teach what we know. We've brought a civilised way of life they never knew, and then this is what we get in return. Just hatred and prejudice. Can you imagine what would happen if we weren't here? Can you imagine the disorder that would follow if we had to leave? Now, tell me, can you?'

She seemed to expect an answer, but Ma Shephard held her head down as though she wanted to forget the charges which were being made against her son and Singh.

'What we call justice is only a way of seein' right an' wrong,' she said, 'but no man can see if his eyes ain't open, and their eyes ain't open, theirs nor the ones they hold enmity 'gainst.'

'The inconvenience of it,' said Mrs Crabbe as though she had not heard a word. 'No light, and now we've tried to get some lamps, they've passed word to the little shops not to sell us oil. What have we done to deserve all this?'

'You must pray,' said Ma Shephard. 'Pray for them, an' for all who have to suffer what happen'.'

Rowley was trying to escape their attention. He wanted to pacify his grandmother with some promise, but he checked himself and turned to look at her. She was waiting for Ma Shephard to say something more hopeful and immediate to the issue which had made her so angry. She did not notice Rowley who had stepped under the archway. He was looking towards the small wicket gate at the other end of the grounds. There was no one in sight, and he seemed to lose heart. He leaned against the car and surveyed the curve of the wall expanding out from the gate. The place looked unoccupied, a desolate and deserted plain of grass and weed cringing under the assault of the heat. His grandmother was beginning to climb the stairs behind Ma Shephard and he saw her turn to look for him. He did not want to arouse any suspicions, and he leapt from the archway into the hall, and ambled slowly up the stairs. He was waiting his chance to escape.

A young doctor appeared at the top of the stairs, and his grandmother paused to talk with him. Ma Shephard continued towards the waiting-room where Crabbe and Penelope were sitting. Rowley saw his grandmother and the doctor pace slowly down the corridor in the opposite direction. He paused, and when they were out of sight he started a slow retreat down the stairs. He was going to wait in the archway until he had seen some sign of the boys. The secret Society was at work again.

Crabbe and Penelope were waiting in a small room on the second floor of the wooden building. The attendant had already told them that they could see Marcia, but they had different reasons for postponing the visit. Crabbe wanted time to speak with Penelope alone, but Penelope did not want anyone to share her afternoon with Marcia. When Ma Shephard arrived, they both agreed that she might go in first; and now it seemed they were waiting for her to leave. Crabbe thought they should all go in together, and he had asked Penelope to wait until his mother and Rowley arrived. Now he wondered whether Penelope would guess that their absence was a kind of arrangement.

'It was very good of you to come,' said Penelope, 'and bring your family, too.'

'Will she be all right?' Crabbe asked.

Penelope thought for a moment about Marcia and felt a sudden reluctance to discuss her with Crabbe.

'The young doctor thinks it's just a case of shock,' she said.

Crabbe noticed the way the voice faded to silence. There was something of a retreat in Penelope's manner, and he hastened to rekindle her interest in their talk.

'This man Kennedy,' he said, 'the chap she's in love with...'

'What about him?' Penelope said sharply.

There was a brief silence, and Crabbe realised he was about to make an observation which Penelope would not share.

'Nothing,' he said. 'One can never really tell.'

'Tell what?' Penelope asked.

'Don't get me wrong,' Crabbe said, and his manner had suddenly grown cautious and defensive. 'They just strike me to be so unusual.'

Penelope was suddenly reminded that she did not like Crabbe, but his manner was cordial, almost disarming. He looked apologetic, as though Marcia's illness was a personal embarrassment which he might have prevented. But it had created the right kind of excuse for his meeting with Penelope. It was a convenient way of talking about Marcia and Mark. And then Bill. He glanced at the window which offered a view of the grounds below, and he thought it safe to start their conversation again.

'How long have you all been here now?' he asked, walking casually towards the window.

'We arrived with Shephard,' said Penelope, and turned to watch him.

He had reached the window, and she could not see his face from where she was sitting. He was playing for time as he leaned his head over the sill and stared across the grounds.

He was not to show any reaction to the name of Shephard, and suddenly he swung round and invited Penelope to join him at the window. His attention was taken by one of the patients who, it seemed, was carrying on a frantic row with a blade of grass.

'Look here,' said Crabbe, pointing his finger at the man.

Penelope got up and walked to the window.

'What a world,' said Crabbe, 'it must be terrible for them.'

'I wonder what it is he has discovered,' said Penelope, recalling her meeting with Shephard.

'Discovered,' Crabbe said, a little perplexed and amused, 'what can he discover in that state of mind?'

Penelope did not answer. She continued to watch the man who was now pacifying the blade of grass. He held it like a lost lock of hair which reminded him of the head where it once grew. His manner was infinitely tender as he watched the grass turning slowly between his hands.

'Has it occurred to you that we are surrounded by people whom we don't understand?' Penelope asked. She was talking to Crabbe as though he were not near and might not hear. 'And they frighten us.'

'Until we find a way of dealing with them,' said Crabbe. 'It is then that we feel safe among them.'

'But we are never sure how to deal with them,' said Penelope. 'How can we be?'

'You learn from results,' said Crabbe, 'you may try the wrong method, now and again, but it's always from results that you learn.'

'Have you ever talked with one of them?' Penelope asked.

'No, I've never,' said Crabbe, 'but in my job I find that the same principle works. You can only try and learn from the results.'

'But when the results are not promising, what do you do?' Penelope said. 'You can try again, but each failure may have a corresponding effect on those you are trying with.'

Crabbe was not at all sure whether Penelope was referring to his work or the lunatics, but his attention was again attracted by the man in the grounds.

'If you're trying to help,' he said, 'you must be prepared for the failures. There are always so many more who will benefit in the long run. It's this faith which compels you to go on trying. You take the failures for granted. But every result to the contrary restores your strength. That's why people can go on working in such a place. They're helping life in some way. It may be small, but it matters, because it is on the side of life. That's why I go on in San Cristobal.'

'Do you think Shephard was really mad?' Penelope asked.

Crabbe gave a start, but his sense of shock quickly receded. Now he seemed more calculating in his replies, as though it was important to give the wrong answer, or encourage a false impression.

'Why did you mention Shephard?' he asked.

'You know he spent some time in this place,' Penelope said.

'Yes,' said Crabbe, appearing to think out his reply. He kept looking at the man in the grounds. 'Shephard may not be mad in the same way that man is mad, but he is mad. There are kinds of madness, and he certainly is mad.'

Penelope noticed that he was agitated, and she waited for him to compose himself. Shephard had become dominant in his thinking, and it had suddenly given his manner a certain warmth. His feelings were involved, but in a way which displeased him.

'Have you ever talked with Shephard?' Penelope asked.

'Not really,' he said. 'In an official way, but how can you talk with a man like Shephard. It's like asking what that man out there has discovered. Their state of mind makes reason impossible.'

Penelope pondered his remark. She had been drawn gradually into this obsession with Shephard, and she was trying to remember something of the conversation on Bird Island.

'That's probably what frightens us,' she said. 'I mean Shephard's state of mind, as you call it, and his conviction that he is on the side of life. Shephard feels he, too, is on the side of life.'

Crabbe turned his back to the window, and looked at Penelope. He was beginning to see himself in an argument, and he remembered Bill's letter, and wondered whether this was Penelope's way of saying that she agreed with Shephard's politics. But he did not show any emotion now. He seemed more formidable in that quiet, assured stance, like one on the job.

'You think Shephard is on the side of life?' he asked.

'I don't know,' she said, 'I was simply trying to give an example of something we said earlier. Trying, as you say, with something we do not understand. If you and Shephard are convinced that you are on the side of life, it is clear you are not talking about the same thing. At any rate if life means the same thing for you, then you don't understand him any more than he understands you.'

Crabbe hesitated, trying to remember the details of Bill's letter. Did it correspond with what Penelope was saying about Shephard? But he could not recall any mention of Shephard in the letter. Yet he was unsure of her meaning. He smiled very quickly.

'As I said,' he began, 'there are different kinds of madness, and Shephard's is one kind. He is mad enough to believe he is on the side of life.'

'I don't think Shephard would say that you were mad,' said Penelope. 'He might say that you were doing what was natural, considering who you are, your education, your background, your whole way of looking at the world.'

'There may be several ways of looking at the world, but there is only one world,' said Crabbe. 'It is my world and Shephard's world.'

'It exists in different ways in different heads,' said Penelope.

Crabbe looked suddenly irritated. 'Are you trying to defend Shephard?'

Penelope was astonished by his directness, and for a moment she wanted to rebuke him, but his manner did not seem to justify a quarrel.

'I'm not defending anyone,' she said.

Her tone was cold and final. Crabbe thought he had blundered, for in no circumstances did he want to antagonise Penelope. He reconsidered all he had said. He smiled and again his manner seemed apologetic. He looked out at the man who was now sitting in a still communion with the grass, and he thought that he might distract Penelope from their talk of Shephard. But he hesitated, remembering Bill's letter. It was a source of much anxiety for him, and he believed that Penelope might have been able to throw some light on something he wanted to know. He fought hard to offer Penelope his goodwill, but it was difficult to change their conversation without creating too obvious a break, and without losing an opportunity to ask Penelope about the letter.

'I can understand the way you talk,' he said, focusing his glance on her. 'But not all of us have that turn of mind, or the sort of courage which goes with it.'

'What courage!' Penelope could not feel any flattery in his observation, and there was nothing she had said which showed courage. She looked at him in a way which suggested that it was his duty to explain. And Crabbe smiled, as one would at another's absent-mindedness.

'I didn't think I could have employed your gardener or what-ever he is,' said Crabbe. 'Not in my house, knowing who he is.'

'It was my husband's choice,' said Penelope, 'and it seems to work.'

'You mean you've never lost anything since Thief joined you?'

'We haven't missed anything,' said Penelope, and she was obviously relieved, now she knew what he meant by her courage.

'Would you like to borrow him?' she asked, smiling. She knew where his talk was leading. Crabbe reflected. He had almost said yes, when the door was flung open, and Rowley ran in, panting for breath. Crabbe was angry with him for interrupting; but Penelope, who saw nothing wrong with his sudden appearance, had already beckoned him to join them.

'I'm hiding from Granny,' he said. The lighter fell from his hands, and he scrambled it quickly, slipping it shamefully into his pocket. Crabbe was about to ask what it was, but Penelope had already intervened to ask him about the small boat which had capsized near Bird Island.

'Go and find your granny,' Crabbe said. 'At once.'

Rowley was no less relieved to be out of the room. Penelope laughed; and Crabbe, feeling a little silly by this show of anger, laughed too.

He closed the door, and walked back towards Penelope, and she noticed that his laughter had not ended naturally. Then he smiled, and passed his hand through his hair.

'We were talking about Thief,' he said, looking through the window, 'could you spare him?'

'You would have to ask my husband,' said Penelope.

'Of course,' Crabbe said, and in the same breath, he added: 'I was only joking.'

He was about to mention Thief again when his mother entered, and the whole room seemed to adjust itself to her presence.

'Have you seen Rowley?' she asked, bowing at the same time to Penelope. 'I don't think he ought to be running about here on his own.'

'He said he was hiding from you,' said Crabbe, 'he must have gone along the corridor.'

'I never like walking without a guard,' said Mrs Crabbe, 'after all, this is not a gymnasium.'

She asked Penelope whether it was time to see Marcia. Penelope nodded. Crabbe did not move. He said he would go in search of Rowley; but when they left, he sat on a chair and tried to organise his thinking.

Rowley had rambled across the grounds towards the wicket gate which was open. The guard had gone, but others had collected in small groups along the road which led from the gate. He glanced over his shoulder to see whether they were likely to stop him, but the men paid no attention. Gradually they dispersed and walked away in different directions. A similar group stood outside the waiting-room. They were still wearing their uniforms, but it seemed that they had finished work for the day. A man rushed out from one of the offices, stuttering angrily as he approached the group. He chopped his hands violently through the air as he signalled orders to the men who refused to move. They watched him for a while as though they were trying to express without words their contempt for his authority. Then they turned their backs and continued talking. The man was working himself up to an uncontrollable fury. He moved nearer, cursing their idleness, as he circled his hand through the air, reminding himself of his duty to those who lived in this institution. But the men were indifferent. They walked further away towards the waiting-room, and the man ambled wearily back to the office.

The grounds were almost deserted. The white buildings rose and spread through the hush of the afternoon, losing their shadows in the still, dark pasture of weed and grass. The grass grew high, and the green blades turned and crossed like a tunnel of ribs which covered the weed. The earth was hidden like a grave under a fresh lid of green foliage, and the afternoon was passing slowly like the grave murmur of the wind under the grass. The walls of the mental hospital stood out, massive sentries in wood which had met in a white and cruel silence, like the fantasies they surrounded. But the sky turned away, leaving a lake of scarlet shadow in the pool.

Rowley had survived his impatience. He saw the boys labouring through the trampled tracks of sugar cane, and he waved them to hurry. He noticed that they could barely support the weight of the cans which they were carrying, but he thought only of the triumph of the secret Society and the surprise with which his grandmother and his father would receive his news that he had got them a supply of oil. He remembered what had happened the night before when the lights went out and his father's guests had to finish their dinner in the dark. He had seen his father's disappointment the night the lights failed, and their party was ruined. His grandmother was almost hysterical and could not be persuaded that it was not her fault that some of the politicians had encouraged their followers to cut the wires now the electricians were on strike. But for the few candles which they had found, the house was in darkness ever since. The maid had failed to get any oil. The rumours were true about the shopkeepers' prejudice against people like his father. He had thought of a way out. He had got the boys to purchase the oil with money from the Society's funds, and he had assured them that his father would pay double. The arrangement was a secret which he could now declare in triumph to his father. It was the secret Society outwitting San Cristobal, and his power surpassing that of his father. They did not really care about the price of the oil and the profits which the Society would make. But the crisis which paralysed San Cristobal had given their secret a new importance.

He saw the boys stoop and rest the cans, trying to catch breath. He glanced behind to make sure that he was not seen, but the guards were all hidden in secretive groups behind the office opposite the archway. The grounds were empty but for the man who stood behind the car in the archway, swaying the blade of grass under his nose. Rowley did not see him. He thought only of the boys who were approaching the gate. He was eager to hear whether anyone had suspected them. The boys crept up to the gate and rested, exhausted, over the cans.

' 'Tis a surprise, you see,' said Lee, 'but it nearly didn't happen.'

'How you get it?' Rowley asked. He was looking at the cans with delight, and he was not really interested in what had happened.

'The shops play hard to fool,' said Lee, 'an' down town they say they won't serve unless they get a paper message from my father.'

' 'Tis only a chance make it happen,' said Singh, 'that we know the shop outside that Lee father own. Lee went in an' was makin' himself useful, when his father's friend ask him to hold on till he get back.'

' 'Tis right there we buy it,' said Bob, 'an' we lucky too it was near 'cause we can't travel for long with this load.'

'Tell you what,' said Rowley, 'suppose we can get it in the car now nobody's looking, and I'll go for my father.'

The boys regarded each other uncertainly. They stared across the grounds, but they did not see anyone. The man with the blade of grass had rambled behind the building. Rowley offered to help carry the cans, and they limped across the grass towards the car.

'We better not wait,' Bob said.

'We don't want nothin' to happen the last time we makin' a work,' said Singh.

'If you say it's my father you're looking for, everything will be all right,' said Rowley. 'They know him here.'

'How soon you come back?' Singh asked.

'Now,' said Rowley, lowering the can, 'he'll come as soon as I tell him.'

They raised the boot and lifted the cans into the car. The man had come up quietly behind them. He was sucking the blade of grass, making it flutter from side to side as he shook his head. He raised it between his fingers and the grass leaned over his hand like hair. He squeezed his eyes as though he wanted to cry, and the boys watched him, incredulous and scared, as though they had forgotten for a moment where they were. Then he took the grass from his mouth and smiled, but they were still transfixed by his action which they were gradually beginning to understand. Singh wanted to run, but his legs had lost their strength. They continued to stare at the man who was caressing the grass with his hand. He came closer to them, smiling, and they tried to feel at ease, but their suspicions had unnerved them. Rowley thought of his father, but he could not move.

' 'Tis how she die,' the man said, 'an' I ain't see her no more after the burnin' cover her head and her hair blow away. 'Tis how she die.'

He waved the grass in the air as though he would have liked to see it drift with the wind out of sight. Then he put it in his mouth and sucked the end.

'An' they put me here,' he said, ' 'cause they think I do it, but I ain't do it, I ain't do it ever. It just happen. An' I beg them to see how it happen, but they won't let me show. 'Cause they know I don't belong here till now they make me what they think I was. 'Tis w'at they do, holdin' me here. An' I beg them to let me show, but they want to hold me here. An' I don't mind they hold me, but I want to show.'

'Show what?' Bob asked, trying to show courage. His voice was hardly audible.

'How it happen,' the man said. He lowered his head, and turned the grass in his mouth. 'Make like you light a cigarette,' he said, turning the grass between his fingers, 'make like you light it.'

Bob hesitated. He was squeezing his hands together, trying to lift them level with the man's mouth, and the man stooped lower and brought his head closer. 'Make like you light it,' he said, and suddenly Rowley thrust his hand out, showing the lighter. He wanted to console the man.

'Light the grass?' he asked.

The man nodded, and suddenly drew his head away. Rowley's hand remained outstretched, but the man had pulled the grass from his mouth. He seized Rowley's hand, and ripped the lighter from between his fingers.

'Where you get it?' he asked.

'It's mine,' said Rowley. He was trembling with rage and fear, as he watched the man.

'You steal,' the man shouted, 'you steal.'

'Ask them,' Rowley said, 'they know it's mine.'

But the man had refused to listen. He looked at the lighter in his hand, and then he turned to Rowley, tightening his grip.

'Why you steal?' he said, 'why you steal? You take everythin' from everybody. Why you take? An' make them hol' me here.'

'It's mine,' Rowley insisted, and tried to release his hand. 'You ask them.'

The boys felt themselves pressed against the car. They hoped someone would appear to distract the man who was staring fiercely at them while he held Rowley's arm. They wanted to escape, but the man's gaze was like a weight which fixed them to the ground. He had forgotten the blade of grass, for the lighter seemed to have started another stream of memory. He looked at it as he champed his teeth, and threatened Rowley with his arm. The boys were overcome with fright. They were pressing themselves further under the open boot of the car. They could not bear their terror any longer. Singh darted under the man's outstretched arm, and stumbled across the grass. He fell flat on his face, and as quickly rose again, running towards the gate. The man released Rowley, and the other boys suddenly swung from behind the car, and dashed after Singh. Rowley stood for a moment, uncertain where he should turn. He was crying, and the man seemed suddenly to lose the anger which had possessed him when he saw the lighter in his hand. His expression was mad and frivolous. He held the lighter as he had done earlier with the grass, and Rowley took the opportunity to escape. He had gone in search of his father, but he did not know what he would say. He wanted to regain his lighter, and he wanted to tell his father about his success with the oil. But he did not know the order in which he should relate the two. He stood on the stairs, frantic and afraid. The three boys had got beyond the gate. They crouched in the grass, panting breathlessly, waiting for some sign of Rowley. They could not imagine what would happen. They watched the man who now stood beside the car, talking to the lighter. He looked around the grounds, and he saw himself alone, and he thought no more of the boys. He treasured this solitude with the lighter and the blade of grass, which he had recovered from the ground. Then he crept towards the car, and closed the boot quietly over him. He would stay there telling his grief to the blade of grass and the metal lighter which had returned like the sad memory of a woman's hair once lost in flames.

The boys lay on the grass outside the iron gate terrified by their silence and their exhaustion. Singh tried to raise his body, but his arms wobbled and fell, and he could feel the repetitive, galloping thump of his heart against his ribs. Bob's mouth was dry, and his throat burnt. He saw the sweat swell and slide like dew over his hands, and he pressed his nose against his fingers, and felt his eyes swim round the narrow black circles which the grass made under them. But Lee had recovered his strength. He was beginning to suspect the future of their labours. If Rowley's father refused to buy the oil, they would probably lose their money; or the guards might take the oil since they were guilty of trespassing on the grounds without permission.

'Think we goin' save this last work?' Bob asked. He raised his head trying to take some confidence in Lee's composure, but his arms were still quivering under the weight of his body.

' 'Tis a last work always the hardest,' said Lee, 'but when he pay, we goin' take a holiday.'

'I ain't makin' no game like this again,' said Singh, ' 'tis too much plannin' an' waitin', an' always you feel something waitin' to take you by surprise.'

'But it work,' said Lee, 'the secret Society really work, an' till this minute we never feel no failure.'

'I goin' take a rest,' said Bob, 'after this the Society got to rest or we can make some other game.'

'But we can tell how it work,' said Singh, 'there ain't nothin' prevent us makin' a boast how we see it work.'

'It work all right,' said Bob, 'I done decide how I goin' tell my father what we do.'

'Me, too,' said Lee, 'after we see what happen here.'

'It ain't matter what happen,' said Bob, 'we can tell what we do, 'cause we succeed every time, an' now don't make no difference. But I tired holdin' the secret. I just want a rest from not sayin' something.'

'Whenever we tell the secret,' said Lee, 'it mean that the Society finish, an' if people know what we doin', there ain't no point doin'.'

'An' they won't give a work no more,' said Bob, ' 'cause they feel they have no business with games.'

'Then we got to walk like boys again,' said Singh, 'if ever we tell the secret we got to start thinkin' like boys again.'

' 'Tis all right,' said Bob, 'I want to stop for a time. Maybe after a rest we start something again.'

'But not like the Society,' said Singh, 'it look too dangerous, after w'at happen with that mad man.'

'But we can't tell the secret 'bout the Society if we don't say what happen this evenin',' said Lee, 'an' perhaps they won't believe that we had to get away from that man.'

'They won' believe, but 'tis true,' said Bob, 'an' once 'tis true I can tell them. It goin' make the biggest story I tell 'bout the Society.'

'Not bigger than the time we nearly drown,' said Singh.

'Perhaps not,' said Bob, 'but nobody ain't help to save us this time.'

'An' that man look more terrible than the water feel that day,' said Lee. 'When I see his eyes, my toes take a long cramp. 'Tis why I couldn't run. I just stand there feelin' the knots tying my muscles up to my knee.'

'Where you think he gone,' said Singh, 'I ain't see him move.'

'He was behind the car,' said Bob, 'but he disappear.'

'He got the sense to know they might lock him in if he look dangerous,' said Lee. 'He was only talkin' a half-mad talk.'

'That talk was mad right through,' said Bob, 'mad from start to the end.'

'Perhaps we been half-mad with all the trouble o' the Society,' said Singh, 'everythin' look mad from here.'

'I ain't mad,' said Bob, 'I was just 'fraid.'

Now he succeeded in raising his body from the ground. They faced each other, sitting on the grass, and their eyes seemed to declare a common verdict on the future of the Society. They were going to make their secret known and retire from the game. Then Bob spoke again as though he had suddenly discovered another secret which had escaped the other's attention.

'But Society or no Society,' he said, 'we goin' stay like before. Just like before.'

The others did not answer. Lee was pointing ahead where the guards were collecting in a line outside the waiting-room. Others

300

emerged from the building, and the queue lengthened. It seemed that all the guards had assembled to join the queue which now moved slowly past the waiting-room, making a semicircle round the building. They moved forward in single file, demonstrating their refusal to work. They held their heads down, hands thrust in their pockets, coursing indolently round the grounds. The tail of the queue disappeared behind the building, and gradually the others emerged in a curve round the other side of the building. They were completing a circle which they would retrace until they were satisfied with their protest. They marched past the wicket gate, and the boys slipped out of sight. But they could still see the men's faces, grim, and angry and fearless.

'They behavin' like the people they take charge of,' said Bob.

'But they know what they doin',' Singh said, 'it seem the strike reach here, too.'

They kept their lips under the grass, talking in whispers, as they watched the queue grope wilfully past the iron gate along the waiting-room and round the building.

'You think they goin' let all the madmen get away?' Bob asked.

'Would be terrible in town,' said Singh. His eyes widened in awe at such a prospect.

'Imagine the madmen takin' over the town!' Bob said. 'There ain't no sayin' what could happen after that.'

'They'll have to shoot them,' said Singh.

'You can't shoot a man who ain't know what he doin',' said Bob. ''Tis cruel. An' it ain't their fault if the guards let them go. Would be more right to shoot the guards.'

'But it ain't the guards' fault that it happen,' said Lee, 'why the others don't give them what they askin' for.'

'Would be murder for everybody if those madmen decide to take over the town,' said Singh, 'you an' me an' the guards an' all the rest.'

'Those who ain't mad would have to fight them,' said Bob.

'You mean the mad in a war against those who ain't mad?' Singh asked.

'But would be like the Ants,' said Lee, 'you can't fight a enemy you don't understand.'

'And suppose the madmen win?' asked Singh.

'Perhaps they'd make everybody else take their place in that building,' said Bob.

'You mean those who mad outside, an' those who ain't mad put away?' Lee asked.

'Sometimes I hear my father say it might be better that way,' said Bob.

'That would soon make everybody mad,' said Singh, 'an' you can't have a whole world in one place mad.'

'But look how the guards behavin',' said Lee, 'like they mad, too. An' when those in charge play mad, then everythin' turn upside down.'

'They should punish whoever make this trouble,' said Singh, 'it could be too terrible to forgive.'

'I think you right,' said Bob, 'it could lead to something too terrible.'

' 'Cause look how nobody seem able to order them back to work,' said Singh, 'an' in a place like this.'

'It mean that we can't go back inside to talk 'bout the oil,' said Lee.

'You mean we goin' lose it?' Singh asked. 'If we lose what we work for I blame those guards.'

'They ain't got ears to listen to nobody now,' said Bob.

'Look there,' said Lee, 'w'at it is she find?'

Ma Shephard was staring at her hands, trying to guess the direction from which the little ball of crocus bag had struck against her back. The man had already slipped the boot over his head, and Ma Shephard continued to stare in amazement at the line of guards emerging on the other side. She glanced at the small bag and then slipped her hand into her pocket. There was a faint smell of burning rubber in the air, but her attention was dominated by the lawless display of the guards moving idly past the small wicket gate towards the office building. She remembered Singh, and looked towards the hut at the other end of the grounds. But no one was there; then she turned again, looking towards the car, and felt a sudden relief when she saw Crabbe hurry through the door. Rowley stood behind him.

Crabbe halted suddenly under the archway, shocked by the spectacle of the guards who had continued walking in a circle round the building. He had lost his assurance. He stood beside the car, holding Rowley's hand, and his mind was incapable of decision. He looked inside the building, and then across at the office, as though he were trying to choose between a personal and a public anxiety. Then he ordered Rowley to return immediately to the room with his mother. Involuntarily, his hand found the car, and the door opened. But immediately he changed his mind. He slammed the door, and hurried across the archway into the office. He was going to order that the police be armed and dispatched at the hospital. The office was empty. He lifted the receiver, and then he noticed Rowley lingering at the door of the building, trying to see the guards. Rowley watched them pass, and then crept behind the car, forgetful of the guards, to see whether the oil was safe.

Crabbe slammed the receiver and rushed to the door to order him back to the building. But his ears were suddenly split, and his eyes bled, and the world of his sense had fallen into an appalling blankness which hissed and leapt before his eyes. The guards fled like a frightened flock of sheep, wild and loud with fear, and the air expanded everywhere in a red ruin that wrapped round the white wooden walls of the mental hospital.

Crabbe fell back into the room, and Ma Shephard tottered forward, speechless with alarm as the dense spiral of smoke rose and covered everything from view. The arch had collapsed, and Rowley, mutilated by the flames, lay beside the charred corpse of the man under a smoking rubble of metal and wood.

The building opened like a tomb. The walls melted in the flame and the wind rode scarlet edifices of cloud in a widening circle over the smoking wood. The voices had joined in a single wail that shook the earth and reached to the sky, until their tongues were stopped by the swelling fists of smoke that turned and pushed to the back of their throats; and their eyes closed, finally scarred by the stabbing darts of flame. The walls had surrendered, but the massacre swept wide, fencing those who were trying to escape. The voices came again, and their feet fumbled through the thick tangle of smoke that burnt blue and sore beyond relief. They struggled alone, beyond aid, in their pain, as they did in their lunacy. For the fire had surrounded their world with a quivering red wall which grew larger and more menacing, transparent and impenetrable. They were isolated from aid until the trenches were opened, and the water burst from the canvas pipeline, falling in a steady, lumbering thud over the smoke which covered the dead.

The town had collected outside the enclosure, mourning the fate of San Cristobal. Their faces were sad and suspicious, and their eyes travelled like the wayward crawl of the smoke, falling heavy over the grass. They looked towards the black wreckage where the guards were working frantically through the charred ruins that smoked hot and wet in their hands. The water came in a fine shower as they passed the bodies like bent sticks, scorched and sweating down the line where the ambulances waited. The mental hospital was level with the grass, and the voices struggled for sound under the throttle of smoke.

But the crowd had not offered their verdict on the disaster which had silenced them. Their feelings were fed by a sorrow which they could not utter as they speculated on the names and number of the dead. It was as though a curse had settled for ever on the hopes of San Cristobal. They had lost their sense of peace. Hope had deserted them.

'Good God, got mercy! Was only wood what house those poor folks.'

'However it happen?' someone asked, 'however it could happen here?'

'Was only wood,' a voice replied, 'was only wood house those poor folks.'

'Lord God, w'at happen?' the other voice shrieked, 'w'at happen here?'

Many had trickled on to the grounds working a way past the police to get a close view of the scene, and to hear what had happened before they arrived. They stopped beside the guards in a similar effort to clear the debris and locate the voices which were cut short beneath the sizzling black wreckage. The police seemed wholly occupied with questions and the various suspicions which some had raised about the origin of the fire, and gradually the crowd began to swell the scene, until they all seemed part of a public inquest. The law was allowing them to help in the defence of the dead, and since the law required an accused, they were beginning to search their feeling for a possible suspect.

The boys had joined the crowd on the grounds, but no one noticed them. They would turn away and as quickly return, lingering round the smoking remains of the car. They were trying to recognise the black heap of burnt iron and metal which the car made in the archway, telling themselves that Rowley was the only person who shared their secret about the oil. And now they were the only three who knew. Rowley had been taken away with half a face, and all his skin consumed before he died in the flames. The boys did not speak, but each knew the other's fear, and their silence described too their grief and their innocence. They were trying to remind themselves that they had nothing to do with what had happened. Their safety was in their silence, for they could not explain to anyone that they were concerned only with the game of the secret Society which proved their unity and their affection. The fire was something which happened. It was outside their intention or their desire, and beyond their control. But the police were already beginning to ask questions, and people had started to substitute their ignorance for explanations and opinions which might seem reasonable in the circumstances.

One of the guards was telling the policeman what he remembered, and the crowd closed in, moving closer to the car. The boys retreated slowly, wondering whether the guard had seen them earlier.

'It didn't start nowhere in the buildin' you see fall down there,' he said. He waved his finger in an attitude of positive denial. 'That much I remember, a noise which break up the squad we make in preparation for strike, an' then we see the top o' the arch there move back an' the car let out all fire an' smoke. An' nobody could get near there till it was no use tryin', when half the building was red. God only know how the boy an' the madman get trap' there, but it ain't no need askin' now, 'cause they can't tell. But it start outside, an' for all I know, it start with the car. Nobody ain't set a fire inside.'

'Perhaps the car bring the trouble with it,' someone said.

The policeman did not register this remark. He called two of his colleagues and they made ready to disperse the crowd. The people lingered for a while, moving reluctantly towards the gates as the police approached. The guards were collecting in one place to give evidence, and another ambulance drove away. The crowd pressed indolently through the gates, pausing outside to consider the tumbled wreckage which smoked wearily through the evening.

The air was heavy and sultry, moving everywhere with the odour of sulphur and burnt wood, as though it would remind the town of its uncertainty. The sunset had failed against the red tides of flame that swooped up from the grounds, and turned, wide and spreading, to the sky. The smoke followed like a gradual, black jungle that rolled over the grass and embraced the trees. And now the night was near.

Ma Shephard felt safer. The night was like a loud whisper in her head, but it took the light from her eyes, and concealed her failure of spirit. She was waiting for a chance to desert the crowd. She was lost in the tumult that swelled as she returned with the crowd to the street. She took no part in their wild surmising about the fire. Her grief was more intimate. She was thinking about her son who was removed from her by an ambition she could not trust; and she wished she could persuade him to renounce his claim to the power which people now praised him for. She saw that his will was a temptation which he could not overcome, and she knew where it would lead. The fire had reminded her of her fears for San Cristobal. It was a warning which had made the innocent suffer, and a curse on those who refused to see that the future of San Cristobal was beyond their power.

She recognised the boys stealing their way to the side of the street. She saw their faces in the early night, tight and grave, as though they were trying to understand a grief beyond their years. She wished that her son was their age. The boys made for a moment of hope in her sad reverie. She wrestled through the crowd, and followed close behind them. She could talk to these boys as she would have liked to talk to her son, and she knew they would listen with an interest which was beyond those whom age had made obstinate in their ignorance and disbelief, like this crowd who would rave until they tired, showing no respect for the truth which a wise experience had brought to her years. And they were dangerous for the boys. It was in that innocence of wonder and simple belief that evil found its readiest soil. She was not only consoled by the presence of the boys; she felt her duty towards them. It was her chance to depart from the crowd.

Singh was scared when he saw her, but she did not recognise their secrecy. She held their hands, and without words steered them away from the main street over the tracks of pebble and sand which skirted the houses. The boys could hardly contain their suspicions. Ma Shephard probably knew what had happened. But they were not guilty of any crime, and they felt she should know that too. They trusted her to understand everything.

The crowd were beginning to separate where the street divided, and the boys were preparing to walk away in different directions. But Ma Shephard signalled them to wait until the crowd had made distance between them. The boys waited, avoiding each others' glances. Ma Shephard was quiet, looking at the crowd which gradually crept beyond her view into the hollow of the night.

'Now we make a move,' she said, pressing Singh's arm. The others hesitated, but she turned to look for them. 'Won't take you long, just join me a little where the roads make a secon' turnin', an' then I can go safe. But the old knees not wearin' well after what we see this evenin', and my heart take more to you as guide than the big ones who hurry past in their wildness.'

She paused, feeling her way beside the boys. They had become more relaxed, but they did not speak, and the old woman did not notice.

' 'Tis that wildness you got to keep clear from,' she said, ' 'cause it can only spell ruin as we see this evening, only ruin. My knees shake with the age o' those hills that hide behind the dark, but I see how it come, an' how it grow, an' my heart feel a lump when I see you in all your simple life not knowin' w'at is danger an' w'at it ain't, 'cause the wildness that surround you is too swift for a young understandin'.'

They listened, but they could not choose between silence and a reply.

'An' there ain't no time to learn,' Ma Shephard continued, 'there ain't no time. Every lesson is a learnin' for a knowledge that won't serve, 'cause it last no longer than the time that make it look important, an' the time is always short, an' they goin' kill San Cristobal as they crucify that poor place this evenin' scarcely gone, and you an' me an' every life that take air from the breeze blessing this land, every breathin' soul goin' weep without even a tear to show pardon. 'Cause there can come a time when the heart turn stone, an' no kind o' pardon can call a tear, not one tear to show that love leave a little moisture in the soul. An' so it must be for those who find their way in secret to set a curse o' fire on the sick. 'Twas a mad act, mad as those poor heads that burn an' couldn't tell what evil take them, but we who live goin' answer for such a sin.'

The boys had not spoken, for words might have betrayed them into a confession which they could not fully explain. And Rowley was not there to prove their innocence. The old woman's prediction had increased their fear. Their secret game had come to an end, but the Society would probably be put on trial. They could not refuse to answer questions, and it was not likely that anyone would believe their answers. They were beginning to feel the need for shelter and the protection of their parents. They wanted the old woman to let them go, but they did not want to arouse her suspicions.

She had paused outside the house. The boys were eager to be relieved of their service, but she seemed to need them. She had remembered the small ball of crocus bag in her pocket, and she asked Singh to see what it was. They stared in silence at the piece of bag opening slowly under their eyes. The lighter was wrapped inside. They were afraid to claim it. They were terrified of their knowledge and they seemed to agree, by instinct, on their role of ignorance.

'I don' know w'at it is,' said Singh.

'It look like a…' Bob hesitated, as he saw Singh fold the lighter back in the piece of crocus bag, and slip it into the old woman's pocket. They wanted to desert her now, but that might have aroused suspicion, and they waited for her to say something. But she had lost interest in the piece of crocus bag. She was thinking of her son as she noticed the lamp filling the creases of the window with light. She wanted to talk with her son, and she wanted these boys to be present.

She fumbled up the steps, feeling for the wooden rails that led to the door. They saw that she was tiring, and it seemed that she could not get past the door without their help. She was waving them to follow her, and instinctively they hurried up the steps and helped her through the door. They stood in the dark passage, but the old woman called again as though her strength had suddenly failed. They led her further along the passage, and then they heard footsteps, and a door opened showing the small lamp which filled the passage with light. The old woman strengthened her hold round them, and suddenly they felt her weight desert them as though she had been lifted off the ground. Shephard was standing in the door, guiding her with one hand through the room. She was still calling for the boys, and Shephard waved them in, and closed the door. And each seemed to think that it was the first time they had met the man whom San Cristobal had sworn to follow. He settled his mother in the chair and looked up at the boys.

'They been a golden help,' she said, ordering the boys to sit, 'an' after what I see this evening, I only want to make a prayer for them, an' for a future that may never see them roast alive. 'Cause it is the ones that size that make tomorrow. No promise, an' no threat o' words that forget a meanin', but a livin' boy an' girl who can't see more than their years, an' who follow only where the old ones leave off. 'Tis only why I beg them follow me, not knowin' to find you here, an' all alone.'

Ma Shephard had recovered her strength, but she had been silenced by the grave bewilderment which she saw in her son's face. Shephard looked as defenceless as the boys who crowded on to the chair behind him. They watched him closely, wondering whether he would speak about the fire. Perhaps they might tell him what they knew. But he seemed unwilling to hear anyone. He leaned across the table, soothing his forehead with both hands. Ma Shephard thought she recognised this attitude. She was afraid of her suspicions, afraid of the curse which he had brought upon himself. She knew that he was in trouble. The boys recognised her fear, and they wondered what she had seen which no one wanted to tell.

He knew they were staring at him, and he looked up from the table and turned to face the boys. Ma Shephard sat at the edge of her chair. She could see his face more clearly in the light. His eyes were like lights that showed up the sullen, pitiful brooding of his face. His brows were arched, black and weary, but there was also the expression of a child's penitence which softened his face. She could not recall him in this attitude of longing and neglect, and it drew her to him, as though he had suddenly lost his years and his power. He was her son, freed from a wayward ambition which had left her without any power of persuasion in his life. Until this moment which was probably too late. She could feel her fear return; but her pity was useless if her suspicions were right. Perhaps it was the fire which had reduced him to this state of contrition. She glanced at the boys, and quickly turned to him.

'But forgiveness is free,' she said, 'if not here, here after, an' there ain't no sayin' what mercy may be in store, bad as this evening was.'

He understood her misgiving, and she noticed that her words had wounded him more deeply. He turned to the boys as though he wanted them to protect him from her charge.

'Do not suspect too much,' he said, talking to the boys, 'suspicion is the end. It will rot everywhere, everything we do.'

Ma Shephard was growing restless on the chair. She had forgotten her prayer for the boys. It was her son who occupied her attention. He was looking at her from across the table, as though he wanted to bridge the time and the worlds which kept them apart, although their wish was the same. But she could not see beyond her faith.

'And if they really kill me for what I've done,' Shephard said, 'there will be others. There will always be others.'

He stood, and the boys leapt from the chair as though they wanted to intercept him. The old woman gazed at them, and Shephard turned to ask what had happened. But the boys were speechless. They could not understand why he had spoken as he did.

'But you ain't do nothing,' said Bob. 'I was there before the fire start.'

Bob paused, and waited for the others to speak. He was afraid he had said too much, and he elbowed Singh to say something quickly.

310

'You never pass near there,' said Singh, ' 'twas only the madman an' the guards, and Rowley who get killed.'

'Why you say you do it?' Lee asked quickly.

Shephard was slow to answer. His mother leaned from her chair, as though she suspected some larger disaster. Could it be that these boys were offering to lie in order to save her son? He had caught them young, she thought, and there was no power which could persuade them that he was wrong.

'How you come to be there?' she asked.

'It just happen we had to pass there,' Singh said lamely, 'it just happen.'

'Like the fire,' said Bob, 'just a chance.'

The old woman raised her body in the chair and looked up at Shephard. She was accusing him of his power over these boys who did not convince her.

'I wasn't talking about the fire,' said Shephard. 'We'll find out what happened, and you must not tell any lies for me or anyone.'

' 'Tis no lie,' said Bob.

But he did not continue. They saw the old woman's eyes turn on them, and they felt they were already called for trial. Their little game had come to an end, but they had already entered each other's future by a secret which they dare not deny.

Shephard opened the door, and the boys nodded to the old woman who raised her hand, and mumbled some blessing. They filed out into the passage, and Shephard watched them drift slowly past the last rim of the light into the night. He returned to the room and sat on the chair which the boys had occupied. His mother waited for him to speak. But he was thinking of the boys and his warning against suspicion, and he recalled the evening in another room when he had met with his colleagues to discuss the strike. It was then that he had been reminded of the contagion which distrust could carry to any heart, and he saw Bill Butterfield turning away from the table, rejected and despised by men who were afraid to trust. And he himself was part of the bitterness which made Singh and Lee suspect the stranger's intentions. They had turned Bill away, and they had done so in the certainty that their instinct was right. And he had accepted.

Now his suspicion had turned against him as though it mocked his judgement. His regret had failed to relieve the feeling of guilt which Bill Butterfield had created. It was Bill he thought of when he warned the boys against suspicion, and it was his intolerable sense of guilt which he tried to express in that warning. He would have liked to see Bill, but he knew it would be difficult to tell in words the measure of his feeling, and he wondered what he could do to prove his need of the other's forgiveness. He turned in the chair, bringing his head down to his knees. His mother raised herself feebly from the seat and went beside him.

'What happen now?' she asked. 'What new trouble you put yourself in?'

'No trouble is new,' he said softly, and he stood, offering her the chair. 'But this concerns me only. And Mr Butterfield.'

She shuffled into the chair while he paced round the room, and he could sense her eagerness to hear what part Bill Butterfield had played in this harrowing restlessness which had come over him. He did not speak. He walked back to the table, and his hand turned slowly round the package in his pocket, and he thought that it must have arrived about the same time the fire was preparing for the total massacre of the mental hospital. And suddenly he remembered the boys, and wondered whether they might find a way to avoid the suspicion which had made a wall between strangers, and which had now placed him for ever in Bill's debt.

The old woman saw his hand crawl quietly over the table, and his eyes turn fearfully over the contents of the envelope which Thief had delivered in the afternoon. Ma Shephard peered through the light, trying to recognise the black leather wallet which was open on the table. But she could not read the name engraved under the square face of celluloid, and she did not know that the letter which he was reading again was Bill Butterfield's short explanation of the way he had come by the crisp fragment of paper which carried the arrangements for Shephard's assassi-nation.

'And there might have been no election after that,' he said to himself. 'But it isn't my death, not so much that as Butterfield's wish to save me… Butterfield on the side of San Cristobal…'

San Cristobal had stumbled quietly like the sun into some familiar territory of silence. The days were dark, and everywhere the weather wandered, reluctant and ominous, with a hidden warning that they would have to postpone their festival. Election Day was gradually losing its appeal. The fire had prolonged their mourning. Some said it was a warning and a judgement against their readiness to celebrate the victory which they were promised. On the eve of their prosperity, they felt a steady weakening of will. It was as though some fearful robbery was about to take place. The fire had started fresh rumours. The atmosphere was tense. Leave had been suspended, and the police appeared in greater numbers. It was generally known that the Governor was afraid. He was always in consultation with his advisers. There was an atmosphere of un-lucky preparedness. Something was going to happen.

Singh had left town on a pre-election campaign in the north, and no one had seen Shephard. A rumour persisted that he was ill, but the opposition were declaring that he was afraid. It was thought that the burden of governing was more than he could withstand. There was a rumour too that he had discussed yielding his place to Singh. But the party had made no statement. The weather had interrupted the pre-election meetings in the town, but Lee and the other candidates had appeared to remind the people of their duty. They were assured that Shephard was well and Singh would soon be back to celebrate their victory. They were asked to remember their polling stations, and they were advised against antagonising the police in any way. There were to be no demonstrations until the results had been announced. The meeting was a personal success for Lee who made a brilliant speech, reminding them of their pledge to the party. He told them that the new police regulations were an obvious attempt to intimidate them. He wanted the election to take place without incident. It had to be a day when San Cristobal displayed impec-cable conduct. He had calmed their fears a little, but it was now four days since Singh had left, and Shephard was still absent.

On the eve of election, nothing had changed. The morning had arrived in mist and drizzle, tired and unwilling like the remains of the previous night. The public clocks looked silly and false as the day lingered, showing no visible sign of progress. It was raw, slow and deceptive. In the afternoon, the light had already darkened. The winds increased, and there were rumours of a storm. But the rain had abated. The shower would last for a while, then fail gradually to a teasing drizzle over the streets. And the drizzle continued into the night. Few people had gone out. The shops remained open, but they were nearly all empty, and the streets were quiet. Business had relaxed into a sulky inertia. But the night had now brought a certain illusion of sameness. It was always black in San Cristobal, but it seemed a little more soothing. It wore the colour of any other night, and it restored their habit of waiting and whispering their intentions towards the following day. They were all thinking about tomorrow. The Administration was still in a frenzy of preparation. Shephard had not appeared; Singh was away. That was the sum of the news that mattered. Everything else was in the nature of prediction and surprise; and everyone waited.

Shephard knew she could not endure much longer, but he needed her to stay awake. He shifted on the bed to block the light from her eyes, and he saw her lips in shadow, a dark, breathing quiver of flesh, pleated like old leather at the corners. She was fumbling for words, but fatigue had dulled her interest.

'Why you hide these las' few nights, my son?'

'I'll hide no more,' said Shephard, 'I see their plan to murder me, but I'll hide no more. Singh gone away, and tonight I want to talk with those I feel intimate with. It is a long long time we talk like now.'

Ma Shephard had pushed herself up slowly from the bed. Her head rested against the brass ball that adorned the bedpost. The lamp burnt low on a wooden stool in the corner, and the light made freckles that played aimlessly over her hands. She heard the shriek of the wind under the jalousies and the slow, familiar patter of rain charging over the roof. The night was a secret which she had learnt. She was glad he had come to speak with her. She looked at her son who sat beside her and then at the stool which showed a dark, melancholy surface under the light. She took his hand and turned her eyes towards the ceiling as though she was going to pray. Shephard was beginning to feel a mild cramp in his leg, but he did not shift. He saw his leg hang lamely over the edge of the lath which jutted out from under the mattress. He felt the aged fingers cling to his hand, and he knew what she was thinking. He belonged to her. He was her son; for ever and ever he was hers.

' 'Tis that very stool holdin' the lamp,' she said, 'the very stool in the same ol' corner. But a boy you was then, my one an' only chil', and there you would sit night after night, an' listen to my prayers. Every night barrin' none you come to give thanks for a day leavin' the lan', an' beg a blessin' that would carry you safe through the night. Like tonight how you come. An' always I know it, but now is my chance to say it. No matter how late or how old, a man will always turn back to his earlies' teachin'. W'at the chil' once do, the man for all his age an' show of wisdom, will try some time to imitate. Like now. Like how the memory bring you back tonight.'

He felt her fingers slip reluctantly from his hand. She was tired, but he wanted her to stay awake. He needed someone to save him from the danger which was luring him slowly beyond control. He had felt it earlier in the evening, and the night had increased its power over his actions. He looked round the room as though he feared someone would enter to deprive him of his mother's company. He wanted to distract her from this nervous agitation which had driven him to her rescue. He could feel her fingers creeping across the sheet to touch his hands, but she was weak with age and fatigue. He did not want to tire her, but he felt it was unsafe to be left alone.

'I didn't like the look in your eye earlier,' she said. 'What it was frighten you then?' She was beginning to doze. He could hear her breathing slower and more restful.

'The dream,' he stammered, 'the dream was with me again last night.'

'The same dream?'

He noticed her eyes close, but he had to keep her awake.

'The same dream, only a little worse,' he said. 'I had to get out.

315

I was trying to keep my seat, but every eye in that carriage just turn on me. Like lights or spears fightin' to pierce through me, everyone lookin', lookin', lookin', till I feel I was shrinking, all of me shrinking to nothing, and I couldn't bear it. I had to get out. And out I rush from the seat to where the carriages join. I steady myself, and climb out. I crawl up the side to where the carriages join. I steady myself, and climb out. I crawl up the side where the carriages join, and reach the top. And there I sit down feeling the train multiply in speed. It just went like mad with me on top, and I walk the whole length of the train to where the driver would be, but nobody was there. Nobody was there at all, and I couldn't tell them to get out. I couldn't tell them to stop. But I wave and keep waving at the train that was coming to us, but nobody wanted to see me, and the two just burst through space to meet one another face to face in full blast. I was waving and waving when they crash asunder, waving, waving...'

Ma Shephard was asleep. Her head had slipped away from the brass ball. Her hands lay open over the sheet. Shephard tried to steady his hands as he pushed himself up from the bed. He stretched across the bed and lowered his mother on to the mattress under the sheet. He thought he heard the crash of the trains echoing through the room, and he stared towards the window where the jalousies rattled with the wind. The chimney looked unnaturally pregnant with the flame that tottered up from the lamp and fell, dead as leaves, on to the stool. He walked to the window and felt for the lock of the door. The wind wrapped round his fingers through the jalousies, and he guessed that his senses were deceiving him. He hurried to the bed to see whether his mother was alive, and then he remembered the wallet. He lowered his head to hear her breathing, considered his hands in the light, and walked to the door to see whether it was real. The spray slapped his face and he heard his voice like a warning following him through the night: 'precaution... precaution...'

The girl had resigned herself to waiting. She wet her finger with saliva and soothed her lids. The mongrel pawed at the empty kettle under the counter, whiffed the air, and sidled up to her leg.

The chain made a noise against the kettle, and the proprietor leaned sideways. The girl stooped under the counter and closed her hand round the mongrel's mouth.

'They goin' soon,' she said, 'they go soon, you hear, then I'll take your chain off, an' let you stretch your leg. You hear, I'll loose you the minute they go.'

The dog yawned and paddled its tongue along her hand.

'Policemen all the same,' the girl said, coaxing the mongrel to be still, 'take off their uniform, an' they don' care for order or law, like any plain criminal in town. But we'll be free w'en they go.' She leaned her head against the dog, and swivelled its tail between her fingers. The proprietor was dozing again. The dog arranged its paws and laid its head against the kettle.

'Good boy,' the girl said, raising herself slowly above the counter, 'they goin' soon. You stay there till they go.'

She pulled the stub of pencil from her hair, and continued to count the figures on the torn sheet of brown paper.

The room smelt of garlic, and in the far corner, adjacent to the half-open door, the two men breathed an odour of stale liquor and peppers. Their shadows showed a faceless deformity of shapes against the window. Their heads touched, and their hands embraced upon the table. The voices were subdued, soft, and prophetic. The short man shook his head in drunken approval of the other's predictions about the future of all friendship. The night and the cheerless dereliction of the shop seemed to darken their spirit. They were celebrating a private vision of despair, the sad and ruined victory of men over the kingdom of beasts.

'Whoever win, the dog will still bark,' he said.

'An' goats goin' carry on eatin' their grass,' said the other. 'Election or no election…'

'No election?'

The short man made a noise like a horse's neigh, cupped his hand under his nose and sneezed.

'Bless you,' said the other.

'Bless the beasts o' the fiel',' he said, wiping the mucus off his sleeve.

'Bless tomorrow,' said the other.

317

'There's a limit to all blessin',' the short man said. 'Tonight I would not bless myself.'

He paused and looked at his friend whose head was swaying gently from side to side.

'How much service you got?'

'We join together.'

'Together,' the short man repeated. 'We join together.'

'An' we rise together.'

'We rise together,' the short man muttered, squeezing the other's hand. 'Why you think Crabbe favour you an' me?'

The man hesitated. He noticed a change come over the short man's face, and he held his hand, patting it like a child's.

'He figure he could trust us,' he said.

'There's a limit to trust,' said the short man. 'I learn there's a limit to trust.'

'You trust Crabbe?'

'There's a limit to trust,' said the short man. 'Last night I went through my las' supper with Crabbe.'

'You eat with Crabbe?' the man interrupted.

'In his house,' said the short man, 'he summon this disciple to his house.'

'You rise above me,' said the other, 'we join together, but you rise above me.'

'I finish risin',' said the short man. 'There's a limit to risin'. Now listen, you listen. I witness the las' supper with Crabbe. I see how his min' was workin'. An' there an' then, he know w'at I know, an' we did not argue.'

'W'at is it you know?' the man asked.

The short man delayed his answer. He was brooding over the empty glass, working his fingers up and down.

'You know there was a move to murder Shephard,' the short man said.

'Murder!' the other whispered.

'To murder Shephard,' the short man said coldly. 'Was the matter he mention over the las' supper.'

'Who? Crabbe?'

'He simply draw my attention to the rumour he receive,' said the short man. 'He was givin' me power to pick a special guard who would keep watch over Shephard. Nothin' was ever to happen to Shephard, he repeat. We could not afford to see Shephard die, he say.'

'Who want to murder Shephard?' the man asked.

The news had made him more sober. He was beginning to doubt the short man who seemed undisturbed by what he had heard. He drained an inch of rum into his glass and washed his throat.

'Jus' imagine for a moment,' he said. 'Imagine you collec' your closes' frien' on a night like tonight for a final feedin' before you say farewell. Tomorrow you settin' out for some glory which is God's reward for a lifetime o' toil. Hard labour an' a sufferin' toil reach you at las' to that reward, but tonight, on the eve o' your deepes' pride, you find your closes' frien', an' in that final feedin', sacred as a church service 'twixt you two, a knowledge o' man's min' strike you sudden, an' you see it clear as sunlight that he, the prince o' your tenderes' feelin', decide to work a treachery 'gainst the glory waitin' to crown your life. An' there an' then, while feedin' on the fat o' lan', celebratin' that sacred farewell, you tell him w'at you know, an' he hear you, an' you finish your feedin', an' part company denyin' nothin', arguin' nothin', but knowin' w'at you know…'

'That las' supper was like gall for those who listen,' the other said.

'For all except Jesus,' the short man said. 'He was glad. My sympathy was always for poor Judas who r'ally believe he was a crook.'

'Crabbe ain't Jesus,' the other said. 'An' Jesus didn't do nothin'.'

'He didn't have to do,' the short man said. 'He was who he was. That was enough.'

'He was the Son of God,' the other said.

'An' the brother o' Satan,' the short man said.

The man drew his hand away and sat erect. He seemed startled as he watched his friend.

'W'at you say?'

'The brother o' Satan,' said the short man.

'Where you fin' that teachin'?' he asked.

'In my own meditation,' the short man said. 'Lucifer an' Christ

319

is blood brothers in spirit. Their ambition was always trouble, but one was more ambitious than the nex'. Christ make his trouble 'mongst men, but Lucifer long before try to make his trouble 'gainst God. 'Tis why we here on earth divided the way we divided. Jesus who try to redeem was a coward, an' Lucifer who make us w'at we is was a fool, a courageous and rebellious fool.'

'Lucifer didn't make me,' the other said quickly.

' 'Tis so,' said the short man, 'nature an' all animal life was God's doin', but Lucifer fashion the spirit you call human. I didn't speak my feelin' to Crabbe. But tomorrow I will follow in Judas' footsteps.'

The short man felt his friend's hand raising him up from the chair. He rubbed his fists on the table as he struggled against the strength of the older man's arms.

'W'at you leavin' for?' he asked.

'You had too much to drink,' the other said.

'Listen, listen…'

'You had too much to drink,' the man said, steering him towards the door.

'Listen, I tell you, listen…'

The voices retreated, and the shop was suddenly still. The bar was deserted. The girl removed her apron and whispered to the proprietor who was leaning over the counter. He dug his nails into his ear, and shrugged his shoulders. The girl untied the black mongrel which pranced between the tables, following her towards the small cubicle curtained off from the shop. She raised herself up on her toes, and peeped over the rod which supported the curtain. She could not leave before the last two customers were finished. She knew it would have angered the proprietor if she tried to interrupt them. She walked back to the counter, drew a chair from under the table, and cuddled the mongrel on her lap.

She could hear the sound of voices behind the curtain, but the words eluded her. She rubbed her head against the mongrel, hoping that each pause was the silence which had ended their talk.

'The plan to murder him may be off,' said Singh, 'but it ain't safe for him to ramble in that state.'

'Will be all right,' said Baboo, 'he jus' keep talkin' 'bout throwin' caution to the wind.'

'What time you say that was?' Singh asked.

'Mid-afternoon I see him,' said Baboo.

'He don't know I back,' said Singh. 'I goin' check, I have to check on what happenin'.'

'You not able,' said Baboo. 'If you see yourself, you'd know you not able.'

Singh fingered the stubble over his chin. The light made black circles under his bloodshot eyes, and the table seemed to extend, increasing the distance between himself and Baboo. The silence was like weight in his ears. He tried to soothe his eyes, but the lids were sore, and he noticed the table again, like a wobble of wood, swaying under his hands.

'You cover more than two hundred miles in those four days,' said Baboo. He was persuading him to rest.

'He was talkin' to himself, you say?'

'Eat,' said Baboo, 'you got to eat.'

He pushed the plate nearer to Singh, and got up from the table. His walk was casual. He returned from the window, and watched Singh for a moment. He was chewing wearily at the slab of meat. It looked like a piece of wet rag sticking out from a dog's mouth. Baboo thought he had succeeded in distracting him from this sudden obsession with Shephard. He lingered beside the table for a while, then turned towards the curtain and slipped it back to see who was there.

A fly had alighted on the strip of wire which coiled in circles round the lamp. The wick showed a blue edge that crumbled into particles of soot which finished between the crease of the chimney. The proprietor opened one eye and noticed the shadow widen through the room. He raised his head from the counter. He was half-asleep. He saw the fly crawl along the wire then nose the chimney for a moment before soaring up to the ceiling in a circle round the lamp. It was cool in the shop. One door was half-open, and Baboo could see the flush of light closing gradually over the road. The proprietor bolted the door, and walked back to the counter. He looked across at the table, and then glanced up at the wire which held the lamp to the ceiling. The fly had crept down the wire. It glided slowly towards the chimney, then dived through the light and collided with the rim of the glass. The body looked like a parched grain of corn shrivelled up beside the burner. The proprietor leaned his head slowly down against his arms and closed his eyes.

'Time to go,' said Singh. He stirred the spoon through the black pool of gravy, and watched the chewed edges of the meat on the plate.

'You better eat some more,' said Baboo. 'It will only waste.'

'Not tonight,' said Singh, 'not tonight.'

'You in no shape to see Shephard now,' said Baboo. 'I see how your eyes closin'.'

'I tired, I r'ally tired,' he said, 'but somebody got to go. If w'at you say is true, somebody got to go.'

'You not in shape to see him now,' said Baboo.

The spoon fell from Singh's hand and the gravy sprinkled the table. The proprietor looked up, and Baboo pushed the plate aside, and polished the grease into the table. He watched Singh rub his eyes and shift his body forward to lean on the table.

'He don't know I come back,' Singh said.

'But you not in shape,' said Baboo, 'you can't carry your own weight from this table.'

'Somebody got to go,' said Singh, 'or he may make a mistake an' leave the house.'

'I know for a fact the plan is off,' said Baboo, 'but you never can tell.'

Singh raised himself from the table and wiped his hands in his eyes. He could hardly recognise Baboo who looked sideways towards the counter. He saw the black slab of meat, wide grained and wet, lying wastefully in the gravy. He belched, and the wind made a ripple over the plate.

'Time to go,' he said, waving his hand at Baboo. 'But do this one thing before you turn in. This one thing…' He paused and shook his head as though he could not remember his words. 'Before you turn in,' he said, looking up at Baboo, 'make straight for his house, make sure he in, an' tell him not to leave till I come. Tell him it important, an' see he don't leave till I come. He mustn't leave. Whether or not I reach, he mustn't leave. You hear that, Baboo? He mustn't leave.'

Baboo hesitated. He glanced at Singh, made as though he

wanted to argue, and then whispered, 'As you say. Nothin' likely to happen, but he shouldn't leave the house.'

Bill leaned against the door and his eyes closed on the darkness of the room. He could feel the water course freely over his skin as he stood in the doorway, trying to remember the arrangement of this room. A week ago this darkness would have been a familiar territory. He would have found his way between the black passage of furniture. But the world in his head had changed. The house was strange. He had returned from Penelope's grave where he had sat for hours in the rain. The house seemed to change places with another environment, older and more familiar than San Cristobal.

He was back in England, and now he could see Penelope entering the room at Fern Row. She was sweeping her hair from the back of her neck over her head. It fell like a veil, black and tattered, down to the line of her mouth. Then she parted it in two with her hands, and her face showed under the light, and he could see her eyes, alive and restless. Those eyes which belonged to that face. There was something she wanted to say, and for a moment he noticed that she was not sure. It was the first time he had ever felt that Penelope really needed his help. He took her hand and arranged the chair, and they talked through the evening until Mark arrived. He could hear her voice asking his pardon if she seemed to complain that their happiness at Fern Row was not enough. And he recalled her surprise when he said that he too wanted a change. She had never guessed this feeling. It was a contradiction which they shared; for he had said that their happiness at Fern Row or anywhere else might not be enough, but they could not get beyond it. It was a duty which they had to bear. Yet he wanted to find some alternative. He had felt this raw and urgent need to do something else. So they had found San Cristobal. It was old and yet new. It had started with strange tribes whose relics told of an ancient time and were the precious souvenirs of students and scholars. Yet it was a beginning, and he wanted to be a part of its promise.

And suddenly he could hear Penelope's voice, a day before she died, begging him to leave. She thought it was fatal to remain in San Cristobal. She wanted to return to Fern Row, but he had refused. They had found San Cristobal, and he would not lose it. He tried to persuade her that the fury of the politicians would not last. He argued that it was necessary, but he knew that it could not last, and he reminded her of the afternoon when they rehearsed the boys for their radio programme. The boys represented something that they could not afford to lose. And Penelope had agreed.

Now he was back in San Cristobal. He shuffled along the wall, and stooped on the sofa which offered him his bearings. The water raced off his clothes and made a puddle where he sat. But he could not feel. Memory had returned that afternoon and the touch of Penelope holding his arm as they walked down the corridor to the studio. He was going to show San Cristobal what it could do. The corridor stretched ahead of him, a narrow passage of wrinkled carpet. It was the success of this programme which had relieved him from worrying about Mark's decision to find another house. He remembered that the main lights were off when they entered the studio. The green bulbs made erratic flickers across the room. The engineers were at work. Then the main lights came on, and the boys were surprised to see him standing with Penelope in the doorway. They waved at him, and Penelope hurried to a table to check the scripts. She sat in a far corner, biting her nails and scratching her head, and occasionally she sipped from a glass of water. The boys seemed unusually thirsty. They were afraid, but he had made the studio a market place with his gestures and his anecdotes.

Flagstead was sitting in the engineers' room. He had come to have a laugh, but some secret ambition, which no one could share, had given the boys their cue. They were reassured when he said that if anything went wrong, it would be the fault of those who worked in the engineers' room. They believed him, and when they took their places in front of the microphones, he felt that he had won. They gave their version of the Tribe Boys' conflict with the Bandit Kings. And the studio was almost silent with idolatry. Only Penelope shrieked her praise, for she had felt a personal triumph in this experiment. It was she who had told him of the story, and later invited the boys to the house. And he remembered Penelope saying that the boys were her discovery. It was that afternoon which made her decide to stay… But now? What could he do now? He had lost Penelope, and she had taken San Cristobal. It might survive, but never again would he want to possess it.

A light crept under the door. He could hear Thief walking down the stairs. He raised himself up on the sofa, and suddenly he felt the weight of his clothes clinging to him. He let his legs slide on to the floor. He fumbled across the room to find the switch. He could hear Thief's voice in the adjoining room, and he paused, trying to catch his words. His hands rambled over the wall, but he decided against the light. He wished Thief would go away. He wanted to be alone. But he could still hear Thief, and gradually he felt that someone else was there. He leaned against the wall and waited for Thief to keep still.

Thief sat on the floor coaxing the monkey to eat. He soaked the bread in a bowl of water before passing it between three fingers into the monkey's mouth. The food fell in lumps over his hand. He leaned the monkey's head on to the sheet of paper, and wiped the thick drool of slaver from his fingers. The monkey was dying; but Thief continued to talk, trying to imagine himself and the monkey in a human dialogue of farewell. He spoke the monkey's questions, and gave its answers, like a child talking to a tree.

'Won't save you,' he said, 'refusin' to feed the way you do. Days an' more nothin' pass your throat, an' I don' want to bury you.'

He paused to indicate the monkey's reply.

MONKEY: You'll bury me with the water. Take me to the canal an' let the rains race me down till I reach the river.

'I don' think the others would have like' that,' said Thief.

MONKEY: The likes of it don' help, an' a burial couldn't bring no consolation. An' the others…

Thief paused and looked up at the window, trying to see whether the night had recovered from the massive showers of rain. They had continued steady and hard for the third day. The morning grass was covered with water, and everywhere the trees leaned as though they could not support the pull of their branches to the earth. The leaves were whipped into a green frenzy until they lost their hold and fell, wet and shivering, over the water which sailed them across the garden to the street.

'It interrupts my hearin' terrible,' said Thief, 'the kick they come with. Is fearful, an' they may las' for a time.'

MONKEY: They won't wash you out of the house, you nor Mr Bill.

'But they could take the house an' all,' Thief said, turning his glance from the window to consider the monkey. Now he wished the monkey could really hear him and reply without his help.

'Won't be long before she says "amen",' Thief said in silence, as though he were afraid the monkey might hear. He glanced at the monkey, then passed a cup with cold tea to his lips. He watched the monkey over the rim of the cup, stroking its head with one hand.

MONKEY: I always say things won't thrive out o' their natural home, like people too. Order an' adventure don' go han' in han', an' there ain't no gain one gain that a loss the other won' lose. But you mustn't worry no more.

'Not me,' said Thief. ' 'Tis the others worry. I jus' watch, an' when things take a turn to terrorise, I make way quick, an' fin' shelter till the trouble pass.'

MONKEY: You got trouble comin' this way?

'Everywhere,' said Thief, 'San Cristobal goin' burn in trouble. Shephard will win, for certain he will, an' then Singh an' the rest…'

And suddenly he felt a wave of resentment sweep through his body. He swallowed a mouthful of the tea and glanced towards the window. He rested the cup and looked down at the monkey, thoughtful, confused; and he realised, as he tried to confess this mood of bewilderment, that it was Penelope whom he was struggling to console. He looked into the cup to make sure it was empty, and then pressed his hand against the monkey's head as though he were beseeching the dead to acknowledge his affection. He relaxed his hand and brought his head slowly down to his arm. He closed his eyes and wished that Bill would arrive. Through Bill, Penelope's dead ear might hear him; and suddenly he thought he heard the monkey speak.

MONKEY: Is anything wrong?

He had taken the monkey's head into his hands, passing the lumps of bread into its mouth, and listened again to his voice repeat the monkey's question: 'Is anything wrong?'

★

Bill opened the door and entered the room very quickly. He watched Thief's hands slipping the bread into the monkey's mouth. The saliva made a little pool on the paper. He looked at Thief and remembered how they had met, and thought that he, too, was Penelope's discovery. He turned to go.

'You are a good friend,' said Bill.

Thief let the monkey's head rest on the floor while he wiped his hands.

'You too,' said Thief. 'An' not only to me, but San Cristobal too. Until the end of time I will remember how you send me with the warning for Shephard.'

But Bill was impervious to any kind of praise. He wanted to forget San Cristobal. He felt a sudden revulsion of feeling when Thief mentioned this service to Shephard. Already he had lost his desire for any share in the future of people like Thief. The future had arrived with Penelope's death, and he could not forgive it. He looked at Thief and considered the friendship which he had offered. And he was unsure of what he had said. Some strange atavistic instinct had taken hold of his reason. He knew that Thief was helpless, like himself, to save Penelope; but this sudden association of people and places had grown like a noise in his head. Thief had become San Cristobal, and San Cristobal was Penelope's grave. He tried to control his feeling, and turned again to say good night.

'Perhaps even friends keep a corner of their mind tuck' away,' said Thief. 'An' it ain't no business of mine to know, but I wonder time an' again why Mr Mark leave.'

Bill did not answer. He was staring at the piece of paper which was wet with the monkey's slaver. Thief was waiting for him to speak. Bill leaned forward again to read the writing which he recognised. It was a fragment of Mark's diary which had been left behind. Thief did not notice.

''Cause he came this evening when you went out,' said Thief. 'An' he look so lonely. I feel for him.'

'Who came?' Bill asked, trying to decipher the words on the paper.

'Mr Mark was here when you went out,' said Thief. 'He asked

that you come see him, 'cause he was expectin' Shephard, an' he didn't want to be alone with Shephard.'

Thief was casual. He lifted the monkey from the floor and carried it out into the rain. He did not want to tell Bill that it was dead. Bill watched the door swing behind him, but he did not feel the spray which the wind blew through the room. He held the paper up to the light, reading the diary which Mark had recorded some months ago. It bore no date, but the words were legible under the green flecks of spittle which the light dried in patches over the paper. He walked out of the light through the darkness which covered the flight of stairs up to his room. When Thief returned, he closed the door, and called out, good night. But Bill did not hear. He could hear nothing but the silence of the paper spread across his hands and the weight of the gun in his pocket.

Thief had carried the monkey to an old dog's kennel behind the house. He wrapped it in his blanket, and left a candle burning where the head rested on the heap of sand. Tomorrow he would perform the rites which a friend deserved. Now he was searching the room for the piece of paper which made a pillow under the monkey's head. He was afraid the wind had blown it into the living-room, staining the floor with the monkey's slaver. He knocked against the door to ask Bill whether he had thrown it away, but there was no answer. He stood at the foot of the stairs, wondering whether he should go up to the room where the light showed under the door. Then he called out, 'Good night,' but there was no answer. Bill did not hear. He could hear nothing but his breathing against the paper which lay across his hands. The room was a whirlpool of light spinning viciously round his head, and the gun grew steadily heavier in his pocket.

For a moment he had lost touch with the ordinary details of the room. The walls sprang to an awkward altitude; the ceiling dozed and sagged above his head. The bed rocked him gently to one side like a raft swimming in circles over a stagnant pool. He could feel a gradual dissolution of things eddying cautiously through the light. The mirror yawned, widening to the furthest limits of the room, and the light broke into a blinding shower of splintered glass entering his eyes. His body was frozen stiff, but he could feel a gradual quickening of the blood cruising through his head. A slow procession of noises alerted his ears, and his eyes were stung into a sudden clarity. He saw the sheet, and the pillows, astonishingly vivid and still. The light grew steady and austere as though it demanded some action to restore its neutral gaze. The room had grown impatient. The night made a nervous shadow against the window. He was feeble with rage while he watched the paper like an explosive in his hands. The letters were recovering their shape, the lines straightened and the words found their original meaning. He was reading the last paragraph again as he pressed his hand against the gun in his pocket. 'It is this passion for revenge which will eventually destroy them. Two weeks ago some workers set fire to three hundred acres of sugar cane in the south. I argued with Shephard that this was a childish and dangerous way to intimidate the Administration. He could have stopped it. His word would have been enough to persuade them against this folly. But revenge is like an illness with them. Power is not enough to soothe their wounds. They need to punish also. Today Shephard was going to send word to the prison warders, calling on them to strike. And there has been talk about a similar plan for the mental hospital. They would like to see the lunatics at large. But I have spoken with Shephard. He knows my decision. If there is trouble at the mental hospital, he will have to consider my action a betrayal. I would give evidence in any charge that is brought against him.'

He started to crush the paper into a ball between his fingers.

'And he's there now,' he said quietly, 'in Mark's house. Penelope's murderer sitting this moment in Mark's house.'

He was crushing the paper against the bed, considering the stages of the journey which would lead him to Shephard. His whole body ached, urging him to free it from this idle stupor. The diary had resurrected Penelope's corpse. It defined his duty. His mind was free from the slightest fear of consequences, closed to any doubt about the origin of the fire. Penelope was his persuasion, absolute, original immediate. She was rehearsing her agony before his eyes; the charred deformity of the skull, the arms skinless and white. He had had one shocking glimpse of Penelope's body, emerging from the parting cliffs of flames that peeled her eyes. 'Penelope, Penelope…' He heard his voice, barely familiar, repeat her name, and his hand stretched tight over the paper. 'He is there now,' he said, 'he's with Mark now.'

His hand relaxed slowly over the paper. He spread it out again, and brought it closer, searching for some further reference to Shephard. He read a line, skipped angrily over a passage which seemed irrelevant to his need, and then continued. The word 'betray' had aroused his interest. He read the passage slowly, waiting for the name of Shephard to increase his frenzy.

'Baboo deceived me, and I feel that he will betray them, Shephard and Singh. He has tricked them into believing that he is the party's spy among the official administration. They knew of his devotion to Crabbe, and the secrets which Crabbe shares with him, and which he, in turn, discloses to them, established his role beyond any doubt. It put him in their favour, and finally placed them in his hands. It was he who broke the news to them that the Administration were planning to get rid of Parnall, but they do not know to this day that it was he who had informed on Parnall, not informed but lied. Parnall was a little sympathetic to both Shephard and Singh, but Baboo's story of a secret alliance between Parnall and the Party was pure invention. He had arranged that Crabbe should overhear their conversation. Nor does Singh know that Baboo's vigilance over the Party members is really his service to Crabbe. His treachery will surpass anything that Crabbe...'

There was no further mention of Shephard. He felt no interest in anyone else, but he felt a certain satisfaction with Baboo. He glanced at the end of the sheet and read the last line: '...he will have to consider my action a betrayal. I would give evidence in any charge...' He thought for a moment of Mark. Perhaps Mark was seized by a similar passion, but he wanted to encounter Shephard alone. His mind had grown frantic with speculation. Mark must do nothing till I reach. Nothing must happen to him before I reach. He rolled the paper into a ball and threw it back on the bed. He was ready to move. The way was clear. He knew what he had to do. For Penelope. For himself. The room was beginning to swim under his eyes. Faces, names, events: his life seemed to assert itself for his judgement.

Nothing was clear but the spectacle of Penelope disfigured by fire. It was the background, unseen yet present, from which every other recollection emerged to form his thinking. They came in fragments, like bits of glass surrounding the weapon which had brought destruction. The fragments multiplied, receded and emerged, changing in their importance each time, and at the centre was the image of Shephard, consistent, unmoved, impervious. It was Shephard he wanted to deal with. It was as though this image had existed with the beginning of his consciousness. Shephard had always been there, a shadow in the dark, brought suddenly to light by an event which had ruined his love. Now that Penelope was dead, it seemed that he existed only for Shephard. The fire had been cheated of its importance by the peculiar bond which the diary created between himself and Shephard. He thought of the services which he might have rendered San Cristobal. He remembered Thief and the letter which hinted the plan for murdering Shephard. He had considered his knowledge a service to San Cristobal, but he was no longer averse to the ways of Crabbe and those who made the official alliance. He thought he understood Crabbe's fear. But the memory of Penelope had obscured the politics of San Cristobal. He wanted to deal with Shephard directly. The image of Shephard hardened. It was fixed. It assumed a substance, offering itself like a challenge, alive and tangible for his wonder: a substitute for grief. It was Shephard who filled, entire, the size of his wild, secret, wounded preoccupation. He wanted to read the diary again, but the clock struck the half-hour, and he leapt from the bed and hurried towards the dressing table. The water dripped behind him, making a trail where he walked. He felt his shoes like a sodden sponge clinging to his feet. He pulled out the drawers. A knob broke off in his hand. He threw the knob over his shoulder, and snatched the brown leather gloves from under a pile of scarves and stockings which Penelope had packed away. He could feel the room close round him, alive and tense with his silent preparations for the night. He left the drawer open, and walked back to the bed. He swept the paper off the pillow and pressed it into his pocket. He slapped his hands against his chest, and felt in his pocket for the gun. He had forgotten to switch off the light, but he thought of Thief as he crept down the stairs. He could hear unfamiliar

331

sounds, like a warning, pursue him through the dark passage, but he moved slowly, cautiously, avoiding any audible collision with the furniture, as he felt his way through the living-room. The door prolonged its creak behind him, and he noticed the light from the bedroom making a shadow over the lawn. He hesitated, feeling for the butt of the gun as he glanced from the lawn to the square of light which showed the window above; then he hurried his hands into the gloves, pressed them into his pockets and ran towards the street.

Mark took another drink, and slid the glass along the table. He tried the edge of the knife with his finger before placing more pages of the diary into the basket. He felt an extraordinary sensation of calm relax his body. The whisky was cool, mellow, anaesthetic. It lingered at the back of his throat, bristled his nerves, and spread, gradual and elusive as a vapour, across his stomach. There was no trace of anguish in his final recollection of what had happened. He had lost his familiar tendency for regret. His disinclination had given way to an attitude of calm and decisive self-containment. He had chosen his way out. He looked at his wrist again, studying the intricate aberration of the veins, and then turned to read the final pages of the diary. He was approaching the end. And he knew with that momentary thrust of certainty which sharpened the knife and showed the lifeless future of his hands that he would not write again. He was reading for the last time the epitaph which described the evening after Marcia's funeral.

'I was walking down the lane watching the clouds distribute their shadow on the grass, and I understood their warning, but I did not feel inclined to turn back to the house. Disinclination had settled my course and put me at ease with the risk my journey was encouraging. The clouds had taken care of my interest, and I could feel their lack of intention. They were moving as I was moving, without interest or desire, and when their burden left them, and they spilt their weight upon the earth, they would go on moving, without malice. And the evening surrounded the trees, passed over the grass like a hand. The lane was empty, and houses were far, and soon the animals would obey their nature and go to sleep. The impatient fireflies, like metal eyes, were peeping from under the week. They watched me and the vagrant clouds which were already beginning to leak. I continued to walk, but nothing changed. It seemed that Marcia had never been alive. I tried to cheat my feeling, rehearsed the role of a man in mourning; but my memory served no purpose. I felt innocent as the clouds which collected overhead. Innocent and free. I was deprived of the ordinary response to the death of one who loved you. In her life I had consumed the resources of her love, and in her death I was without the virtues of guilt or regret. And now her absence, like my total lack of feeling, reminded me that something which probably remains alive with every man, had never been truly born in me. It was then that I decided I was seeing the last of San Cristobal.

'But I like it here in the evening; for the evening in San Cristobal is a final rebuke to all decision. It does not change places with the day, gradually, obediently, at the customary coercion of the season. The day does not slink away as though it wanted to stay. It cannot. The evening arrives. It arrives with a show of militant displeasure, and it declares its wish for solitude and the absence of light. It is arbitrary and firm. It knows its own mind, and its action is prompt. The day hesitates for a while, like a man who doesn't want to lose face. It tries to put up an argument but its methods are feeble, and it has got used to its defeat. So it slips away meditatively, in an attitude of mild outrage. And the evening quickly surveys its territory, relaxes its black frown, and stretches lightly, lazily over the land. It is amiable and harmless. An innocent occurrence which travels always with its own apparatus of enjoyment. Like a miser, at first, it offers a little light here and a little there, and considers the effect. It is pleased. Flattery tempts it; and suddenly it turns prodigal with its gifts. The land crouches, a little closer, it seems, the sky gets its order to perform, and a galaxy of eyes are open in the awakening sky. The land holds its breath, stays steady, easy and unmindful under a smouldering twinkle.

'Now I know gratitude, for it is this night which reminds me of myself. It is on my side. I am not alone in this combination of elements which constituted one thing whose parts cannot be distinguished. The night, whose arrival I witnessed, clear and single and separate like a man, has let itself slip senselessly into the sky and the land, until it has become them as I have become the disinclination which possesses me. It is not the hidden piece of earth and those shining open eyes, puncturing the sky with their scrutiny, which have made the night. They are the night as I am now this total lack of feeling.

'And now, if I may speak to you, as one man to another, two presences which share the same negative endowment, a similar lack of desire, reprieved from registering choice or favouring a promise, I would ask you, the night, to stay: the only miracle which my disinclination would join me in sharing. Surprise every waking eye with a dark dawn, animals, birds, and, above all, those who are stricken with duty and a large desire to be doing. Deprive the day of its incredible need to return, and teach a new terror, bloodless and unfamiliar. Break down like a wheel that refuses to run, and train men to move in a tolerable dark. Make the dark your tenure for a while. Fold up the sky, and pocket the stars, and hide each from the other's eye. Give the living unlikely season and yourself an inexplicable reign. One miracle would have been enough to make my reason wonder, and an improbable dark would be the dearest to me.'

He put the sheet aside and took the knife from the table. The room seemed to resent his presence. For a moment he felt like a traitor amidst the furniture. He remained on the sofa, scraping the leather-bound side which supported his elbow. He saw the basket, stacked with the diaries, and beside him, clean and neatly scribbled, the one page which he had just read. He did not want to remind himself that Bill might arrive. He had forgotten Shephard. Unthinkingly he continued to make the sudden little thrusts with the knife, until the leather split and its belly of brown fur began to fall in small tufts on to the floor. He pulled the knife from the split of the sofa and threw it on the table. It became part of the pattern of objects which seemed to watch him with a silent and unerring contempt.

Here he was in a world of objects which were not only equal in their lack of life. They were unanimous in their dumb understanding of his solitary presence in the room. He got up and walked round the room, scraping the furniture feebly with his shoes, past the sofa, the small table where he worked, the large mahogany table where he and Marcia had their meals together, and the chairs which, after each meal, were always put back against the walls. He stood, looking at the photograph of a black mule stretching its head forward in an attempt to drink some water from a small pond surrounded by bush. He passed his fingers round the edges of the frame and reconsidered the scene. It was late afternoon light, thin and obscure, that uncertain and illusive passage between the day and night in San Cristobal. The sun was beginning to lose its way between the turning folds of cloud, and the mule had got its tail caught erect in the wind.

From the near corner, Marcia stared, smiling, out of a gilt frame. He paced further along, tapping his heel against the floor as he scraped his fingers over the walls. He held the light up to her face and saw again the thin red hair which ran with the wind down her neck, and that wild delight which was the special attraction of her eyes. She had kept her innocent glance on the mule which stared across the room with its naked behind. He walked to the window and held his head against the pane, looking out at the night which had fallen heavily round the house and over the hedges which surrounded the garden. Somewhere in that black absence Marcia's body had found its eternal shelter. Soon he would follow his inclination to join the night. Not for Marcia, but for himself. Marcia was dead. He did not care to impress the dead. It was his life which now charted his way. His life had become identical with this soothing lack of feeling. He was identical with death.

He walked back to the sofa, touching the chairs and the table and the frayed edges of the leather which the knife had made. His hands returned from their touch, cold, empty and resentful. He sat on the sofa and let his eye discover the possibilities of the knife. It lay on the table, an ordinary little instrument which would obey his hand. It would rest obediently in his fingers, and its point, burning brightly in the ray of light that traced its shape, would follow the direction which his hand had ordered. And gradually he glanced from the knife to the picture of the black mule. The water refused to stir and the mule held its ground, displaying its longing and its patience; he turned his head and looked at the night that dropped, curious and abrupt outside the window. He reached for the knife and held it by the handle, following it from its point down the curve of the blade until it disappeared under his fingers. Like the still black pools of water, waiting to receive the thirst of the mule, it was a symbol of possibility. He turned the point down and watched his fist tighten its grip, and felt the point make its probe against his knee. The pool mirrored the mule, singing its willingness. He had chosen his way out.

The knife fell. He looked at his hand, stricken by his sudden failure of strength. The wind swept freely through the room and a shadow broke across the light. Shephard was standing in the doorway. The door swung heavily behind him and the noise startled Mark. He watched Shephard making towards the table. He was trying to recover the knife from the floor. He did not speak. Shephard approached the table. He was silent, smiling, elated. Some new excitement had quickened his step, and enlarged his sense of power beyond control. Mark looked puzzled by this frenzy of enthusiasm. Shephard seemed to mock his own intentions. Mark could not speak. He felt reduced to the meek curiosity of one who watched and waited for some extraordinary revelation of authority. Shephard had stolen his attention from the knife. Mark watched him slap his fat, black hands on the table. A frenzied look of delight now ruled his conduct. He looked at Mark, then glanced round the room as though he suspected another person there. Finally he considered his hands, raising himself full length above the table. He seemed to see the world concede its worth to his touch, and he grinned. A sinister delight had prepared his feelings for this moment. Mark was beginning to recover his calm. He remembered the knife in his hands, and he felt a sudden thrust of anger. For a moment he ignored the look on Shephard's face. He felt his plans were going to be aborted. He wanted to be alone. He was going to ask Shephard to leave, but his courage failed him. He could not find the strength to send Shephard away.

Shephard stood before him like a guard obstructing his escape from the wretched imprisonment of the room. The darkness filled the windows, the walls narrowed round him, and the ceiling seemed to move in a gradual descent which would soon crush his body against the floor. He considered the point of the knife, and waited for Shephard to sit. It would have been easier to bear his presence from a lower altitude. But Shephard was indifferent to his wish. His hand emerged from his pocket, and he leaned forward to rest the black object on the table. Mark saw the wallet and thought of Bill. He had glanced at his watch and seemed to abandon all hope of seeing Bill. He had to endure the presence of Shephard alone. He wanted to shout, but his throat was dry. Words raced through his head, then halted and turned to a frozen clot in his mouth. He was uneasy. He could not bear the startled look of pleasure which showed on Shephard's face. He was indicating the wallet as he turned his gaze on Mark.

'I scorn the thought of precaution,' he said, glancing from Mark to the wallet. 'Tonight or any night, the hand that raise to murder me will perish before any action take place. Many, many are called my dear Kennedy, but few, very few are chosen. And every man chosen moves in a charmed life. A charmed life, Kennedy. Tonight or any night, I will move as the spirit charms, and no force in San Cristobal can make me hide behind the precaution any ordinary man may make. But tonight, Kennedy, tonight...'

He paused and lowered his body on the chair. Mark tried to avoid his eyes, but Shephard's presence, tense and stern in this moment of scrutiny, was like an order which demanded his attention. Mark was no longer free to choose his actions. He could only relieve himself from the concentrated power of Shephard's glance by yielding to it. He saw the wallet and the knife, and Shephard's hand, like a nervous claw, shaking lightly against the table. He tried to speak, but Shephard raised his hand to silence him. He wanted Mark to share the ecstasy which shaped his words. He had chosen Mark, above all others, for this moment of intimate disclosure.

'I choose you, Kennedy, you I choose to share my feeling.'

Mark wanted to disengage his hand, but Shephard's grip became firmer. The chair rocked sideways, and he brought his head closer. His eyes were delirious. Mark's body was a blur obstructing his vision of the night that thickened outside the window. He glanced at the chair, leaning dangerously to one side under his weight, and Mark felt the fingers tighten round his hands. He wanted to suggest that they should have a drink, but Shephard had made him speechless.

'We carry a secret,' said Shephard, and his teeth showed behind the spreading black lips. It seemed that he would burst with laughter, but suddenly his mouth contracted. He steadied himself in the chair and relaxed his grip. Mark leaned further away, but Shephard came closer. His manner was confidential. His voice was calm.

'Tonight she recall the golden days,' he said, and his eyes softened, pleading with Mark to share his recollection. 'She remember when I was a boy taking my place on the stool, the same old stool...'

He paused as though he wanted Mark to show some recognition of those days. 'You remember? You remember?' he whispered. He slapped Mark gently on the knee, and folded his arms above the chair. 'You remember.' His voice was meek, nostalgic, and his eyes wandered vaguely round the room. 'Now I see you there,' he said, indicating the chair on the other side of the sofa where Mark sat, 'I see you kneeling there, waiting my words, and the chairs kneeling too, waiting my words also. You remember? You remember how I bless them? How they stand and kneel as we tell them, and then they hear my words and rejoice? You remember it? Can you see them now? My wooden children waiting my words and you kneeling there till it was time to bless them goodbye, and you depart, you depart carrying my secret. You remember it? Tonight she was recalling the golden days where you and I belong when we were boys... you remember...?'

Mark nodded, but he could not bear the terrible delight which showed in Shephard's eyes. He made to get up, but Shephard leaned the chair to block his way. He was smiling again. He stretched his hand out and lifted Mark's chin up to the level with his eyes.

'You I choose,' he said, 'I choose you to share my feeling as you share my secret then. You remember? You remember my children, you remember how they kneel at my bidding? And how

338

they stand in a silence to respect my prayer. Tomorrow it will come to pass again. It will come to pass, and you will share my feeling once more, you will carry my secret…'

His hands fell away from the chair. He stood erect, considering Mark who was staring at the photograph of Marcia. But Shephard did not notice his distraction. He swung his leg over the chair and paced like a tethered animal round the table. Now and again he halted at the chair, rested his hand on Mark's head, and then continued his frantic patrol round the table.

'Comrade of my golden days, victory is mine.' He paused and looked at Mark for understanding and agreement, but Mark was unthinking. Confusion had stolen his senses. His eyes rendered Shephard an obedient service, but he could hardly see him. Shephard was eloquent, irrepressible.

'Tomorrow, respected comrade, I shall hold this land in the palm of my hand, and bend it like a wheel to meet my intention. I shall call on the earth to clap and the water to sing and every living thing shall tell its pleasure in a humble service to my sovereignty on an island that once slept under water. But tonight, Kennedy, I shall walk the water and for a moment consult with my Maker.'

He continued pacing round the room, ignoring Mark who had turned quietly to watch his movements. He walked back to the sofa, and rested his hands on Mark's shoulder, and for a moment it was not clear what he intended.

'Kennedy,' he said, 'let us drink to an eternal alliance.'

Mark waved his hand towards the table. Shephard poured some whisky into a clean glass. He passed the drink to Mark and emptied his glass at one shot. He had not noticed that Mark had rested his glass on the floor. This enthusiasm had ruined his awareness. He poured another for himself, and raised the glass slowly above Mark's head in an act of blessing.

'Join me in my endeavours, respected comrade, and prove loyal always.'

He finished the drink and put the glass on the table. 'Now you will join me,' he said, taking Mark by the arm.

'Join you,' Mark whispered.

'To the Point,' said Shephard, 'I shall go there to offer a prayer.'

'To the Point,' Mark whispered again.

'You will join me,' said Shephard.

'Join you,' Mark whispered again.

He found himself repeating Shephard's request. He saw Shephard's head lift and swing across the light, and he felt a sudden dizziness obscure his mind. He felt lured by Shephard's improvisation of speech and gesticulation. He let his hand rest tamely in Shephard's, while his eyes started a tireless scrutiny of Shephard's face. He had seen that face before in a similar aspect of fantasy: the taut, ecstatic lips and the eyes lost in an eagerness of unnatural vision. Shephard spoke with his eyes. A dark delirium had settled over them. Their gaze contained a terror which Shephard could not control, but a similar occasion had taught Mark their meaning. He understood their warning. Shephard had slipped beyond the normal habit of his reason, and Mark was beginning to feel rebuked by his lack of sympathy. He felt Shephard's hand tighten on his.

'You do not smile, comrade, and you are pleased, are you not?'

'Very pleased,' said Mark.

'With our victory,' Shephard added.

'Victory,' Mark murmured. He tried to smile, but Shephard's enthusiasm had plunged him into words. He had found in Mark the perfect occasion for his declaration of joy.

'The elements shall laugh at a marvel they cannot utter,' said Shephard. He released Mark's hand and paced round the room, sailing his arms like wings through the air.

'What you witness now, comrade of my golden days, our colleagues shall consider my neglect of their favours. To have seen their leader in the fullness of that light which led us to victory, and with an ear made perfect for wonders. Such a large pleasure is mine that you are what you are. And so you must attend my prayers at the Point.'

Shephard turned his back. He walked over to the telephone. Mark drew his legs up and made to stand, but he heard Shephard's voice, calm and decisive, making its request. He hesitated, watching the point of the knife. To the Point. And he felt a sudden strength possess his limbs. He was going to join Shephard in this dark and illogical journey to the sea. He saw the wallet, then he looked towards the photograph which showed Marcia. To the Point… He stretched his hand to take the knife, and glanced in the direction of Shephard. He was beginning to feel an emotion like gratitude towards Shephard. He glanced at the photograph and decided that his wish was still possible. Shephard had suggested it. He would go to the Point. To the Point… He heard the sea whisper a melancholy welcome in his ear. The waves made wreaths of foam over his body slipping to its ultimate rest upon the coral seabed.

He slipped the knife in his pocket, and glanced at the page beside him. He felt for a moment rebuked. The words seemed to rise from the page, reminding him of his wish. They soothed his anxiety about Shephard. He looked at the page, repeating his contract with the night. He felt the knife probing the corner of his pocket, and he lingered over the words.

'Deprive the day of its incredible need to return, and teach a new terror, bloodless and unfamiliar. Break down like a wheel which refuses to turn, and train men to move in a tolerable dark. Make the earth your tenure for a while. Fold up the sky, and pocket the stars, and hide each from the other's eye. Give the living an unlikely season and yourself an inexplicable reign. One miracle would have been enough to make my reason wonder, and an improbable dark would be the dearest to me…'

He turned to have a last look at Shephard in the light. He had finished with the telephone. He walked towards the table, indifferent to this change of decisive calm which had come over Mark. He poured some whisky into his glass and raised his empty hand to encourage Mark. Mark lifted his glass from the floor and drank slowly, staring past Shephard at the photograph of Marcia.

'To the Point,' said Shephard, 'there to offer my prayer.'

'I shall join you,' Mark said quickly, returning the glass to the table.

'Comrade,' Shephard cried. 'Comrade of my golden days.'

He took Mark's hand, and they looked at each other as though they were about to swear, in silence, to an eternal alliance.

Bill was waiting. He had avoided any doubt which he might have had about the origins of the fire. It was Shephard's responsibility, and he was going to avenge Penelope's death. It became a duty which defied evidence. He needed no evidence to justify his action, since this poison had seized upon Shephard as the reason for Penelope's death. Shephard had become the source of any misfortune which he had witnessed since his arrival. He was an accident which San Cristobal would never survive; but, above all, he was his enemy. It was Shephard who had burnt Penelope. And yet this was the man whom he had tried to protect from the conspiracy which Crabbe and others were preparing for him. He remembered the incident on the plane, as though he saw in it the logical reason for his hatred of Shephard. It was Penelope whom Shephard had chosen to humiliate; and later, after he had forgotten what Penelope must have suffered during that flight, he had tried to save Shephard's life. He had persisted in foiling the plans which Crabbe had devised for putting an end to Shephard. It made him feel like an accomplice in her death.

This knowledge was no longer useful. He knew now that those arrangements had been cancelled, but he was going to join in this conspiracy which Crabbe could not carry through. He was going to murder Shephard, and he felt that his wish was also part of the hope for San Cristobal. It was Penelope who had fed this desire beyond any reason which might make him alter his decision. San Cristobal was a grave. It contained one corpse which would always tell its misery until he had done his duty.

He was waiting, patient as the night, for Shephard's departure. His hand felt slack round the weapon, but he was not afraid. He tried to anticipate the order of his actions, and then he thought of its consequences. But he had no misgiving. Perhaps they would find Crabbe's wallet and the letter which would show that there were others who wanted to murder Shephard. Crabbe would have to explain that as best he could. Or would they suspect Mark? He had not thought of involving Mark, but now it did not matter. Mark would have to explain why Shephard had visited him that evening. He could not be bothered with the details of the future. It was Penelope who determined his relation to the future. He crept closer, and his hands grew firm and cold round the metal in his pocket. He could see Shephard's head swinging in the light, and he thought he heard a voice. He moved closer, and the voice came again. He decided to wait. There was no need to hurry. He would wait until the night was a little older.

He crawled cautiously over the dry stubble of grass, and he could hear the earth making its night noises under his feet, a chorus of animals and insects like a perpetual argument against the night. It entered his ears, and his senses seemed lost in a conflict which which raged at the back of his head. His solitude was loud with names and voices fighting like swords in the hot tower of his skull. He put his hand against his face, and the moisture stuck like dying wax against his skin. But he was not afraid. The voices protected him from any anxiety which he might have felt. Flagstead explaining why it was necessary to defend oneself against Shephard, and Penelope in her final agony. They were ordering his action, and he knew, without their consent, that he was right. Shephard had to die. It was a duty which had saved him from the stain of murder. It was not the thought of murder which made him sweat. He thought only of Shephard's future which resided in that neutral wheel of metal which would soon release its load. Then Penelope's end would be redeemed and his own hatred stilled. This would be the end of his excitement. His wish would have had its reward, and the rest San Cristobal could decide.

He wiped his hands over the seat of his trousers, and raised his head slowly up to the level of the sill. The room was now in half-darkness, lit only by a small standing lamp in the far corner. Shephard's back was turned to the window, but he could see Mark, sitting erect under the light. He was holding the point of the knife against his knee, as though he were trying to prevent the blade from plunging into the bone. He stared at Shephard with incredulous eyes. His glance was calm, deliberate and certain, and Bill wondered whether Mark, too, had felt a similar need for revenge. He searched his pocket and secured his grip round the gun. He could see Shephard's back, wide and vulnerable as the window pane, waiting, and he heard Penelope's voice swelling the night with a cry that rose with the chorus of insects out of the earth.

Bill was straining against the window. He could see Shephard's hands swinging through the air, while Mark remained on the sofa. He tried to hear what Shephard was saying, but the words seemed to dissolve in a whisper of syllables, a shadow of noise that could not pass beyond the window pane. His hand leaned casually over the gun as though this sudden curiosity had obscured his mission. His ears had become alert and stinging, devoured by a hunger which his hearing could not satisfy. He could feel his eyes dart here and there as though Shephard's body was a magnet which regulated his glance. For a moment he seemed lost in this incredible atmosphere of the room. He had forgotten the night which swept in a wide and silent embrace about the house.

And suddenly he saw himself caught in a yellow flush of light. His hand found its grip, but he was unsure of his decision. He had no time to think, and he remained where he was, trying to block his eyes from the glare of the headlights. He had not heard the low throttle of the engine until he sprang back from the window and saw the car nosing into the driveway. The driver made a noise with the horn, and Bill knew he was seen. Shephard was about to leave, but the driver now became an obstacle. It would have been unwise to hide, and he was not going to miss Shephard. He had not moved when the door opened, and Mark appeared on the steps. Shephard was standing behind him, making ready to approach the car. Bill felt his fingers tremble. He was ready. His throat was tight, and he could feel his hand wobble as it crept up his side. But he remembered the driver and the sudden flush of light which had showed him under the window. He decided to announce his presence. Mark started at the voice. Bill walked in the arc of the headlights towards the steps. He did not speak.

Mark was trying to decide how he could get rid of Bill. He was determined to leave with Shephard.

'I thought you weren't coming,' said Mark, 'and I have got to…'

Shephard leapt from the steps and stood between them, slapping his hands on Bill's shoulder. Bill felt for the gun. He was beyond himself with rage, but Shephard had succumbed to this blinding spell of unreason. He spoke like a man whom drink had made forgetful of certain details.

'The plane,' he said, leading Bill towards the car, 'I remember the plane. You remember? You remember, Kennedy?'

He turned to look for Mark who was following close behind.

'We share a secret too,' he said, pulling Bill beside him in the car. 'Not the golden days, but a secret that was important too.' He was feeling in his pocket for the wallet. They had left it in the house, but the driver interrupted to ask where he should take them.

'To the Point,' said Shephard, 'Paradise Point.'

Mark sat beside him, feeling the point of the knife in his pocket. Shephard was silent and thoughtful as though a sudden loss of excitement had returned his judgement. He muttered something about the plane, but Bill paid no attention. He was calculating the chances of his success as he pressed his finger against the gun. The car felt its way through the night with an intolerable caution, but they could hear the sound of the wind, and Bill knew his task was clear, simple. The night wore the right colour for his undertaking. He thought for a moment of his future. 'Tomorrow San Cristobal will be confounded, not knowing whether to weep or to rejoice. The leader's death shall be as large as his victory.'

BOOK THREE

ON TRIAL

PART ONE

1

Ten thousand feet in the asphalt yard, crushing the yellow berries to a flat, wet pulp. Taken from their stems at every interval of wind bending the branches, the useless fruit, with their large reputation for poison, fell from a great height down the green trees, and died, flattened, with a fine yawn of their flesh closing quickly under the numerous feet which waited or wandered in an eager shuffle over the asphalt yard. The Court had never seen evidence of such a morning before.

FIRST VOICE: Today is a day.

SECOND VOICE: Believe me, it is. Most certainly.

FIRST VOICE: A day of days, I tell you.

THIRD VOICE: In my lifetime, to be sure.

FIRST VOICE: In the lifetime of any of us standing here this bright Monday morning.

THIRD VOICE: You are right, upon my word, you are. 'Tis a case for history. An' a fair trial it will be. If all goes well.

FOURTH VOICE: You've spoken a mouthful, my son, saying as you say a minute ago, if all goes well.

FIRST VOICE: They will be hanged.

SECOND VOICE: By the grace of God, they goin'. When all is heard of what happen that night. The Law will heal what they do.

THIRD VOICE: An' may the good Lord have mercy.

SECOND VOICE: As men, His mercy they deserve, but as beasts they will bury with a rope round their neck.

THIRD VOICE: A most shameful murder they make.

FIRST VOICE: And of one who was truly call' to lead us into the light. As it was with our Lord and Saviour Jesus Christ, wasn't it?

FOURTH VOICE: You speak a word, my friend, so it was with our leader, Shephard.

THIRD VOICE: He would have us see the light, and he die' for it. But they will find out their mistake, the criminals, oh yes, they will. Let's leave everything to God.

FOURTH VOICE: An' the Law.

The Law was present in the pair of scales, most carefully worked in stone on the square, patient face of the court; and the police, taking their turn round and about the yard in a most leisurely patrol, urging order and quiet; and beyond, the white walls spiked with sharp points of iron, where the red prison waited on a small hill for the court's decision; and still further, not blocked by houses or hill or any obstacle between, making an end of the view from the yard, the little cemetery of the damned, overgrown with weed, and carrying a single tombstone, long gone green with moss, which was to serve the evil memory of all who were buried within.

FIRST VOICE: Give me a pauper's funeral any day. With my children hidin' their heads in shame for fear of the neighbours knowin' they couldn't carry their father to a grave that cost a right an' proper sum.

FOURTH VOICE: 'Tis true there's little difference 'twixt the appearance of two such graves, no one showin' a respectful remembrance with some sort of flowers. But a pauper is better off where he rest his head than any criminal in the hole over yonder.

SECOND VOICE: He is, an' he goes in grace when he goes, an' can wait, safe an' sound for the call of the Master on that great day that is comin' by and by.

THIRD VOICE: There won't be no room there for these two, poor devils.

FIRST VOICE: There can't be. Not among the righteous.

FOURTH VOICE: I live in fear an' tremblin' that no such disaster visit me nor mine. Nor any standin' here in waitin' this mornin'. So I try to train my children, mornin', noon an' night. That no envy, no jealousy, no bad feelin' that follow you roun', an' try to enter your heart to push you into damnation, take them by surprise an' teach them the evil thereof. I always ask Heaven to help me.

The judgement and the fear of voices, reaching across the yard and up to the face of the court, showing justice in an even measurement of stone, made a large murmur from top to bottom, end to end on all sides of the arena which the public had made their gallery. The police were signalling silence, pacing to and fro in a strict and special pomp, trying to match the meaning of the day with their manner.

FIRST VOICE: An' to think the Law is never in sight, like on that night, when somethin' so bad is 'bout to happen.

SECOND VOICE: These police can never prevent any evil doin'. Whenever they arrive, they arrive to ask what happen. An' then every mouth stay shut. Stop right up, by God, for fear it get itself in a new set of trouble.

FIRST VOICE: Never, never, you will never find a policeman in his right position when evil decide to take a turn on a woman or child, the poor or the helpless.

FOURTH VOICE: 'Tis true as every written word of Gospel, they arrive in time to ferret out what happen. Like you an' me who never know what of evil is happenin' round us.

THIRD VOICE: Like they have nothing to do but wait for wages week in week out. An' then to play they gettin' mad when nobody take the risk to say what they see.

SECOND VOICE: But you can always find them on a day like today, makin' a great parade of how powerful they can be, orderin' poor innocent people 'bout like they own you. Tellin' you to shut up, to stan' back, to go this way an' that.

THIRD VOICE: An' sometimes to leave altogether.

FOURTH VOICE: Indeed! As if they own you.

SECOND VOICE: Well I be damn' if I take it upon myself to stop talkin' on a day like today. It would be rage and riot an' hell fire self in here today if one o' them ever get it in his head to lay a han' on one limb o' me. So help me God, I'll be by your side in any kind o' commotion they try to make with their great airs.

FIRST VOICE: Puttin' on the grand manner like a peacock on holiday. Today is our day.

FOURTH VOICE: Yours and mine in commemoration of the murderin' o' a man who nearly make you an' me better men.

THIRD VOICE: An' woman too.

FOURTH VOICE: To be sure. He was for all.

And all had arrived, in unusual numbers to get within the yard to have a view of the court and hear without mistake or deception the words which would be spoken from within. Every trade and profession which Shephard had lived for was there, reviving their memory of what he was and how he died, each who laboured daily for bread had made a sacrifice of work to come to the courtyard. And for once the idle had found a reason for their presence. They had come to dream what might have happened if Shephard had survived his labours. And their wish for another death was wide, a unanimous hope that the Law would share their judgement and join in their lack of pardon. The feet were multiplying, and their press together had left no opening over the asphalt for the berries which dropped now and again, making a brisk hop from head to head, and rolling briefly over the crooked lines of feet, squeezed painfully close. The little yellow balls collided and rolled to a rest in the sink of their toes, and no one, in the end, seemed displeased. The ropes which marked the limits of the public premises were slackening, and the police were erecting new poles to enlarge the area for the increasing crowd. Whenever the crowd extended to touch the ropes, and the press made it again uneasy to move, the police were going to close the gates; and that, for the time being, would be the end of all coming and going through the yard. The yellow berries were beginning to slide on to the asphalt, uttering a sudden snap and moan as they flattened under the feet. The sun entered gently through the new spaces starting little thrusts of light on the asphalt like wet fingers playing indolently over the window pane. It had to stumble through the leaves of the wide evergreen, before finishing its fall on the asphalt; and when the shade of the branches shifted, the light opened and closed on the asphalt, and the whole yard seemed to sway under the berries, yellow and crushed between the tiring feet. But it was hardly noticeable to those who were preparing to sit. They shuffled down, impatient and weary with waiting.

THIRD VOICE: Nine o' the clock.

FOURTH VOICE: An' a whole hour to go.

SECOND VOICE: Have patience, my friend, nothin' happens before it's time.

FIRST VOICE: We wait years to fin' a man who would show us the way. An' then we lose him, dear God, just like that. So we can wait now, an hour or more for the callin' o' the Court. But there won't be no losin' our wish for all those who had a han' in this doin'.

FOURTH VOICE: Who was it say, Death come like a thief in the night?

SECOND VOICE: It goin' come to the guilty in broad daylight for every eye to see, an' all ears to harken.

THIRD VOICE: Sit, an' give your limbs a chance to catch themselves.

FIRST VOICE: An' pray that the Law let us rejoice in the punishment o' the guilty.

SECOND VOICE: O' the accuse' as they like to name them at this stage o' their lastin'. An' rightly accuse', too, with not much lastin' in them.

FIRST VOICE: Indeed, not much lastin'.

The Court is quiet. The defence counsel has described the manner in which he will hear the evidence, and all eyes turn to watch Ma Shephard take her stand. It is her hands which first compel attention. Frail and unfit, they eagerly attempt to test her weight, leaning lightly on the rails. Her fingers in their crooked clutch are like a bird's dead claws that cleave unnaturally to the curve of the rail. Her nails are broken and brown, frozen scabs that have been stuck fearfully into the hidden moisture of her flesh. They are a remnant of limbs feeling at random for contact and support. Her wrists are an abrupt arrival of bone. She leans forward, and her testimony follows without interruption.

WITNESS: The manner in which he die on that bad beach I shan't know, an' it ain't in my power to say how, an' I am not one to pretend to know what didn't come within the reach o' my two eyes. But he is dead, never to come back on this earth, not in this life. An' whoever do it, that terrible thing, I am not wise to say, but it is the end o' a long long worry for me; for without meanin' to, he wasn't really a bad child, he bring in his time much botheration to my life. I never ferret out his ways from a chil' upwards to when he was a tall an' strappin' man, and I withdraw an' leave him to himself. If he was goin' to bring downfall on his life I had nothin' but prayer, and if, by the grace of God, he bring glory I was glad.

But from a chil', his luck was bad. Little girls used to laugh at him, and even when he was full grown, not only one woman I know of rob him. Oft times, I say to him, Isaac, let the worl' go its way, for God in his own good time will give you the life you deserve, but he was proud. He always feel he could conquer, and that was one of his bad faults. He had it in him to conquer. Now he gone, he can forget all that worry, and San Cristobal must find a new man to plague. My son, as I say, was ambitious, even as a chil', an' 'tis the reason he take up himself as he do, some years gone by, an' sail all the way up to England. This England was in his blood, an' 'tis what bring final ruin to him. Whatever happen there I cannot in a manner of certainty speak, but he had a bad experience which teach him to rebel, an' it come out in his dreams. Many a night I hear him shout out in sleep, using the worst words, which was a great change, 'cause he never swear to my knowledge, the most awful language he could fin', he painted those who make his experience painful. I was afraid for him, poor chil'. Whatever they do to him there I don't know, but he came back here, full up with a great hate for that England, an' the only way he could work it off was in the great fight he start for the poor workers. But that too had its bad side.

The day before he died, not knowin' his end was so near, he call me to talk like he was a child again. His nerve was wearin' down, an' he start to talk in a way which frighten me. Was the very night he visit the two men on charge for murder.

Some say he was 'fraid Mr Kennedy would enter politics an' take the lead from him, but he never bother with that. They say in the rumour 'bout the plane that he was bad to Mrs Butterfield, an' the lady who die in the fire was Mr Kennedy' make-believe wife, an' many people feel that the night they went down to Paradise Point was arrange' beforehan'. I know for a truth, an' I want to speak without taking any sides, my son always did want to show some sympathy to Mr Kennedy for what happen in the fire, that's why he went that night. But the truth will come out, if not now, some time, an' if they are guilty of such a terrible act, they will suffer, if not here, then hereafter.

He never return that night. Ten o'clock strike an' pass, then eleven, an' no sign o' my son. But a voice wake me in the middle o' the night to ask if he was in. I never recollec' who the voice belong to, but it was familiar all right, an' not thinkin' any evil so near, I say from my window where he went. An' the voice went to fin' him in the house where the taxi collect them for Paradise Point. He never come home that night.

Ma Shephard pauses and bows her head as though she is too exhausted to continue. Counsel for the defence nods, and the clerk helps her back to the seat, holding her arm, and stepping patiently beside her as she fumbles with the stick. Her feebleness is irksome, and the Court feels impressed with her performance. Heads nod in approval of her conduct and wonder about the voice which she does not remember. The Chief Justice is patient. He watches the clerk deposit the old woman and return to his seat, then he passes the back of his hand across his brow, and props his chin on his clenched fists. There is a hurried rustle of paper on the clerk's desk, as the men mutter in consultation about the proceedings. Counsel for the accused is leaning forward with his arms sprawled over the desk. His eyes are hidden by his hands, but no one notices him. The Chief Justice lowers his head and receives more papers which he shuffles mechanically from side to side. A shadow floats across the court which is about to break its silence.

The clerk announces a name, and the Court rehearses its privileges again and waits for the witness to speak. His tongue stumbles through the oath, and his hands dodder over the rails of the wooden dock. He seems to think that every witness is on trial; that he too is accused of murdering Shephard. They signal him to begin, and he avoids the faces of the accused, and stares at the Chief Justice, beseeching him to believe.

WITNESS: To be plain, sir, it was not my intention to come here, an' if I could have find a way out I would not, indeed, have put a foot outside my house this mornin'; for 'tis the first time in all my born days, believe me, that I ever set foot in this place, although, an' you can ask any of the ones outside who set eyes on my face before an' know me, I live just outside the wall that surround this court house. An' this, as I say before, is my first time, a man gone fifty mind you, in such surroundings, sir, I will tell the truth, the plain truth, an' nothin' but the truth, but, an' I will ask your favour not to cast misbelief on my word, I ain't got no truth to tell.

The clerks of the court, whispering their impatience, look at each other, and try to suppress their amusement and their irritation. The audience seem lightly moved to laughter by the witness's confession, and regard the man with eager and anxious curiosity. The witness notices that his delay has naturally caused some concern in the court, but the Chief Justice, whose head is bowed in grave and authoritative silence, waves his hand impassively towards the witness, requesting him to continue. Counsel for Mark and Bill is about to make some suggestion when the witness continues, scratching the back of his neck as he slaps the other hand in a furious declaration on his chest.

WITNESS: Sir, I am a sinner save' through grace and washe' once an' for all in the blood of the Lamb. This is no place for me or any chil' o' God who die' in Christ an' rise again through the sheddin' o' his blood on Calvary.

The audience are astonished, and the Chief Justice, whose head is now raised, looks at the witness with an expression of pity and rebuke. Then he speaks in a voice, fastidiously gentle and betraying in the drop of the syllables a tone of irony and boredom.

JUDGE: The witness is only asked to state as clearly and as briefly what he heard and/or saw during the period of his hire from the residence of the accused to the seashore on the night in question. And this Court, I may remind and assure the witness, is not of necessity a place to avoid. Its function, during my jurisdiction, is not to ruin but rather to protect and ensure, as far as is possible and within its right, the life and the dignity of all citizens who are, in all good cause and reason, summoned to it. Will the witness please continue.

WITNESS: My ears, sir, hear not one thing from any of those lips behin' me on the night you make mention of. They talk' no talk at all, sir, until, as any man who make his living by a taxi may expect, whichever gentleman it was pay the fare just say good night.

The Chief Justice scrapes his head with an indolent hand and fingers a stack of documents which are laid before him. He does not appear to read the documents, but the witness is apprehensive, and is waiting anxiously to have some word of confirmation or dismissal from him. Counsel for Mark and Bill, who has already suggested that evidence be given with as little interruption as possible, has attracted the attention of the judge.

COUNSEL: Everyone appreciates the difficulty of the witness on an occasion like this, since it is his first experience of the Law at work in a chamber of this kind. But every attempt must be made to remember, as far as is humanly possible, the details of that night. There is already some conflict in the evidence of the witness on a previous occasion. Then he recalled bits of conversation which he had overheard.

The witness keeps his head down until counsel has finished. His hands shake nervously as he clasps them in front of him. The judge continues his vague survey of the papers before him, while the audience wait, in a nervous sympathy, to hear the witness make his correction. There is a flicker of voices which come abruptly to an end as the judge lets his eye rove in a reminder of contempt to the farthest limits of the room.

WITNESS: 'Tis not me, sir, but my memory which speak through me, an' if I falter for fear or a natural forgettin', I would ask, sir, not to put the blame on me. The memory will carry so much an' no more, sometimes more now than then an' the other way roun', but if it was not forbidden me to take the name of the Lord in vain I would swear by that name, even in this place, that what I fail to remember, I ain't fail to remember for a purpose. That night, as the gentleman say, not tryin' to accuse me of a mistruth I pray, I did hear a few words pass in a drunken manner from the dead man, God rest him in his grave. They talk 'bout what happen in the plane, but I say to myself they was all mad to make this journey to the sea of all places at that time o' mornin'. But they wus drinkin', sir, from the way I hear Shephard talk, I say to myself he had some liquor in his head. He was talkin' wild, but his words miss my ear. 'Twas two thirty, as I'm standin' here, to my surprise, sir, when I put those three gentlemen down at Paradise Point on the night in question. And that, sir, with the help o' God, is what I hear or have to say in the business o' that night.

JUDGE: There is no need to hurry, and it will be more convenient for all concerned if it is not necessary to call you here again for further evidence.

WITNESS: One voice say, but I never make no distinction betwixt the voices, so I can't say who say, the voice say: 'It was a disgrace how you treated my wife,' an' at that turnin' o' their speech, which didn't seem no more joke, I turn off my hearin', not knowin', sir, if it was the plane or a later time they wus makin' mention of, I mean in the matter of the behaviour and the wife. Somethin' 'bout their behaviour scare me, an' only the grace o' God save me from takin' a life, 'cause I make such a reckless haste I nearly finish my life in collision with a car standin' still in the road which run down to the beach. That, sir, if you would take my word as a Christian who could not for the sake of eternal life afford to let a deliberate lie enter past my mouth, that is all what I hear the voices say in the sad business o' that night.

COUNSEL: Thank you. That is all.

The witness bows respectfully to the Chief Justice who does not notice, and walks at a hurrying pace, uncertain of his step, back to his seat beside a short black woman who snatches his hand and rests her head in a gesture of encouragement on his shoulder. He is wet all over, and afraid, but he does not release his hand to wipe his face. Suddenly the woman takes a handkerchief from her bag and performs this little service with an elaborate and loving attention. Everyone looks at them with sorry smiles, nodding their understanding of the man's dread. He has never felt any distinction between the court and the jail, and he is sure that anyone who enters the first eventually and inevitably will spend some time in the other. He keeps his glance on the Chief Justice, who, in his enormous lack of concern, seems to him an infinite source of power. He would be pleased if the Chief Justice would smile approvingly, or even in vague satisfaction at him. He does not turn to regard those who are sitting behind him, or to the side of him; for it is only the Chief Justice who matters. The Court is his and the Law and all who ramble within their power.

The wife continues her silent attentions, wiping his hands and, with as little show as possible, his neck and the sides of his face.

The Chief Justice looks up, letting his glance travel beyond the limits of the building to the asphalt yard, where the crowd have revived their interest, and are holding forth in noisy judgement on what they have heard. A man leaves the court to remind the police outside that the hearing must proceed in quiet, and the Chief Justice, whose wishes are made known only by the peculiar mannerisms of his body, lowers his head, and pushes the papers before him from side to side. A sudden quiet overtakes the crowd who are irritable and impatient, contemptuous of the police, and revengefully concerned about the future of this case. The Court is quiet like a waiting witness while the Chief Justice pinches his hairy nostrils and passes a hand, with supreme complacence, across his mouth. He can smell the perfume which sterilises his natural odour. It is a comic face, soft and black, under the wig that carves his head like a calabash, arrogant eyes and an upper lip that is made unnaturally severe by the need to press upon the teeth that are too large for his mouth. His expression is one of indifference as though a fear of being thought very ugly continually reminds him of his power and fills him with a professional and protective spite.

From the preparation of names and numbers, another witness emerges. A man with a firm face and huge loyal arms that are remarkably bent at the elbows. His hands are heavy and sure, and the veins rise and ramble over the back up to the roots of his nails which sink deep into the fat white flesh. The tackle has given his hands all over the sharp, raw scars of his fishing trade. His legs look thin and awkward under the stiff starched khaki, and his waist is narrow, but his body widens at the ribs, and his chest, barely visible under the diaphanous blue shirt, unbuttoned at the top, shows great staying power, efficient and reliable. He does not rest on the wooden rails of the dock, but stands erect with his arms easily folded across his chest. He is comfortable and astonishingly calm, almost aloof in his expression of patient forgiveness which he turns occasionally on those who sit nearest him. His presence makes the Chief Justice and the surrounding paraphernalia of the court seem irrelevant, ridiculous, absurd. He is present because he has no place to go. It is a harmless favour to grant, his knowledge of the sea, and the information he can give. It is his wish that the men should die if they are guilty, but it is not the deceased who occupies his attention. It is the Chief Justice and the strange, irrelevant paraphernalia of the court. He wants to humble them with his passion for the sea.

CLERK: We have had some difficulty in ascertaining the full name of the witness.

The judge seems a little puzzled and the audience show a mild excitement about the disclosure the witness will make.

WITNESS: They call me Rockey.

There is a quiver of fun in the court. It does not last. It subsides at a gentle thrust of the Chief Justice's head upwards. He looks briefly at the witness, but on this occasion the language of his movement is not to be interpreted. The witness is unmoved, and does not speak, because he considers he has said all he need say about his identity. The clerk risks a quick glance at the Chief Justice and then addresses the witness, who is neither puzzled nor amused by their lack of understanding.

CLERK: When you were summoned here, we accepted, for convenience, the name you have given; but we must have something more substantial for the records. What is your real name, your full real name?

WITNESS: I come or go, as is the case, if I hear Rockey.

The clerk lowers his head in a suggestion of annoyance, and the witness seems of a sudden slightly irritated. The audience is apprehensive, and the Chief Justice suppresses a yawn and shows a lack of attention. It is one of the tricks he uses in preparing for some sudden assertion of his authority. The witness ignores him; it is the clerk who seems to arouse his anger. He does not understand the mystery they are making of his evidence. He feels a sudden impulse to shout at the clerk; for he is not used to prolonged misunderstanding in a matter that seems so simple, and as a man whose work requires speed and unerring efficiency he loathes people who make a mystery of what seems quite simple.

WITNESS: If you like plenty names I can make them up, but Rockey is all I know, or my mother before me, or my men who fish with me. An' if Rockey won't do, you can let me go.

The judge suddenly intervenes with a studied caution. He looks at the witness for a while, feels a strange bewilderment about him, and then leans forward to address the clerk.

JUDGE: Let him proceed.

WITNESS: Now I may speak I will begin.

There is a pause while the clerk lowers his body in the chair. He looks rebuked, and pretends disinterest. He turns to say something to one of his colleagues, but he does not get a hearing, because the man is watching the witness with a grave misgiving. The witness is silent as though he is preparing for some lengthy and deeply moving discourse. He looks round the court, at the flags and the photographs and the mouldy monuments of fame, showing like flotsam. His life is not a game of questions and answers. His life is the sea where Shephard was murdered, and he will first tell them something about the sea, which wears no wig and tolerates no questions from those who explore her for food. He has taken a day off from the sea to speak about the sea. He shows a certain pleasure in the opportunity. He lets his hands fall lazily down to his sides, and suddenly, as though it seemed an unbecoming stance, he folds them again across his chest. He is relaxed, calm, resourceful.

WITNESS: I enter the ocean at an early age, a strip of a boy beside my father, helpin' to raid the fish of the sea, all class of fish in every kind of sea-water. No fish none of you can name that I din't down with harpoon or hook or haul flyin' in with these said same hands you see here. An' I defy any son of man livin' or dead who know Paradise Point to contradict me. There be many matters an' ways o' the sea which knowledge of education cannot teach; for experience is the only rule and master of the tides. An' fish can be smart, smarter than humans, and stronger than most humans. Take a black jack, for the sake or argument.

At this point counsel intervenes apologetically to ask the witness's indulgence. They ask him to limit his remarks to the night in question at Paradise Point. At first he seems slightly taken aback. He hesitates before continuing as if questioning their authority to make him speak as they wish.

WITNESS: Night and day is two sides of the same coin, one side maybe is heads, the next side maybe tails, but the same coin, an' 'tis the same with every man who chase fish, maybe 'tis nightlight, maybe 'tis daylight, but there's only one time, that's fishing time. An' fishin' time is all time. An' the time I hear you call the night in question catch me fishin' off Paradise Point.

Now Paradise Point ain't really no Paradise at all at all, an' those who tuck on that name to the place was only forming the

361

fool. An' what you call the night in question was, I recollect, no bed o' roses at Paradise Point. It was a complete blackout of light for the night, and it take a reg'lar piss-to-win'ward to say he settin' out for a swim in that sea.

There is a brief interruption while the clerk asks for some clarification of the term, piss-to-win'ward. It means simply a foolish man, one who was observed in the witness's example making water with his organ held up to the wind, so that the urine was returned in his face.

WITNESS: There's two sets o' seas at Paradise Point as any man who fish there will verify. There's the sea where the fishin' move forward in velvet water; the wind don't pay no great visit there, that's the east or angel-island side o' the Point. An' there's the side o' the Point where the ocean is thistle and thorns, an' then you don't only have to outsmart your fish, but contend with a truly riotous nature. The body o' the dead man was on that side. That's where I pick it up. Not disrespectin' the dead, I must say that at first, my eyes not suspectin', I thought it was a dead dog, or sheep, or some animal o' that nature. The Point was a no-man's-land o' night, the darkness was so deep. There was no question 'bout what you call the night in question. 'Twas an outrage to every light that ever was or will be. Now for the man I pick up, lying there with the sea inside him. He was not yet dead, but any man with a head for the nature o' the drownin' would know that man didn't have no great claim on the livin'. But I was in time to hear his voice. 'Twas me Heaven choose to hear his las' words. He believe it was Butterfiel' holdin' his sleeve, an' he groan, 'Turn in the letter, Butterfiel'. Don't burn the letter, Butterfiel'.' Then he whisper some word 'bout his people, and sudden so he give up the ghost, an' his mouth refuse to surrender whatever meanin' his head was holdin'.

The witness seems less assured, for an awful quiet has come over the court. He waits, looking from the clerk to the Chief Justice, and gradually from side to side at the audience. He has become more important than the occasion, for he was the last person to see Shephard alive. It is the first disclosure the Court has heard of this evidence. The Chief Justice is scribbling carefully on the paper before him, and two clerks are talking quietly.

A new interest has awakened them. A timid whisper scurries round the court, and the clerks raise their heads to suggest silence. The Chief Justice continues writing, and the witness waits, gradually regaining his control. He, too, feels a new interest, for he can feel their glances declare him the only man among them who matters. He sweeps his hands over his head and down the sides of his face, then rubs them vigorously together, slippery with his sweat. He seems a little pleased with himself, as he watches their efforts dictated by his evidence. He has much more to say about the deceased but he will not oblige them until they have heard him again on the miracles of the sea off Paradise Point. He wants to describe in greater detail the quality of the night, the heavy wilderness of trees which screen the sea from the land and which make a shade for fishermen in the idle afternoon. He is trying to invent a language of darkness and absence to convey the black splendour that surrounded him, alone in a hazardous labour, off Paradise Point. He is sure they will listen. The Court has not yet recovered from its excitement, and the noise is increasing in the yard where the crowd are beginning to challenge the right of the police to silence them. The Chief Justice summons one of his clerks, and a man disappears with a threat. The asphalt yard suddenly becomes an enquiring whisper. The man returns, bows obsequiously to the Chief Justice and takes his seat.

Crabbe enters, whispers to the clerk who passes an envelope to the Chief Justice. The Court is silent. The Chief Justice reads, and his face reflects the urgency of the note which Crabbe has delivered. A little light falls reluctantly on the faces in the court; but they are alive with wonder and anticipation. The witness has suddenly assumed a heroic role in their awareness. He scratches the palm of his hand for luck, and suggests that they let him continue without more delay. Words are becoming unruly in his head. Paradise Point puts itself up for sale before his eyes, and the darkness of the night in question settles deliciously over his senses. The sea rolls in his ears urging his acclaim, and his small boat which has dared every occasion of ruin for his sake puts out its sails before him. The sea sails hilariously in his blood. And suddenly, overcome with memory, he smiles and rubs his hand, positive and assured. The Chief Justice looks up and notices his face, almost ecstatic with excitement, and feels a certain misgiving. He glances at the clerks, makes another scribble on the paper and then stands, a heavily built man, preoccupied and disdainful. The Court rises.

JUDGE: The Court will adjourn.

An awful quiet unites the crowd. The Chief Justice raises himself slowly, crunching his teeth as he sweeps languidly down the narrow flight of steps to his office. He lifts his hands to his eyes in a gesture of fatigue. The room awaits him, silent and sacred with custom, but suddenly the corridor seems to shake, and the air is defiled with a familiar violence. He hears the voices of the crowd, hysterical with rage. He pauses and glances over his shoulder at the receding corridor, familiar with carpet and decay. The walls look weary and afraid under their ancient and foreign display of royal faces and legal company. He lingers for a while outside, observing the late sovereign countenance which smiles from a gilt-edged frame above the door. Then he enters, quietly, throwing the envelope on to the table, and checks his powdered wrinkles in the mirror. He whiffs the fragrance of his soft black hands, and again the echo of the crowd intervenes, with a chant which lingers outside the window.

> *'Over land and over sea*
> *Freedom shall prevail*
> *Man was made for liberty*
> *And Freedom shall prevail.*

'Friends in mournin' we must sharpen the sword. We will sharpen the sword an' prepare, 'cause this law can let you down. Justice ain't sugar you can weigh by the scale, an' the scales can't measure your feelin' nor mine. Prepare your sword if this law decide to let you down.'

'The law will be we.'

'Over land and over sea.'

'Freedom!'

' 'Tis freedom they arrange to murder.'

'Never… never… never…'

There was a soft knock on the door, but the Chief Justice did not stir. The heat had spread like a fever under his gown. His body poured with sweat. The fan buzzed and spun as it made its half-turns to the opposite corners of the room. A fly climbed the worn white curls of the wig which lay on the table, made a circle round the glass and alighted on his head. It nosed slowly down the groove of his neck where the hair divided like rows of black shrub, and washed itself. He did not feel. The curtain flapped and fell, and the noise continued, soaring over the courtyard. The voices rose everywhere, drunk and helpless with revenge. The crowd waved their fists in anger when the car rode Mark and Bill through the yard. They threw the yellow berries into the dust which trailed behind, and shook their fists again. The police were persuading them to disperse, but they had begun to make a show of their reluctance. They would not leave.

He raised his head and listened for the knock on the door. It was his habit to answer ten seconds after the first knock, but his attention was divided between the noise of the crowd and the leisurely crawl of the fly down his neck. He saw the curtains balloon and glide across the window, and he tried to decide whether he should close the window. Then the wig and the glass competed for his attention. He was going to put the wig on the chair, but his hand lifted the glass instead. He took a mouthful of water. Some trickled over his lip. He cupped his hands under his chin and sawed two fingers across his mouth. He put the glass on the table, and crushed the false curls of the wig under his hands. The knock came again. He scraped the chair back and pressed the button. The door closed quietly behind Crabbe. The Attorney General had walked ahead. He pulled a chair up on the opposite side and waited for Crabbe to sit.

'Is it really true?'

'I suppose you knew already,' the Chief Justice said, looking at Crabbe. He was angry, and they understood.

'No one knew until an hour ago,' said Crabbe.

'When are they coming?' the Attorney General asked. He looked relieved as he fanned his gown over the chair and waited for the noise in the courtyard to subside.

'The troops will arrive soon,' the Chief Justice said curtly. 'My orders are to prolong the case until they get here.'

He took another mouthful of water and banged the glass on the table. Crabbe did not speak. The Attorney General was uneasy. He understood the man's irritation, but he did not think this was a time to insist on minor issues of prestige. It was irrelevant whether Crabbe had got his information before the Chief Justice, and it was certainly dangerous to have him feeling disgruntled in a moment of crisis.

'You do agree with the decision?' the Attorney General asked.

'I have nothing to say,' he said, 'except that I don't like having to pronounce judgement in this case.'

'The troops can take care of that,' said the Attorney General.

'Can you hear that crowd?' the Chief Justice asked. He was looking at Crabbe. 'It will be worse if the men are found innocent.'

'And if we proved them guilty?' the Attorney General said.

'What difference you think it will make?' the Chief Justice answered. 'What difference! Who is going to tell them…'

There was a clatter of bottle and glasses. The Chief Justice half stood, looking at the mess of broken glass in the corner. An enormous photograph of his predecessor had fallen face down over the table. The floor was strewn with splinters. The Attorney General stared up where the nail showed, headless, in the wall. Crabbe rubbed his hands over the table, indifferent to the spectacle of the twisted picture frame lying in the crystal dry pool of glass. The Attorney General got up and walked to the window. He saw the crowd milling slowly about the courtyard. He drew himself behind the shelter of the curtains and watched. The Chief Justice pressed the button, and a messenger arrived to tidy the mess.

But the Chief Justice had decided not to stay. He watched the man squat in the corner, lifting the frame from the thick wreckage of glass. He would have liked to be blunt with Crabbe, but he thought his silence was enough. He collected the wig, squeezed his papers into the briefcase and walked away.

'Leave the mess,' the Attorney General said.

The man looked up, bowed, and hurried noiselessly out of the room. Crabbe did not turn. The Attorney General left the window and drew his chair closer to Crabbe's. His hands shook as he waited for the noise to subside.

'I know what you're thinking,' Crabbe said.

The Attorney General seemed to waver. He was trying to avoid an admission of defeat or fear. The future seemed terribly near like the voices of the crowd.

'How can we get the letter?' he asked.

But Crabbe did not answer. And the voices returned, distant and clear, preparing the crowd for revenge.

FIRST VOICE: 'Tis plain as daylight what they do.

SECOND VOICE: All arrange' in order like a war the night they finish him off at the Point. Drunken him first, 'tis what they do, drunken him first, an' then empty his life in the sea.

THIRD VOICE: That letter will be witness too. Whoever holdin' that letter will be better off after, if he surrender it now. The man who hold it back tryin' to hide what they do better turn in his secret to the court.

SECOND VOICE: Court or no Court somebody got to dead. They got to dead who murder my leader at the very height o' his doin'.

THIRD VOICE: 'Twas the springtime o' his power they choose to finish his rule. But one eye goin' close for a next eye, an' one tooth got to fall out for a next tooth.

FIRST VOICE: Will be more than tooth or eye, I tell you. If I got to put my neck to the rope I goin' see them pay for his murder. Adjourn or whatever word they choose for holdin' this operation up, one thing stay certain an' sure, that judge can' adjourn his job.

SECOND VOICE: Nor the sentence his duty demand. He can' adjourn the rope which goin' swing them to hell. 'Twas murder deliberate an' cold that they do. They murder my leader, yours an' mine. The very man who bring San Cristobal in step with the outside worl' an' teach us how to run with the times, they make it their business to murder him.

FIRST VOICE: An' the letter will tell more. The letter will expose any who help in the crime that bleed my heart an' yours too. Shephard's red blood was mine too.

SECOND VOICE: An' mine.

THIRD VOICE: His blood make all o' us bleed.

SECOND VOICE: An' it will last, I tell you it will last, his blood goin' soak San Cristobal. 'Cause a feelin' tell me there's more than two, there's more than two authorise his end.

FIRST VOICE: I feel it too. 'Twas no personal grievance make them murder. 'Twas a reason that touch you an' me an' all San Cristobal. The mention o' that letter show me once an' for all 'twas more than two.

THIRD VOICE: They do it, I have no doubt, nor you, nor you, that they do it, but I feel as you say there's more than two behin' all that happen. An' if the law don't work, we will teach it how to. I swear by Moses an' all the saints, includin' Jesus himself, that I will swing for any man who stay alive 'cause his name an' privilege spare him. Let him hide. His time will run out. An' whoever the evidence prove guilty, today or a year from today we goin' wait for. We goin' wait. His time will run out.

SECOND VOICE: But letter or no letter those two can count their stars. They can start to count their stars. An' it make no difference what the Court decide 'cause it is plain as daylight what happen.

FIRST VOICE: 'Tis plain, 'tis plain what they do. But I will rejoice if the letter turn up, 'cause I feel there's more than two who make that murder.

SECOND VOICE: 'Tis more than two.

THIRD VOICE: Something tell me a plan was at work, an' the two set o' hands which nasty the night with what they do, had orders from somewhere else, 'cause 'twas no personal grievance. An' after these two dead an' gone, an' they goin', by God Almighty, they goin', long after I will worry to know who else. We not leavin' a single soul uncover'. 'Tis why I achin' to hear what that letter tell.

FIRST VOICE: Maybe it will never turn up. Maybe those who know done burn it.

SECOND VOICE: Then we will make them talk. Butterfield will have to talk, 'cause he can tell what it say. They should make them talk if it call for torture.

THIRD VOICE: But you know the enemy you opposin' now. In death they get more stubborn than ever, an' if one see plain that he goin' die, it is hard to make him talk. He will turn dumb for those the letter expose.

SECOND VOICE: 'Tis true. They never give way.

FIRST VOICE: Let that bastard adjourn the hearin', let him adjourn. We goin' wait.

THIRD VOICE: Look round you an' see how every face tell its

feelin'. Every man declarin' his stand. Consider, jus' consider what Shephard do. He make a bond between you an' me an' every race that live with sufferin' in San Cristobal. He heal whatever difference divide them, an' when his real work was 'bout to begin, they snatch his life, an' deprive San Cristobal o' that future which Heaven was preparin'. 'Tis what they do. 'Tis what they do the night his blood cry out all over the sea.

Crabbe was alone in the room. The curtains were drawn. The fan was still. The heat sprang a silent furnace round his ears. The sweat was a river smothering his body, breaking quietly through the pits of his arms to mark frontiers of wet and dry patches over his clothes. It was like his vision of hell: the intolerable boiling, the exhausting wait for some relief, the fury of the crowd, the stubborn and irrelevant face of the clock trying to devour time. This was eternity seen in a moment of dread. He walked to the window and eased the curtain away for a view of the courtyard. He watched with one eye and wished for the absence of the crowd.

This was their day. The death of Shephard was a time to abandon the Law. He saw his power shrink to a relic, obsolete and useless as the yellow berries that cried under their feet. Who murdered Shephard? Was it his letter? Or the accused? The crowd did not care. This death was an occasion to purge their feelings. And the troops? How many would survive the ruthless discipline of the troops? They could not argue with bayonets and tanks. He was beginning to anticipate the future which would smother them noisily with lead and steel. But it was not enough to exterminate them. They were unkillable until you had found good reason for seeing them dead. Their death would be a waste without some moral justification for the troops. He heard them, loud and inarticulate as the day, deciding the future of San Cristobal, and he knew that his wish was right. Shephard had to die if the future of San Cristobal was to be rescued from chaos. The troops had to come if San Cristobal were to be saved from their savage and passionate hunger for blood. The order for troops was justified. His duty was beyond any argument. But the letter? How could they proceed without the slander which the letter had caused?

He had to know for certain that the letter was destroyed. And if it was available, he had to find a way of concealing it from the evidence of the court. The letter was the only obstacle to controlling with decency the anger of the crowd. But was it the letter which really murdered Shephard? Or was it really the accused? He had been assured that no one had carried out his order to shoot Shephard. But there was still the letter and the possible innocence of the accused. Who had really murdered Shephard?

In the far corner, separated from the crowd, he could see Flagstead and Thief. When the court resumed it would be Thief's turn to give evidence. Apart from Mark and Bill, Thief was probably the only other man who could say what had happened to the letter. And he knew Thief's loyalty to Bill. He knew that Thief and Flagstead would provide any evidence, or undertake any risk to save the two men. He could not risk a confidence with Flagstead or Thief unless he had a way of saving Mark and Bill. There was no hope of paying Thief to destroy the letter, and he was sure Flagstead was capable of any sacrifice on behalf of Bill. If Thief was in possession of the letter and Flagstead knew, there was only one thing he could do. But would they take him at his word? Would Thief surrender the letter before he was sure that Bill would be saved? Shephard was safe, and the troops would restore order, but his life was in danger if Thief offered the letter as his evidence to the court. His mission would come to an end in San Cristobal. The troops could not save his honour. He brought the curtains together and shut the light out. He stood at the window, head bowed, and watched his hands in the dark, and thought that never in San Cristobal or elsewhere had he been afraid to die, but the loss of honour, to be discovered not playing the game: this was his only sense of damnation.

He returned to the chair and tried to anticipate what order the night would take. The court would not resume until the following day, but the trial would continue. Not the trial of the accused whom he could help to escape the judgement of the court, but the trial of his own honour before Thief. He could never meet Thief with a simple request for help. Nor could he bribe him with promises. In one way or another, by argument or deception, he had to win Thief without any concession of his rule in San Cristobal.

He heard a knock on the door. He pressed the button and watched the door swing briefly to let Baboo in. Baboo watched him as he guided the door behind him to a close. Crabbe saw his face in the half-dark and felt that his difficulties had begun. He was forgetting the signs which helped him to interpret Baboo's feelings. He pointed to the chair opposite and watched Baboo bend slowly to the seat. He kept his hat on and glanced uncertainly from Crabbe to the window. Silence was always their code for bad news, but Baboo's eyes did not show the customary melancholy which he had always noticed when he felt disappointment. Crabbe was waiting.

'The news not so good, sir,' Baboo spread his hands on the table and considered his surroundings for a while. He noticed the absence of the picture from the wall, but he made no comment. 'The news not so good, sir,' he repeated.

'You spoke with Butterfield?' Crabbe asked.

'All alone in his cell, sir,' said Baboo. 'He wouldn't believe at first, but I get him to understan' I was serious, when I tell him how we decide to do it. Was mention o' Flagstead which make him believe. Then I talk with Kennedy. He won't move unless they leavin' together, so that is fix'.'

'An' the letter?'

'That's where the news not so good,' said Baboo. He looked up at the fan, and Crabbe noticed how his hands grew restless on the table, as though he wanted to avoid offending him with the news. He made it difficult to break his information. Crabbe was anticipating the worst. He leaned forward and rapped his hands on the table.

'You didn't mention the letter before talking with Thief,' Crabbe whispered. He was shaking for fear that Baboo had done things out of turn. But Baboo was unmoved. He had followed every instruction as he remembered them.

'Nothin' happen out of order,' he said. 'Not a word cross my lips to Butterfield 'bout the letter. He only understan' that Flagstead is payin' for what I decide to do.'

'Go on,' Crabbe said quickly.

''Tis Thief who stan' in the way,' said Baboo. 'He won't part with the letter till he see Butterfield safe on the ship an' out the harbour. Then he will destroy it in front my eyes.'

'An' Flagstead…'

'Don' suspect nothin',' said Baboo. 'He too busy with the arrangements this moment. But all set an' only waitin' for tonight…'

'Is that all?' Crabbe asked.

Baboo was twiddling his fingers over the table, and Crabbe thought he was scared. But he was distracted by his own arrangements for deceiving Thief. He looked at Baboo again, trying to discern whether there was something he had failed to say. Baboo continued to tap his fingers nervously on the table. Crabbe understood this sign. He was trying to choose the right moment to say something important. Crabbe thought he was reluctant to offend and he was not always sure when he was risking his privilege by offering. He watched Crabbe swing his leg over the chair and pace up and down the room. That, too, was a sign that it was time to leave. But Baboo did not stir. Crabbe lingered at the window, certain that there was something Baboo wanted to say.

'What is it?' he asked. 'What else is there?' He turned to face Baboo.

'If it not rude, sir, what that letter 'bout?'

Crabbe walked forward to the table. He tried to look at ease as he watched Baboo waiting for an answer.

'I'll tell you later,' he said. 'Meet me at ten sharp. Corner of Cross Roads and Bel Air.'

'Very good, sir.'

Baboo stood. His eyes avoided Crabbe as he turned to the door.

'Hold it,' Crabbe said suddenly.

'Yes, sir.'

'How many years service you have now?'

'Fifteen.'

'And the Superintendent?'

' 'Bout the same, sir.'

'Thank you,' said Crabbe. 'Ten thirty sharp.'

2

'If only I had that letter in my han',' said Rockey, 'if only I had the chance your privilege give you the mornin' you find it in the house o' the accuse'…'

'You'd do the same,' said Thief, 'if you had my feelin' for Butterfiel' you'd do the same.'

'But your conscience, Thief, your conscience…'

'Your conscience couldn't stop you,' said Thief, 'with any feelin' you'd surrender that evidence too if you see a way to save him.'

'An' hide those who do that crime?'

'Butterfiel' ain't do it, Rockey, I swear Butterfiel' ain't do it.'

'They had no han' in what happen?'

'I'd go to my grave for what I feel,' Thief cried, 'Butterfiel' ain't play no part in that night.'

'Then who it is Baboo tryin' to hide?' Rockey asked. 'Why he demandin' the letter too when he done get his money for what he doin'? Why he make you surrender the evidence, Thief?'

Thief hesitated. He felt his fingers tremble in the grooves which they had made through the sand, and he leaned his head forward, staring idly at the dark movement which they concealed. He wanted to calm Rockey's suspicions and dispel the doubt which these questions had started.

'You know how you feel for me,' he said, 'an' you know that feelin' can match any risk when you see a frien' in need. No question ever enter your head when you see a las' chance to set a frien' free…'

'But who Baboo tryin' to hide?' Rockey insisted.

'I don' know, Rockey, I don' know,' Thief cried, 'but from now to this mornin' is a short time. An' when Baboo claim the letter plus the money too I didn't have no time to argue. For the moment I didn't question myself who murder Shephard, if surrenderin' the letter would help Butterfiel' escape…'

'An' if it was Butterfiel'…?'

'I swear, I swear,' Thief cried, 'it ain't Butterfiel' who do it nor the next one too.'

Rockey raised his head and looked at the half-moon which stared like an eye, solitary and sightless, through the wide, black kingdom of the sky. The corners were wrapped in blood. The sky was a ceiling that sucked up the sea, striding leisurely up the sand. He could not distinguish Thief from the formless space which made a distance between them. But he heard the wind and the occasional shriek of the leaves, and he looked towards the wood that spread with insect noise like some nameless, unfamiliar vegetation which the night had sprung across San Cristobal. The darkness was like a conquest. It made him nervous whenever he thought of the reason for his meeting with Thief at this hour.

' 'Twas a night like now poor Shephard finish,' he said, 'an' not a star to tell what happen, an' the court won't have no accuse' no more.'

'Not if Baboo mean business,' said Thief, 'an' we get them on that ship 'fore sailin' time.'

'An' if Baboo don' come?'

The voice sent a shudder through Thief's body. He jerked his fingers from the grooves of sand, and stared in the direction of Rockey. His doubt was much sharper now.

'They'll bury under San Cristobal,' he said, ' 'cause even if the court don' bring them guilty, the crowd waitin' watch outside will divide their bones. 'Tis why I risk what I risk with Baboo...'

Rockey was silent for a while, considering Thief's fear of the crowd. They had already chosen the accused as their enemy. He remembered the angry gathering in the courtyard, and his suspicions returned, urging him to question again the innocence of the accused. He was loyal to Thief, but this undertaking made him uneasy.

'Who kill Shephard, then?' he asked.

'Not Butterfiel',' Thief answered, 'I swear now an' for ever, nor the other one too. They had nothin' but a good hope for Shephard.'

'An' Baboo believe that too?' Rockey asked.

'Baboo don't have time to believe,' said Thief. 'He jus' arrangin' a work for Flagstead, an' Flagstead won't see Butterfiel' hang whatever it cost.'

'An' Butterfiel' know yet what happenin'?' Rockey asked.

'He'll know when he see Flagstead on the ship,' said Thief. 'He waitin' there.'

Rockey paused, turning questions in his mind, impatient to learn the truth.

'Who else in this business?' he asked.

'Nobody but those I mention,' said Thief. 'Apart from Butterfiel' himself an' his frien'.'

'Baboo say he will bring them here himself?' Rockey asked.

'An' we will row them to the ship,' said Thief, 'where Flagstead waitin'.'

He let Thief finish, but already he had forgotten what he wanted to say. He sat silent, trying to trace the stages of this argument which he waged in silence with himself. He had already chosen his decisions. He knew that he would yield to Thief. And it was too late to withdraw, but he had to appease this gradual conflict that grew like fever in his brain; his loyalty to Thief and his need to avenge Shephard's death. He could not refuse Thief's plea for help; yet he wanted to persuade him against what they were doing. For the time being he gave no thought to the accused. It was Shephard and Thief who persuaded his feeling. He tried to accept Thief's devotion to Butterfield, and gradually the feeling returned, denouncing his role in Thief's undertaking. He saw himself as part of the conspiracy against Shephard. He was helping two men whose innocence he could not accept. Yet this loyalty to Thief kept him wavering, and he noticed how his questions changed as though his passion for justice had deserted him.

'You think you can trust Baboo?' he asked.

'Not me,' said Thief, ''tis Flagstead who payin' him. The money won't let him deceive Flagstead.'

'Money can grow,' said Rockey, 'from one offer to a next.'

'Only the law would compete in this,' said Thief, 'an' the law don' pass money in these matters.'

'Baboo deceivin' the very law he serve?' Rockey asked.

'I tell you before an' again I tell you,' said Thief, 'a man like Baboo don' believe in nothin'.'

'But why he force you to surrender the letter?'

'Perhaps he know who murder Shephard,' Thief said.

'An' he want to hide him?'

'I don' know,' said Thief, 'a man like Baboo don' let you make no kind o' prediction. 'Tis hard to tell with people who don' believe in nothin', God, frien's or the devil himself.'

They were silenced by the sudden alarm of the ship. It had lost its shape in the night, but a few lights made a loop above the sea flashing signals across the harbour. The waves came wild up the shore, and the men could hear the hiss of the spray suddenly caught and carried with the sweep of the wind. There was nothing to recognise but the signal of the lights showing the ship, but Rockey was beginning to anticipate his way through the darkness that covered the sea and swept his boat out of sight. He held his waist, slackening the rope which joined him to the boat some yards away. Thief sat beside him making holes in the sand.

'In all the nights my eye close on,' said Rockey, 'none match like now an' when Shephard leave this life, the night I find him full with water.'

'Midnight near,' said Thief.

He was trying to avoid any mention of Shephard until Bill and Mark were safe on the ship. He knew Rockey was not convinced that he should help in their escape. He had come to please Thief who had begged him to take them to the ship in his small boat.

'Thirty-seven years I work this sea,' said Rockey, 'an' I see many a man finish with the sharks, but I never help no shark to his own harbour, not me.'

'The man we help ain't no shark,' said Thief, 'nor the other one too.'

'Who lead Shephard to the Point?' Rockey asked. 'He didn't come all by himself.'

'They only follow to save him from his ravin' that night,' said Thief.

Rockey remained quiet considering the suggestion that Shephard was mad. He did not want to argue with Thief, but he was curious to know how he had come by this information. The two men had already disappeared the night he had found Shephard's body on the beach, and suddenly he remembered the feel of the dying hand in his, and Shephard's voice like a noise under water. Perhaps, Shephard was trying to say what had happened. It was he who had announced San Cristobal's dark day. Now Thief was trying to contradict his feeling by starting a rumour that the men were innocent.

'W'at dead an' gone I done with,' said Rockey, 'an' Shephard for all his place in fame can't come 'twixt me an' tomorrow. I go back to my business with the sea where I belong. I never witness the action exact that stop his tongue an' turn his hearin' cold, but I report w'at my feelings order the night my foot collide with his. That is that, an' I finish with that. But 'tis those two you propose for safety who make the dead walk back. An' I ask you before an' again I ask you Thief, w'at business bring them here that night.'

Thief was slow to answer. He turned to look at Rockey, but they were only shapes in the night.

'I want you to weight my words,' said Thief, 'an' balance my feelin' right. I believe w'at Butterfiel' tell how they come to watch poor Shephard pray. He choose the time himself to talk with God 'bout San Cristobal, an' so Butterfiel' say it happen. He enter the boat, an' then a bullet take them by surprise.'

''Tis mad you sayin' Shephard was?' Rockey asked.

'His mind hold a demon,' said Thief, 'an' a right ambition turn his senses wrong. I watch him travel to power, an' you too see him collect every heart San Cristobal own, an' he gallop the way the hurricanes move, but something split him down the middle in two, an' one half never make a new meetin' with the next. He divide like a river runnin' for different direction. An' his mind wasn't just right or wrong complete, but all two both as the moment strike. An' 'twas a special moment strike the night before San Cristobal declare him Lord o' the day. You hold my word, Rockey, that Shephard won't happen again, but San Cristobal goin' grow from his grave as it rise from the water that wet his breathin'.'

'You softenin' me to make a risk for Butterfiel',' said Rockey.

'Maybe so,' said Thief.

The sea made a choking noise up the sand, and Rockey made to turn, but Thief's words had started a strange emotion which he struggled to contain. He wiped his hand across his mouth and felt a gradual moisture soften his eyes. He turned to see Thief, but the darkness was uniform, and this sudden silence seemed to spread like the night. Something held him like a claw round his throat while it avoided contact with his skin. He worked his tongue against the roof of his mouth, and pumped a frugal spurt of saliva through his teeth.

'Thief!'

'Yes, Rockey.'

'What it is bind you to this man, Butterfiel'?'

'If you can tell me what bind you to the sea,' said Thief, 'then maybe I fin' a way to say.'

'The sea is my life,' said Rockey. 'It show me my weakness an' my power too. But this Butterfiel' is only a man you hardly know.'

' 'Tis more than the man himself that hol' me in reverence,' said Thief. ' 'Tis the way, Rockey, 'tis the way he take me in his house an' his trust was something bigger than the man himself, like the truth which always seem more powerful than the tongue that tell it.'

'An' you never take?'

'Never,' said Thief, 'till that time with the wallet.'

'You never take from his house?'

'Never, never, never,' said Thief. 'But if I see him safe on that ship this night, I wonder how I will manage with the change he help me make.'

Rockey turned to face Thief, and his hand moved blindly over the sand to touch Thief's. For a moment he had forgotten Butterfield and their arrangements to bring about his escape. He thought only of Thief and his unlucky career, and he started to wonder about their future.

'Tomorrow ain't got no name but the name you make,' he said. 'An' if you want to keep your change, you can make a new name.'

Thief felt Rockey's hand brush against his as he stared towards the wood and suddenly he remembered Rockey in the days before Shephard returned. And he tried to recall his own life as he imagined Rockey in his labour at sea.

' 'Tis a strange turn of feelin' that will let me answer to the name of Thief. I carry the name of my callin', like a good man who for some natural reason his neighbours christen him angel. Thief is a thief, an' I oft times puzzle to fin' which come first: Thief or a thief, my name or my callin'.'

'Your hand is unholy,' said Rockey, 'an' how many times I tell you to speak to it. Not once, not twice, not several times, but always. Always and for ever, I tell you, Thief, take that hand, one by one, look it good in all the lines an' the fingers that complete it, and say to it, one after another, "Hand, don't again for the love o' keeping whole, don't reach me forward to my neighbour's goods."'

'My hand will not hear, Rockey. I take it not once, not twice, time over time, I take it, an' I say as you speak a minute ago, "Hand, now, Hand," but the fingers come down in a sad closing, and when I open up again, lo and behold, there's a fearful reckoning to make, something's already inside. 'Tis just so, Rockey, just as I say. Things trespass my hand like those monkeys in the trap.'

'Take a turn at fishing,' said Rockey, 'your callin' would be clear there, and the more the sad reckoning you mention, the richer will be your reward.'

'Fish are alive, Rockey, only dead things search for my palm. Money, food, garments I never gear myself in. For the completing of my point, Rockey, I will confess, never in my history have I taken a live fowl.'

'For no reason I can remember,' said Rockey, 'I feel it in my heart, you are a good man. Many a night, sitting on the water, with my little boat swimming under me, your face come before my face, and I wish you'd just take a turn with the oars, try the temper of the tides for once, feel the nerve of a fish in the challenge and the battle for catchin' an' escapin'. 'Tis a wondrous trade, Thief, and also 'tis a saving grace. Oh, yes, Thief, the sea is a saviour. Many a man who'd be a murdering evil on land is an angel in the ocean. Believe me when I speak, Thief, 'cause my words carry a weight of wisdom in their syllables, and I've been with the sea in many a conflictin' season. I've seen the waves wonder what force it was interfere with them, and I've had the water beg my boat to move, everything was so ordinary with stillness.'

'You speak like a brother, Rockey, an' you make an unnatural water wet my eyes when you advise.'

'Maybe 'tis my pride,' said Rockey, 'but my heart was like miser that morning, with a big, big store of joy and pride when I hear you speak an' say, "He's the only man who know how to make a headway in a turnin' sea." I search the market and the avenue to find you, and it was then I promise you can reckon with Rockey any night of any hour to offer a service, if it be within the possible, and the possible make honest sense.'

'Perhaps I may try one hand with the water,' said Thief.

' 'Tis a thought worth turnin' in your mind,' said Rockey.

'It will take a new lot of learnin',' said Thief, 'and an' old head is unwilling.'

'Every man hide many sources,' said Rockey, 'an' there's no tellin' till the lids be taken off.'

'Where you get your heart, Rockey, 'tis high as any hill with hope. You never say no.'

' 'Tis the habit of the sea,' said Rockey. 'Just keeps roaming an' returnin'. I'll bury this same body in the ocean, Thief, and what I take from the fish, I'll surrender to the fish. Any man who chase fish should fetch his bones to the fish.'

He paused, waiting for Thief to make a promise with the sea, but a torch had flashed a spot on the night, and his hand found Thief's arm as they watched the light ramble up the beach and return to trace a circle round the boat. They knew why they were waiting, but the sudden flash of the torch had forced them into a state of wonder, and they tried to distinguish the wash of the waves up the shore from the gradual crunch of feet making intervals over the sand. The light showed against the boat like a white hole in the night, and they heard the feet coming nearer.

'Here they come,' said Rockey, feeling for the rope round his waist.

'Light the lamp,' said Thief.

Rockey crawled over the line of the rope towards the boat, but the feet had stopped, and he whispered to Thief, 'This wind troublesome.'

'They waitin' my signal,' said Thief. 'Must be Baboo came ahead the car.'

'The wind make no difference w'at happenin'.'

'You light the lamp,' said Thief, following close behind.

They pushed themselves through the sand and watched the light make its nervous shudder against the boat. Rockey climbed into the boat threading his fingers through the bars of wire which enclosed the chimney. The waist of the lamp made a split that let his fingers through, and a flicker of light filled the chimney. Thief had crept up to the side of the boat trying to show himself under the eye of the torch; but the spot of light had retreated, making somersaults over the sand. Then it relaxed in one place, and quickly disappeared.

'Only the light can see,' said Rockey.

'Hois' your lamp,' said Thief.

He sat up letting his back lean against the boat. The torch went on again, and the sound of the feet returned. Rockey tied the lamp to the bow and slipped his feet out of the rope. They watched the light of the torch fumble towards them like a crab.

'It makes you nervous not seeing what you know comin',' said Rockey.

'They nervous too,' said Thief, 'not seein' what they know wait.'

'Yet my nerves never talk when I fish,' said Rockey, 'no matter what sea it is surround me there.'

'We could scare hell out o' them if we just disappear,' said Thief.

'I just want to dump them safe an' finish,' said Rockey.

'Me too,' said Thief, 'everything ready.'

They stood on either side of the boat slipping the oars through the hollow fists of iron which held them. The light showed their hands against the blue-black floor with its surface of pitch rough with sand. The light was a frozen white shadow wrestling with the wind, and the lamp rattled like rats' noise. The howl of the wind grew loud and the boat leaned suddenly as the sand loosened and slipped away with the sea.

'We near enough to slide her in easy,' said Rockey.

'This wind goin' play hell with the light,' said Thief.

'The lamp familiar with this weather,' said Rockey. 'She will shake till the wick turn blue for goin' out, but the flame always fight back.'

'Yet I goin' keep watch for any rocks,' said Thief.

'Not here,' said Rockey, 'you have no hindrance like rocks risin' here. From now to where the ship sit still is plain sailin'.'

'If you say so,' said Thief.

' 'Tis so,' Rockey replied.

They were ready. Rockey made another lap with the rope round the lamp, and Thief stepped aside to follow the light of the torch crawling slowly towards them. The light dipped and fell like a large insect tossed dead on the sand, then rose again level with his eyes. He blocked his eyes and made an angry signal with his hand. The light returned to the sand travelling cautiously towards the boat, and the spot leapt from the sand and covered Rockey's chin with a sparkling white flame. Then the torch went out, and the night seemed to swell round the lamp stammering its solitude over the bow now turned towards the sea. Thief returned to the boat and stood beside Rockey.

'I would creep an' crawl like you say for life,' said Rockey. ' 'Cause if they guilty, they goin' carry their own trap 'cross the sea.'

'Don't make the night more difficult for them,' said Thief.

'Not me,' said Rockey. ' 'Tis them who make their own night-time. But before they put a footprint in my boat, I goin' remind their memory that in every man conscience work like a clock that won't ever stop tickin' till time himself drop dead.'

The torch went on again, and the light rambled over Thief's body, and rested finally on his lame hand. He glanced towards the sand and his eyes caught the circle of light which showed, like an accusation, the three stumps of black knuckle between the two fingers on his hand. His anger gave way to a feeling of humiliation, and he turned to Rockey, but words had suddenly deserted them. The torch had traced its orbit back to the trees, and they looked at each other with an expression of stupefaction and defeat. It seemed that this corner of the night had collapsed to make way for an incredible break of day. The night cracked like a wall and made way for the torrent of light which leapt from the edge of the wood to show their faces. They looked at each other and then at Crabbe who stood before them making signals with the torch. Behind him the light was advancing across the sand and the trees slipped out of light into the ordinary stillness of the wood. Crabbe put out his hand, and the light was steady again, spreading like a fan across the sea.

Thief felt his feet wobble forward as though he had not yet

recovered from the shock of the light, but he noticed Crabbe's hand waving him back to the boat, and he stopped, feeling blindly about him for Rockey. His hand fell down his side as though his muscles had turned to wool, and he felt his tongue locked in a muteness which shook his spine and turned a terror through the silence which raged in his head. Rockey helped him back to the boat. He sat at the edge, trying to steady his hands on his knees. And then the ship's siren alerted them. Crabbe looked at his watch and Thief seemed to find his strength.

He heard the sea gallop up the shore and he thought of escape, but Crabbe stood before him, and the light which pressed against his eyes reminded him that the law was present. He recognised the light which had discovered them, and he knew that behind it there were men armed with weapons and instructions for his capture. And he thought of Rockey who sat like a stone beside him. He could not find the effort to ask his pardon. His mouth was slack, a wet hole which let the light through to the black silence which smouldered in his guts. Crabbe was armed. He knew that. He could not attack him, and they could not hide like those pebbles which were receding with the tide in a wild dispersal under the water. The ship's horn raised another alarm, and he saw Crabbe come closer. The light stayed still, worked by hands which were waiting to seize him. Crabbe crept leisurely towards them, and Rockey held his head down as though he wanted to make his grave in the sand.

'We haven't much time,' said Crabbe, 'so you have got to be quick.'

His voice was strangely calm, and the words seemed to hurry through the air, brief stabs of noise which travelled without echo. He waited as though he wanted to help them prepare themselves for an answer, but Rockey remained distracted, thinking that his presence at this hour was an act of folly to which he had surrendered himself. The sea came between Crabbe's voice and his hearing. He was finished with the whole affair, and he wanted to leave or be taken. It did not matter.

Crabbe moved sideways towards a tree which rose behind him, a solitary partition against the light. He thought of the letter as he watched Thief, and prepared himself for the exchange which would persuade Thief to surrender it. He had to persuade Thief without making a direct request, and he could not risk a refusal. But he noticed that the men were afraid. They did not anticipate his arrival, and they could not have guessed how much he knew. But time was running out. He had to be swift and unhurried. He needed all his powers of deception to put them at ease. His manner was cautious, almost protective, and his voice was calm.

'The facts are simple,' said Crabbe, 'and you know them. You are here to help in the escape of two men on trial for murder. The men have already escaped custody. They are on their way here. You are to take them to the S.S.... where a friend is waiting, and this ship sails within an hour.'

Crabbe paused and jerked the torch towards Thief.

'You agree this is true?'

Thief hesitated. He was wondering why Crabbe had not ordered their arrest at once, and it seemed that this delay had helped to restore his confidence. He wanted to ask Rockey's advice, but they were no longer free to share any secrets. Crabbe was becoming impatient.

'Is this true?' he repeated.

'W'at it is you waitin' for?' said Thief. ''Tis no question you makin', but facts, as you say, which bring me here.'

'Is this true?' Crabbe asked again. 'Yes or no.'

'I ready to walk wherever you take me,' said Thief, 'an' 'tis a strange thing you askin' me to take sides with the truth since you know me by name. I don't have no traffic with truth.'

He had given up all hope of saving the men and he told himself that Crabbe was lying about their escape from prison. Having heard of the plans to help the men, it was obvious that Crabbe would have made sure that they were heavily guarded. But it was part of his job to play this kind of deceit, and Thief was not going to let himself be fooled in this way. He had already been betrayed, and that was enough.

'You know what this could mean for both of you,' Crabbe said, and it seemed that he had already decided their fate.

Rockey shuddered, and Thief noticed the sudden shudder of Rockey's hand in the light. Crabbe had become patient. His brief silence was like a preparation for something they could not guess. Thief suddenly remembered what had happened to Crabbe's son, and as though his feelings were open to any assault, he thought of Rockey, and felt a sudden thrust of guilt. Alone, he might have found the strength to defy Crabbe. He could take some comfort in this final act of defiance. But Rockey's innocence had put him completely at Crabbe's mercy.

'The men will arrive any minute,' said Crabbe, 'and you two might have to prove that you didn't help in Shephard's murder.'

Rockey found himself standing. His hands rambled up and down as though they tried to trace the feeling which had lifted him from the boat. His body moved; but it was no longer his, just a weight, foreign and irrelevant, like the charge which Crabbe had hinted, clinging to him. His hands continued to grope across his stomach. His mouth twitched and his ears seemed to swell with a noise which had paralysed his hearing.

'And what is interesting,' Crabbe continued, 'is the fact the two men swear they are innocent. Nothing can make them confess they murdered Shephard, yet they can't say what happened.'

He watched Rockey as he swung the torch round his finger. Then it stopped and struck out like a finger at Rockey.

'And you were the last man to see Shephard alive,' Crabbe said. He had raised his voice to a shout. He watched Rockey sink slowly back to the boat. Thief tried to take his hand, but he had lost his nerve. Their silence was like defeat.

Thief was beginning to believe Crabbe's story. It would not be long before Mark and Bill arrived, and he wished they would not. Could the Law really stretch the charge of murder to include himself and Rockey? He was not familiar with the details of the law, but he knew that when Crabbe spoke there would probably be no limit to what could happen in the name of the Law. Baboo had tried and failed, but for the moment he was not concerned with the fate of Baboo. He had to find a way of saving Rockey. He looked over his shoulder and noticed how the light fell like a swollen arm over the water. He heard the pebbles again racing idly down the slope of the sand, and remembered Rockey saying that tomorrow he would return to the sea where he belonged. He could feel his lips move in a feeble mutter, but the words made no sound although the question had already taken shape. 'Should he make a false confession in order to save Rockey?'

'Have you made up your mind?' Crabbe asked.

Thief seemed to shake in his seat on the boat. It was as though he had heard Crabbe's voice for the first time forcing him to make the confession which was taking shape in his mind. He made to speak, but Crabbe did not notice. He was losing patience.

'Are the facts true or not?' Crabbe asked. His voice was angry, almost violent as he waved the torch at Thief.

Thief turned to talk with Rockey, but Crabbe interrupted.

'I will tell you what happened today,' Crabbe said. He had become quiet again, talking slowly as though he wanted to help Thief's memory. He was going to give him the details of what he knew. His change of manner was unbelievable. His calm was like the light which they could not have anticipated. It seemed that patience was a gift which he could summon at will. Thief and Rockey were giving him their full attention. And Thief hoped there might be a flaw which would help him to reply on Rockey's behalf. He turned his fingers round the oar which rubbed against his back.

'When the court adjourned you saw Baboo,' Crabbe said, 'and he told you that everything was arranged with the ship. Everything depended on your getting the fisherman to help with his boat, because this was the safest way to leave.'

Crabbe paused now and again, as though each interval was a chance for Thief to contradict what he had heard. But Thief did not stir. He was beginning to think of Baboo.

'You asked Baboo why he was doing this,' Crabbe continued, 'and he showed you a certain sum of money which was his reward. You had already spoken to the person who was paying, but to Baboo's surprise you didn't want your share because you were only interested in seeing Butterfield and his friend free. Is that right?'

Thief did not answer. He thought only of Baboo.

'Baboo told you that he was not on duty tonight which made it easier,' Crabbe continued. He was swinging the torch rapidly round his hand, jerking it towards Thief whenever he paused. 'It was easy because Baboo knew how to get duplicate keys to the cells, and he would not be responsible for what had happened. You didn't know if it would work, but you said you would see to it that the boat was ready at midnight. Is that so?'

Crabbe did not seem to care whether Thief answered. He knew what he was saying was true, and Thief felt that he was taking some pleasure in proving his knowledge. Now he understood why Crabbe was in no hurry to have them arrested. He was waiting for the men to arrive, but it was an unusual risk of double-crossing which Baboo had achieved. He had earned Flagstead's money by arranging for Butterfield's escape, but he had also arranged for them to be caught after he had fulfilled his obligations to Flagstead. Both jobs were complete. Rockey turned his head away, and his eyes fell on the small lamp which showed a tottering blue flame through the crushing white limb of light that plunged beyond the bow into the sea. He turned his head into the light again and looked at Crabbe. He felt his boat like a gift under his hands, and he tried the strength of his feet, arching his toes in and out of the sand. He could see Crabbe staring at them, and he wondered for a moment whether he was really telling the truth. Thief had not told him all the details, and he could not ask Thief at this moment to confirm what he had heard. Yet it was not likely that Crabbe would have risked faking such evidence. Thief knew what Baboo had told him after the trial, and now it was clear from his silence that he had no way of contradicting Crabbe. Rockey had resigned himself to the future which Crabbe was making for him, but he would find a way to survive it. He would find words for his innocence, and neither Crabbe nor the law could come between him and the heart of San Cristobal. He was beginning to feel his certainty again, and he watched Crabbe with a suggestion of contempt. He wished he understood what was really happening between Crabbe and Baboo? Was Crabbe lying about the men's escape? Or was this Baboo's way of earning promotion? He turned to Thief and then he looked up at Crabbe as though he could no longer control this sudden violence of feeling.

'How many murderers it will make includin' the man waitin' on the ship?' he asked.

Crabbe felt the change of voice, and he decided not to answer. But Rockey had become indifferent to his immediate fate. Like

Crabbe, he was not interested in answers. He asked questions as a way of talking.

'An' who Baboo r'ally workin' for?' he asked. 'You, me, or the next man?'

'Baboo works for the law,' Crabbe said crossly.

'Meanin' who?' Rockey put in quickly.

'Meaning the law,' said Crabbe.

'Which law?'

'You will soon see,' said Crabbe, and his voice trailed to a whisper.

They could feel his refusal to engage in argument, and Rockey relaxed into his original silence. He was no longer afraid of Crabbe but he was mumbling curses against himself for following Thief into this trap which Baboo had prepared for them. Thief thought only of Baboo and wished that the men would not arrive. If the men were caught before they reached Paradise Point, there might be a chance to spare Rockey the fate which Crabbe had threatened them with. He would deny the conversation between himself and Baboo. But he would deal with Baboo afterwards. His career was going to end in crime. Baboo would never survive the promises which Crabbe must have made.

He saw Crabbe glance at his watch before knocking the torch against his side. Then he glanced over his shoulder towards the wood, and Thief wondered whether Crabbe too was anxious that the men might not arrive. He wanted to say something but Crabbe seemed distracted. The men would arrive any moment. Crabbe considered the decisions he would make. He wanted to force a confession from Thief before it was too late, and he could not allow them to suspect his reason for trying to implicate them in the murder.

They were conscious of the silence which separated them at this moment. Rockey scraped his hands down the side of the boat cursing his error, while Thief encouraged his wish that the men would not arrive. And Crabbe thought of some way to make Thief yield to his request.

He had not told Baboo why he had really undertaken to let the men escape, and he wondered how he could safely avoid a scandal if his plan had failed. But he thought he understood the temperament of men like Baboo and those who worked the light which charged from the wood across his face to a splintered white edge over the sea. His secret was a burden which reminded him of his role in San Cristobal. And suddenly he tried to rebuke himself for thinking things might not have happened as he had ordered them. Yet it seemed that the men might be late. Perhaps Baboo had made a mess of his instructions. It was not unlikely that Baboo could make a mistake in these circumstances. He was efficient and ambitious to please, but he had very little tact, like most people who had worked always under someone else's orders. But he recalled there was no detail which Baboo could not have followed without arousing suspicion. The men did not know how their escape was being conducted, but it would not have been difficult for them to accept Baboo's word. He was going to use Flagstead's car which Butterfield would recognise. He would take them from the cells at midnight, and they would leave with Baboo, each in the uniform of a prison warder, through the private gate which was used by the senior staff.

The police whom he had chosen for the occasion were to dim the light when they heard the car approach, but they were not to interrupt while Baboo led the men to where the boat was waiting. Then he would make his final decision. But now it was important to make Thief talk.

The light softened, and Thief looked up rubbing his hands into his eyes. Crabbe tightened his hands round the torch. The light was playing tricks with Thief's eyes. He turned to talk with Rockey, but the light suddenly dimmed to a faint white wobble through the night, and they were alert. A car was moving cautiously towards the light, but the wind had taken every other sound away. Rockey became restless. He moved nearer to Thief, and they stared ahead, in silence, waiting for something to happen. Suddenly the light broke, and night swept across their view, cooling their eyes. They could feel the gradual return of the light as the car nosed in slowly into the night. Thief shook his head, and crossed his hands over his face. Crabbe relaxed his grip on the torch, and tried to compose himself. It was his last chance to make Thief talk. He wanted to make him yield before the men reached the boat. He shifted his weight and struck the torch out at Thief.

'They are here,' he said. His voice was grave, and suddenly charged with intent. 'And only one thing can save you now.'

Rockey glanced at Thief. He expected him to speak. Thief stood, trying to think how he might protect Rockey from the charge which Crabbe would bring against them. He saw the torch like a black bone in the light and he looked at Crabbe.

'What evil make you do them that?' he said. 'No plea can make them look innocent when you take them back.'

'Think of yourself,' said Crabbe. 'You'll be going with them unless you tell the truth.'

'What lie you forcin' me to tell?'

'It's no lie that you stole a wallet, which is now in your possession…'

Thief made to speak and suddenly stopped himself. For a moment he was at a loss to understand what Crabbe was getting at. This was a fresh charge which had nothing to do with Shephard's murder and the escape of the two men. But it was true. He was trying to choose his answer, but Crabbe had become almost frantic.

'Where is the wallet?' Crabbe asked.

Thief felt his hands tighten round the oars. He could not guess Crabbe's intentions, and he did not want to make any confession which would leave them without defence against the charges Crabbe might make. Crabbe straightened himself, letting the torch fall abruptly against his leg.

'It's the only chance you've got to save yourself or your friend here,' said Crabbe. His manner was decisive.

'What is it you want?' Thief asked.

'If you can produce the wallet as it was when you stole it,' said Crabbe, 'you and your friend are free to go.'

For a moment Thief could not decide what he should say. He thought only of his duty to Rockey. He had to save Rockey, but he could not trust Crabbe's offer of freedom. Did Crabbe really believe that he had the wallet with the letter? It was the signal for him to do something that would save Rockey. But he had to delay his action. If he had the letter, he would have given it to Crabbe without any argument, but now he was unsure what he should do. Should he pretend that he had the letter? Or should he tell Crabbe that he was lying? He could not be caught guessing if this was his last chance to save Rockey. He steadied himself and tried to test Crabbe with his show of agreement. Rockey was waiting.

'Let my friend here go first,' he said.

Crabbe glanced over his shoulder in the direction where the car had stopped. He was going to agree to the bargain which Thief had offered, but Rockey interrupted.

'It make no difference,' he said, 'I goin' stay till this whole business finish.'

'Don't make things hard for me,' said Thief. 'You go.'

He was encouraging Rockey to raise himself from the boat, but they were distracted by the sound of feet coming across the sand. The men were approaching, and Crabbe waited anxiously for Thief to continue. He could not press Thief to answer while the men were present, and time was against him. But everyone's future depended on the answer which Thief would give. The men might escape, or Thief and Rockey could be convicted on a false suspicion; but his loyalty was exclusively a matter of his own safety and his authority. His future depended on the answer which Thief would give. He heard the men shuffle through the sand, and suddenly the sound was devoured by the tedious noise of the wind finishing through the trees. But they were near, and his anxiety was like a spasm which seared his throat.

'What about the wallet?'

Thief was silent. He watched Crabbe retreat behind the tree until his body became a shape at the edge of the night. He wanted to warn the men that they had been deceived, but it was useless. No one could escape. The night was only a temptation, and the sea could only show the way.

'Everything too far gone,' said Rockey, 'here or a next time they got to walk to the gallows.'

'What you goin' do?' Thief asked.

'Surrender till tomorrow,' said Rockey, 'tomorrow is all we got.'

'The law won't listen,' said Thief. 'Will be like the past that put that wallet in the way.'

'I will make San Cristobal hear,' said Rockey, 'innocent is innocent.'

'An' if Butterfield innocent too,' said Thief, 'what difference it make?'

'How my action innocent I know,' said Rockey, 'like I know my face.'

'But it ain't matter what you know,' said Thief, ''tis what the next man don't see.'

'I can talk,' said Rockey, 'innocence can talk.'

'It ain't got no language,' said Thief, 'unless the next man lend you his belief.'

The voices flickered to a whisper and died. The men entered the light stepping nervously towards the boat. Thief held his head down, but Bill had felt already that this enterprise was a failure. He was a prisoner under orders, waiting to return to the judgement which this journey had finally decided. He was beyond sympathy, but he felt a growing need for vengeance. Who had betrayed whom? He could not tell, but he wanted to justify his death which he felt was near. Thief watched him stalk towards the boat like an animal made desperate by its defeat.

'Where is Baboo?' Bill asked.

'Baboo!' Thief's voice was no more than a noise describing his surprise.

'Where is he?' Bill asked, as though he suspected Thief.

Bill suddenly stopped and turned, as though he heard the night itself accuse him, and he saw his own anxiety and surprise confront him. Crabbe stood before them, imprisoned in the wide bar of light which showed his misgiving. The torch trembled like a hand.

'Who brought you here?' he demanded, trying to support his authority.

Bill seemed to forget the details of his journey from the prison. Crabbe's presence was a shock which quickened his awareness of this sordid drama on the beach. Now he understood the light which had waited to receive them. He turned to Mark who was staring in the direction of the car where Baboo had given them their last instructions for getting to the ship. He had gone ahead to make sure that Thief and Rockey were there. They were to follow the light which would show them where he was waiting with Thief and the fisherman. Bill stared across the sea and then towards the wood, but he could not speak. He saw Crabbe moving slowly towards them, and he understood Baboo's absence.

'Who brought you?' Crabbe asked again, fidgeting with one hand in his pocket.

Bill could not answer. He turned to Mark for support. Mark remained silent. Crabbe seemed to regain his control. He walked towards them, knocking the torch against his knee. It was the moment to assert his authority or capitulate. The law was in danger of defeat. They could feel Crabbe's uncertainty. But he continued in his role as though nothing had really happened. He was pretending to trick them with his ignorance. Baboo's absence was his secret which he would use against them.

'Let's go,' he said, jerking the torch towards the wood.

Bill hesitated. Thief took a step forward, then turned waiting for Rockey to join him.

'What 'bout my boat?' Rockey asked.

'Put out the lamp,' said Thief.

'Let's go,' said Crabbe, and he struck the torch out again.

The sea followed them up the sand swinging its noise through the wind and the night that travelled everywhere around them. The sand slipped behind them in a line of empty cradles which had received their feet. And the wind whipped the trees into a fury of leaves and branches that snapped and fell through the dark disorder of the wood. When the wind paused, the trees made an interval of silence that trespassed briefly over the night, and fear possessed them like the light that led them blindly to their future. Mark and Bill knew what form it would take. It was only an interval between this moment and their final disappearance. Certainty had dulled their feelings and put their waiting beyond suspense. But Rockey trusted to his innocence, while Thief argued with himself about the charge which Crabbe might make. Would it be theft or murder? He would not know until Crabbe had given his instructions. But his future was not certain as it was for the men who had escaped from prison; nor was it wholly lost. He could wait.

Crabbe had been denied any similar expectation. The future

393

was neither part of his certainty nor his suspense. It did not exist. He was isolated by his own knowledge of what he had planned, and until Baboo appeared, it would be impossible to predict what would happen. But the men had arrived, and he had to know who had arranged their escape. Was it one of the warders whose assistance might have been necessary at the last moment? It was possible that Baboo could not manage on his own, but it was not clear why he had not arrived with the men. He saw the scandal which would develop if Baboo had been careless in his choice. He had to be sure about this before he decided anything.

The light suddenly dimmed, and Crabbe stopped. The others continued up the sand as though nothing had changed. But Crabbe felt a shudder ripple through his body, and he hurried up the sand, narrowing the distance which the men had made. Then he paused, and cupped his ear against his hand, as though his hearing had deceived him. The car was moving further along the road away from the light.

'Stop it,' he shouted at the men behind the light.

The others waited while Crabbe dashed from behind signalling the torch towards the wood. But no one seemed to move. The light softened, and Crabbe stood, staring helplessly towards the wood as the car increased its noise in the distance. He wheeled round as though he would smash the torch against Bill's face.

'Who drove you here?' he shouted.

They were shocked by this sudden show of violence, but Bill seemed suddenly indifferent to Crabbe's orders. What did it matter now whether Crabbe knew who had brought them? Bill did not answer, and Crabbe turned to face the light which was yielding gradually to the night.

'What the hell you think you're doing?' he shouted.

But as quickly he turned again and assaulted the air with the torch.

'Who drove you here?' he asked.

There was a pause, then a voice spoke from behind the light. 'The law.'

Crabbe stared at Bill, as though he could not locate the origin of the voice. Then he steered his body round towards the light, and his hand crawled towards his head like an animal's paw.

It seemed that his memory had deserted him. The world collapsed before his eyes, an abandoned ruin, black as the wood that hovered over the light. The policemen had disappeared, surrendering their position to the men who waited on either side of the metal tripod which supported the bulbs. Crabbe's eyes burnt dry, and he felt his skull like a roof of splinters dissolving round his body. His future was beginning to take shape from the silent ruin of his work. The policemen had gone; his power had disappeared like a crutch refusing service to some helpless cripple.

He could not see the man who lay on his stomach directly behind the tripod, but he saw Singh, standing erect, his chin thrust forward and his hands clasping the gun across his chest. Lee squatted on the other side tapping a revolver against his wrist. It was like a miniature spectacle of the mob eager to avenge the death of Shephard. He was armed, but he could not try to defend himself. He would have to shoot both Lee and Singh, but this would have left him defenceless against the evidence of the others who were waiting to see what would happen. He would have to shoot the whole lot. It was impossible. His hand struggled over the rim of his pocket and fell, empty, down his side. Singh was coming towards him. The others watched, silent, alarmed.

'Not a year nor a day,' said Singh, 'but a lifetime I been waiting for a moment like now.'

'What have you done with my men?' Crabbe asked.

'To the end,' said Singh, 'to the very end you will behave like a ruler.'

'I ask you what happened to my men?' Crabbe repeated.

'And after you see clear as day you have nothing to rule you will be the same,' Singh said, ignoring Crabbe's show of courage. 'Like the leopard changing his spots. Knowing your life as one thing you cannot feel it different, no matter what change.'

Singh paused, considering Crabbe's face in the light. The temples were like burnt rubber and the eyes worked like black marbles spinning out of their sockets.

'How I feel,' said Singh, 'how I feel you will never know. Never. 'Tis the first time I ever look you clean and straight in the eye.'

Crabbe shifted his glance towards Lee. Thief moved closer to

Rockey. Mark held his head down avoiding the light in his eyes. Singh smoothed his jacket and slipped one hand into his pocket.

'You say two men disappear,' said Singh.

'I arrived here with two policemen who had certain instructions,' said Crabbe.

Singh hesitated. He glanced behind him at the tripod, then turned to Crabbe.

'Can you ever believe you never saw the two men?' Singh asked.

'I am not mad,' said Crabbe.

'No, you are not mad,' Singh said, 'but you have to believe you never saw them.'

'Where are they?' Crabbe's voice had become more confident.

'Don't worry,' said Singh, 'you won't want to see them again, so you must believe you never see them tonight or any time after.'

Singh came closer, burying his hand deeper in his pocket. He was within an arm's reach of Crabbe, and the men thought he was going to strike. Crabbe held his ground, and they stared at each other.

'From tomorrow,' said Singh, 'I must believe that I never ever see you here in San Cristobal or anywhere else. From tomorrow I learn to believe that. The two men will believe that too, and when the next tomorrow come, nobody will have to believe. It will be true like the first alphabet lesson. There was never no Crabbe in San Cristobal.'

He paused and the men watched him lift his hand from his pocket. His voice had changed its tone of casual recollection. It was decisive and grim, suddenly equipped with the terror which made every suggestion an order. It made argument impossible. It was the kind of voice which Crabbe might have used on many occasions, but never with the same passion and intent.

'What are you going to do?' Crabbe asked. He suspected violence, and his words were barely audible.

'Not me,' said Singh, 'it is you to decide.'

'I am going,' said Crabbe. 'I will leave this matter until tomorrow.'

'Tomorrow is mine,' said Singh. 'Tonight you will talk.'

The voice had worked its terror. Crabbe had suddenly become

defensive, almost apologetic in his attempt to explain his presence on the beach.

'You know why I came here,' he said, pointing at Mark and Bill.

'To escape a charge of murder,' said Singh.

'Murder…'

'Yes, murder,' Singh repeated. 'These two only witness what you had to mind. They never join you to plan that murder, and I know now for a certainty that one o' them warn Shephard 'bout that night. They only witness what you had in mind.'

Thief felt for Rockey's hand as though he had heard the case concluded in favour of the accused. The trial was over, or at any rate it was Crabbe who was now on trial. He glanced at Bill and Mark, trying to communicate his relief, and then he heard Singh's voice resume its charge against Crabbe.

'You know the evidence,' said Singh, 'but you don't know the result. I decide the result, and it is you to decide your future.'

He whipped his hands in his pocket, letting his fingers ramble for a while under the leather bands which held some papers. Gradually his hand emerged, and he kept his glance on Crabbe. Thief and Rockey seemed to move closer, trying to see the package in his hand. Crabbe averted his glance, staring aimlessly at the arch which his boot had made in the sand. Singh held his hand out, and Thief made a grunt of surprise and pleasure.

'There you see,' said Singh, throwing the black leather wallet on the sand.

Crabbe did not move. He felt an urge to stoop and reclaim the wallet, but his hand was reluctant. It was no longer a part of his action, and the wallet lay on the sand, at once a stranger and familiar like the night, telling his motives. He was alone, without secrets, dispossessed. Each had seen it at some time, and they knew in different ways what it signified.

Singh picked it up and held it out for the men like some article which is passed around in a court for the witness to examine. He had set the scene for another enquiry. The Court which was considering the circumstances of Shephard's death had adjourned, but the trial was still going on. Singh was both advocate and judge.

He would argue their case and decide their fate also. He held the wallet before Crabbe, inviting him to speak.

'This was your possession,' he said.

'I had nothing to do with the man's death,' said Crabbe. His voice was low, as though he spoke without any interest in what he was saying.

' 'Tis always so,' said Singh, 'the guilty never present when such a murder happen.'

Crabbe did not reply. It seemed useless to tell Singh that he had played no part in Shephard's death. He was exhausted by the light and the tension he felt ever since Singh appeared. He wanted to be alone.

'You say to yourself San Cristobal would be better without Shephard,' Singh said. 'Shephard was bad for what you know is good.'

Crabbe did not answer. He was tired to the point of collapse. But he thought that he was doing a job. He did not care about Shephard or Singh or anyone else. He had a job to do and he wanted certain results. That was all. The power he represented had been betrayed, but his action was neither right nor wrong. It was expedient. That was all; and he had failed. He looked towards the light where Lee squatted, and wondered what Singh intended. He would have liked this failure to be seen as something personal. It had nothing to do with anyone else. The plan to murder Shephard was an error which he had started without anyone's knowledge or consent. He wanted to be judged without any reference to those who ruled San Cristobal. His purpose was a deviation from all that was really intended for those who had followed Shephard. But he had lost the will to argue. He felt his silence surround him like an enemy proving their suspicions and his guilt.

'They will go on the ship,' said Singh, thrusting the wallet above his head towards the sky. 'You will stay with me. To the end.'

Crabbe started. He swung his head towards Singh and he could feel the sweat make drops falling from his chin on to his neck. The shock had crushed his effort to speak, and Singh watched his lips labouring feebly to make a way for words.

The ship was making another alarm. Singh beckoned Lee who came forward with the gun pointed level at Crabbe's stomach. Singh put the wallet in his pocket and edged sideways towards Mark and Bill. They watched, speechless and alarmed as Lee sidled past Crabbe, tightening the grip on the gun. Crabbe stiffened. Lee had him covered with the gun while Singh moved nearer towards Thief and Rockey. His movements were swift and precise. It seemed that he was in a hurry to be through with these preliminaries of investigation. He wanted to be alone with Crabbe. The men waited anxiously to hear him speak. He signalled Bill to come forward, then struck his hand in the direction of Rockey. He was asking them to close in as though he wanted to share a confidence. But his manner was uncompromising. The scene was set for orders. He stared at Bill as he spoke.

'I know now for a certainty,' he said, 'that you once warn Shephard 'bout that night. An' that you would warn him and want to murder him too, I do not believe. And there is no way now to clear this matter up. The crowd will crucify you. Innocent or guilty, you would finish like a dog in San Cristobal. But your warning to Shephard, it is for that you can go. No kindness on my part save you now, only the warning you once make to save Shephard.'

He paused and looked towards Thief and the fisherman.

'The two will go as arrange before,' he said. 'Was someone within the law who murder Shephard. But you will leave.'

There was no argument. Thief turned and sauntered towards Rockey. The light brightened, and they saw the lamp show a burning blue circle above the boat. They were beginning again on the same adventure. The sea was swimming leisurely up the sand, and the ship waited. Nothing had changed. They were still part of a conspiracy which they could not understand. Crabbe had given orders, now it was Singh's turn to make them obey. And they followed their safety, defenceless.

'I go too,' said Lee, tracing a line down Crabbe's back with the gun. He spoke quietly, and the voice was gentle and sure. He had spoken without any show of feeling. He had not yet learnt to regret, and he was not capable of the turbulent delight which Singh seemed to feel when he gave his orders. His calm was original and absolute. But Crabbe could feel the warning probe of the gun against his back. He knew Lee would not fail to make it work.

'You wait with the fishermen till that anchor leave the water,' said Singh.

'And Flagstead, how he choose to reach land?' Lee asked.

'He know his own arrangement,' said Singh.

'You wait me here?' Lee asked.

'Till whatever hour you reach with these two,' said Singh.

They watched Thief hurry towards the boat. Singh and Crabbe stood alone like shapes growing suddenly larger out of the sand. Lee sat in the stern looking towards the wood, anticipating what would happen on his return. Rockey and Thief worked feverishly with the oars. Bill sat alone, impervious to the splash of the water. His body was gradually losing its shiver. He wanted to speak with Thief. But he felt a sudden anguish throttle him. He would never again be able to make his peace with Thief. Neither Singh nor the law nor his imminent escape occupied his mind as he watched Thief fighting triumphantly with the oar. He wanted, more than his escape, to make his private peace with Thief. He wanted to tell him that it was only an accident which had saved him from murdering Shephard. He had gone to Paradise Point to murder Shephard, but another's bullet, which took them by surprise, had deprived him of the wish he felt that night. He was beginning to feel he could not endure his freedom until he had heard Thief's judgement on his intention, but he could not speak now, in the presence of Rockey and Lee. His escape was about to make an infinite gulf between himself and Thief. He heard the oars slap the water and he turned his head away. He could not endure the silence which embraced them, and he struggled to say something which would bring Mark to his rescue.

But Mark sat beside him, half an arm's length away, a shadowless blur against the water. He was aware of nothing but the black, unspeakable contingency which joined his life to the sea. He looked at the water which had already smothered his wish, and thought that he could not even summon the will which had formerly urged him to redeem the meaning of his life by freely choosing its end. His death in San Cristobal would have been a waste, and the ship which waited could offer him no alternative. He sat alone, feeling the water spray his hands, and wondered for a moment why he had joined Bill in this escape from the prison. But he could not tell, for he felt nothing but a strange absence of regret, some familiar and anonymous void that widened within and around him, denying all expectation. He had become superfluous to life, unfit to die. He avoided Bill's glance, and watched the light slip with the water behind him.

Crabbe did not turn to see the boat slipping slowly beyond the edge of the light. He felt the sweat course down his face and settle like a wet lump in the quivering dimple of his chin. The men would escape. Singh had the letter; yet he hoped that something would happen before Lee returned. Perhaps Baboo would arrive, but the police were not there, and he felt for the first time that all was lost. Perhaps Singh and his men had intercepted Baboo who had probably suffered the same fate as the policemen. He could not rely on Baboo's arrival. He remembered the gun in his pocket, but the light showed his hands, and he could not avoid the murderous vigilance in Singh's eyes. His strength seemed to drain away under the relentless scrutiny which Singh directed on him. He felt faint, but Singh's voice gave him a jolt. It was sudden and sharp like a needle thrusting through the nerve. He stiffened and watched his adversary through the steady gaze of the light. Singh's voice was like an assault, a smouldering passion which consumed the sudden muteness of the night.

'There never was a man who make me feel more deep than Shephard,' he said, 'an' never will be. Whatever difference might set us apart from time to time, always a little voice like conscience would come back to tell me what Shephard was worth. Such a man never happened in San Cristobal before, never. He take the struggle which I start and turn it to a movement that was now more than losin' or winnin'. Win or lose, it could not matter no more when I watch that man work with me, telling me his open ambition which all San Cristobal know, but also his private grievance too. He expose himself to me in a way I never learn to do to any friend however near. An' through him I learn, I learn for the first time what it could mean to feel loyal, not only to the cause but loyal to the person too. I come as near to lovin' Shephard as any man came to lovin' a next, and it was his murder twist my heart like it was my own son dying in front my face…'

His voice was weakening, but he held the gun firm as he watched Crabbe. He felt a clot thicken in his throat, and his eyes burnt. His hand wavered, but the feel of the gun reminded him that he could not let this recollection of Shephard come between himself and Crabbe. It was getting beyond control. Shephard's corpse seemed to struggle from the sand vivid as the light which framed Crabbe's body against the wailing density of the sea. It grew like the night, a monument of despair. The wind was the dead man's voice, and the light made eyes which reminded him of Shephard's, burning holes through the mute, frozen stupor of Crabbe's face. He had met Crabbe. It was the wish that his hatred had always urged. But the memory of Shephard had intervened. It was the only flaw which the night had worked against his purpose. He would murder Crabbe in behalf of the cause for which Shephard had given his life. But this was not enough. He could kill Crabbe in behalf of the cause, but Shephard's death would not be avenged. This bond which his memory had renewed demanded a personal vengeance. He steadied his hand and watched Crabbe in the light.

'What there is between me an' you,' he breathed, 'no court can settle. That's why I arrange to come here, to meet you face to face on this sand, on the very spot where my comrade fell down dead.'

He paused and ripped the wallet from his pocket, showing it to Crabbe. The paper showed an edge under the rubber band which fumbled nervously with his fingers. His hand shook as he held the paper up to Crabbe.

'What would prevent me surrenderin' this evidence to the court when they meet,' he said. His hand shook as he struggled to tighten his fingers round the wallet. 'Tomorrow I could decide to show them this, an' leave it at that. But no court, Crabbe, no court can ever settle what come between you an' me. This is for one man to a next, in personal meetin', face to face.'

His hand leaned gradually down his side. He pressed his fingers against the gun as he eased the wallet back into his pocket.

'Tomorrow is mine,' he said, 'but tonight you must talk.'

He walked forward, steadying his glance on Crabbe. Then he

paused, raising the hand which held the gun, and Crabbe saw his eyes burn black and bright. He thought he should defend himself against Singh. The law was still on his side, but there was someone behind the tripod. He dare not move while the light showed his hands. His eyes showed a tottering blur where Singh stood, and he felt again the urge to defend himself, but the light stopped his hand. He had to make his peace with Singh. He was beyond surrender. He would never yield to the threat which Singh was about to accomplish. He was not afraid to die. But he wanted to redeem the cause which he served. He wanted to avoid the slander which the letter would perpetuate through-out San Cristobal. To the end he would be loyal to his mission. He would sacrifice his life in order to retrieve the letter which soiled the meaning of his power in San Cristobal. He would bargain his life to conceal the fall which a general knowledge of this letter would celebrate for all time. His mission in San Cristobal was larger than his life, more urgent than his death. He felt his strength return as he watched Singh. He stared ahead trying to see the man who lay face down behind the tripod. Then he glanced at Singh who had sensed this change of mood. The blood raced under his skin, warm and rich, swelling his ears.

'You can't get away with this, Singh,' he said. His voice was quick, erratic, defiant. He had lost his sense of danger. 'Whatever your thugs did with my men will be discovered. Too much has happened, Singh. You can't get away with this.'

Singh moved sideways to see him more clearly. He was beyond provocation. His patience was like a trick which he had mastered. He was not going to shoot until he had heard the last piece of evidence extracted from Crabbe. It was all he needed to appease the memory of Shephard. He had already outlined with Lee the method of torture that would make Crabbe talk. He watched him for a moment, glanced quickly at the tripod, and then took a step nearer.

'Until the leopard change his spots,' he said, 'until then you will be the same. Talkin' 'bout your men. Your men. Can't you understan' what Shephard help to make possible in San Cristobal? Can't you understan', Crabbe?'

403

Crabbe was silent. Singh paused, a noise of feet rose briefly behind the tripod. The light seemed to blink and shiver from the aimless trespass of the wind. The sea was an echo receding gradually down the sand. Singh soothed the barrel of the gun with his thumb. Crabbe stood firm, waiting for Singh to take some action, wondering what had happened to the men whom he had brought to work the light.

'You are loyal to your feelin',' said Singh. 'You know where your interest is. You know your duty, but it never seem to you that other men may be the same. That they have a loyalty to their feelin' too, that they know their interest no less. 'Tis a revolution that happen in front your eyes. You have no men in San Cristobal, Crabbe. Where you think I get my knowledge 'bout what was happenin' here? I will tell you, Crabbe. Was your favourite spy, the very man you choose to do your dirty work was always with me hand in glove. 'Tis what take place tonight in front your eyes. This ain't for logic or reason, Crabbe. Any ordinary feelin' can understan' what happenin' in San Cristobal...'

They heard the ship's alarm. Singh's words were lost in the distant echo which rose and faded shrilly through the night. Crabbe bit his lips, and turned his head away, avoiding Singh's glance. The light tottered and shrank, and beyond he saw the wood wide and deep, spreading like a jungle which reached everywhere in permanent conspiracy with the night. He could not hear the ship declare its last alarm, nor the impatient wrestle of the feet behind the tripod. Singh was a shape, wraithlike and foreign, growing more and more monstrous in the leprous exposure of the light. His blood froze, useless and still in his veins. He felt the muscles of his hands swell and fall, contracting slowly like a rat's body losing life under a trap. The night opened like a wound, treacherous and black with age, and his vision of the light turned crazy. But the sand was firm as rock under his feet. The sense of touch had returned to the scene, and Singh's voice, sharp and swift as an axe severing his ears. Your favourite spy... my favourite spy... Now he understood what had troubled him earlier when he met Baboo, cautious and hesitant, but without that trace of melancholy regret which always showed when things went wrong. My favourite spy. And the light sharpened, showing his hands, eager to slip inside his pocket. His body was alert, urging him to defend himself. But the tripod checked his impatience. He was about to move, when his eye caught it, steady as a hand behind the light, warning that he was not alone with Singh. He glanced from Singh to the tripod, and heard the words again, my favourite spy. They were together in a conspiracy he had never anticipated. Baboo and Singh. He repeated Singh's phrase, your favourite spy, and felt their names like knives lacerating his tongue. He knew what had happened. He understood the secret of Shephard's assassination, and he felt a sudden surge of strength persuade his feeling. Singh's passionate homage to Shephard had made him feeble; but now he felt strong. Something had cleansed his doubt. He was redeemed by his knowledge of their obscene alliance. He looked up and spat.

'You can finish your filthy work,' he said.

Singh felt his hands shake with rage. His blood was in revolt. Muscle and bone stirred like needles under his skin. He stepped nearer, grinding his heel into the sand where Crabbe had spat.

'Not yet,' he said, and the angry throb of his breathing seemed to smother his speech. 'Not yet, Crabbe, not yet.'

'Go on, shoot,' said Crabbe.

'Not yet, Crabbe, you will bleed…'

'What you do will stink for ever.'

'We will make you bleed, Crabbe…'

'What are you waiting for?'

'Only one thing,' Singh whispered, 'just one last thing.'

'There's nothing you don't know now…'

'Only one thing, Crabbe, only one thing, and you will tell. We will torture you till you tell.'

He waved his arm towards the tripod and took a few paces back, steadying himself.

'Who was it get the order to shoot Shephard?' he asked.

The tripod was jerked to one side; a gunshot whistled and exploded through the light that showed Crabbe's hands clenched and quivering over the red hole which opened in his stomach. His body stumbled forward, and his voice, like an animal's yelp, stopped sudden when his legs collapsed, and his head plunged lifeless into the sand. Singh stood, helpless as a stone, staring at the white pile of flesh pouring blood on to the sand. He felt his body shake, and he looked at the gun, cold as ice in his hands. A gradual stupor had seized his body. His passion froze and died like the memory of Shephard. He was still waiting as though he expected to hear Crabbe's voice. He turned, hesitated for a moment to see whether Crabbe might be alive, then spread his hand over his eyes to block the light. He was feeling his way, like a man walking in his sleep, towards the tripod. The echo of the gunshot seemed to linger in his ears, returning the shock which rent his hearing as he stood, wordless and alone, waiting for Crabbe to speak. His mouth opened and closed. His lips twitched and parted, making an idiot's yawn in an effort to ask what had happened. He looked at the gun as though he doubted its silence, and watched Baboo raise himself up from behind the tripod. The light narrowed round them, and Baboo emerged, looking all shadow in the black uniform, formless and grave as the wood which hid him. He held his head down observing the wet patches of blood which stained Crabbe's hands. He avoided Singh's glance and let his eyes ramble over Crabbe's body. It was ordinary as wood. The blood made a noise like water under the open stomach. Baboo let the body occupy his attention as he waited for Singh to speak, but Singh's silence was like a betrayal. He watched Baboo, and hoped that his suspicions were false. Crabbe's untimely death, like the memory of Shephard, had come between them. He saw Baboo pause and shovel his boot through the sand. But he was afraid to repeat the question which Crabbe could not now answer. Baboo walked towards him, making a painful journey of the narrow stretch of sand which separated them. A saint whose martyrdom served no purpose. His loyalty had betrayed him. He wanted to go closer, but the body lay between them, and he saw Singh's face like two uneven profiles divided by the light, beyond recognition. Singh's eyes had lost their fire. Meek as ashes, they stared through space, crazed and blinded by some infinite vision of defeat. The moments stretched like an eternity of torture. Singh's passion was useless; his knowledge had become unimportant. He saw Baboo stretch his hands out, and he heard his voice, almost innocent in its cry of sad and despairing solicitude.

'Was only for you, Singh, was only for you I do it,' he whispered, 'from infancy I dream to see someone like myself, some Indian with your achievement rule San Cristobal. My only mistake was to wish it for you Singh, was only for you I do what I do…'

The wind crept like a hand round Singh's throat. His eyes fell to the dead body which made a bridge between them, and his silence was like a plea for the night to lift.

PART TWO

Crows were collecting again over the iron shed, and the flies were busy round the wet entrails of fish stacked high on the coarse crocus bags. It was hot and the men were wet and rough. Far from the lethargy of this waterfront they heard a horn hoot, and the rails seemed to rock and scream under the spinning wheels. The flies dispersed in terror, and the crows fled reluctantly away. All the clocks were contradicting each other, and it was only the weather which seemed consistent with its oppressive steam, and the stale drifting odour of the water. A dog crept fearfully round the wire pots, sniffing hungrily at the rot of naked black bones and the dead grey scales until a man kicked it out of the street.

Each road was like the beginning of a chase which led involuntarily behind the houses, through crooked lanes of withering brown shrub, across sudden flat areas of sizzling red marl towards the iron shed which expanded in all directions with its chaotic increase of scrap iron.

The little boats were swaying idly on the water. The workers had parked their small carts beside the pier waiting for stolen cargo.

The Indians worked furiously with small push carts, hurrying up and down along the pier. They were cruel with labour to their bodies, and their faces were strained with secrecy and spite and expectation. They were going to rob the future of what was left. The Negroes sat heavy, large, indolent, unwilling and destructive. They rebuked all possessions by a show of indifference. They were killing time with their hands. Their labour was irrelevant and misplaced. The Chinese moved everywhere with severe and stoic reservation. They were not worthy of any interruption, and they were now no part of any alliance, but they were going to earn their share of everything. They were the tribe of willing exiles, who watched the weather, and anticipated every occasion of danger.

The policemen stood at the brink of the pier, pretending not to notice anything. Their visits had become a formality, infrequent and harmless. They talked playfully with their friends, collecting bits of information about the progress of the day. But when they arrived they had left the Law behind them. They were part of the conspiracy of disorder. The troops had usurped their authority.

'I feel like bees or ants or some sort of insect keep marchin' through my head. I can' take it much longer. An' if the troops lose their hold, something terrible will happen.'

'I don' mind what I do that night, I don't feel bad 'bout that.'

'But we arrive in the name of the Law, an' if the Law collapse nothin' can hold. Nothin' can hold.'

'I did not like Crabbe.'

'But we arrive in the name of the Law. We work that light at Paradise Point in the name of the Law, an' when we know what was goin' to happen to Crabbe, it was the Law we agree to deceive.'

'We had to serve two masters, an' I decide which I would suffer. I choose 'gainst Crabbe.'

'He was not a right an' proper man, but my heart was in my hand when we walk off through the wood an' leave him to the murder that happen later. It was the Law we leave, an' now these troops take over, an' if they lose their hold something terrible will happen.'

'Let it happen.'

'I do not like these troops, but it is Law which call me to my senses. If the Law disappear just like that, something terrible must happen. An' it disappear that night at Paradise Point. We make it disappear when we meet to help them murder Crabbe.'

'I can't feel for Crabbe. I just can't feel where Crabbe is concerned. It is the fate Singh will get that make me frighten.'

'Lee won't be able to carry on.'

The policemen walked to the end of the wooden pier and watched their reflection projecting from the pier: two irregular shapes laid out like dummies on the surface of the water. It made a black ripple round their uniforms which showed no colour but that of the sea riding noiselessly up to the pier. They saw how the helmets lost shape and cleaved to the shadowy outline of face and skull, and one kept wishing that the water would wash his shadow away. He turned and continued his patrol along the pier. He wanted to see his shadow stir. Then he stopped, but would not glance at the water.

'You on duty tonight?'

'Not after the curfew call.'

'Then we must go see those boys. We got to warn them not interfere, or they may only cause more trouble.'

'It was a lucky thing the troops didn't slap them down.'

'The kids were just carryin' out some kind of game.'

'But it was a dangerous game. The Inspector was thinkin' he should order them for treatment.'

'We goin' all need it soon if some change don't happen.'

They saw Baboo walking towards them, and they continued leisurely down the pier. He passed Thief and Rockey who were sitting on the iron rail where a few row boats were tied. They did not speak. Thief showed a false interest in the view of the hills which were rimmed with a scarlet flush of sunset. Rockey held his head down as though he were counting his toes. They glanced at each other like men who know what they have done. Innocence was an art which they had agreed to practise, and each waited for the other to suggest some flaw in his demeanour. But they were perfect, alike in everything but their uniforms. They shook hands like strangers, and Baboo turned and marched in step towards the iron rail. His voice was quiet and austere.

'You see what happen this mornin'?'

'It was nothin',' one said, 'the kids were carryin' out some fancy game. They just turn them away, but we goin' warn the mothers not to let them out till things are over.'

'It was the strain on Singh's son,' said the other, 'an' the next two probably feel they should join in. Some game they start when Shephard was alive.'

'But Ma Shephard won't talk,' said Baboo. 'I went to see her after what happen this mornin', but she won't talk. Just sit in a spell, an' won' talk.'

They noticed one of the troops making in their direction, and they paused. Then Baboo started a violent remonstration with his hands, and the policemen looked towards Thief and Rockey, as though they were eager for some sort of action. The young soldier was within reach. Baboo took a step forward to meet him.

'Don't like them loiterin' like that,' he said, making a flurry of gestures in the air. ''Tis trouble enough on your hands an' mine.'

The young soldier looked bored. He glanced to where Thief and Rockey were sitting, and then slapped Baboo amiably on the shoulder.

'I wouldn't play it too rough,' he said. 'And the chaps look quite harmless.'

Baboo pretended to be rebuked, and the policemen looked disappointed. The soldier forced a smile and passed on. The pier made distance between them, and the evening burst with the sound of bells from the Saragasso cemetery. Baboo stood fast, making a fuss with his hands, noticing too that the soldier had reached the end of the pier. The soldier lit a cigarette and squatted for a while on a huge bank of rope.

'You think Singh will manage a way out?' Baboo asked.

'News is scarce,' said one, 'but the odds seem 'gainst any kind of wishin'.'

'No mention of Crabbe?' Baboo asked.

'None,' said the other policeman. 'We can call that safe. The rumour at Headquarters is that he probably drown himself 'cause of what happen to his mother an' son. They makin' a search for the body.'

'An' Lee?' Baboo asked.

'The order is that Lee will go free the moment they finish the trial of Singh.'

'They want to leave Lee alone,' said Baboo. 'They know he won't be able to do nothin' alone.'

'Lee won't be able to carry on.'

'Then we must beg them to put us in order,' said Baboo.

He glanced at the water and spat. He watched his spittle drift towards him, floating white towards the rotting edge of the pier.

'I thought those boys had start some real trouble,' he said. 'Now you tell me 'twas just some game.'

411

'We mustn't tamper with young ones,' said one of the police-men. 'Whatever happen, let's leave them out. A boy is a boy.'

They separated where the pier leaned to meet the road. Baboo leapt on to the road and the dust spiralled round his boots. The policemen turned round and ambled back to the bank of rope where the soldier rested.

'Would you do it again?' one asked. 'Could you use the Law an' the special favour it grant you in a similar deceit?'

'I could do it again,' said the other. 'I could do it again. It was Crabbe who choose me to help catch these accused, an' it was me who tell Singh how we could catch Crabbe, an' I had no feelin' for what would happen.'

'But Crabbe hold you loyal,' said the other. ''Tis why he choose you that night.'

'An' I was loyal in my fashion,' he said, 'I was loyal. I can do it again, till Crabbe an' all like Crabbe learn not to take this face for granted like some rock you don't care to read. My face hold a meanin' too, an' any stranger here must read me like one man learn to read another he hold in friendship. I was loyal an' I could do it again.'

'Perhaps Crabbe was loyal too,' said the other.

'Crabbe was loyal too,' he said, 'but one loyal is more than a next, an' mine was right. Shephard used to say that what he do, he do in the name of every man, whether here in San Cristobal or elsewhere. I could do it again.'

'Would you teach your son the sort o' rule you follow?'

'I never had a son.'

'But life favour me with a boy,' said the other, 'an' sometimes I don't know what to say when he put his questions concernin' San Cristobal. An' I remember those boys this mornin', and wonder whether it was something Shephard say which make them go crazy outside the court. Whatever game it was they carry out, it didn't feel like ordinary play. Not when the old woman weep in her chair.'

'Not when Ma Shephard was weepin',' said the other. 'They carry their fun too far.'

'You agree with me there?'

'I agree,' said the other. ''Twas the first time I see her old age shake.'

412

The soldier heard them approaching. He turned to welcome them, and they watched his face like a familiar object which now revealed some strangeness in the light. The flesh burnt red from the sun, and the down which sprouted in soft white threads under his chin had betrayed his wish for a beard. His hands were strong and steady round the waist of the gun, but his eyes were moist with longing and wonder now he watched the sea. He invited them to smoke, but they said it was a privilege of the troops. He took another puff and threw his cigarette in the water. He did not speak, but they wanted to say what they had recognised. He was young and a stranger. They turned away and stared in silence towards Paradise Point.

'Five o' the clock,' said Thief, 'Saragasso in mournin' with the Saints.'

'The dead better off where they lie down,' said Rockey, ''tis the livin' who can't tell what future have for them.'

'Now is a time to steal,' said Thief.

They paused and looked at Baboo who stood alone, apparently unaware of the troops.

There was no trace of guile in his eyes. Cold and melancholy, they seemed to restrict attention to the dark enclosure of their sockets. Passion was now forbidden. His glances seemed effortless, incurious and without intention, as though some instinct of dumb and bored credulity had defined their function. His eyes revealed no possibility of doubt; no tendency for surprise or expectation was entertained. His eyes were casual, unhurried, almost reluctant, as though they had refused to trespass beyond those objects that interrupted the ordinary line of his vision. He did not look. His attention had to be seduced. It surrendered to the thing which it could not avoid, lingered for a moment, and then withdrew, innocent, without calculation, impartial. It seemed that it was now his duty, even his total nature, to lose interest. He did not look. But he saw. Baboo saw everything. That look of innocent renunciation was the mask which neutralised his interest, and led everything finally within the range of his motive. His treachery was faceless, transparent, freed from any form of visible intrigue or cunning.

A tank rolled slowly up behind and the children followed close, collecting the dust which made a tail turning languidly over

413

their heads. A voice shouted orders and the children scattered, while the soldiers wheeled and marched away in pairs. The tank laboured forward, filling the width of the road. A woman steered one of the children into the gutter to make way for the troops, then looked at the sky and swore. The crows circled over a finished heap of garbage, clapped their tongues and swooped through the afternoon. The bells at Saragasso were chiming.

'Just two hours to go 'fore the curfew call,' said Rockey. 'Nine days gone since these watchmen arrive, an' the town takin' shelter when their bell bang seven. 'Tis nine days gone, and tomorrow may be worse than now.'

'Now is a time to steal,' said Thief.

' 'Tis nine days gone too that Crabbe dead on my hands,' said Rockey, 'an' I watch my little boat burn.'

' 'Twas the only way out,' said Thief, 'when Lee in his murderin' mood bend the body in your boat an' mince it like meat, 'twas the only way out. That blood was too abundant for any water to wash. 'Twas the only way out.'

'You never had a boat,' said Rockey.

'But 'twas the only way out,' said Thief. 'My eyes burn too like I was seein' a last revelation, but 'twas the only way out. Nine days gone, an' nobody make mention what happen to him, an' they can't find him ever unless Lee give way an' Baboo talk.'

'Lee goin' hang,' said Rockey, 'tomorrow Lee may hang. An' Singh too.'

'You think 'tis true what they say Singh do?' Thief asked.

' 'Twas terrible what he do if 'tis true,' said Rockey, 'an' I would hang him too. 'Tis more terrible than how Lee mince Crabbe up, an' bury him once an' for all.'

' 'Twas like a last revelation,' said Thief, 'when they reach Saragasso an' open up the grave where his son was dead, an' put them together for good. Then they cover it back like nothin' ever happen.'

'Baboo work like he do it before,' said Rockey, 'he handle the dead like a newborn babe.'

'An' now no mention made anywhere how Crabbe disappear,' said Thief, 'an' when the boat burn 'twas the only way out.'

' 'Tis thirty an' more years burn in front my eyes,' said Rockey.

'Thirty years I been fighting fair with fish. Those troop boys don't understan'. They don't understan' what it mean to be dead when you livin'.'

'Now is a time to steal,' said Thief.

'What will happen tomorrow?' Rockey asked.

'Tomorrow is tomorrow,' said Thief.

He watched the troops pace up and down, and the uniform assumed a life real as the men who now watched the roads with guns hanging idle from their shoulders. They became a target that provoked his temper, but he dare not show his anger, or talk beyond the whisper which passed between himself and Rockey. The bells at Saragasso were still chiming.

Rockey was resigned. He had seen his life turn to fire on the sands at Paradise Point. His boat had fallen like a corpse, and the ocean carried the wreckage away. He had not yet given his bones to the fish, but his boat had gone before sailing in a black dissolution of dust and ashes for ever through the sea. A day later he had visited the scene where Lee made meat with Crabbe's red corpse, but the sands were washed clean. Nothing remained of what happened. The men had escaped and Baboo had made an end of his work. They had quartered Crabbe's body and parcelled it like meat beside his son. Every evidence of his end lay buried where the bells now chimed through the annual ritual of wreaths and candles that mourned the graves at Saragasso. San Cristobal had ordained a saint, and the crowds were hurrying before the curfew called to swear once more their homage to Shephard.

'What will happen tomorrow?' Rockey said, as though he were talking to himself.

'Tomorrow is tomorrow,' said Thief.

'Thirty is a lot o' years for a man to struggle with life,' said Rockey. 'But when my struggle was real an' help to make more life, I could struggle again an' again till the Almighty call me home. A man must struggle, Thief, 'cause that is what man was fashioned for, but his struggle got to keep a clear meanin' in his head an' heart, or else...'

The voice faded into the hoarse rumble of the tank far behind them. They walked away from the pier up the twisting stretch of road that led to Saragasso cemetery, where Shephard was buried.

They saw the evening swoop down the hills in a drift of mist that seemed to tease the thirst of the trees. The hills were rusting with drought. The earth looked old as iron, hard and unturned. The river was a scorched valley of pebble and weed like a lake that had returned to the land. Rockey remembered the sea as he watched the arid land with a sorrowful eye. Thief counted the fingers on his disfigured hand, and thought of his calling. He did not want to abandon his hands but their nature had reminded them of an unruly hunger. They were like a pair of wicked agents which ordered his actions and measured the meaning of his life. They were his hope and his disenchantment.

'A man can turn wild,' he said, 'turn wild or just lose all feelin' complete an' never move one way or a next. Just like that man Kennedy who couldn't say yea or nay. But Butterfield had a heart to say yea, only time wouldn't let him. The time was wrong for his wish to say yea.'

'But even here an' now,' said Rockey, 'in San Cristobal that was plain as daylight, 'tis like a certain darkness confuse me. Take the charge they charge 'gainst Singh. What sense it make to any common, plain mind if he do what the charge say happen?'

' 'Tis like Shephard,' said Thief, 'something split a man right down the middle in two, an' one half never make a meetin' with the next.'

'An' what will happen tomorrow?' Rockey asked.

'I say only tomorrow is tomorrow,' said Thief.

'But San Cristobal uncertain,' said Rockey. 'We see what happen when Crabbe die, but nobody witness the charge 'gainst Singh. An' now the troops invade, an' ordinary law is no more, it seem certain that he will swing. An' what will happen next?'

'Tomorrow ain't got no name,' said Thief. 'Time an' time again I hear you say it.'

The bells at Saragasso had stopped. From now on they would only make a solitary chime to warn the mourners that time was short. The curfew would begin at seven, and the town would retire to consider the night in a whispering alternation of rumour and prayer. Thief was restless. Rockey looked at the sky and waited for the echo of the bells from Saragasso. The afternoon was scarlet where the sea waited to receive the last burning folds of the sky. The hills turned cheerless with dark cloud, and the town seemed to prepare itself for an early silence. The troops looked a little bored now. They had arrived ready for a war which did not happen. In the morning the children would play hide-and-seek round the tanks, but the adult population avoided the troops. After nine days there hadn't been a single incident, and at night some of the troops would disguise in civilian clothes to go whoring in the slums. It was then that they talked, and often the women repeated what they had heard. The heat was getting them down, and the lack of any action made it worse. They wished something would happen. But they did not know, as Thief had learnt, that the whores were paying attention to their talk. They were organised, waiting for the judgement which would decide the future of Singh and Lee. Hatred was beginning to grow, collecting candidates like a plague. And Thief was among them. He wanted to return to the trade which had made his reputation throughout San Cristobal. He would surrender his hands to some extraordinary act of violence. Already the troops had ruined his affection for Bill Butterfield.

'My sense will make no difference now 'twixt one face an' a next,' he said. 'As every bee is a bee, so every skin that show white qualify for the same crucifixion.'

'But San Cristobal can't claim no special colour,' said Rockey. 'It hold every race that woman an' man can make, an' every colour too.'

'Yet some colours more sacred than the rest,' said Thief. 'An' it goin' take a terrible, terrible crime to make them meet in a common place.'

' 'Tis like the sea,' said Rockey, 'not every fisherman understan' the tides, an' some, through a careless manner, make the ocean swim over them without mercy. 'Tis like the sea, Thief, life ain't got no favours to give but the favour each man can take. An' if you choose a murderin' evil, whatever reason you choose it make no difference, then you buildin' a tabernacle that can only house one breed, an' the sun goin' set a lastin' disgrace on the bones that help you build. For ever an' ever, Thief, till time change to eternity it will go on an' on…'

'But a man don't make his feeling,' said Thief. 'They just hold him an' hold him, till he an' it come together as one. An' 'tis a feelin' that hold me when I watch these troops.'

'It hold me too,' said Rockey, 'an' 'tis why I ask what will happen tomorrow.'

'Tomorrow ain't got no name,' said Thief. 'It ain't got no name you can go by.'

'Nowadays I get a cramp with tryin' to think,' said Rockey, 'an' it seem that not only here in San Cristobal that end a islan' every eye can see, but all the world, Thief, all the world wherever different interest an' claims for the earth collide, it happen, a murderin' evil just waitin' to hold mankind. I get complete cramp with thinkin', Thief, a cramp that weaken my belief.'

'Me too,' said Thief. 'It move me too.'

The night was beginning to slip through the stagnant ridges of mist that surrounded the hills. The sky receded, and the air winced and squirmed from the careless spasms of black wings that fluttered down to the lamps. A street light went on, and the bats dived and circled the hood of glass which now shed yellow over the post. The evening was losing its way behind the houses, the trees were collecting their shadows from the ruined passage of twilight. And somewhere in the cemetery a child's voice emerged from the dark whisper of the crowd. The voice was soft and near as the night, feeling its way through the innocent and unpractised recollection of the words. And the crowd seemed suddenly still, possessed and fixed in their attention as though they had been suddenly freed by a miracle of strength to share in the elements which that voice celebrated. There was a pause as the child struggled to catch breath, and then the voice, innocent of danger, rode calmly through its obvious flaw of breathing with the words which her memory had returned.

> *Now the day is over*
> *Night is drawing nigh,*
> *Shadows of the evening,*
> *Steal across the sky.*

The silence gradually failed, and Thief's eyes were alerted by the shocking burst of flame which filled the street lamp. Another lamp repeated the signal, and soon the lamps started a hurried procession of light that worked like an invisible relay, leaping from post to post along the street. The bats burst from the trees and swished the air in a furious swoop that pitched them sightless into the light. They grew dizzy in a mad pursuit of shapes, colliding like lines on a map before swinging skyward through the wide, soothing obscurity of the night.

'In the land o' the blind,' said Thief, 'the bat is king.'

'The lights come on sooner than necessary tonight,' said Rockey. 'P'raps they smell trouble inside Saragasso.'

'They can' stop the crowd payin' their homage,' said Thief. 'Till the curfew go, they can't hinder them.'

People were filing slowly out from the cemetery, pausing here and there to exchange rumour about the events in San Cristobal. The island had been shocked into a general fear. They were mourning for Shephard. Now Singh and Lee were safely hidden, taken beyond the reach of any public appeal. No one could say what had happened to Crabbe. But rumour was abundant. His absence had created a kind of doom in the minds of those who could not guess what had happened. Thief watched the people disperse as they entered the street, and Rockey slowed down, trying to catch the fragments of talk that rose and vanished like the invisible flight of the bats overhead. He drew Thief's attention to the group of women who were collecting under the sycamore tree which faced the cemetery gate. The soldiers were moving towards them but the women did not notice, and the soldiers seemed reluctant to order them away. They had recognised the occasion, and it made them lenient towards this group. At the centre, in a long, loose-fitting black dress, stood Lee's wife. The night was beginning to obscure the moisture of her eyes, but her voice was a frail, demented shriek like the wailing sigh of the sycamore branches. She was an ordinary citizen, without much information, and like those who surrounded her, in search of news. She wanted to know what her husband had done. She wanted someone to prophesy what would happen. But the women only listened, patient and grieved, as she described the morning they took her husband away. She kept repeating how it was a black morning, long before the dawn made light in any house. Even the cocks, she went on, were still resting, and when they started to crow, her day was already news and mourning.

'My face make water an' water when they take him from under the sheets,' she cried. 'An' when he was ready to go I see his eye makin' water too. I couldn't talk. I jus' stan' in the corner by the bed, an' I never ever know human bones behave the way mine shake. An' all I say, callin' him by his bedtime name, "Tell them you ain't do nothin'." He won't talk. He just won't talk, an' then he walk with them like he agree what they was doin'.'

'But how they charge him that mornin' time, Mrs Lee?' The question was like an agreement that her grief was so much greater than theirs. No one turned to see who had spoken, but they continued to look at her, patient and solicitous.

'They jus' say they make investigation here an' there,' she said, 'an' some special evidence they receive make their action clear. An' the charge was what they name by a word call' menace, that my husban' was a menace to me an' his son, an' every single soul in San Cristobal who ask for a little peace. Is how they charge him the night they knock an' enter. Three o'clock o' the mornin' some days after those who kill Shephard get away an' the officer Chief Mr Crabbe leave town.'

'So I hear it too,' a woman said. 'When Mr Crabbe leave town, it was a secret mission they send him on.'

'He it was who arrange for these troops,' another woman said. 'The way he walk out San Cristobal is a secret like a murder under cover, I know a bad turn was comin' our way.'

'An' now my son gone wild,' said Mrs Lee. 'They take my husband an' put my only chil's min' in flight.'

The bats scurried through the air and the sycamore leaned as the wind wrapped round its branches with a shrill and melancholy murmur which lingered over the night. The bells of Saragasso were chiming, the air tolled with panic, and the bats retreated from the light in a mad disorder to the trees. The chiming came to an end, and Thief nudged Rockey to hurry. They wanted to make their visit to Shephard's grave. The troops were beginning to remind them that time was short. After the curfew they would become less lenient. Thief and Rockey walked through the gate and made their way towards the cemetery. They could see the women draw closer, and they heard a voice, loud and hysterical, rise behind them. But they did not stop. They continued, silent with wonder, as they watched the earth tremble everywhere with candle flame.

The women were shaking their heads, bowed with waiting and rumour. They saw two soldiers draw nearer, but their attention was fixed on Singh's wife who had arrived in a fit of despair. She was looking for her son. Someone pointed towards the cemetery in the direction of Shephard's grave, but the effort was a waste.

'No, he not there,' she said. 'I look but he not there.'

'Is grief make them run wild,' Lee's wife said. 'I ain't see mine since what happen' this mornin'.'

'Mine leave not long with a candle,' said Singh's wife, 'an' I say he was makin' for Shephard's grave. But he not there. He never make his visit there.'

'I see them both short time after it turn dark,' someone said. 'An' they had candles each, but what happen…?'

'Is the old woman,' said Singh's wife, 'the old woman do them something.'

'Who, Ma Shephard?'

'She do them something,' said Singh's wife, 'what it is I don't say for certain, but she do them somethin'.'

'She was there when the trouble happen this mornin',' said Lee's wife, 'but what happen…?'

'Is something happen between she an' my boy,' said Singh's wife. 'He swear 'fore he leave home he could murder ol' Ma Shephard.'

'Murder…'

There was a flutter of air as though the women were all catching for breath at the same time. They were silenced by the blasphemy of Mrs Singh's information, but they did not know the details of the incident which had taken place in the morning. Singh's wife was convulsed with tears, her small black hands were weary with wringing the sodden handkerchief that dried her face. Lee's wife seemed more composed. She was staring towards the gate where the light made a wide circle round the post. They were silent for a while, almost frantic with guessing about the whereabouts of the boys. A solitary bat dived headlong from the syca-

421

more tree, settled its flight upon the magic of the light, and abruptly finished its journey in a fatal crash against the post. It struggled for a moment to find its wings, caught a brief current of wind, and rolled finally under a dark bed of weed that grew from the gutter. No one noticed. The bells at Saragasso were chiming as the last queue of worshippers filed out into the street. The women moved nearer to look for the boys, but the troops were beginning to order them away. It was soon time for the curfew.

Rockey and Thief were hurrying towards Shephard's grave. They remembered the spectacle of the troops outside, and slipped the candles from their pockets. They felt a sudden fear of the troops who followed the traffic of the mourners from the street to Shephard's grave. The regulations made it illegal for people to assemble in groups of more than five or be seen out of doors after the curfew. They saw Ma Shephard kneeling beside the grave. She was alone. They lit the candles and quickened their steps through the narrow avenues of flame.

Every grave was honoured with candle flame, but the earth seemed different where Shephard was buried. The candles were numerous, irregular in length, but bright with flame that melted them down to pale, swollen stubs of wax which burnt the earth.

'It look like a million lights shine now,' said Rockey. 'A million an' one lights mournin' the livin'.'

' 'Tis the dead an' the livin' they celebrate at the same said time,' said Thief.

'San Cristobal get hit hard,' said Rockey, 'we get hit hard with the times.'

'Tomorrow is tomorrow,' said Thief.

'But tomorrow is more than me an' you,' said Rockey. 'Tomorrow is the children who continue long after we lie down like the dead who don't know what these candles tell. With next to nothin' of experience, Thief, how you hope they can shield whatever evil come?'

'Troops an' revolution don't frighten them,' said Thief. 'They too young contend with thinkin' 'bout the grave, but while a force like Ma Shephard last, it frighten them. Whatever truth her old age tell put a fear in their heart. An' 'twas the same when we was young. A certain age could always call you to order.'

' 'Twas the same with me,' said Rockey. 'But what will happen tomorrow?'

Thief did not reply. The shadows stooped from the trees to announce the night, and waited for the candles to die. Thief felt for Rockey's hand, and they stood, silent and perplexed, hearing Ma Shephard's voice.

She was praying aloud, shaking with reverence and fear, in a voice that seemed to burn with anguish through the wide enclosure of the night. Thief had removed his cap, and Rockey held his head down, innocent and docile as any child in this moment of worship. They could not catch the words of her prayer until the voice rose in a cry of agony through the spreading illumination of the night. The candles sputtered over their hands, but they did not move. The voice grew like a force surpassing the threat of the troops who occupied the town. And she too seemed afraid.

' 'Twas only that afternoon nine nights ago that I find what I find,' she cried. 'Not a minute before, and nine nights I wrestle with You, Lord, and now my heart is whole an' clean, I hope, in every corner. But this terrible turnin' in those boys must make me wonder what was wrong in the early days. I will not trifle with the temper of my God, so teach me, Lord, an' tell me where my faith fall down. Was it the doing of my son that turn their heart? Or was it me? Was it me not able to hold your fort, Good Lord, an' make them trample on my word till old age fall in disrepute?

'Or is it the doing of my son that make a soil for such evil seed in their heart? I do not know, I dare not say what reckonin' you make. But you know my stand, Good Lord, an' if my feet fail on that rock You build, I ask Your strength to make me straight once more. I beg Your strength. For the pity of men is a failing refuge like the old rooftop that shelter and leak on me at the same, said time. In death here now, where every candle is a love that shine on these Saragasso graves, the heart wax soft, soft, soft in every one. But the mood to conquer can remain, an' any ambition that will not point Your way must begin with a false start. 'Cause love 'mongst men is not enough when any small deceit can work on their weakness. 'Tis a hard sayin' I know, but true, I feel, Good Lord. Love is not enough when man meet man in some evil opposition their heart cannot hold. Their love is not enough. An'

I wonder, an' beg You, Good Lord, why those boys deny me now. Time was I could reach them with one turn of my eye, an' hold them safe for Your comin'. But today, You witness what happen. You see how they trample my wish, an' deny my word. 'Tis not my power to curse their years, for my own womb deliver one whose soul is now in Your care, an' I must pray for them as I pray for him. Help them out of their mistake, Good Lord, an' do not send us a new sorrow. But go with them in a gradual way, Good Lord. For 'tis the first time I really fear the will of man. This mornin' they bring it on. An' it was worse a moment ago. You witness how worse, Good Lord. My bowels burn when they scorn my call, an' all I beckon they would not come. They carry their candles elsewhere an' would not come. I cannot say what evil understandin' order this terrible turnin' in their hearts. But I was afraid. I live in a fear an' tremblin' of the time that teach this change. An' I beg in a humble manner that may be wrong to change us first. You change us, Lord.'

Her head had fallen to the ground and she folded her hands over her face and wept. Her elbows reached to her knees, and her back curved like half a wheel. Thief fixed his glance on the candle, and was afraid when the flames rambled near to touch her hands. But she did not hear them arrive, and they did not speak. The sun had finished behind the houses and the candles showed like the first streaks of a morning suffusing the night. The evening surrounded her in a black and yellow season of blossoming and death. She seemed an essential part of their order, inevitable and old. But the day had darkened her spirit. She was beyond all simple, human comfort. Only God could cure her misgiving.

She scraped her hands in the dirt, and gradually pushed herself up. But her hands were weak. Rockey stumbled forward and Thief followed close, and they raised her to her full height. Thief stuck the candles into the grave.

'The curfew near,' he said, 'we will have to move soon.'

'Is Ma Shephard all right?' Rockey asked.

She nodded, drawing her hands away from the two men. Then she pointed to the ground. The hand was stretched out, waiting for the handful of dirt which Rockey had scooped from under his feet. He put the dirt in her hand, and she nodded, sifting it through her fingers on to the grave. Then she turned to go, and they walked beside her towards the wall where the troops were barely visible under the arch which led to the street.

'You remember me?' she said looking up at Thief.

'Like the first day my eyes realise San Cristobal,' said Thief. 'They say you bring me into the world, but that I ain't see. I only remember you like I remember the first time I really see myself.'

'You remember me?' she said again, turning to Rockey.

' 'Twas you who tell me all I know 'bout the islan',' said Rockey, 'how it rise from water, an' what tribulation it meet in the days before I was born. An' 'twas you too who bring me in the world.'

They were silent. She struggled between them, trying to find their hands. She could feel a weight lodge somewhere in her head, pressing against her eyes, and her hands trembled. But the men held her, keeping time with the feeble crawl which her feet made towards the wall.

'An' would you ever charge me with an' evil doin'?' she asked.

'Evil!' Thief exclaimed.

'Would you ever charge me with an evil doin'?' she repeated.

'I would not believe my ears if you say it happen,' said Rockey.

'The lie deliberate is an evil doin',' she said, 'an' 'tis what those boys believe.'

'Singh's boy?'

'An' the two who travel with him together everywhere,' she said. 'This mornin' they look at me with an evil eye, an' a moment ago when we all come to respect the dead, an' remember what fate in store for man, they curse me with a silence I never know. They turn their backs an' would not speak. But I am innocent, innocent as the day that now leavin' this land. I was innocent an' whole in what I do.'

Rockey wanted to say something to Thief, but he faltered. He tightened his grip round the old woman's hand and waited for Thief to break the silence. They were thinking of Singh.

'You believe Singh guilty?' Thief asked.

Rockey's hand trembled in the old woman's and he saw the wall close in on them. The troops were near, but he waited for the old woman to speak. He could not remember what she had said about the boys, and it did not matter now he was about to hear her

425

verdict on Singh. He did not know what had happened in the morning, but a rumour had shaken San Cristobal.

'Nine nights I wrestle with the Lord,' she said, 'nine long nights, an' the spirit win in the end, an' my duty was to show what I find. I sin when I remember what evidence I hold an' would not speak, but when the spirit enter to challenge my will, I could not last. "Vengeance is mind," saith the Lord. That I remember. An' much as I treasure what is right, an' feel that the islan' was wronged, this San Cristobal nearer to me than any rock elsewhere was truly wronged, I say to myself that right must not travel by an evil road. An' I show what I find. But some madness possess those boys, an' make them confess to a terrible lie. They say they see what happen, an' they start to put the blame on the innocent dead, but the law won't let them speak no more.'

'You think Singh guilty?' Thief asked.

' 'Tis the boys,' she said. ' 'Tis the boys, how at that age such an evil could enter. An' they shake my faith like never before.'

'What will happen tomorrow?' Rockey asked.

'Tomorrow,' said Thief, 'tomorrow.'

They had reached the wall, and Thief suddenly refused to speak, and they walked past the troops in silence.

Soft and docile, like a leaf relying entirely on the wind, the evening gave itself up to the last visible corners of the sky. The night was near, neighbouring the wind and the sky and the hidden procession of tides that tossed their echo up from the sea. The houses leaned forward, large and obscure, surpassing the wall which contained this familiar colony of the dead; and windows opened to watch the candles that smoked and rained a trickle of wax on to the dust and weed which covered the dead. The season had returned, and the town had honoured their promise to celebrate the souls of the departed. Now they turned, away, leaving their grief, long or lately felt, behind them.

Only the boys remained. Alone, convulsed with weeping and outrage over Rowley's grave.

They could hardly see the candles gradually lose height, multiplying nervous little tongues that leapt fearfully into the night, freckled and polished with flame. The angels, so reverently sculptured in stone, seemed to walk out of their frozen cells to trespass unnaturally through the whispering grass. The air trembled, and the candles seemed suddenly uneasy. And some went out. But the flames continued in a brief and burning fury, hopeless and passionate like mouths that open and shut and open again in a silent effort to make some utterance. And suddenly the church bell chimed, a solitary and triumphant shriek, like a whistle calling for order. The angels obeyed. The stone wrapped itself about their naked feet, the effigies were restored to their area of vigilance. And the dead were safe. The boys watched through their tears the candles which they had bought for Rowley's grave. The wind made marks in the narrow pools of wax where the flames strained upwards like a root, taken slowly, gently from an invisible soil. The petals on the wreath showed like fresh blood. The weed was an unfamiliar vegetation, alive and restless like worms fighting to surface completely. They had entered the ritual which the cemetery celebrated, brooding over the three candles which they had offered. Then the wind hurried, and everywhere the flames were agitated and leaned like petals ready to fall. For a moment their attention rambled on wherever the night showed the vivid white fire of the diminishing candles, and they could only guess the farthest limits of the graves by the tumbled treasure of light which embraced the dead. Now they were together as people may be, in special moments, when they are caught by the same wonder. They saw the candles and felt the nearness of the grave, and the memory of Rowley broke through their tears.

'To the end I goin' remember him,' said Singh, 'to the very end, an' when my father let loose from prison, he can fret like that church bell buryin' the dead. I goin' remember him.'

'Me too,' said Bob. 'He hold a place equal to me an' you in the Society, an' so he die. Could be you or me lying dead under where that candle shine.'

'He was equal,' said Lee, 'equal equal.'

'An' dead as we know him dead there,' Bob said, 'the recollection make him real, real, like he was listenin' from the next side of the grave.'

'He was real all right,' said Lee, 'different like me an' you born an' raise different, but equal real like you and me, 'cause never before was my nerves this safe with the dead so near.'

'They reach round you everywhere,' said Singh, 'little dead and big dead, but while we last he can count himself with the livin'.'

'An' with the Society,' Bob added, ''cause although it finish we can't ever make a single work without him standin' in some sort o' remembrance. 'Tis why we make his candles the biggest an' best in the whole, wide cemetery, to keep the feelin' for something real which now dead an' gone.'

Singh struggled to make fists with his hands, which he buried into his eyes, hiding his tears. They could scarcely recognise his voice breaking with words through the violent sobbing which squeezed his throat. He bounced his knuckles against his eyes, and rubbed the moisture from his cheeks. They heard his breathing, militant and broken like the noise of the sea.

'Rowley dead,' he said, 'and the grave take his feeling an' leave him free. But they just hold my father, an' punish my father with a false charge.'

Singh was trying to recover his courage. He tossed a spray of dirt over the grave, and the candle wobbled and sputtered a bubble of light. Bob looked up, surprised, and Lee leaned forward and straightened the candle. Singh looked equally surprised by his action, then he scooped up a handful of dirt and sprinkled it through his fingers. The dirt made a small mound which he levelled carefully over the grave. He saw Lee looking towards him, and he sat erect, making a level surface with the dirt as he brushed the tears off his nose.

'The Society start as a game,' Lee said, 'but it ain't a game no more.'

'Once a man always a man,' said Bob, 'and hard as hard can be, a man got to stop his eyes from makin' water.'

'My father face make water the mornin' they take him from under the sheets,' said Lee. 'When he was ready to go I see his eye makin' water.'

'They can't kill them,' said Bob, 'they can't kill them.'

'They can kill them,' Singh said sharply. 'They can kill them.'

Bob was uncertain. He wiped his eyes, and turned abruptly to face Singh.

Singh brought his hands to his forehead. The sweat made circles which slid down his face. For the first time he seemed terrified by his knowledge. He avoided Bob's eyes, staring towards the square of dirt where his fingers had left its print round the base of the candle. Lee did not speak, but his muscles tightened, and he could feel a gradual moisture warming his skin. Singh's hands were beginning to shake against his legs thrust forward towards the edge of the grave. He was afraid. The others could feel his silence, a presence like his hands, and they hoped that he would speak because they wanted him to say that there was some mistake. There might have been some consolation if they could contradict each other. He knew they were waiting, and it made him nervous. But he was determined to play his part by saying something. He was going to argue their innocence, his and his father's, and the innocence of the Society. He looked at the candles, and the grave became a sudden reminder of what had happened, and he saw Rowley, scarlet with excitement, hurrying across the grounds of the mental hospital. And suddenly, as though he could not bear his silence, he cried: 'For the madhouse fire they charge my father, for the madhouse fire.'

They were silent, rehearsing the incidents of the evening which, it seemed, had now become part of the future which Shephard made his theme. The church bell chimed again, and the night seemed to reawaken, agitated by a fresh burst of candle flame.

They sat in silence, trying to contradict the memory of the scene which had already made them news throughout the town. They had challenged the troops with stones in order to gain entry into the small chamber of the court where a committee of the Bishop, the Chief Justice, and two other officials had met. They were hearing, in private, the last piece of evidence which Ma Shephard had offered in the charge against Singh. The crowd had broken into cheers of rapture and anger when the boys rebelled. An emissary had hurried from the court, and there was an uneasy pause while one of the troops explained that he could not understand why they wanted to enter the court. The emissary spoke to the boys, and some moments later they were led through the scattered groups who stood in the court towards the chamber where the committee had met. But it was not long before they returned, crestfallen, and without a word for anyone. It was like a bad joke magnificently started, but blasphemous in its failure to continue. They looked sick as they walked away. And they had not spoken again until this meeting at Saragasso.

'It was their faces make me go soft,' said Singh, 'the way they set their faces to make me look foolish, an' she was sittin' in front with her eye on me like I was mad. It had 'bout a minute before my mouth could open, an' then I try to tell them how the little Society work, and what happen before Rowley burn. But before I could get to the part where we meet him with the oil, they finger the man at the door to take me out. They say I was wastin' time…' The tears shot down his face.

'I didn't know what you say, or I might have start different,' said Lee, 'but when you came out an' I went in, 'twas almost the same except that the man in the red robe was smilin', an' Ma Shephard hold her head in her hands, an' only look at me like she was the Lord in wrath. An' I try to say how we celebrate the day Rowley join the Society, but they wouldn't let me finish to tell what we give him an' how we get it. 'Cause I was wantin' there an' then to tell everything, but I feel the hand on my shoulder, an' the man lead me out. I was goin' to shout like when we try to hit the troops, but my tongue won't talk, all I try my tongue won't talk. They make me look so foolish…'

'The Society start as a game,' said Bob, 'but it was no game no more.'

He was thinking of the moment they entered the chamber together. They did not want to hear from Bob, but they had lined them up for a stern warning. And they wanted to express some sympathy towards Singh and Lee. But Ma Shephard was already on her feet. They saw the faces of the men tighten as they turned their eyes towards the centre of the table. Gradually the boys recognised the object which the old woman indicated, and they felt a sudden relief. Now they could explain. The Society had become real once more. But the old woman had started to speak. She was anxious to save them from error.

'Nine nights I wrestle with the Lord,' she said, 'but my will would not last, an' I offer up what I find that terrible evening.'

She pointed at the lighter which showed a deep black scar on top. The boys had made to claim the lighter, but a hand withheld them, and the Chief Justice said sadly, looking at Singh: 'It bears your father's name.' And the boys leapt forward again to claim the lighter, but the hand withheld them. Then the old woman said: 'An' he was there that evening.'

And Singh screamed at the top of his voice: 'You lie, you lie,' and the others carried the chorus like a sudden lunacy had possessed them, 'You lie, you lie, lie.'

'An' 'tis Rowley's lighter,' Bob shouted, ''tis the lighter which Rowley had from the Society.'

In a moment it was over. The guard led them from the room and hurried them out of the court. And the Chief Justice asked, when the door was closed, 'Who is this Rowley?' and the Bishop replied that it was Crabbe's son, and the Chief Justice turned, as though he were bored beyond feeling, and asked the old woman: 'Are they mad, or what?' But she did not answer. She had collapsed in her chair, barely conscious of the frenzy which those voices had hammered into her head.

'For the madhouse fire,' cried Singh, 'they charge my father for the madhouse fire.'

He was weeping into his hands, spread frail and clammy against his face.

Bob ploughed his fingers into the dust, crushing the tiny veins of root which his fingers touched. The weed fell in dark velvet heaps under his feet. For a moment he had lost touch with the others. Singh and Lee seemed to compare their misfortunes. Each had seen his father arrested, in black morning, long before the day made light in the houses.

They looked at the graveyard and remembered Rowley, no more than a box of bones, lying faceless under their gifts of a wreath and three candles. And Lee was repeating the verdict which they had reached when they brought the candles and sat by the grave. He was an equal part of the Society. Singh wanted to speak, but he noticed Bob sitting like a fallen log, silent and vague and beyond feeling. His mood was a secret which he could not share. He was thinking that he, alone among them, had been spared the sadness of a father imprisoned on false charges. It would have been better if his father was one of the leaders. He did not want the boys to suspect this feeling, because it isolated him. And he thought of the

431

Society and glanced at the tottering flames of candle which now linked them to Rowley. He shook with the memory of the fire, and wondered what would happen to Singh's father. He glanced at Singh, and then turned his head abruptly to question Lee.

'What kind of punishment you think they punish for something like the madhouse fire?'

The boys were alerted. It seemed that they were now beginning seriously to connect the charge with some kind of punishment, and they stared at Bob, trying to guess his feeling, afraid that he knew something which they had not heard.

'Would they deal with it like murder?' Lee asked anxiously.

'Murder!' Singh said, and his voice suddenly failed. He had not thought of murder.

'Was the fire that kill those folks inside,' said Lee, 'not a human hand in the same moment. Was the fire that kill them.'

'But if they say...' Bob said. He paused to reconsider his words. The sentence was taking on a dangerous surmise, and he hoped his silence would tell them what he feared.

'But it wasn't we who do it,' said Singh. 'It wasn't we either who do it.'

He raised himself and threw his hands down flat over the grave. His knees failed gradually under his weight, and his body leaned to one side, slipping nervously down the soft slope of dirt.

'But it wasn't we,' he repeated, and looked at the grave as though he were asking Rowley to speak. They noticed how he looked at the candles.

'If the grave could talk,' said Bob, ''tis the only hole that got a real name, but it can't talk.'

'Was only we left to talk,' Lee said. 'Only we left to talk.'

'But it wasn't we who do it,' Singh repeated, thrusting his head high to show his innocence. 'It wasn't we either who do it.'

'An' they won't believe what we say,' Bob said gravely. 'Only we left to talk, an' they won't believe.'

They were silent. Lee stood, then Bob and Singh followed, and they held their heads down, not really seeing the grave, but staring through the candlelight in a similar bewilderment and fear. And Singh kept repeating Bob's fear that no one would believe what they said. The Society had no power to persuade anyone who did not understand and could not believe what they had done. Their secrecy belonged entirely to them. Then Singh whispered, like someone making soft noises in sleep, ' 'Tis almost like the Tribe Boys an' their trouble with the Bandit Kings.'

'What we goin' do?' Bob asked. 'What we goin' do?'

His voice was clipped and urgent, and the question turned and turned like an order in their ears. They saw Bob shake with excitement, and his eyes seemed to burn holes through the night, and they thought they knew what he was thinking, and wondered at the terror of their challenge.

'My father free,' said Bob, and he was struggling to give his voice all he felt. 'Of the three of us left, 'tis only my father free.'

They understood what he wanted. He would have liked his father to be with theirs, and he felt deprived of some honour which was theirs. He had made them feel guilty.

'But it ain't your fault,' Singh said, 'it ain't your fault your father ain't taken.'

But he did not seem to hear. His mood was set, obstinate and decisive, and his eyes waged war before them. He was ruled by a wish which made them speechless.

'If they don't hear what really happen,' he said, 'if they turn we down, an' take off the leaders to swing…' His breath made a clot in his throat, and he paused trying to compose himself.

'We can't fight them,' said Singh, 'if we just had what it take to fight them…'

Bob did not seem to listen. He was bullying his throat with his fists, waiting to continue. Then he swallowed, and they watched his hand lean easily down his sides, and heard his voice calm and firm and terrible.

'If they make them swing,' he said, 'I goin' do as the Tribe Boys do.'

'Like the Tribe Boys!' Singh whispered. His breath was hot as the burning air that leaned the candles lower to the grave.

They were standing, speechless and reverent with fear for the memory which an island's legend had churned. The air was like acid, cleansing their eyes, and all their years congregated and fled down a long legendary tunnel that swung a refuge through the dark, volcanic heart of San Cristobal. The night was a black tormented desert where a regiment of ants were waiting, patient and furious, to devour the flesh of the living. But the hills revolted and grew fire where pepper trees were planted, and the air was torn by the slow, deceptive waves of smoke crawling wilfully into the sea.

'Twas that human will complete... 'twas that human will you talk 'bout... Nothin' else... an' the Tribe Boys who remain walk out like they surrender... walk out like they surrender... but they won't... but they won't... an' they walk without stoppin', an' the Kings only watch them walk like they join a trance, like they join a trance... right to the top o' Mount Misery... an' there they kiss on the cliff for ever... for ever... for ever... kiss on the cliff for ever... an' then lean their heads down in a last-minute dive... to their own funeral...

'Like the Tribe Boys do! Like the Tribe Boys do.'

The name had made an echo that loitered unnaturally through the night. It cleaved to the air like the candlelight. It quivered for a moment and sank finally into a sad and perfect silence which surpassed simple reason and made, for ever, a captive of their fear. It was a moment which entered them like steel, one accident of time exploding from the whole accumulated muddle of their past. It opened the earth under their feet to honour their fantasy and their hope; and, in a moment, impartial as the sky, returned them baptised by a new and cruel desire. Anger had almost deserted them. The silence was disturbed, and they could hear, from afar, the gradual stride of the sea labouring heavily towards them. The wind hurried over the candles, and the flames lost their hold and crashed into the sudden moisture of the weed. It had started to rain, but they did not stir. The candles were closing rapidly everywhere like eyes surrendering to the night. But Rowley's grave was still lit. The flames looked triumphant under the press of the wind bending the candles nearer the dust. But they survived, and the rain halted for a while.

The moment had worked its magic and returned them to an ordinary awareness of the night. The darkness made fearful strides towards them, and they noticed how the candles wasted away, and the flames collapsed and died. But the earth grew light where they stood. Their gifts still made a quivering fire over

Rowley's grave, and they felt that it was he who kept their candles alive, that they would burn for ever in a legend which told San Cristobal and the world why they had followed their wish to climb that steep and pitiless cliff which carried the Tribe Boys to their death.

'Tomorrow is the trial,' said Bob.

'Tomorrow an' maybe till a next tomorrow it last,' Singh said.

'But hardly more,' said Bob, 'tomorrow an' a next tomorrow.'

Lee did not speak.

The curfew rang, ordering every street to be empty. But they would not stir. They sat in silence beside the grave. And the sound reached them again, irrelevant as the noise of the sea, an ordinary part of the night, like the howl of a dog shut out. The Law could not now enter their feeling.

ABOUT THE AUTHOR

George Lamming was born in Barbados in 1927. He won a scholarship to Combermere High School where he had the good fortune to have Frank Collymore as one of his teachers. As editor of *Bim*, Collymore encouraged Lamming's early writing career. In 1945 Lamming went to Trinidad, where he worked as a teacher. In 1950, he came to England, on the same ship as Sam Selvon.

He is the author of several of the most important Caribbean novels of all time, including *In the Castle of My Skin* (1953), *The Emigrants* (1954), *Of Age and Innocence* (1958), *Season of Adventure* (1960), *Water with Berries* (1971) and *Natives of My Person* (1972). His departure to England led to the seminal prose work, *The Pleasures of Exile*, which, amongst other subjects, explores the relationship between the West Indian writer and absence from the region. He is recognised as one of the Caribbean's most important thinkers on the issues of political and cultural independence. He has been a visiting professor at the University of Texas at Austin and the University of Pennsylvania and a lecturer in Denmark, Tanzania, and Australia and granted several honorary doctorates. He continues to visit and lecture in the USA, but is now mostly resident in his native Barbados.